MEETING OF WARRIORS

Suddenly they were surrounded by mounted Comanche warriors. Clay Allison spoke to them fluently. Finally one of the braves nodded to Allison, and he rode on, Dan following. As they progressed, Comanches seemed to appear from behind every bush and tree.

They reached a clearing where the cook fire still smoldered, an early morning breeze fanning the embers. A young Indian stood before them, dressed in buckskin. Dan couldn't believe that the young chief was the notorious Quanah Parker.

With his hands, Allison made the buffalo sign, and then pointed to Dan. Quanah shook his head, raised both hands, spreading all his fingers. He then spoke to Allison.

"He says all white men deserve to die," Allison translated for Dan. "Just as Black Kettle and his people died under the guns of Custer and his soldiers."

THE DODGE CITY TRAIL

Ralph Compton

St. Martin's Paperbacks

This is a work of fiction, based on actual trail drives of the Old West. Many of the characters appearing in the Trail Drive Series were very real, and some of the trail drives actually took place. But the reader should be aware that, in the developing of characters and events, some fictional literary license has been employed. While some of the characters and events herein are purely the creation of the author, every effort has been made to portray them with accuracy. However, the inherent dangers of the trail are real, sufficient unto themselves, and seldom has it been necessary to enhance their reality.

THE DODGE CITY TRAIL

Copyright © 1995 by Ralph Compton.

Cover photograph by David Heiser / Getty Images.

Map on p. v by David Lindroth, based upon material supplied by the author.

For information address St. Martin's Press, 175 Fifth Avenue, New York, NY 10010.

EAN: 978-0-312-95380-5

Printed in the United States of America

St. Martin's Paperbacks edition / January 1995

20   19   18   17   16   15   14   13   12   11   10   9

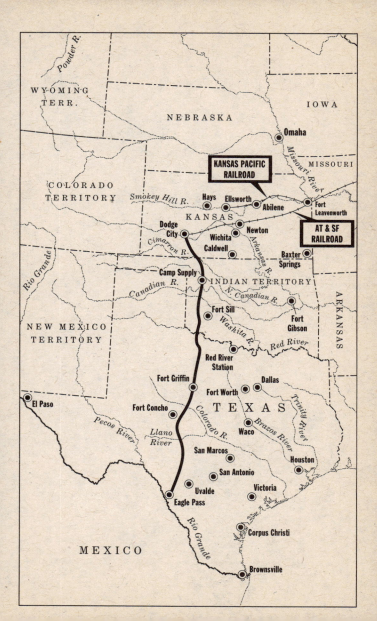

AUTHOR'S FOREWORD

In March 1865 the military commander at Santa Fe sent troops to occupy a strategic river crossing in the southwest quarter of Kansas, which eventually would become Ford County. The post commander at Leavenworth dispatched a force against the Indians, with orders for his men to establish and garrison a post on the Arkansas. In April a detachment of cavalry founded Fort Dodge, and with Indian hostilities continuing for almost two decades, the fort became a bastion of safety on a barren prairie where pale buffalo grass stretched away to merge with the blue horizon. The site's location —soon to become Dodge City—was ideal, with its proximity to the fort and its southernmost position on the Santa Fe Trail and to the vast buffalo ranges of the southwest. Speculators were quick to see the commercial possibilities, and a settlement soon arose to the west of Fort Dodge.

In July 1872 nineteen individuals—some local merchants, some officers from Fort Dodge, and some army contractors—formed a corporation formally known as the Dodge City Town Company. It was their intention to develop the town, but the Town-site Purchase Act of 1867 denied them the 320 acres they sought. So large a tract demanded more occupants than the speculators could produce, so they had to settle for a modest eighty-seven acres, at a cost of $108.75.

The Atchison, Topeka & Santa Fe railroad reached Dodge on September 15, 1872. Already the fledgling town had become a mecca for buffalo hunters, and long before a depot could be built, business was booming. The first railroad office was set up in a boxcar, and dozens of cars a day were loaded with buffalo hides and meat. Incoming trains brought carload after carload of grain, flour, and numerous other provisions. The streets of Dodge were strung out with wagons, bringing in hides and meat, then loading up with supplies from early morning until far into the night. Meanwhile, conditions in earlier cattle towns had begun to worry railroad officials. By 1874 the Santa Fe had become concerned that the settling of the country around Wichita would force the cattle drives farther west. More and more they favored Dodge as a major shipping point. New regulations adopted by the military aided their decision. Stronger measures were being taken to curtail Indian depredations south of Fort Dodge which might discourage cattle drives trailing so far westward. With an eye for business, merchants in Dodge reduced their prices on liquor, cigars, tobacco, and other goods, while restaurants and hotels rushed to improve their accommodations or to build new ones.

The herds of Texas longhorns came, driven by money-hungry Texans, weary of the ravages of reconstruction, eager for a good time. The whorehouses, saloons, and tinhorn gamblers were ready, willing, and able to accommodate them. The fast guns—men who walked on both sides of the law—came to Dodge. Those who wore a badge, in Dodge or elsewhere, were Wyatt Earp and William B. ("Bat") Masterson. Famed killers included Doc Holliday, Ben Thompson, and Clay Allison. A drunken John Wesley Hardin fired through the wall of his hotel room one night, killing a man in the adjoining room who was snoring.

Ironically, insofar as the Texas trail drives were concerned, the railroad was alpha and omega, the beginning and the end. As the rails moved west, so did the farmer, and with the advent of barbed wire came the fences. One by one—Abilene, Ellsworth, Wichita—they were tamed by encroaching civilization, until only Dodge remained. Those who walked her streets have proclaimed her the greatest of them all, the queen of cattle towns. Those of us who have walked there in spirit—through the pages of western history—can only agree.

PROLOGUE

Uvalde, Texas. December 16, 1869.

*H*e rode a rawboned gray mule, and if appearance meant anything, they were fit company for one another. The mule bore scars of rope or whip on its lean flanks, was missing half its right ear, and traveled at a shambling gait as though it cared not where they were going or if they ever got there. The rider had no saddle, guiding the weary mule with a makeshift rope bridle. While he was but twenty-nine, Daniel Ember looked and felt ten years older. His hair, once the color of wheat straw, was almost white. His eyes, once a friendly blue, had become slits of blue ice. His haggard face had the look of a man who had been to hell and back, maybe more than once. A red flannel shirt hung loose on his gaunt frame, while his gray Confederate trousers were all but threadbare at the knees. There was a hole in the crown of his hat, and countless rains had drooped its brim like the wings of a sick bird. But on his left hip, butt forward, he carried a Navy Colt revolver in a thonged-down holster.

It had begun to rain, and he tried to hunch deeper into the flannel shirt. Through the holes in the soles of his boots, a chill wind found its way to his sockless feet. His left knee ached and there was a stiffness in his left shoulder, reminding him of the wounds that had kept him in a Yankee hospital for a year following Lee's surrender. Now he rode the same dusty trail that had led him away seven long years ago, and the multitude of

tracks told him it had been used regularly. Somebody
had spent an almighty lot of time at his old place, and
might still be there. He slowed the mule and the tired
animal staggered. Ember sympathized with the beast,
and dismounting, led the mule. Whatever lay ahead,
he'd feel better facing it afoot. Before he was within
sight of the cabin, a horse nickered and he could hear
voices. Because of the spreading oaks, he saw the barn
before he could see the house. To his amazement, he
found the barn had been enlarged and a horse corral
had been added. Two men had come out of the barn,
and seeing him approach, had mounted and ridden to
the cabin. Dismounting, they stood in the yard, thumbs
hooked in their pistol belts. While they had made no
hostile moves, there was no welcome in their eyes, and
tension flared like prairie lightning. Ember halted, dropping the mule's rope halter, freeing his hands. The sig-
nificance of it wasn't lost on the hard-eyed pair, and one
of them spoke.

"You got business here, mister?"

"I have," said Daniel Ember coldly. "This is my
place."

"It ain't no more," said one of his antagonists. The
other man laughed.

"Who's claiming it, and by what right?" Ember demanded.

"I am," said a third man, who had stepped out on the
porch. "I am Burton Ledoux, and I bought this place
last year by paying the taxes. Now you just leave the way
you come in, and we'll forgive you for botherin' us."

"This is my place," Ember repeated, "and I'm taking
it. You coyotes can mount up and ride, or make your
play."

"Jared, Slade," Ledoux shouted, "cut him down."

But Ember had anticipated the move, and his Colt
was blazing before the two men cleared leather. Only
one of them got off a wild shot, and it struck Ember's

gaunt mule in the head. The unfortunate beast dropped
in its tracks. Burton Ledoux had scrambled back into
the cabin, and Ember could hear him shouting orders to
unseen men. There was a commotion at the barn as
shouting men came on the run in response to the shooting. Daniel Ember had but one chance. Holstering his
Colt, he sprang into the saddle of the horse belonging to
one of the dead men. Heading south, he kicked the big
black into a fast gallop. Behind him there were gun-
shots, but he was soon out of range.

"I want him caught and gunned down," Ledoux
bawled to the rest of his outfit.

"He's headed for the border," a rider said.

"Well, by God," said Ledoux, "it's fifty miles, and
there's a dozen of you, so take extra horses and ride him
down in relays. Don't give him the time to rest his horse
for even a minute. This Rebel scum killed Jared and
Slade, and if we don't make an example of him, there'll
be no controlling the rest of them. Now ride."

They rode, led by a Cajun giant known as Black Bill.
He had killed men with the lethal blacksnake whip
coiled on his burly right arm, and as he rode, his lips
skinned back in a wolf grin of anticipation.

Ahead, Dan Ember slowed his horse to a slow gallop,
sparing the animal. Bitterly, he considered his situation.
He had gunned down two men, but damn them, they
had given him no choice, and if that wasn't enough, they
could string him up as a horse thief. He rode on, knowing his only chance lay in reaching the border and Mexico, knowing he hadn't a prayer. When his horse played
out he would be forced to take a stand, selling his life as
dearly as possible.

With fresh horses on lead ropes, the Ledoux riders
gained on their quarry, and soon Ember could see them
coming. Eventually they would get him, so there was no
sense in riding his horse to death. Ember began looking
for a place to make his stand. But they denied him even

that. His pursuers split up, flanking him left and right, and shot him out of the saddle. Warily, they approached, but their caution was unnecessary. Ember lay facedown, his unfired Colt in his hand.

"We tote him back to the ranch?" a rider wondered.

"You can if you want," said another. "With all that lead in him, he ain't goin' nowhere. Besides, Black Bill ain't done with him."

The burly Cajun had dismounted and was shaking the coils from the deadly blacksnake whip. He seemed not to notice when his comrades rode away. They had all seen Black Bill perform, and none of them had the stomach to witness it again.

"One day," said a rider with a shudder, "we're gonna have to kill that crazy sonofabitch. He ain't human."

Slowly, methodically, Black Bill applied the whip to the helpless Daniel Ember, ripping the clothing from his body. When he was finished, he regarded the bloody mess with satisfaction, mounted his horse and followed his companions.

There was no sound except distant thunder and the sigh of the rising wind. Buzzards circled in the darkening sky, harbingers of death awaiting their grisly time. When the rain began, the bloody mass that was Daniel Ember shuddered with the chill, and what might have been a final groan of agony was lost in the rumble of thunder. . . .

1

Eagle Pass, Texas. December 17, 1869.

*A*n hour before first light, thirteen-year-old Denny DeVoe awakened to the sound of rain pattering on the cabin's shake roof. He crawled out of the old straw tick, seeking to avoid waking his mother and sister, only to stub his bare foot against the leg of a chair. "Damn," he grunted. His sister Lenore giggled.

"Densmore DeVoe," said his mother sternly, "you watch your tongue. Your daddy would have taken a strap to you for that kind of talk."

"Ma," the boy said tiredly, "he ain't comin' back. You know he ain't. He's been gone since 'sixty-one, and come spring, the war will have been over for five years. Leave him rest, and let me be the man of the house. Ain't I been bringin' in meat since I was seven?"

"You have," Adeline DeVoe sighed, "and I'm proud of you, but you're still just a boy. I don't like you riding north alone. Why can't you do your hunting along the river?"

"Because the Mex border patrol keeps all the game scared off," Denny said hotly. "They're staked out, just waitin' for some reb to try and sneak across the border. Then they'll shoot the poor bastard."

"Denny!"

"Sorry, Ma," the boy said, not sounding sorry at all.
"I aim to get us a deer. I found tracks around a spring a
few miles north."

Sixteen-year-old Lenore laughed at his self-confi-
dence, while his mother only sighed, but all of it was lost
on young Denny. He had found his clothes and worn
boots, and dressing in the dark, his mind raced ahead to
the sign at the spring and the anticipated deer. Wearing
an old flop hat that had belonged to his father, Denny
headed for the log barn.

The mules, Banjo and Fiddle, heard him coming.
There was no saddle, for that and their only horse had
gone to war with Barnabas DeVoe. Denny bridled
Banjo, and the animal balked, not wishing to leave the
barn for the cold rain and chill wind. Denny appreciated
the mule's reluctance. He wished he had brought his
coat, but chose to go on without it. A return to the
house would invite further fussing from his mother. A
canvas sheath kept his rifle dry, and that's all that mattered. It was a Maynard carbine for which Barnabas
DeVoe had paid twenty-five dollars in 1859. The
weapon was .35 caliber, with a folding back sight. It was
only thirty-seven inches long, with a twenty-inch barrel,
and had an effective range of thirteen hundred yards. It
weighed just six pounds, and was one of the first to fire
metal case cartridges. Barnabas DeVoe had bought a
thousand rounds and presented cartridges and carbine
to young Denny on his seventh birthday. Now, as he
rode the unwilling mule into the rainy predawn darkness, Denny DeVoe couldn't help thinking of his father,
and a lump rose in his throat. He swallowed hard. Despite the bitter words to his mother, he wanted to believe that Barnabas DeVoe was alive and would return.

Denny rode on, as yet unable to see, a little on edge
as a result of his mother's fears. In the predawn darkness, with the continuing rain, he had to depend on the

surefootedness of the mule, and had it not been for the animal, he wouldn't have found what was left of Daniel Ember. Banjo shied, reared, and Denny slid over his rump.

"Damn you, Banjo," he said. He threw his weight on the bridle, but Banjo refused to move. Shucking his rifle, Denny moved cautiously ahead, and immediately fell over something. He went to his knees, and to avoid sprawling belly down in the mud, flung out his left hand. But his hand didn't touch the muddy ground. Instead it rested on the back of a human head, in sodden hair. Heart in his throat, Denny lunged to his feet and backed hastily away. He had stumbled over a dead man! But after the initial shock, reason took over and he realized what must be done. Whoever the poor soul had been, he deserved a decent burial, and that meant riding back to the cabin for a spade. That, he thought gloomily, would result in yet another lecture from his mother over the danger of his riding alone.

Despite the overcast sky and continuing rain, first light was fast approaching. When at last he could see, Denny again approached the body, and was sickened by what he saw. He turned away and threw up his supper, and it was a while before he could look upon what he believed was a dead man. The body lay facedown and had been literally beaten to a bloody pulp. The clothing had been cut away, and the whip had ravaged him from his shoulders to the tops of his worn-out boots. Denny believed the man had been shot, but with all the blood from the beating, he couldn't be sure. Futile as the gesture seemed, the boy knelt and took the stranger's left wrist, seeking a pulse. To his dismay, it was there! Denny snatched the bridle of the grazing mule, mounted, and kicked the beast into a fast gallop. The wounded man had been through hell, and Denny knew he needed more help than he alone could provide. He received no lecture from his mother. Adeline DeVoe was a frontier woman, and immediately began preparing to rescue the wounded man.

"Denny," she said, "bring Fiddle to the house. Lenore and me will be ready when you return."

Denny bridled the second mule, and when he reached the cabin, helped his mother and sister to mount. He then mounted Banjo and led out.

"How far?" his mother asked.

"Maybe five miles. He's been whipped, Ma. His clothes are gone, and he ain't decent, but there wasn't nobody but you I could ask for help."

"You did exactly right, Denny," Adeline said. "No man is considered indecent when he's hurt and can't help himself. Your sister's a woman now—sixteen—and I was tending wounded men when I was younger than that."

The wounded man lay just as Denny had left him. A pair of buzzards sat on a cottonwood limb, waiting patiently. Adeline found a stand of buffalo grass and spread the two blankets she'd brought, one atop the other.

"We must get him on one of the mules," Adeline said, "but first we're going to wrap him in blankets. He'll catch his death, if he hasn't already."

"It's gonna be hell—hard on him," Denny said, "wrappin' him in blankets with his back tore up like that."

"Nothing can hurt him more than he's already been hurt," Adeline replied, "except the exposure. Denny, you take his arms, I'll take his feet, and when we lift him, Lenore, take the shears and cut away what's left of the clothes."

The girl's face went white and she looked as though she was about to be sick, but she obeyed. With trembling hands she cut away what remained of Daniel Ember's sodden, muddy garments. Adeline and Denny then carried the naked man to the blankets and wrapped them about him.

"He'll have to ride belly down," Denny said, "and it ain't gonna be easy gettin' him on the mule."

Neither of the mules wanted the macabre burden.

"Lenore," Denny shouted, "catch one of them damn mules and hold it still."

Sharing Denny's exasperation, Adeline said nothing. Lenore glared at her brother, seized Fiddle's bridle and forced the animal to stand until the wounded Daniel Ember had been draped across its back.

"You and Lenore mount up," Denny said. "I'll walk alongside and hold him in place."

The rain had let up by the time they reached the cabin, and a pale sun crept from behind diminishing clouds. By the time Denny and Adeline had the wounded man in the cabin and on a bunk, they were exhausted. Without being told, Lenore stirred up the embers in the fireplace and put on a kettle of water to boil.

"We should of took his pulse before we brought him in," Denny said. "He may not even be alive."

"You're right," Adeline said. She tried his right wrist but found nothing. But when she tried the left, there was a feeble pulse. "He's alive, but not by much. Lenore, get the rest of the muslin. We're going to have to wash off the blood, apply a thick mud poultice where he's been whipped, and turn him over. He's suffered more than just a beating. I think we'll find that he's been shot."

Ember groaned once as Adeline began cleansing his mutilated back, and she caught her breath as she made a startling discovery. Two slugs had struck the man high, entering just below the right and left collarbones and exiting above the lungs. The exit wounds had been concealed amid the blood and torn flesh resulting from the savage beating.

"He's been shot at least twice," Adeline said, "but the slugs didn't hit anything vital. That's the only reason he's still alive."

"He's still a mess of blood," Denny said. "There may be more wounds."

"Lenore and I will look for them. I want you to take the big wooden bucket down to the spring and fill it with the black mud along the runoff. Lenore, take some of the muslin, dip it in the kettle and help me remove the rest of this caked blood."

Denny took the bucket and a spade and headed for the spring. Soaking a strip of the muslin in the hot water, Lenore began bathing the blood from Ember's thighs and lower back. She blushed when she became aware that her mother was watching her, and Adeline laughed.

"You'd as well get used to it, daughter. Men are forever getting shot up, cut to ribbons, and their bones broken, and it's the women who have to patch up what's left. When I was just thirteen, I had to help Mama patch up my own daddy."

"Was he . . .?"

Adeline laughed. "He was. Jaybird naked. A grizzly pawed him across the backside, ripped his trousers to shreds, and there was nobody but Mama and me to tend him."

Mother and daughter continued their joint effort, more at ease with one another, and they were ready for the mud when Denny returned with the first of it.

"Dump it on the hearth, Denny," Adeline said, "and go back for some more. We're going to have to coat him with it from his neck to his feet."

When Denny had emptied the bucket and gone for more mud, Lenore looked at the pile and shuddered.

"That stuff looks like cow droppings," she said.

"I suppose it does," Adeline said, "but there's something in it—oil perhaps—that heals. Fold some of that muslin to cover his gunshot wounds. Two pads the size of your hand. I'll get the whiskey."

Barnabas DeVoe had been a drinking man, and he'd left behind a full gallon of whiskey. Adeline poured some into each of the exit wounds, then soaked the muslin pads and placed one over each wound.

"I can see how we're going to cover him with the mud," Lenore said, "but when we roll him over, what's going to keep the mud in place?"

"We cover him with a blanket," Adeline replied, "and tuck it tight on both sides. It'll take both of us, but when we roll him over, the blanket will keep the poultice in place. We'll have to change the mud often, so it can draw the fever out of him."

With bandages protecting the gunshot wounds, Adeline and Lenore began applying the black mud to Daniel Ember's torn flesh. They spread it thick, and Denny made four trips to the spring before the application was complete.

"Take a rest, Denny," Adeline said. "We can turn him on his back." She suspected Lenore was going to blush again, and she sought to spare the girl the embarrassment that might result if Denny were present.

"I'll go rub down Banjo and Fiddle," Denny said.

"Now," Adeline said when Denny had gone, "we'll roll him over and have a look at the other side of him. Ready?"

"I . . . I think so."

"You hold the blanket tight against his knee and thigh," Adeline said, "and I'll take care of the rest."

They worked together, timing their movements, and turned Daniel Ember on his back without displacing any of the carefully applied mud. To their dismay, the women found themselves looking into cold blue eyes. Almost immediately the eyes closed, and Lenore was the first to speak.

"Why he's . . . his hair's white, and I thought . . ."

"He's not as old as I am," Adeline said. "He's had a hard life, and it ages a man."

"There's another bullet wound," Lenore said, "and it looks worse than either of the others."

The slug had torn into his left side just above the belt line, and from the bleeding, the wound might have been mortal. But the lead had struck a rib and had ripped its way free.

"Thank God all his luck hasn't been bad," Adeline said. "That one hit a rib, and it could just as easily have gone the other way, right through his vitals. Hand me the whiskey jug."

When the third wound had been treated and bandaged, Adeline brought more blankets and covered the wounded man. She then turned to Lenore.

"You did well, Lenore."

"He's a handsome man, Mama. Who could have done this to him, and why?"

"He has some old wounds," Adeline said, "and from the looks of him, he's been to war. God only knows what's happened to him, considering some of the terrible people who have followed the Union soldiers who occupy Texas. Such as the gunmen who were here last fall with Burton Ledoux, the new tax collector."

"I remember him," Lenore said, "and I was afraid of him. Denny and me were outside when they left, and I . . . I didn't like the way he looked at me. He said something I couldn't hear, and the others laughed."

"He'll be back," Adeline said. "With Texas under Federal occupation, I fear there are troubled times ahead for us all. God knows what we're going to do when they come demanding taxes from us."

Lenore turned away, her eyes on the silent, blanket-wrapped man on the bunk. When she again faced her mother, there were tears on her cheeks and fire in her eyes.

"Damn them," the girl cried. "Damn them all."

* * *

For three days and nights Daniel Ember's life hung in the balance, and none of the DeVoes slept. Only a curtain separated the wounded man's bunk from the room where Adeline and Lenore tried to sleep. Daily, the two women changed the mud poultice, while Denny uncomplainingly hauled more mud from the spring. It had become an Armageddon, a struggle between the living and the dead for the feeble spark that was Daniel Ember's life. They washed and dried his filthy blankets, poured whiskey down him and listened to his ragged breathing, dreading the moment when they might hear it no more. But before noon of the third day, the fever broke.

"He's sweating, Mama," Lenore cried.

"Thank God," Adeline sighed. "We did for him the best we could."

As though in response to their words, the sweating man groaned and again the eyes opened. The lips moved but there was only a rasping rattle. Quickly Adeline brought a tin cup of water, lifted his head and allowed him to drink.

"Thanks," he said. The single word was no more than a whisper, and all he could manage. His eyes closed and he sank back on the sodden pillow.

Five days after Daniel Ember had thanked Adeline for the water, he spoke again, this time to young Denny. Adeline and Lenore were down at the spring, washing blankets. Denny sat on a stool, nodding.

"Pard, could I . . . have some water?"

Denny almost fell off the stool. He brought the tin cup, helping Ember to drink. Ember did so, sighing with satisfaction. His weeks' growth of beard was mostly silver, like his hair, but his haggard face was softened by a half smile.

"How did I get here, and who . . . ?"

"I found you," Denny said, "and me, my ma, and my

sister brought you to our place. Ma and Lenore are down at the spring, washing blankets."

"I'm Daniel Ember. My friends call me Dan."

"I . . . I'm Denny. Denny DeVoe." He suddenly became shy and could think of nothing to say, but Ember seemed to understand. He had more questions.

"How long have I been here, Denny?"

"This is the eighth day," said Denny. "I was lookin' for a deer when I found you."

"Lucky day for me and the deer, I reckon. I'm obliged to you."

The conversation ended when Adeline and Lenore returned. It was Daniel Ember who seemed shy when confronted by the two women, and it was Denny who came to his rescue.

"Ma, this is Daniel Ember. Dan, this is my ma and my sister."

"My pleasure, ladies," Ember said, regaining his composure. Again there was the fleeting smile. Adeline spoke.

"I'm Adeline DeVoe, and this is Lenore. I suppose this is a foolish question, but how do you feel?"

"Like I've been dead and resurrected. Denny, would you bring me some more water?"

"What I meant is," Adeline said, "how is your back? You had been terribly beaten, and we had no medicine, nothing but the mud from the spring runoff."

"Nothing better," he said, "and I don't hurt, if that's what you mean. But I've been a burden, ma'am, and frankly, I don't know what to say. When you're owin' your life, there's no fittin' words."

"And none needed," Adeline said. "Are you hungry? I could heat up some beef stew in just a few minutes."

"That would be as near heaven as I ever expect to get. I've had no decent beef since leavin' Texas in 'sixty-two."

Lenore stirred up the fire and began heating the stew

in an iron pot. The conversation lagged. They were unable to question him beyond the state of his health, for western etiquette forbade inquiring too deeply into a man's past. What he wished them to know, he would tell them. This, Ember understood.

"You took me in when I was more dead than alive," he said, "and I reckon I owe you some answers."

"You owe us nothing," Adeline said, "but if you wish to talk, we'll listen. But not until you've eaten. I'm sorry we have no coffee. All we can offer you is cold spring water."

"There's whiskey," Denny said helpfully.

"Denny," said Adeline, "I believe Mr. Ember's had enough of that."

"Thanks, Denny," Ember said, "but I've had more than enough. I'm not a drinking man. I'd want nothing better than cold springwater, and I don't like bein' called 'Mister.' Call me Dan."

"Very well," she said, "if you'll call me Adeline. Lenore has the stew ready. Now eat."

He devoured the first bowl of stew, asked for another, and finished that. He drank his fill of cold water, and when he again spoke, his voice seemed stronger.

"Adeline, before I talk, I'd like to ask you something. What do you know about Burton Ledoux?"

"Only what we've heard in Eagle Pass, the village to the north of us," Adeline said, "and nothing that's been good. Ledoux is the Federally appointed tax assessor for that portion of Texas south of San Antonio. From what we hear, he imposes impossibly high taxes and then takes the land when the owners are unable to pay. He and some men came to Eagle Pass last fall, calling on all the little spreads along the river. He even called on us, claiming he wanted to 'get acquainted.' From what I hear, he's taking the larger spreads to the north, working his way down to us."

"That's about what I expected," Ember said, "but he

won't be botherin' you. Once I'm on my feet, I aim to destroy Burton Ledoux, and then I'm goin' to kill him."

"It was him that was after you," Denny said.

"His band of killers," Ember said bitterly. "One day I'll tell you about that . . . about me . . . but not now."

Eagle Pass, Texas. February 12, 1870.

Daniel Ember slept little, spending much of his time wandering beside the river. Adeline left him alone with his thoughts, careful to see that Lenore and Denny respected his privacy. After days and nights of virtual silence, Daniel Ember surprised them. One night after supper he joined them on the front porch. After a painful silence he spoke.

"I've never thanked you proper—all of you—for what you've done for me. I've had things on my mind, questions needin' answers."

"When you feel like talking," Adeline said, "we'll listen."

He *needed* to talk and after he began, the words came easier. He told them little about the war years. Only that he had been wounded and had spent almost two years in a Federal prison. He told them of returning to his hard-won ranch, of finding Ledoux in possession of it, and of the forced shootout. As he spoke of his futile ride for the border, young Denny's eyes were afire with anger, while Adeline and Lenore clenched their hands into fists. When he had finished, there was a long silence. Adeline was the first to speak.

"I can understand how you feel, wanting revenge, but there's so many of them. And they'll have the support of the Union army."

"I don't aim to fight them alone," Ember said. "From what you've told me, Ledoux's called on all the little spreads, softenin' them up for the kill. Suppose we all banded together and stood up to him, built ourselves one giant herd of Texas longhorns and drove them north?"

"Jiminy," Denny shouted, "I'm goin' on the drive."

"It would be a grand thing to do," Adeline said, "but where are you going to get the cows? When Ledoux takes over a spread, he's going to claim all the cattle."

"Only the branded ones," Ember said. "The rest are mavericks. When Texans went to war, their cows went wild. By law, we have as much right to that unbranded natural increase as Ledoux. He may steal our ranches, but he can't steal our cows. Soon as I'm able, I'll find a rancher willing to stake me to a horse and saddle."

"I want to help," Denny said. "That old bastard's comin' after us too."

"Denny," Adeline said, "watch your mouth."

"Thanks, Denny," Ember said, "but it wouldn't be safe for any of you to be associated with me. Once Ledoux learns I'm alive, there'll be a price on my head, and I don't aim to endanger any of my friends."

"But Denny's right," Lenore said. "We can't hide from them, and if we're caught up in this anyway, why can't you stay here?"

"You're welcome to remain here," Adeline said. "What you've said about the unbranded cattle makes sense. We had more than a thousand head when my . . . my husband Barnabas left in 1861. He had dreams of driving them to market, but now he never will, and now there must be four times as many."

"There's a railroad that's comin' west," Dan said. "The Atchison, Topeka and Santa Fe. It's a ways off, but we'll be a while gathering our herd. I reckon there's some truth in what you say. If Ledoux aims to gobble up your place, he'll do it whether I'm here or not. If you're with me in this gather, maybe that will influence others."

"We have an old wagon that could be patched up,"

Adeline said, "and two mules. Perhaps I could drive to the other spreads along the river and talk to people. I can't believe any of them will allow Ledoux to steal them blind without making some move against him."

"I hate for you to take the risk," Ember said, "but the longer we can keep Ledoux thinking I'm dead, the better off we'll be. All the spreads may not be friendly to us, and those that aren't, we'll have to count them as bein' in Ledoux's camp."

Eagle Pass, Texas. February 15, 1870.

Daniel Ember resoled his worn-out boots, and Adeline had given him two pair of Levi's pants and several flannel shirts that had belonged to Barnabas DeVoe. It was a mild February day and Dan was at the barn, working on the old wagon. Denny was with him and Lenore had just brought fresh water from the spring.

"I think I'll take Dan some fresh water," Adeline said.

"You do that a lot," Lenore replied with a giggle.

"Hush," Adeline said.

She was halfway to the barn when she saw the scarecrow of a man coming down the trail that led to Eagle Pass. His left arm was missing, his ragged coat sleeve flapping loose in the light breeze. There was something familiar about him, and as he came nearer, Adeline felt the hair rise on the back of her neck.

"Oh, dear God," she cried, dropping the water bucket. Barnabas DeVoe had come home.

2

When Daniel Ember and Denny heard Adeline's startled cry, they left the barn on the run, and the scene that followed was painfully awkward. Barnabas DeVoe halted ten paces from Adeline, and with the wind to his back, she could smell the whiskey. That and the stink of a long unwashed body almost overcame her. DeVoe's dirty gray hair trailed down his shoulders, and his beard was halfway down the front of his ragged shirt. His trousers were much too large for his wasted frame, and were secured with a length of rope. The uppers of his brogans had split, revealing his sockless feet. But what frightened Adeline the most was his eyes. In them was a look of madness, and they did not linger on her or the children. Instead, DeVoe fixed them on Dan Ember, and when he spoke, it was with a snarl.

"Got you 'nother man, huh? Whilst I'm away bein' shot to hell, you had this sonofabitch sharin' yer bed." He took a menacing step toward Ember.

"No, Barnabas," Adeline cried, getting between them. "This is Dan Ember. He was hurt just before Christmas, and we took him in. It's the truth. Ask Denny and Lenore."

"You lyin' wench," DeVoe shouted. His fist caught

Adeline on the shoulder, and she would have fallen if
Dan hadn't caught her.

"Damn you," Denny shouted, "you leave my ma
alone." He brandished the hammer they'd been using at
the barn.

DeVoe looked at the boy as though he'd never seen
him before. Then he returned his attention to Daniel
Ember.

"You," he said through clenched teeth, "whoever you
are, git the hell off'n my place, an' don't come back."

Daniel Ember said nothing. Without a backward
look, he walked away, taking the trail that led west to
Eagle Pass.

"Dan!" Denny shouted, running after him, "Dan!"

Ember waited until the boy caught up to him.

"Dan, don't leave us," Denny cried. "Something's
wrong with him. He wasn't like that."

"Whatever he is, he's still your daddy," said Dan.
"Give him time."

"Do you have to go?"

"You heard him," Dan said. "There's no room here
for me. Adios, pard."

Denny was so choked up he couldn't speak. He
watched Daniel Ember for as long as he could see him,
until he disappeared in a stand of cottonwoods. Then he
walked slowly back to where his mother and father still
stared at one another. Lenore was biting her lip, her
troubled eyes on the derelict who was her father. Again
DeVoe spoke.

"Git in the house, woman, and fix me some grub."

Adeline turned and walked toward the house. Anything was better than looking into the fearful eyes of
this stranger who claimed to be her husband. Lenore
followed her, and Denny had returned to the barn, none
of them yet able to accept this change that had dis-
rupted their lives. Adeline stirred up the fire, preparing
to warm up what remained of the beef stew.

"Damn him," Lenore cried, "why did he have to come back now?"

"Hush, daughter," Adeline said. "He's your father."

"No," Lenore said. "My daddy died in the war. Mama, that man, whoever he is, is mad. I . . . I couldn't look into his eyes. He looked right through me, as though I wasn't there. He drove Dan away, and I . . . I liked him."

"So did I," Adeline said. "Perhaps too much."

"Mama . . ." The girl blushed.

"What is it, daughter?"

"Is he . . . going to sleep in your bed?"

It was Adeline's turn to blush. "Lord, daughter, I just don't know. If he chooses to, then what choice do I have?"

"I won't let him," the girl said hotly. "I'll sleep with you just as I have since he left. He'll have to throw me out."

"Bless you, daughter," Adeline said.

While she was ashamed of her negative feelings toward this man who was legally her husband, her fear and revulsion overcame her shame. But she dreaded the night and the consequences it might bring. In the larger of the cabin's two rooms—where the cooking and eating were done—there were two bunks. One was Denny's, and the other had belonged to Lenore, before Barnabas DeVoe had gone to war. Would Barnabas take the extra bunk, or force his way into her bed? Adeline wondered. Her thoughts were interrupted by DeVoe's entry into the cabin. Without a word, he kicked a stool near the table and sat down. Adeline took the pot of stew from the fire and set it on the table along with a long-handled, homemade wooden spoon. She then brought a tin cup of springwater. DeVoe took one swallow and poured the rest on the floor.

"Damn you, woman, bring me some whiskey."

"There is no whiskey," Adeline said, "and if there was, I'd pour it on the ground before giving it to you."

He flung the tin cup as hard as he could, and it narrowly missed her head. Adeline retreated to the bedroom she shared with Lenore, and found the girl white-faced and trembling. The two of them remained there until they heard DeVoe go out. Shortly afterward Denny came in.

"He's settin' on the porch, Ma, lookin' off toward the river," Denny said. "What are we gonna do?"

"There's nothing we can do," Adeline replied. "He's your father, and he's the head of this house."

Barnabas DeVoe sat on the porch the rest of the day, staring vacantly toward the Rio Grande. He seemed not to hear when Adeline timidly invited him to supper, and when Adeline and Lenore retired to their bed, he was still sitting there. Far into the night he entered the cabin, and Denny lay awake in the darkness, hardly daring to breathe. DeVoe ripped away the sack curtain that covered the doorway to the room where Adeline and Lenore slept, and they could see the shape of him in the darkness. Suddenly he laughed.

"No need to hide from me, woman. You're trash. I ain't one to take another man's leavings."

He turned away and flopped down on the extra bunk in the outer room.

"Mama," Lenore said, "why does he think you and Dan—"

"I don't know," Adeline whispered. "I think something that happened during the war has affected his mind. He's not himself."

For five days the uneasy situation continued, and on the afternoon of the fifth day, a horseman rode along the river trail. Burton Ledoux reined up in the yard and, without waiting to be asked, dismounted. Barnabas DeVoe sat on the porch, saying nothing. Ledoux spoke.

"I'm Burton Ledoux, the Federal tax assessor from San Antonio. I'm here about your taxes, Mister . . ."

"Barnabas DeVoe," the one-armed man snarled. "You and your taxes be damned, and I catch you on my place again, you Yankee bastard, and I'll kill you. Now git."

Without a word, Ledoux mounted and rode away. Adeline and Lenore peeked fearfully around the edge of the door. DeVoe hadn't moved from where he sat on the porch.

"Ma," Denny said, "he shouldn't of done that. You know what they done to Dan. They're likely to come back tonight and burn us out."

"Perhaps," Adeline said, "but we have no money for taxes. Whatever Ledoux does he would likely have done anyway."

But the night passed without incident, as did the following day, and the uneasy solitude itself got to them. Barnabas DeVoe sat on the porch as usual, ignoring the call to supper. Whatever had unbalanced his mind hadn't dampened his caution, for he had taken Denny's carbine and leaned it against the wall behind him. There was no moon, and the riders came just after dark. Reining up in the shadow of an oak, one of them issued a command.

"Come out here, DeVoe. We got business with you."

DeVoe responded with a blast from the carbine, and there was a cry of pain. But it became DeVoe's final act. A dozen guns roared out of the night, and the only sound was that of the riders galloping their horses south along the river trail.

"They killed him, Ma!" Denny cried. "The bastards gunned him down!"

"Light the lantern, Denny," Adeline said, her voice shaking.

Denny found the lantern, raising its globe with a

shriek. All the coal oil they had was in the lantern, and they used it sparingly, when they had to.

"Ma," Denny said, "you and Lenore stay inside. I'll go look."

"No, son," Adeline said, "this is more of a burden than you should have to bear alone. I'll go with you."

"I'm going too," Lenore said. "I have the feeling this is the start of something terrible, and I won't be able to hide from it."

Barnabas DeVoe had fallen with his back against the wall, and he might have been sleeping. With shaking hands Denny stretched him out on the porch.

"Dear God," Adeline cried when Denny had unbuttoned the bloody shirt, "he's been shot seven times." It was a futile gesture, seeking a pulse, and she released the lifeless, bony wrist.

"Ma," Denny said, "you and Lenore go on back in the house. Just bring me somethin' to cover him. I'll stay here with the gun until mornin', so's the varmints don't get at him."

Adeline and Lenore lay awake until far in the night before drifting into troubled sleep. Young Denny remained with the body of his father until first light. He then took the spade from the barn and began digging a grave under a big poplar near the river. Wrapping the wasted body of Barnabas DeVoe in a blanket, Adeline and Denny lowered him into the grave. Adeline read from the Bible, barely making it through the Twenty-third Psalm. Finally the three of them broke down and wept for the gentle man who had left them in 1861 and had never returned. . . .

Denny had filled the grave, returned the spade to the barn, and gone to the house. The meager breakfast was a silent affair, nobody eating except Denny. Lenore hadn't fully recovered from her weeping, and it was her cry that broke the painful silence.

"Now what are we going to do? They won't leave us alone."

"I'm taking one of the mules and riding after Dan Ember," Denny said. "If we have to fight, then let's build an outfit that can win."

"Denny," Adeline said, "you're the man of the house now. You've just made your first decision, and it's a good one. Just be careful, son. Tell Dan we have to fight, so he won't be hurting us. Ask him to come back to us."

With regret, Daniel Ember had left the DeVoe place and headed for the little town of Eagle Pass. All he had was the clothes on his back and his Colt, and now he would have to risk Burton Ledoux discovering he was alive before he'd had an opportunity to organize any opposition. But one thing hadn't changed. He still was determined to destroy Burton Ledoux, if it cost him his life. He hoped the little town of Eagle Pass would be insignificant enough to have been overlooked by Union soldiers and carpetbaggers, and to his relief, he found that to be the case. The doors and windows of what had once been the town hall were boarded up. The only other buildings were the mercantile and the combination blacksmith and livery. Dan tried the livery first. On a board above the door, in crude black letters, somebody had painted: *Ab Jenks, prop.* Jenks was a big man, gone to fat, and friendly enough.

"Hell, pardner, I don't need no help. Ain't had a payin' job in weeks. If I had anywhere to go, and could afford to go, I'd close up and leave. You might try old Silas Hamby, at the mercantile. He's got a ranch, and neither of his two boys has come back from the war."

"God knows I could use some help at the ranch," Hamby said when Dan approached him, "but I can't afford to hire anybody. But that may not make any difference. That new Federal tax man from San Antone was here, and he's doubled my taxes. I may lose the place."

"Don't worry about the pay," said Dan. "I'm just back from the war, and I'd be satisfied with grub and a place to sleep. I was born and raised south of Uvalde, and when I came home, I didn't have one. They've already taken my place."

Silas Hamby looked Daniel Ember over carefully, his old eyes lingering on the tied-down Colt with the polished walnut grips. Ember waited patiently, his fierce eyes and haggard face a picture of defiance.

"Make yourself to home," Silas said. "I close at six, and we'll ride out to the place. Something's got to happen. Maybe it'll be for the better."

Denny DeVoe had no idea how he was going to find Daniel Ember, but he knew that somehow he must. The nearest town west of Eagle Pass would be Del Rio. Denny had never been there, but he had heard that it was fifty miles or more, a formidable distance to a man afoot. That left only Eagle Pass, with nobody from whom a man could beg a meal, unless it was from Silas Hamby. Old Silas had lost both his sons to the war, and he seemed to feel a kinship to the DeVoes, for they had lost a father. In his haste to be gone, Denny hadn't asked the advice of his mother, and now he must rely on his own judgment. Certainly he would have to tell Silas about his father having been gunned down, but how could he justify his search for Dan Ember without betraying Dan's secret? Silas would be hit hard by the increased taxes, and he should be one of those desperate ranchers to whom Dan wished to appeal, but could they trust Silas Hamby? This was Daniel Ember's plan, and Denny desperately needed Dan's advice. Denny tied the mule to the hitch rail and reluctantly entered the store.

"Come in, Denny," Silas said. "Your pa was by here last week, and he looked poorly. How is he?"

"We buried him this mornin', Mr. Silas."

The news hit Silas Hamby hard, especially when he learned how Barnabas DeVoe had died.

"I feared it would come to this," Silas said. "Is there anything I can do, Denny?"

"No, sir," Denny replied, "unless you can help me find Dan Ember. He was helping us fix up our place, but Pa didn't like him, and . . . and Dan left. I need to find him, Mr. Silas, because them Yankee bastards that killed Pa will be back, and . . . and there's nobody but me. . . ."

"I think I can help you with that, Denny," Silas said. "When I close the store, you can ride out to my place and stay the night."

Daniel Ember seemed surprised to see Denny, and greeted him warmly. Denny wasted no time in telling his story, and for a long moment after he became silent, Ember said nothing. When he finally spoke, it was to Silas.

"I reckon you just lost a hand, Silas."

"Under the circumstances," Silas said, "I can't say I regret it. This is somethin' that's touchin' us all, Dan, and something's got to be done. If I ain't gettin' out of line with my tongue, I'll back you if you're aimin' to fight this Burton Ledoux."

"I'm aimin' to do just that," Dan said. "Let me tell you why, and then I'll tell you what I aim to do. I'll need your help and that of as many other Texans as we can gather."

For half an hour Daniel Ember talked, and when he had finished, old Silas slammed his fist against the table. Then he slapped Dan on the back, roaring his approval.

"You're Texan to the bone, by God. I knowed it when I laid eyes on you. I'll back you till hell freezes. When and how do I start?"

"You can start by loaning me a horse and saddle until I can pay you," Dan replied.

"You got 'em," Silas said. "What else?"

"Get word to every rancher you can trust," Dan said, "and get a commitment from them. You'd better get a vow of silence too. Until he have enough of a gather to set up an armed camp, Ledoux's killers can pick us off one at a time, just as they did Barnabas DeVoe. We're going to need riders too, and I don't mean just the ranchers themselves. Tell them to hire hell-for-leather Texans who'll work for forty and found, to be paid at the end of the drive. Promise a bonus of a hundred dollars for every man who finishes the drive."

"That's what I wanted to hear!" Silas shouted. "What else?"

"For as long as we can get by with it," Dan said, "we'll keep the herd split, on individual ranches, but with a common brand. Then when we have at least ten thousand head, we'll bring them together in a common herd with a twenty-four-hour-a-day guard until we can drive them north to market. Have every rancher riding with us brand his cows with a circle star, the sign of the Texas Rangers."

The following morning, with Silas Hamby's support enthusiastically assured, Dan Ember and Denny DeVoe rode back to the DeVoe place. Silas had mounted Dan on a big black, with a double-rigged Texas saddle. With just such a need in mind, Silas had hoarded ammunition, and in an old saddlebag, Dan now carried a thousand rounds for his Colt. From his limited supplies, Silas also sent other needed provisions neither Dan Ember or the DeVoes could have afforded.

"You'll have money at the end of the drive," Silas said. "Pay me then."

Adeline and Lenore had seen them coming, and when Dan dismounted, he was embarrassed when Adeline threw her arms around him. He pulled away from her while Denny and Lenore laughed.

"I'm sorry," Adeline apologized, "but you seem like one of the family."

Dan grinned. "I feel that way myself, but I wish I was returning under happier circumstances. But I don't think you'll need to drive around to the ranches. Those who can be trusted will quietly be given the word. Denny and me took care of that last night."

Dan told them of Silas Hamby's support, of the proposed circle star trail brand, and of the plan to hire extra riders.

"You may have trouble finding riders," Adeline said. "So many went to war and never returned."

"We could sneak across the border and find Chato," Denny said. "He's a Mex Injun. Him and his amigos ain't scared of nothin'."

"You'll do no such thing," Adeline said. "The border's patrolled by the Mexican soldiers."

"That don't make a damn to Chato and his pards," Denny said. "They come and go as they please."

"Denny DeVoe," Adeline said, "the next time I hear you use a swear word, I'm going to take your trousers down and switch your bare backside."

Denny turned red, while Dan and Lenore laughed. Then Dan got serious.

"Denny and me are going to make us a circle star iron, and tomorrow we'll start branding these Texas mavericks for the trail. Come dark, we'll sleep with our guns handy. I figure it's just a matter of time until Burton Ledoux gets word of our gather, and if he can learn that much, he'll soon know I'm behind it. When that time comes, I'll move out into the brush. I won't put the rest of you in the line of fire."

"Then why don't we all move into the brush and set up camp?" Denny asked. "Long as we're here, they can ride in anytime and surround us."

"Good thinking," Dan said, "but you're moving too fast. Once we have a large enough herd to set up an armed camp, then we'll all go there. For now, you're as safe here as you'd be anywhere. We'll let Ledoux make the next move. He's gone this far, and he'll come calling again."

Ledoux did come, and it was in the early afternoon while Dan and Denny were down river, branding cows. Adeline heard a horse coming, and by the time she and Lenore reached the porch, Ledoux was dismounting.

"I heard about your husband," he said suavely, "and came by to pay my condolences."

"You hypocrite," Adeline said bitterly. "It was you who had him killed."

"Those are harsh words, Mrs. DeVoe, and you can prove nothing."

"I have all the proof I need," Adeline said. "I've heard of you, and I've heard what happens to those who can't pay your impossibly high taxes."

"Speaking of taxes," said Ledoux, "yours will be due July first. Two hundred dollars, I believe."

"We can't pay," said Adeline, "and you know it. But that's the idea, isn't it? You want to drive us out, to take the land and what little we have."

"Now, Mrs. DeVoe, I'm not one to take advantage of the less fortunate. I'm sure we can work something out that will be satisfactory to the both of us. I am quite taken by your beautiful daughter, and I have much to offer a woman. If she looked favorably on me, you could just forget about the taxes. What have you to say, my dear?" He was speaking directly to Lenore.

He was just near enough for Lenore to slap him, and she did. He almost fell, and his hat went reeling.

"You murdering beast," Lenore hissed, "I wouldn't spit on you if you were on fire."

Ledoux recovered his hat, and when he spoke, it was to Adeline.

"You are going to be very, very sorry, Mrs. DeVoe,

and this little hellcat of yours is going to be even sorrier. Good day."

When Ledoux had ridden away, Lenore said, "I'm sorry, Mama, but I just couldn't stand it. I'd rather be dead than . . . with him."

"If you hadn't hit him, I would have," Adeline said.

It had been a shameful proposition, and Adeline avoided telling Dan. She finally did, but it was almost a week after the incident, and it came about in a way she hadn't expected. Daniel Ember often sat on the porch long after the others had gone to bed, and Adeline often wondered what he thought about as he sat out there alone. One night when she thought Lenore was asleep, she got up and slipped out to the porch, wearing only her long gown. Dan sat on the steps, and she could see him in the starlight. She sat down beside him, and he said nothing.

"You smell like sweat and cows," she said.

"Did you come out here to tell me that?"

"No," she said, laughing. "It was just the first thing that came to mind."

"Somethin' I've been meaning to ask you," he said. "What did Ledoux have to say?"

"How did you—"

"I read sign," he said. "Tracks. I couldn't think of anybody else who would have come calling."

She told him of Ledoux's impossible tax demand, of his shameful proposal to Lenore, and of the girl slapping him. She concluded with the threat Ledoux had made.

"Just some more reasons for me to kill the sonofabitch," Dan growled.

"Do you really think killing him will solve anything? You would become an outlaw with a price on your head, and Washington would appoint another man, maybe worse than Ledoux."

"Would it bother you if I were outlawed, on the dodge?"

"It would," Adeline said. "You're too good a man to throw your life away. Don't you want something better than being shot, hiding out long enough to heal, and then being shot again?"

"I reckon you've got a pretty good handle on it," he said. "The Yankees got lead in me twice, and I'd just managed to heal when Ledoux's bunch of lobos gunned me down."

"You didn't answer my question," Adeline said. "Don't you want more from life than that of a wanderer, of shooting and being shot?"

"You mean put the gun away, swap it for a woman and a place of my own."

"That's what I mean."

"When the time comes I *can* put the gun away, I will. Until then, I'd want a woman who understood the need for the gun. Do you understand that need, Adeline DeVoe?"

The moon had risen, and like an inquisitive bird, she cocked her head just enough to see his face. When she spoke, it was in a whisper.

"I understand the need, Dan, but that doesn't stop my being afraid for you."

He reached for her and their lips met. For just a moment she drew away, then went to him again. When they eventually parted, they sat there in silence for a while. It was Dan who finally spoke.

"Have I answered your questions?"

"One of them," she said, "but you've raised another that disturbs me even more."

"I reckon you're about to tell me what that is," he said dryly.

"You know how I feel about you, Daniel Ember, and I believe you have some feeling for me. You could have taken me just now. You wanted to, and you knew I wanted you to, but you didn't. Why?"

"Because this is not the time or the place," he said. "You know there's something I have to do before I can put the gun away. If I had taken you now, you would have become a part of me. So much a part of me that every time I'd pull the gun, you'd be standing in the way. I aim to finish what I've set out to do. Then, if I'm still alive and you'll have me, we'll do it legal and proper."

"Damn you, Daniel Ember," she sighed, "I suppose I'll have to wait. I'll try not to tempt you too much, but I'll tempt you some, just so you don't forget."

"I won't forget," he said, "and I reckon I can handle some temptation. Let's try a little more."

3

After a week of wrassling longhorns out of the brush, Dan gave up on the mules. Neither of them had cow savvy.

"If Denny aims to be a cowboy," Dan said, "he needs a cow horse and a Texas saddle. Maybe Silas can help us again. It's time I was talking to him, anyhow, to see if we're gathering any support."

Dan found Silas still enthusiastic but a little disappointed.

"I got word to twelve of 'em," Silas said, "and they're all interested, but they want a meeting. They need to hear what you've told me, but they need to hear it from you. Damn it, I'm an old galoot that's so used up, a good day of cowboying would kill me stone dead. All these hombres is just as fed up as I am, and mad as hell, but they're all followers. They need a gent with sand and a fast gun to lead 'em."

"Set up a meeting here at your place," Dan said, "and I'll talk to them. I'll see you again a week from today. One more thing. Can you spare me a saddle and a cow horse for Denny? The boy means well, and he can drop a loop as well as I can, but that mule ain't worth a damn for ridin' backup."

Dan returned to the DeVoe place leading a bay horse

with a double-rigged Texas saddle. He told them of the meeting Silas had requested, and Adeline was against it.

"When you speak to them more than one at a time, Dan, there's a chance a traitor may slip in and report back to Burton Ledoux."

"I've thought of that," Dan replied, "but getting them together in a group is the best way. It's the kind of thing where each man's willingness may depend on the support of his neighbor. It has nothing to do with courage or the lack of it. Only a fool jumps into a fight where everybody's shootin' at him. That's why I'm willing to meet with these ranchers who should be ready, willing, and able to join us in the fight against Burton Ledoux. Like you say, there may be a Judas in the bunch, but it's a chance we'll have to take. We'll face that when and if we have to. Besides, we have plenty to do right here and right now. Denny has a cow horse, a Texas saddle, and we aim to rope and brand some longhorn cows."

Eagle Pass, Texas. April 2, 1870.

"I think we should go with you to that meeting at Silas's place," Adeline said. "Most of the men you're going to meet will know us."

"All the more reason why you're not going," Dan replied. "If word gets back to Ledoux, besides having his bunch of killers after me, I'd have to worry about them gunning down the rest of you. I'll be going alone."

It was Saturday night, and Dan purposely reached Silas Hamby's ranch after dark. Even if Ledoux hadn't infiltrated their ranks, he could have been told of the meeting, and by having the house watched, know who attended. The men Dan were to meet hadn't been as cautious, for they were all waiting for him, some of them impatiently. Surprisingly, they were all younger than Silas, and Dan quickly decided they had avoided the war. That, or they had come through it in remarkably good condition. Their lack of participation might become a sore point, if anybody pushed it. His place had been taken from him while he had been at war, while the men he was about to meet had remained in Texas and had lost nothing. But they were about to, and they knew it, and he had that in his favor. Silas had brought in ladder-back chairs, and the visitors were lined up along one wall of Silas's big living room. Some of them smoked, one near the fireplace chewed, while the rest just waited. Silas wasted no time, beginning the introductions the moment Dan stepped through the door.

"Gents, this is Daniel Ember, and he's got some talkin' to do. Dan, these hombres, startin' nearest the fireplace, is Wolf Bowdre, Boyce Trevino, Tobe Barnfield, Rufe Keeler, Spence Wilder, Ward McNelly, Rux Carper, Duncan Kilgore, Skull Kimbrough, Palo Elfego, Monte Walsh, and Aubin Chambers. They represent Maverick, Kinney, Uvalde, and Zavala counties. I'm hopin', after you've had your say, they'll talk to their neighbors."

The men nodded to Dan, and that's all the greeting he got. Silas said no more. The rest of it depended entirely on Dan Ember, and it was a while before he spoke. He began with Wolf Bowdre and concluded with Aubin Chambers, allowing his hard blue eyes to meet theirs. In several there was shock, in several more doubt, but in more than two-thirds of them he saw approval. To a man they focused on the butt-forward, tied-down Colt on his left hip. Finally Dan Ember spoke.

"I reckon Silas told you Burton Ledoux took my ranch for taxes, and I'd say those of you with the savvy God gave a *paisano* know he plans to take yours the same way he took mine."

"Before you go on," Skull Kimbrough said, "answer me one question. If Ledoux has already took your spread, what's your stake in this fight?"

"This," Ember said. He unbuttoned his shirt, shrugged out of it, and turned his back.

"*Sangre de Cristo,*" Palo Elfego said. Even Silas Hamby hadn't seen the terrible result of the beating, and he swore along with the rest.

"That's just part of it," Dan said, turning to face them. "See these holes? They put three slugs in me before the bastard with the whip took over."

"You got reason enough to kill the sonofabitch three times over," Rux Carper said. "I ain't denyin' that. But he's got the damn army sidin' him. They took your spread, just like they aim to take ours, and there ain't one damn thing we can do to stop 'em. The best we can expect is a dose of what they give you."

"You're right," Dan said. "I can't recover my ranch and we can't stop Ledoux from taking yours, but by the Eternal, we don't have to sit here on our hunkers while he takes our cows. I'm suggesting we brand our cows with a circled star, gather them in a common herd, and drive them north to market. The Chisholm Trail is glutted with cattle, and graze is already a problem. The railroad is moving west, and it should reach Fort Dodge late next year. A town's being planned, and I aim to have a herd there to meet the rails."

"All we got is your word," Duncan Kilgore said. "I ain't heard nothin' about the railroad comin' to Fort Dodge or a town bein' built."

"I was in New Orleans last fall," Dan said, "and I read about it in a St. Louis newspaper. By driving north to the rails, you have a chance of coming out of this with a stake, something besides the clothes on your backs. Stand pat, and I can guarantee you a busted flush. Burton Ledoux will pluck all of you clean as Christmas geese, and if you resist, you'll end up like I did. I'm alive by the grace of God, and because some good people found me in time. The rest of you may not be so fortunate."

"Count me in," Silas Hamby said, "if they ain't nobody but me and you. By God, I can see the handwritin' on the wall, and I'm readin' it just like you have."

"I'll go," Wolf Bowdre said, "but what do we do if we get there ahead of the railroad? These things always take longer than anybody expects."

"Western Kansas is virtually unsettled," Dan said, "and the buffalo are being slaughtered. It's still free range. We'll put our herd out to graze, watch them get fat, and gather the natural increase."

"Something's still botherin' me," Tobe Barnfield said. "How do you aim to get these cows out of Texas?"

"By appealing to the Union army commander at San Antonio," Dan replied, "if it comes to that. Like I've told you, I can't stop Ledoux from taking your land for whatever tax he chooses to slap on it, and if all your cows are wearing your brand, then he'll take them too. But with the war going on, and with the Yankee occupation, how many of you have bothered branding your herds at all?"

"Hell, none of us," Boyce Trevino said. "Couldn't none of us afford the drive to market, and if we could, we was scared to leave our range and our womenfolk. Them new taxes has been hangin' over our heads like an ax for four damn years. I'm goin', whatever it takes, but we'll be almighty short on provisions."

"I'll clean out the store," Silas said, "and we'll use that as long as it lasts. I'll figure what it's worth, and when we sell the herd, each of you can kick in a percentage."

"That's damn decent, Silas," Monte Walsh said, "and we can always eat beef. I'm in the game, win, lose, or draw."

One by one the others shouted their approval, and Daniel Ember shook their hands.

"Two things we ain't talked about," Silas said. "We

need to get word to the other ranchers, and we need to hire some riders with fast guns and the sand to use 'em."

"We're going to talk about those things before we leave this room," Dan said. "Now that you're committed to this drive, I want each of you to do two things. Silas, we'll need a pencil and paper for this."

"I thought of that," Silas said. "There's pencil and paper on the mantel."

"Now," Dan said, "I want each of you to think of at least one neighbor who stands to lose his spread to Burton Ledoux for taxes. These people must be trustworthy, with the courage to make the commitment you've just made. I want you to talk to them, tell them what we aim to do, and ask them to join us. I'll speak to them as I've spoken to you, and I'll do it a week from tonight. Is there any who can't think of at least one other man who might throw in with us?"

Dan looked for a sign, some negative word, but there was none. On the sheet of paper, Dan quickly wrote the names of the men to whom he had just spoken. Finished, he turned to them.

"Speak to these men you have in mind. If they won't come willingly, let it go, and be here yourself. I'm counting on your judgment in avoiding those who aren't strong enough to stay to the finish, or who might spill their guts to Burton Ledoux. One more thing. We're talking about an eventual herd that could number more than twenty thousand head. Figurin' one cowboy for every four hundred cows, we'll need at least fifty riders. Including yourselves and members of your families, how many riders can each of you account for? Wolf Bowdre, I'll start with you."

"Just me and my woman," said Bowdre.

Dan nodded to Boyce Trevino. "Three," Trevino said.

"Two," Tobe Barnfield said, without being prompted.

"One," Rufe Keeler said.

"Three," said Spence Wilder.

"Two," Ward McNelly said.

"Two," said Rux Carper.

"Three," Duncan Kilgore said.

"One," said Skull Kilgore.

"Cuatro," Palo Elfego said.*

"Two," said Monte Walsh.

"Three," Aubin Chambers said.

"There's just me," Silas said, "and I don't know how much help I'll be."

"Including myself, I can account for four," Dan said, "and that's thirty-two. I reckon we're countin' everybody over twelve, includin' womenfolk, and we're coming up short on riders. We could use thirty men, hombres who can and will fight, but we can't pay them until the end of the drive, when we've sold the cattle."

"That's one hell of a tall order," Wolf Bowdre said. "Might be easier just to cut back on the size of the herd."

"If we come up with a dozen more ranchers willing to join us, and cut back to five hundred head for each of us, that's still twelve thousand head," Dan said. "The other ranchers will be contributing some riders to the drive too, and that might make up the difference."

"If we're goin' to do this at all," Rux Carper said, "then let's make it worth the gamble. I say let's set a limit of a thousand head for each of us."

"Amen to that," Ward McNelly said. There were shouts of approval from the rest of them.

"We're in agreement, then," Dan said. "We could have an eventual herd of twenty-four thousand head. That's one hell of a bunch of cows, amigos, and we've just raised our number of riders to sixty or more. I have

* Four

a feeling that, even after these other ranchers join our drive, we're still going to be short on riders."

"But we don't know that," Spence Wilder said. "Why don't we wait until our next meeting, see how many more riders we can account for, and go from there?"

"I'll agree to that," Dan replied. "When you speak to these neighbors of the drive, remind them of the need for secrecy. If Ledoux learns of this before we can come together as an outfit, his bunch of killers can shoot us down one at a time. For those of you who can, it wouldn't hurt to begin branding your trail herd right now, and try to separate them from the rest of your stock, in case some of Ledoux's dogs come sniffing around."

One by one they rode out, and when only Dan remained, Silas turned to him with a grin.

"By God, you done it. I got to admit I had my doubts, but I ain't got no more. I just hope these jaspers is strong enough to bring us a new bunch for the next meeting."

"I believe they will be," Dan said, "because I'm living proof of what's going to happen to them if they don't stand up on their hind legs and fight."

Time had flown, and Dan found all the DeVoes on the front porch waiting for him.

"We were afraid something had happened to you," Adeline said. "Tell us what took place at the meeting."

"The dozen men Silas talked to were at the meeting," Dan said, "and they're going to each tell a neighbor of the drive, men who stand to lose everything. Everybody's running scared, and I don't think we'll have any trouble getting these men to join our drive. We've agreed on a thousand head from each ranch, and that means we could have an eventual herd of at least twenty-four thousand head. These ranchers have no hired help. They've depended on wives, sons, and daughters, and after our meeting next Saturday night, I think we're going to be hurting for riders."

"Lenore and me can ride," Adeline said, "and you've already made Denny a cowboy."

"I'm counting on all of you," Dan said, "but besides being short on riders, we're short on good cow horses as well."

"There's Chato and his Injun pards," Denny said. "They got good horses."

"I've been thinking of them," said Dan. "We need riders with cow savvy who can and will fight."

"Dear God," Adeline said, "this Chato and his band are thieves and killers. They rustle horses on both sides of the border, and it sickens me having Denny look up to them."

"They ain't killed nobody but Mex soldiers along the river," Denny said. "I met Chato once when I was hunting, and he was nice to me. He gave me a piece of Mexican silver."

"I'd like to meet Chato and his Indian pards," Dan said.

Adeline frowned. "You're not serious," she said.

"Dead serious," Dan replied. "They can ride, they can shoot, and if they're not too proud to do some cowboying, they may be exactly the kind of men we'll need."

"Some night in the dark of the moon," Adeline said, "they'll rustle all the horses and head for the border."

"Ma," Denny cried, "you don't know that."

"I know it's very late," Adeline said, "and well past your bedtime. And that goes for you, Lenore."

"I reckon I'm a bad influence on him," Dan said when the two had gone unwillingly into the cabin.

"Not where this Chato's concerned," Adeline replied. "That incident took place long before you came. Of course, your considering hiring him and his bunch for the trail drive hasn't helped."

"Sorry," Dan said, "but I believe in fighting fire with fire, and I doubt Chato and his bunch are any more cold-blooded in their killing than the Ledoux varmints that gunned me down."

"Damn you, Daniel Ember, why must you always have good reasons for every blessed thing you want to do?"

"Swear at me, woman, and I'll give you a dose of what you promised Denny. I'll haul down your britches and take a switch to your bare backside."

"There's no moon. You'd never find a switch in the dark."

"Then I'll use the flat of my hand," he said.

She whispered something in his ear, and he carried out his threat. In the dark, in his bunk, Denny grinned.

The new cow horse made all the difference, and Denny DeVoe quickly became an excellent backup rider. When Dan dropped his loop over a cow's horns, Denny swiftly rode in and caught the animal's hind legs in his own loop. The cow was quickly thrown, and with the two horses holding the brute helpless, the riders tied the front and hind legs with piggin string. They then rode on to rope another cow. Later, when the longhorns secured with piggin string had worn themselves out, it was a simple matter to lead them with a horn loop to a holding pen. On Saturday the week's gather would be thrown, hog-tied, and branded with a circled star.

"We caught and branded twenty-five of them this week," Denny said proudly. "Next week, we'll get even more."

"Maybe you're not such a bad influence after all," Adeline told Dan. "I've never seen him so excited. But how are you going to get the unbranded cows from your range without Ledoux discovering you're alive?"

"Maybe I'll send Chato and his bunch after them," Dan replied.

* * *

Eagle Pass, Texas. April 9, 1870.

When Dan rode in to Silas Hamby's ranch, he found only seven of the expected ranchers had shown up. Wolf Bowdre, Rufe Keeler, Ward McNelly, Duncan Kilgore, and Palo Elfego met him outside. Wolf Bowdre spoke for the five of them.

"We done our best," Bowdre said, "but some of these damn fools think they can reason with Ledoux. We reckoned it was better to talk to you out here, so's not to hurt our chances with them seven that had the sand to come."

"Smart thinking," Dan said.

"I got a bad feelin' about them that ain't joinin' us," Rufe Keeler said. "Sure as hell, somebody's gonna spill his guts to Ledoux, hopin' to gain favor with the varmint."

"Maybe," Dan replied, "but we didn't know who would join us until we talked to them. Even if Ledoux gets word of the drive, we won't make it easy for him. I'll tell all of you what I have in mind after I've met and talked to these new men. Let's go in and get started."

Silas wasted no time introducing Dan to the new arrivals. "Gents, this is Dan Ember. You been told somethin' about what he aims to do, and tonight he'll be tellin' you the rest of it. Stand up when I say your name, so's Dan will know who he's talkin' to. Dan, startin' on your left, these seven hombres is Chad Grimes, Hiram Beard, Garret Haddock, Kirby Wilkerson, Sloan Kuykendall, Walt Crump, and Cash Connolly."

Silas called their names slowly enough for each man to stand, and when he had finished, Dan began his talk. He touched on all the points he'd covered the previous Saturday, without interruption. When he had finished, there was a prolonged silence. Finally, Cash Connolly got to his feet.

"Ever'thing you've said is gospel. We're about to be skint like coyotes caught in a trap. The seven of us that come in tonight, we been talkin', and we're addin' eighteen riders to what you already got. But that's includin' our women and the kids that's old enough. Now, we ain't got a prayer of gatherin' such a herd as this and takin' it north to the railroad without a fight, and the riders we're countin' on is more'n half of 'em women and kids. We need hard-ridin', fightin' men, Ember, and I'd like to know where you aim to find 'em."

"I don't believe we'll find them in Texas," Dan said. "I've been hearing talk of a man called Chato, a Mexican or Spanish hombre with a band of Mexican Indian followers. They seem to have a bad name in Texas as well as Mexico, but they're whang-leather tough, and they're not afraid to fight."

"They sure as hell ain't," Sloan Kuykendall said. "They'll gut-shoot you at the drop of a hat, and one of them will drop the hat. Then, before you've breathed your last, they'll be across the border with your hosses. By God, I'd draw the line at takin' on that bunch, even if they was willin'."

"That's somethin' else we got agin us," Hiram Beard said. "We ain't got that many good cow horses, and this drive is goin' to need one hell of a hoss remuda."

"One thing at a time," Dan said. "We won't *need* a horse remuda unless we can hire some hard-riding, hard-fighting men, as Cash here put it. I realize Chato and his bunch aren't the kind you'd invite to Sunday dinner, and I don't know that we could hire them, but what other choice do we have?"

"Hell," Kirby Wilkerson said, "they're outlawed."

"So am I," Dan said, "the minute Burton Ledoux discovers I'm alive. I gunned down a pair of his killers."

"Ain't no law agin killin' some varmint that's pulled his iron and is aimin' to kill you," Garret Haddock said.

"Texas is occupied by the Federals," Dan said, "and

the law's what they say it is. We're not here to discuss written and unwritten Texas law. I want to know how many of you—if any—are opposed to us hiring Chato and his riders. That is, if we can find him, and if he's willing. If you don't want him, then we'll have to come up with somebody else, and I'm open to any suggestions."

"I know how to reach him," Silas said. "Whether he'll join us or not, that's another question."

"Damn it," Chad Grimes said, "this is a hard way to go. We got to beg the varmints that's been rustlin' our horses to save our bacon."

"Wrong," Dan said. "We're not begging them for anything. We're offering to pay them fifty dollars per month per man, with a hundred dollar bonus for each of them at the end of the trail. Payable, of course, when the herd is sold. I'm allowing for four months on the trail, so that would leave us owing each of them three hundred dollars."

"God A'mighty," Cash Connolly said, "I ain't seen that kind of money all at once, in ten years, and we're aimin' to hand it out to a bunch of thieves that's been stealin' us blind."

"Hell, they ain't gettin' it for nothin'," Silas said. "We're payin' for a chance to sell our cows, forty dollars an' more a head."

"That's what it amounts to," Dan said. "Besides, maybe we can buy some horses and pay for them at the end of the drive."

"Hell's fire," Rux Carper said, "we're likely to end up buyin' back the very hosses they stole from us."

"Yeah," Skull Kimbrough said, "or hosses they stole in Mexico."

"Damn it," Dan said, "we need horses and we need fighting men. Now I reckon we're all agreed that Chato and his bunch are outlaws, guilty of horse stealing, and God knows what else. The question is, are you going to let their wrongs stand in the way of your right to save yourselves and your families from being destroyed by Burton Ledoux?"

"You've just brought it home and dropped it on my doorstep," Wolf Bowdre said. "I'd say we swallow our pride and hire this Chato and his bunch, if we can."

Agreement was unanimous. Not because they approved of Chato and his band, but because there seemed to be no suitable alternative. It was bad means to a good end. Dan nodded to Silas, and Silas looked at Palo Elfego. Elfego nodded, but he looked extremely uncomfortable.

"I told you I know how to reach Chato," Silas said, "but that's just partly true. What it amounts to, I know somebody that knows how to reach him. You all know Palo Elfego. He's one of us, and I'll personally gut-shoot any man that lifts a finger against him because of what I'm about to tell you. Chato Guiterrez is the brother of Palo's wife. It's a real sacrifice Palo's makin', allowin' me to tell you this, and you can understand why he ain't exactly proud of it. Now I'm askin' the lot of you to authorize Palo to get the word to Chato, promisin' him and his bunch what we've agreed to pay and offerin' to buy some horses. All payable at the end of the drive, of course."

"I say let Palo set it up, if he can," Ward McNelly said. "We ain't thinkin' hard of you, Palo. A man ain't accountable for the things his kin does. God knows, I'd hate to be."

"Well, hell," Sloan Kuykendall said, "Chato and his bunch lives across the river. They won't be outlaws in Texas."

"Ah," Palo sighed, "I only wish it was so. Chato and his *companeros* are rebels, *Indios* stolen at birth from Texas by *Mejicano* dogs. Chato and his kind are hated in Mexico because they band together and take what they want. There is a powerful man, Santos Miguel Montoya, who has put a price on the head of Chato and his men. They are wanted on both sides of the border."

"Sounds like their enemies are all south of the border," Dan said. "In Texas they'll be earning honest money. We don't even know if they'll be interested until Palo makes contact."

"It's all up to you, Palo," Silas said. "When do you reckon you'll be knowin' something?"

"Per'ap in a week," Palo said.

"Let's make it two weeks," Dan said, "and give Palo enough time."

4

Eagle Pass, Texas. April 23, 1870.

"*T*onight," Dan said, "we'll know whether or not we'll be making the drive."

"Everything depends on those Mexican outlaws, then," Adeline said. "If Chato turns you down, we're finished."

"The big drive is," Dan said. "I'm not. One way or another, I still aim to destroy Burton Ledoux. But there's no way I can take more than twenty thousand head of Texas longhorns to Dodge City without some fighting men and a decent horse remuda."

"Chato will help us," Denny said.

When Dan again rode to Silas Hamby's ranch, he didn't share Denny's confidence in Chato Guiterrez and his gang. The money was generous enough, but only if the Mejicanos were willing to trust a gringo outfit all the way to Kansas. Of course, Palo Elfego might have some influence on his infamous brother-in-law, but they couldn't depend on that. When Dan reached the Hamby ranch, he found everybody there except Palo Elfego, and his absence had done little to reassure the rest of the men. Nobody said anything, but doubt was running high, and Dan could sense it. He even found himself suspecting Chato had refused their offer and that Palo was ashamed to show his face. Palo was as aware as any of them that theirs was a long shot, and that without fighting men and more horses, their cause was all but lost.. Suddenly there was the sound of approaching horses. Two riders. But when the door opened, only Palo Elfego entered. He knew every man in the room was awaiting some word from him, but he took his time. Finally he spoke.

"Your request has been delivered to Chato," Palo said, "and he wishes to speak to you. He comes in peace."

"Have him come in," Dan said. "Whether he accepts our offer or not, he won't be harmed. I'll shoot the first man that pulls a gun."

Palo stepped out the door, and when he returned, the eyes of every man in the room were on the rider who accompanied him. Chato Guiterrez was all one would have expected of him. He was dressed entirely in black, from his polished riding boots to an expensive Stetson with silver conchos worked into the band. His short black jacket was embroidered in red, and instep chains on his big roweled silver spurs chinged when he walked. But it wasn't all show. He wore not one pistol belt, but two, with a tied-down Colt on each hip. Every loop on both belts held a cartridge, and a leather thong around his neck suggested a Bowie knife down the back of his shirt. He didn't get too close to the waiting men, remaining near the door with his back to the wall. Palo Elfego nodded to Dan, and Chato turned to him.

"You are the segundo?"

"I'll do," Dan replied. "Say what you wish."

"Senor," Chato said in careful English, "I have been told of your need and of your offer. For the danger, senor, it is inadequate. Could we, as you Tejanos say, sweeten the pot?"

"Maybe," Dan said. "How much?"

"One hundred dollars each month for each of us, as long as we are on the trail, senor. We will wait until you have sold the cows. But we do not tend the cows. We are fighting men, senor."

"That's twice what we expected to pay," Dan said. "We'll have to talk among ourselves before I can give you an answer. Now what of the horses? Can you sell us some mounts and collect for them at the end of the drive?"

"You will need a large remuda, senor, and you could not pay what they are worth. Per'ap Chato sweeten the pot for you, eh? You will be allowed the use of one hundred fine *caballos*. They will become your remuda until we reach the *soldado* fort and the railroad. Then you will sell them for us."

"What about a bill of sale?"

"If one is needed," Chato replied, "you will write it."

"We need to talk," Dan said. "Give us a few minutes."

Chato nodded, stepped through the door and was gone.

"By God," Tobe Barnfield shouted, "four months on the trail, with a bonus, that's five hundred dollars a man."

"Split twenty-one ways, that's about twenty-four dollars a month for each of us," Dan said. "That's not much for fighting pay."

"It could be," Skull Kimbrough said. "How many riders has he got?"

"Fifteen," said a voice from outside the door.

Most of the men looked surprised, Palo Elfego was embarrassed, and Dan would have laughed if the situation hadn't been so perilous. He spoke quickly to prevent someone else cursing or saying something that might jeopardize the shaky alliance with Chato.

"Sixteen men at five hundred each comes to eight thousand dollars," Dan said. "It'll cost each of us about three hundred and eighty dollars at the end of the drive. Is there any one of you who thinks that's too much?"

"I think it is," Sloan Kuykendall said, "if they ain't gonna help us with the herd."

"We can manage the herd," Wolf Bowdre said, "even if we have to make riders of our women and kids. As I understand it, we're hirin' Chato and his men to help us reach Dodge City alive. If they can do that, we can handle the rest."

"Amen to that," Rux Carper said.

"I'm willing to pay," said Spence Wilder. "When we get the herd sold, we can afford to."

"Let's decide, one way or the other," said Dan. "Any one of you who's unwilling to accept Chato's offer, speak up."

Nobody said anything, and all eyes shifted to the uncomfortable Sloan Kuykendall.

"Well, hell," Kuykendall said, "three hundred and eighty dollars is a pile of money when you're broke. But Spence is right. When we've sold the herd, we'll have money. Let's hire them fightin' hombres and get this drive on the trail."

"Now that brings us to the horses," Dan said. "Are there any objections to Chato's offer?"

"I reckon that depends on who has to sign that bill of sale when the horses are sold at Dodge City," Ward McNelly replied.

That drew some grim laughter, for every man in the room knew what he meant. The horses were almost sure to be stolen, perhaps some of them in South Texas.

"I'll sign the bill of sale," Dan said. "Is there any more discussion?"

Nobody said anything, and Dan nodded to Palo Elfego. He went to the door and spoke to Chato, who stepped back into the room.

"We're accepting your offer, Chato," Dan said. "We

won't need the horses until we're ready to begin the drive. We will get word to you through Palo."

Chato nodded, stepped out the door, and there was a patter of hoofs as he rode away.

"One thing we ain't talked about," Silas Hamby said. "When are we aimin' to start this drive? I reckon every man in this room has been told his taxes is due July first, and if I was a bettin' man, I'd bet ever' last one of you is as unable to pay as I am. Now where are we gonna stand July first, besides out in the yard?"

Nobody laughed. Dan picked up the slack in the conversation, aware of where it was headed.

"We'll have to move out before July first," he said. "I want every one of us in a single outfit, an armed camp."

"I can see the need for that," Aubin Chambers said, "but we got to set a time to finish this gather."

"The last day of August," Kirby Wilkerson said, "and we can start the drive September first."

"Hell's fire," Rufe Keeler said, "some of us may not be ready by then. I ain't got even one man—or woman, for that matter—to ride backup."

"Damn it," Silas said, "this is gettin' us nowhere. Dan, what do you think?"

"I don't think we need a hard and fast date to finish the gather," Dan said, "and I don't think we should all remain separated until July first, when we're to be evicted. I believe we should throw all the outfits together now, as much for our own protection as for getting every man's gather done. We can take the gather one ranch at a time, every available rider roping and branding stock until that ranch has its thousand head ready for the trail. Then we move on to the next range, and when the last gather has been done, we're ready for the trail."

"I like that," Duncan Kilgore said. "When do we start?"

"Monday morning," Dan replied, "if everybody

agrees. Nobody gets hurt, because the drive won't begin until the last gather has been done. What it amounts to is, we'll all be together in a moving camp. Ledoux's killers can't gun us down one or two at a time, and we'll post guards at night so they can't take us by surprise. Now who's in favor of what I've just proposed?"

"I am," they shouted in almost a single voice.

"Then I'll put twenty-one numbers in my hat," Dan said, "and we'll draw lots. Your gather will be done according to the number you draw."

Dan took a sheet of paper and tore off twenty-one strips. Numbering them, he put them in his hat and invited each man to take a number. Quickly they did, and when there was only one left, Dan took it.

"Twenty-one," he said. "Faro. The luck of the draw."

"Whoa," Silas said, "we forgot somebody. What about the DeVoes?"

"I haven't forgotten them," Dan said. "I'm taking responsibility for their gather, and we'll do it after we've finished mine. The DeVoes will be part of our moving outfit, and young Denny and me will work as a roping team. So where do we begin Monday morning?"

"With me, I reckon," Silas said. "I got number one."

"I'm going to make a permanent list of names and numbers, so there'll be no disagreements or misunderstandings later," Dan said. "Starting with two, sing out the number, and then your name."

One by one the men called out their numbers, beginning with Sloan Kuykendall and ending with Spence Wilder.

"That's the order of your gather," Dan said when they were finished. "Those of you who have a good wagon, we can use as many as six, and we'll have to depend on the women to drive them. You'll be bringing only your clothing, grub, your weapons, tools for eating, and utensils for cooking. Those with extra wagon canvas, bring it. We'll need it for shelter. Since the first gather will be here, I'd suggest that you get your outfits together and be here tomorrow night. Those of you who are too far away, we'll look for you on Monday. Do you have any questions?"

"Once we abandon our spreads," Hiram Beard said, "there's no way to keep Ledoux from gettin' wise. Do you really believe he won't try to stop us?"

"He won't care about you quitting your place," Dan replied, "but I think he'll purely raise hell when he learns we're takin' a thousand head of cows from it. Just one more reason why we're pulling everybody together into one big outfit and ending each gather as quickly as we can. The best we can hope for is that Ledoux won't learn we're planning a drive until we're almost ready for the trail."

"We can't nowise count on that," Wolf Bowdre said. "There was five gents that was asked to this meetin' that didn't show. I'd bet my saddle at least one of the five will spill his guts to Ledoux before Monday morning."

"It won't hurt us that much," Dan said. "Ledoux will still count on intimidating us one at a time, and we'll all be together in a single outfit before he can make a move."

When the men had ridden out, Dan put on his hat, preparing to return to the DeVoe place.

"I got just one question," Silas Hamby said. "How'd you manage to draw the twenty-first gather for your-self?"

"I didn't drop twenty-one into the hat until the rest had drawn."

Uvalde, Texas. April 24, 1870.

Two men sat on the porch of the cabin that had once belonged to Daniel Ember. It was a lazy Sunday after-noon, and they passed a bottle back and forth. Sud-denly, the silence was broken by the patter of hoofbeats, and both men got to their feet to greet the approaching rider. The pair had been among those who had ridden down Dan Ember, and they stepped off the porch as the horseman reined up. He had a thin, ferret face, and his anxious eyes were on the pair of Colts facing him. One of the gunmen spoke.

"You'd better have business here, bucko. Have you?"

"I . . . I'm Dud Willett," the horseman stammered, "an' I got a place over in Zavala. I need to talk to Ledoux . . . uh, Mr. Ledoux. It's important."

"Mr. Ledoux ain't here," said the second man. He's in San Antone, and won't be back until sometime next week. Whatever you got to say, tell us and we'll pass it on. Git down."

Willett almost fell from the saddle, relaxing a little when his hosts put away their guns. Quickly he told what he knew of the planned trail drive. Finished, he looked for some sign of approval from the pair of impassive gunmen. There was none. He turned to his horse and mounted, eager to be gone. But before he rode away, he had a final request for the pair of surly gunmen.

"Please see that Mr. Ledoux gets my message. I . . . I hope he'll take care of me."

"Oh, he will," one of the men replied with a contemptuous half smile. "Believe me, bucko, when the time comes, he'll take care of you."

"It's going to be a little scary," Adeline said, "leaving the cabin and moving out into the open. We'll have no privacy."

"I can't wait," Denny said. "Who needs privacy?"

"A woman does," Lenore said.

"You ain't a woman," said Denny. "You're just an old persnickety girl."

She went after him, but he escaped out the door and leaped off the porch into the night.

"You won't be able to take anything except your clothes, whatever food you have, your eating tools, and cooking utensils," Dan said. "I doubt your old wagon can be patched up enough for the drive. We can use the mules to carry packs. Silas loaned us two more horses, and they're in the barn. I brought them back with me tonight."

"What about saddles?"

"Saddles too," Dan said. "They belonged to Silas's two sons. Double-rigged Texas saddles. You and Lenore will be riding like men."

"We can," Adeline said, "and we will. We have Levi's pants and shirts."

Lenore had gone to bed, and Denny came in off the porch.

"It's time you were in bed," Adeline said, "and it may be the last time you'll see a bed for months. We're leaving here tomorrow evening."

Sunday morning dawned clear, the sun warm, the grass green, and new leaves on the live oak and elm trees rustling in a gentle wind.

"Before we go, I want to go to the shallows and take a bath," Lenore said.

"I wouldn't mind that, myself," Adeline agreed. "Dan, what about you and Denny?"

"I don't want no bath," Denny said. "I ain't takin' my britches off with you and Lenore around."

"I think I'll pass," Dan said. "I wouldn't feel comfortable without my gun. Where is this shallows?"

"Downriver a few hundred yards," Adeline said. "The water there's not more than knee deep, and there's a sandy bottom."

"I'd better go part of the way with you," Dan said. "Things being the way they are, you shouldn't be down there alone. You comin', Denny?"

"No, sir," Denny said. "Last time, Lenore caught me and threw me in."

Dan followed Adeline and Lenore along the river until they were well away from the cabin.

"There's a bend in the river just beyond that stand of elms," Adeline said, "and that's where the shallows are."

"I'll wait this side of the elms," Dan told her. "If you need me, sing out."

They went on, and Dan wondered at the look of relief on Lenore's face. He knew she liked him, but she seemed wary, uncertain. He thought it might have something to do with the disgusting proposition Burton Ledoux had made. Even if everything else had been in order, he was old enough to be Lenore's father. Dan stretched out, his back against an elm, his hat tipped over his eyes. He was half dozing when a scream snapped him instantly awake. He sprang to his feet, cocking his Colt as he ran. Dan found the two women standing in the knee-deep water. Lenore seemed frozen where she stood, and it was Adeline who spoke.

"Lenore saw somebody, or thought she did," Adeline said. "Over there in the brush, on the farthest bank."

Dan could see nothing through the brush. He would be a fool to charge a concealed foe. He ran along the river, seeking to cross, to flank or get behind his adversary. The patter of hoofbeats told him he was too late. He returned to the shallows, finding Adeline and Lenore dressed. Briefly, the girl's eyes met his, and she turned away, blushing. Adeline had some trouble hiding her smile.

"There was somebody over there," Dan said, "but he got away before I was able to get across. He had a horse and was staked out here for some reason. He couldn't have known you and Lenore were coming here. He was here for some other reason, and you just caught his attention. He's gone now. You can still have your baths."

"I don't think so," Adeline said. "I'm out of the mood. What about you, Lenore?"

The girl only shook her head, blushing all the more furiously.

"Let's get back to the cabin, then," Dan said. "We should be getting ready to move out."

Denny was on the porch, cleaning his carbine. "I'm ready to go," he said.

"That's what you think. You and me are goin' to load the mules. Since we have no packsaddles, we'll have to load everything in gunnysacks. And we'll need a blanket for each mule's back, so they don't get rubbed raw."

"Do you want Lenore and me to begin filling the sacks," Adeline asked, "or do you have your own way?"

"I have my own way," Dan replied. "Just bring everything out on the porch, and bring as many gunnysacks as you have. We can only put so much in each one, because we'll have to load them in twos, with the necks tied together and slung across the mules' back. If we don't get a good balance, it'll be hell on the mules."

An hour past noon they were ready. Dan led one mule and Denny led the other, and they moved out. Adeline and Lenore lagged behind, taking a last look at the cabin that had been their home for thirteen years. Barnabas DeVoe had come to South Texas from Alabama, bringing with him his young family and his dreams. Now they were leaving him on the banks of the Rio Grande, where his lonely grave would be lost to the ravages of time. She choked down the lump in her throat and kicked her horse into a lope, catching up to Dan and Denny. Lenore was still looking back at the old cabin, and continued to do so until it was lost to view in the live oak and mesquite.

When Dan and the DeVoes reached Silas Hamby's place, they found fourteen families already there. Of the twenty-one men, only four—Silas Hamby, Rufe Keeler, Skull Kimbrough, and Dan Ember—had no wives. Spence Wilder, Duncan Kilgore, and Palo Elfego had sons Denny's age or a little older. Boyce Trevino, Palo Elfego, Aubin Chambers, Chad Grimes, Garret Haddock, and Cash Connolly all had daughters.

"When the others arrive," Dan said, "there'll be fifty of us, every one able to ride."

"I've lived here thirteen years," Adeline said, "and I know none of these people except Silas Hamby."

"A month ago I didn't know any of them," Dan said, "and I still don't know their wives, sons, and daughters. Let's put our horses and mules out to graze and go meet some of them. I reckon most of them will be strangers to one another. The trail drive is bringing us together."

Dan thought it strange that with so many families involved, there were only three sons, and then it hit him. These remaining sons had been five or six years old when the war had begun, so their older brothers must have gone to war, and like Silas's two sons, they had not returned. It was a sensitive subject and he put it out of his mind. Instead, he made the rounds, talking to the men about the roping teams. He learned the order had already been established. The men with sons already had their backup riders, while the rest had pretty well teamed up on their own. It was Wolf Bowdre who spoke to Dan about Silas.

"We know Silas is willin'," Bowdre said, "but he's got some years on him. We done some figurin', and we're one man shy of thirteen ropin' teams. That makes Silas the odd man, and . . . well, damn it, a man has his pride. How can we handle this without him feeling like he ain't man enough to take part in this drive?"

"I'll think of something," Dan said. "I see we already have five wagons, and Silas has one, and there may be another on the way. Why don't we have Silas drive his own wagon and put him in charge of all the others?

They'll need wheels greased, teams hitched and un-hitched, and those of us who don't have wagons will need space for our clothing, bedrolls, and the little we're taking with us. The wagons will have to be loaded carefully, so that we're not unloading them every eve-ning and reloading them the next morning. I reckon, except for Silas, we'll be dependin' on the womenfolk to drive the wagons, and it should make them feel better, havin' a man as a kind of wagon boss."

"I like that," Bowdre said, "and the others will too, if you can convince Silas. With five females at the reins, his might be the toughest job of all."

But Dan had no trouble convincing Silas of the im-portance of his duties. If the old-timer suspected they were trying to make it a little easier on him, he said nothing. Instead, he became acquainted with the lady drivers and made arrangements to grease their wagons and help to ready them for the trail. The wives and daughters reached some agreement regarding the cook-ing, and by suppertime a dozen cooks were at work, preparing a meal for the entire outfit. Silas approached Dan after supper.

"I'm givin' you credit for this, Dan. Frankly, I had my doubts about it ever comin' to pass, and it had nothin' to do with you. I just never seen so many folks come to-gether this quick and work together so well."

"We're not to Dodge yet," Dan said, "and it's likely Ledoux hasn't heard about us. I agree we're doing well, but we can't become overconfident and let our guard down."

"I don't aim to," Silas said. "Tomorrow, while the rest of you are busy ropin' cows, I aim to take my wagon and empty the store. I'd not be a mite surprised if Ledoux and his bunch don't burn the place to the ground once they learn what we're doin'."

"I admire your thinking," Dan said. "Why don't you take a couple more wagons with you, instead of having to load your own all the way to the bows? If you'll talk to some of the women, they'll go along and help you load. If you have more ammunition, with its weight, we'll do well to spread it out among all the wagons."

"I got plenty," Silas said. "I seen this day comin' back in 'sixty, 'fore the first shot was fired. I reckoned if it come to that, me and my boys could fort up and hold out for a while. I even got a keg of black powder."

"Bring everything," Dan said, "and when this drive is done, I'll see that you're paid for it."

"That ain't botherin' me," Silas said. "Way things is goin', without this trail drive, I'd be ruined anyhow. I figure I owe you plenty already, and I just want to say this, while I got the chance. If anything happens to me, and I don't ride this trail to the end, whatever I got comin' from this drive, I want you to have it. Agreed?"

For a long moment Dan said nothing. When his eyes met those of the older man, he understood what Silas hadn't been able to put into words. His sons were gone, and there was nobody to whom he could leave the little that he owned. Rather than have it lost, he wanted it to go to someone who meant something to him.

"Agreed," Dan said. He offered his hand, and Silas took it.

5

Maverick County, Texas. April 25, 1870.

*T*he gather began as scheduled on Monday morning at first light. Silas, accompanied by the Bowdre and McNelly women in two extra wagons, drove to his store. The other five families arrived before noon, Kirby Wilkerson's wife driving yet another wagon. They now had seven. The roping teams rode in at noon for a meal of fried steak and beans.

"We're gettin' in the swing of it," Dan told them. "There's more than a hundred of the brutes in the holding pens right now, and we'll double that before dark. We'll just about finish a gather in four days."

"Won't hurt if we go over the limit a little," Rux Carper said, "since we'll lose some on the drive. We can divide up the extry when we get to Dodge."

The sun was an hour high when Silas Hamby and his three wagons returned.

"We cleaned the place out slick as a whistle," Silas said, "and I'd of been two days by myself. Miz Bowdre and Miz McNelly is a fine pair of teamsters."

Come sundown, Dan's prediction proved accurate. The first day's gather had resulted in 220 longhorns in the holding pen. After supper, Dan announced the order of the watches for the night.

"There's twenty-one of us," he said, "and we each have a number for our gather. Those of you with the first seven numbers will take the first watch, from sundown to ten o'clock. Those with numbers eight through fourteen will take over at ten, to be relieved at two o'clock by those of us with the last seven numbers. It may be too soon for Ledoux and his bunch to try anything, but we won't risk it. Whether your watch is done or still ahead of you, don't shuck anything but your hats, and keep your guns handy."

Silas Hamby, Wolf Bowdre, Boyce Trevino, Tobe Barnfield, Rufe Keeler, Spence Wilder, and Ward McNelly—the riders for the first watch—saddled up.

"Circle the entire camp area, including the holding pen," Dan told them, "and don't hesitate to wake everybody if there's a need to."

Although surrounded by other people, the DeVoes had staked themselves out a sleeping area beneath an enormous oak. Dan had been spreading his bedroll there, and nobody questioned his presence. They all knew of Barnabas DeVoe's fate, and on the western frontier, a woman needed a man. Adeline DeVoe was the envy of many of the women, yet she had quickly made friends. It had been her turn to help with the cooking and the cleanup that followed, so it was a while before she joined Dan, Lenore, and Denny in the area where they slept.

"Lord," she said, "I'm tired, but I'll have to agree this is exciting. I'd never met these people until yesterday, but they're just like we are, and I really like them. Lenore, you have to get over being so shy. And Denny—"

"I reckon Denny don't feel much like socializin', after ropin' cows all day," Dan said. "Give it time. We're just into the first gather, and there's a long trail when all the gathering's done."

"We'll be done with this gather before the week's out," Denny said. "Do we brand these cows or move on, come back and do it later?"

"We'll do this from start to finish," Dan said, "and that includes the branding. I reckon we can do it in a day, easy, with twelve roping teams at work. And when we're done, we'll take the herd with us to the next gather."

"That's going to be dangerous," Adeline said, "when we get to your range. You said Ledoux's using your cabin for a headquarters."

"Far as I know he is," Dan said. "Before we get to my range, I aim to talk to the rest of the men. We'll still be a week away from taking the trail, but I'd like to go ahead and bring in Chato and his bunch. I believe they're equal to anybody Ledoux can send after us."

"If you're going to use them at all," Lenore said in a rare outburst, "I don't see why you didn't hire them starting July first. That's when everybody's taxes are due, and that's when he takes our land. After that, can't he just claim all the cows on each ranch and stop us from taking them?"

"Lenore," Adeline said, "you're out of line. This is men's business."

"No," Dan said, "she's done some serious thinking, and she's touched on something that may become a problem. As we near that July first deadline, I aim to talk to the men about this. We may well have to negotiate some more with Chato. We'll finish the first gather this week, includin' the branding. Working seven days a week, we'll have sixty days before Ledoux's tax deadline. That means we can likely finish a dozen gathers, following this one. We'll have eight gathers ahead of us before we can begin the drive, so we can't take the trail north before September first. That means we'll have a good eight weeks of branding cows off range we no longer own. That's what Lenore's lookin' at, and it's an important possibility we can't afford to ignore."

For a moment Lenore's eyes met his, and then she turned quickly away. There was a prolonged silence, eventually broken by Adeline.

"Dan, if you must have a thousand cows, do you have to risk your life by taking them from right under Burton Ledoux's nose? With all the natural increase, we can easily gather two thousand head from our place, and without the risk. Please don't let your pride get in the way of your common sense."

"Well, if we're going to be sensible about it," Dan said, "do we *need* a thousand head for you and a thousand head for me?"

"Not as far as I'm concerned," Adeline said. "I'm surprised somebody hasn't objected to us having twice as many cows as everybody else. Instead of risking a fight with Ledoux's bunch over cattle from your old range, why not just take a thousand head from our place and let it go?"

"That would likely get the trail drive started a week sooner," Dan said. "I'll suggest it to the rest of the outfit, and while I'm about it, I aim to at least have them consider Lenore's suggestion. Once we're past Ledoux's tax deadline, I don't doubt he'll try to claim every cow on every spread he's able to get his hands on."

When Dan began saddling up for the third watch, he found Adeline awake.

"I'd like to ride with you awhile, if you don't mind," she said. "I can see we're not going to have much time alone."

"I'll saddle your horse," Dan said.

The seven riders circled the area, three in one direction and four in the other. Dan and Adeline rode awhile in silence. Finally she spoke.

"I don't know what came over Lenore tonight, but

you handled it well. It was . . . well, like she wanted you to notice her, to approve of her."

"She seems skittish around me," Dan said. "That time I went with the two of you to the river, I don't believe she thought I was goin' to stop shy of watching the two of you get into the water. Then, when she saw somebody in the bushes and screamed, I came on the run. I reckon I really got on the bad side of her over that."

"It wasn't your fault. She knows that, although it embarrassed the life out of her. So much has happened in the past few weeks. After Denny found you, I made her help me tend your wounds. Then Barnabas—her father —came home, and it seemed like he'd lost his mind. God help us all, we wished he had never come back, but I think it hit Lenore the hardest. She was just getting to know you, and you were forced to leave. Then Barnabas kept us all scared half to death until he was killed. And finally, that disgraceful move that Burton Ledoux made toward her . . ."

"I reckon she's more of a woman than she realizes," Dan said. "God, my ma was just fourteen when I was born."

"You've never spoken of your parents."

"No reason to," he said. "They died in a Comanche attack when I was not quite nineteen."

"I'm sorry," she said. "That's a meddlesome question I shouldn't have asked."

"It doesn't matter. Time has a way of healing just about everything."

Their first night with the growing herd passed uneventfully, and after the second day's roping, their gather lacked reaching five hundred by only a few head.

"We can step it up some," Cash Connelly said, "and finish a gather in four days. On the fifth day, we can wind up the branding."

"I think we can start the drive a week sooner than we

might have," Dan said. "I'd like to suggest a slight change in plans, and I'll talk to you about it after supper, before the first watch rides out."

When supper was done, after the women had begun the cleanup, Dan spoke to them about eliminating the twenty-first gather, which was to have been his own. Instead, he proposed that he and Adeline take a thousand head from the DeVoe range. He said nothing of their personal feelings or of their plans when the drive was finished, but every man understood and approved.

"I'm in favor of that," Wolf Bowdre said, "for more than one reason. Is there any of you that don't think it's a smart move? Let's hear it for Dan and Miz Adeline."

There were shouts of approval from the men and smiles from the women. But Daniel Ember wasn't finished.

"I appreciate your support," he said. "Now I think there's something else we ought to consider. We're all facing the same tax deadline of July first. After that, we're going to be roping and branding cattle from lands that legally belong to Burton Ledoux. We'll still be two months away from starting our drive, and we'll be wide open to whatever retaliation Ledoux may choose. It's been suggested to me that we bring Chato and his men across the river two months early, to watch our backs while we rope and brand cows, and to guard against sneak attacks at night. I believe it's worth considering. What do the rest of you think?"

"Hell, no," Rux Carper bawled. "Not at a hundred dollars a man for two more months."

"Them's my sentiments," said Aubin Chambers. "Damn it, there's twenty-one of us, and our womenfolk can shoot if they have to."

"Forget I mentioned it," Dan said. "I reckon we'll just wait until after July first and see what happens."

Chambers looked upon Dan with some disfavor for having made so foolish a suggestion, but the time was coming when he would regret the small victory he thought he had won.

"I tally one thousand and fifteen head," Dan said late Thursday afternoon. "Tomorrow we'll brand them, and Saturday we'll move on to Sloan Kuykendall's place."

Uvalde, Texas. April 29, 1870.

On Friday, Burton Ledoux returned to his headquarters near Uvalde, the cabin that had once belonged to Dan Ember. The two men Ledoux had left there relayed the message brought to them by Dud Willett.

"One of you ride to San Antonio," Ledoux said. "I want you to fetch Vance, Sumner, Byler, Rowden, Collins, Savage, and Campbell. I think we'll call on some of these cow outfits and see for ourselves."

Ledoux bit off the end of a cigar and spat it on the floor. On one wall hung a tattered calendar, and he studied it, counting the days. So they had banded together, preparing for a drive, had they? There was no way they could rope and brand enough cows before his July first deadline, and then the cattle would no longer be theirs. Damn them, they had some learning to do, and he would be the one to teach them.

Maverick County, Texas. May 1, 1870.

On Sunday morning Silas and the seven wagons led out, bound for Sloan Kuykendall's place. The women, sons, and daughters followed the herd, riding drag. The men were split up into flank and swing positions, keeping the herd moving. The few days in the holding pens, followed by branding, had done little to civilize the longhorns, and they attempted to break away at every opportunity. The seven miles to the Kuykendall place took most of the day.

"Well, hell," Spence Wilder said, "it'll cost us a day between each gather, just gettin' to the next place. We haven't counted on that."

"It's not time wasted," Dan said. "By the time we begin the drive, most of our herd will be trailwise. The last three or four gathers will need some settlin' down, but seventy-five percent of our bunch will have realized they're a herd by the time we take the trail north."

They set up camp two miles south of the Kuykendall cabin, preparing to begin the gather on Monday morning. Thunderheads began moving in from the west, and they barely managed to get through supper before the rain began. Many of the families had brought extra wagon canvas, and there was shelter for the bedrolls. Dan and the DeVoes shared shelter with the Kuykendalls. When Dan was awakened for the third watch, the rain had ceased. Dawn broke with clear skies and laughter around the breakfast fires. Optimism ran high, and with thoughts of the first successful gather strong on their minds, they began the second.

Maverick County, Texas. Monday, May 2, 1870.

Ledoux and his seven men reined up before the deserted DeVoe cabin.

"Collins," Ledoux said, "take a look inside."

Collins dismounted, peered through the cabin's half-open door, then stepped inside. In a moment he returned.

"Nobody there," Collins said. "Bunks is all been stripped, and no clothes that I could see."

"They've pulled out, then," Ledoux said. "We'll ride on to Hamby's store."

Ledoux led out, and they rode to the village that had been Eagle Pass, to find it completely deserted. Even the livery had been closed.

"Come on," Ledoux said. "Let's try Hamby's ranch."

Finding Hamby's cabin deserted, they rode eastward, toward Kuykendall's, and eventually struck the trail left by the cattle gathered on Silas's range.

"They're trailin' right smart of a herd," Vance said. "What are we goin' to do when we catch up to 'em?"

"Just follow my lead," Ledoux said, "and don't do anything unless I tell you to."

They came upon the holding pen first, quickly erected so that the cattle could drink from a spring runoff. The plain was flat, and in the distance was the white of wagon canvas beneath a stand of live oak.

"Must be nearly a thousand cows in that bunch," Byler said, "and I'd swear I've seen that star-in-a-circle brand somewhere before."

"Hell, Byler, you should have," Campbell said. "Ever' Ranger in Texas is wearin' it."

Ledoux and his companions rode on, reining up well before they reached the camp. Confronting them was Amy Wilder, Fanny Bowdre, Tamara Elfego, and Adeline DeVoe. The four of them had rifles cocked and ready, and it was Adeline DeVoe who spoke.

"You aren't welcome here, Ledoux."

"Ah," Ledoux said, "it's come to this, has it? I regret that I have no time for you ladies. I believe it's time I had a serious talk with your men."

"We can save you some time," Fanny Bowdre said. "Our men will tell you to turn your horses around and ride away from here, and that's what we're tellin' you to do."

Ledoux trotted his horse forward, and Fanny blasted a slug into the dirt beneath the animal's feet. Frightened, the horse threw Ledoux and galloped back the way it had come. One of Ledoux's companions caught the reins as Ledoux got up and recovered his hat. Some of Ledoux's men had their hands on the butts of their Colts, but Ledoux shook his head.

"You will be seeing me again, ladies," Ledoux said

coldly. "You and your men." He mounted, turned his horse and rode away, his men following.

"*Perro,*" Tamara Elfego said, "*hijo de asno.* Chato kill you dead."

Dan, Wolf Bowdre, and Rufe Keeler rode up just minutes after Ledoux and his men had ridden away.

"We heard the shot," Dan said. "Ledoux?"

"Him and seven others," Adeline replied. "Fanny fired and frightened Ledoux's horse. It threw him. Before they rode away, Ledoux said we'd be seeing him again."

"I've been expecting this," Dan said. "Somebody talked, and Ledoux came to see for himself. He's seen our gather, and he won't have any trouble figurin' out what we aim to do. When he's had time to think about it, he'll know we can't possibly finish these gathers before his July first tax deadline. I don't doubt he aims to come after us, but I think he'll do it legally. He has time on his side, and it's our enemy."

They all returned to their duties in a more somber mood, taking word to the rest of the outfit. After supper, Adeline spoke to Dan.

"I'm dreading July first. Like you said, he'll hide behind the law. Why shouldn't he? Even with your beard grown out, I'm afraid he'll recognize you and send the law after you with a murder warrant."

"He only saw me for a few seconds before the gunplay," Dan said, "and I was skin and bones. The only two of his men who saw me close enough to know me are the two I killed, and if we're attacked, I doubt Ledoux will ride with his killers."

Even as Dan sought to reassure Adeline, he wasn't all that sure himself. Ledoux would know that somebody had organized the gathers and planned the trail drive, and he would likely have his doubts that any of it had been planned by the ranchers he expected to intimidate. After the July first deadline, there would be problems yet to be discussed with his outfit. One of them was the fact that the cattle they had gathered could no longer be grazed or watered on the land seized by Ledoux. The growing gather must be kept on free range, with riders to guard against stampedes. This, he thought bitterly, would have been suited to Chato and his men.

When the day's gather had been done and supper was behind them, Dan called the outfit together before the first watch saddled up.

"I reckon all of you know Ledoux and his riders were here today," he began, "so he knows what we're planning to do. Today he didn't have a legal leg to stand on, but after July first, we'll be changing positions with him. What I aim to talk to you about is not an immediate problem, but it's not too soon to consider it. Once we've forfeited our spreads—including grazing and water—we'll be forced to find free range for the cows we've gathered. By my figures, we should have thirteen thousand head by July first, and amigos, that's goin' to take one hell of a lot of graze. I reckon we can manage that, and I'll come back to it, but there's more. Wherever we graze these cows, we must have armed men there to protect them during the day, while we're all at work on these final gathers. We leave them unprotected, even for a day, and Ledoux's bunch will stampede them from hell to breakfast. As I see it, we'll have to leave at least half our riders with the gather, heavily armed, just to prevent a stampede by Ledoux's men."

"Hell, no," Cash Connolly shouted. "With half the riders, it'll take us two weeks to do a gather. We'll still be brandin' cows come Christmas."

"Leave our gather untended long enough for Ledoux's bunch to stampede it," Dan said, "and we'll still be here next *spring,* roundin' up the cattle we've already branded."

"We should of talked about this 'fore we got neck deep in this damn trail drive," Rux Carper said. "Now we're caught between a rock and a hard place. We got to use half our riders to protect the branded stock, leavin' us only half the men we need for the rest of the gathers."

"Talking about it sooner wouldn't have changed anything," Dan said. "We'd still be lacking the men necessary to guard the herd while we finish the gathers. I told you I'd come back to this, and I aim to. It involves graze and water for the cows already gathered and branded, after Ledoux takes over everybody's range on July first. I want all of you to get together and draw up a rough map of Maverick, Kinney, Uvalde, and Zavala counties. I need to know where your boundaries adjoin one another, so that I'll have some idea as to where the free range is. We can't use any of your graze or water after July first, or we risk having Ledoux claim the gather. Do all of you understand what we have to do?"

"I do," Aubin Chambers said, "and it's startin' to look more impossible all the time."

"As I recall," Skull Kimbrough said, "it was you that was agin us bringin' in Chato and his bunch for protection startin' July first, so's we can finish these gathers."

"It was, by God," Chambers said heatedly, "and I'm *still* against it. Why risk our lives getting a herd to market, and then pay out all the profits to a bunch of damn renegades?"

"You have a little time," Dan said. "None of this is likely to become a problem until after July first. Just keep in mind that I need that rough map of your boundaries, so I can begin looking for some free range we can use."

The riders on the first watch saddled up and rode out. Silas Hamby and some of the other riders wanted to talk to Dan.

"That wasn't such a bad idee," Silas said, "bringin' Chato and his riders on across the river. I'm thinkin' that last two months of ropin' and brandin' cows may be more dangerous than the drive itself. You reckon I ought to talk to the rest of 'em, and see if we can't override Chambers?"

"No," Dan said. "With all our other problems, we can't afford a fight within our own ranks. All of us agreed that we need more fighting men once we take the trail. I believe once Carper, Chambers, and some of the others have thought about it, they'll see the need for more men *now*. But if they don't, if they still need some convincing, then I expect Burton Ledoux to take care of that."

Dan was awakened for the third watch at two o'clock. The skies had clouded, with only an occasional star peeking through. The seven riders circled wide of the sleeping camp and the drowsing herd. When trouble came, it was from the sky, trailing sparks from a fast burning fuse. Dynamite! A second charge was only seconds behind the first, and they both let go above the herd. A tidal wave would have been easier to control than the stampede that resulted, but that wasn't the worst of it. Rifles roared out of the darkness, and slugs ripped into wagon canvas, and there were cries of pain. Dan and the riders on the third watch fired at muzzle flashes, but their own muzzle flashes drew fire. It all ended as suddenly as it had begun. A cow bawled somewhere, and a woman was screaming. Some of the riders had ridden after the running herd, while some of those who had been sleeping were firing from within the camp.

"Damn it," Dan shouted, "hold your fire. It's over. Those of you from the third watch, come on in."

There was the dull glow of lanterns through canvas shelters, and cries from those who had been wounded. Fanny Bowdre was bleeding from a wound in her left shoulder. Skull Kimbrough had taken a slug through his left thigh, Rux Carper had a bloody burn across his backside, and there were other wounds that Dan had to investigate later. He was working his way toward the shelter where the woman had been screaming. The screams had subsided into heartbroken sobs, and in the dim light of the lantern Dan could see Aubin Chambers with his face buried in his hands. He and Odessa knelt before the bloodied body of their only child, fifteen-year-old Alesia. Dan knelt beside Chambers, a comforting arm about the man's shoulders, and Chambers broke down, sobbing with his stricken wife. Others soon were there, including Adeline DeVoe, and someone spread a blanket over the dead girl. Adeline knelt beside Dan with a whispered request.

"Lenore's been hit. It's not serious, but she's scared. I wish you'd go talk to her. Denny's there, but he's not much help."

Dan found Lenore with Denny, as well as Kirby and Hattie Kuykendall. Lenore lay on her back, a bloody bandage around her right thigh. Adeline was right behind Dan, and when she nodded to the Kuykendalls, they left. Denny, for once, didn't need to be told. He followed the Kuykendalls. Dan knelt beside the silent Lenore.

"I think," he told the girl, "your suggestion was a good one. I don't believe this would have happened if we'd had Chato and his men out there with us. We're goin' to boil some water, and then we'll take care of your wound. Is it hurting you?"

Lenore said nothing. To his surprise, she reached for him, and he held her close while she wept. When her tears and trembling had ceased, he eased her down and got to his feet.

"Get her ready," Dan said. "If somebody doesn't have a pot of water on the fire, I'll see to it. Then I'll find Silas. He has a medicine chest in his wagon."

Silas already had a fire going, and so did several others. Most of the men wandered through the camp with their rifles, seeking to comfort those who had been wounded. To Dan's surprise, Aubin Chambers stepped out of the night, into the light of the fire where Dan and Silas stood. Chamber's face was twisted with grief, but there was fury in his eyes, and Dan prepared himself for the worst.

"Ember," Chambers said, "I've been a damn fool. You were right, and God help me, I've traded my little girl's life for what it would have cost to pay for some protection. I'm going to finish these gathers, finish this drive, and by God, if you don't kill Burton Ledoux, then I will. Come first light, I want you to call everybody together and let's talk about bringing Chato and his men across the river. I don't care if they are killers. I'll side you till hell freezes. Will you take my hand, after what I've done?"

"I will," Dan said, and he did.

6

Nobody slept the rest of the night. Only Alesia Chambers had been killed, but there were a dozen wounded. There had been little Dan could do, and he had assisted Adeline in the cleaning and disinfecting of Lenore's wound. As Adeline had already determined, it wasn't serious, although it had seemed far worse as the result of much bleeding.

"Now," Dan told the girl, "we're even. You helped patch me up, and I've done the same for you."

A grave had been dug for Alesia Chambers, and the girl was laid to rest at sunrise. From a worn Bible, Silas Hamby read the word over her, and before Spence Wilder and Duncan Kilgore filled the grave, the rest of the outfit walked sorrowfully back to camp. The women set about preparing breakfast, and even before it was done, Aubin Chambers had called the men together. Without asking permission from anybody, he spoke.

"Gents, I want every man of you to know I made a big mistake, and I paid for it today. You remember Dan Ember suggestin' we bring Chato and his men north for our protection durin' the gather? Damn fool that I was, all I could see was what it would cost us. Now look what it's cost me. I'm backtrackin' on everything I said. I say let's hire Chato and his riders to stick with us through the rest of this gather, as well as takin' the trail to Dodge at the end of it. And I say we offer 'em the same money to ride with us here as we're payin' 'em on the trail."

Dan said nothing. His eyes were on the rest of the men, and their eyes met those of their women. Chambers's words were strong, but not nearly as strong as the memory of young Alesia Chambers being lowered into her grave.

"He's right," Ward McNelly shouted. "Let's do what we should have done when Daniel Ember suggested it. Ledoux's got his killers. Let's hire some fighting men of our own. Let's send for Chato and his bunch, and do it now."

There were shouts of approval from the rest of the outfit, with some of the women joining in. Dan turned to Palo Elfego.

"You heard them, Palo. Get word to Chato. Tell him he's needed here while we finish the gathers. A hundred dollars a month for him and each of his men for as many months as it takes to finish this gather. Fighting wages."

"*Si*," Palo said. He beckoned to Pablo, his fourteen-year-old son. The boy listened as Palo spoke swiftly in Spanish. Pablo then mounted his horse and rode south in a slow gallop.

"That's all we can do until we hear from Chato," Dan said. "The blasts killed three cows. Some of you dress them out, salvage the hides and as much of the meat as you can. The rest of us will begin gathering the scattered cattle."

Wounded, Skull Kimbrough was unable to go. Silas Hamby took it upon himself to skin the three cows, and Ward McNelly offered to help.

"Let me go with you," Odessa Chambers said. "I must have something to do, or I'll lose my mind."

"I go," Tamara Elfego said.

Dan and the rest of the men who were able to ride set out to find the stampeded cattle. From the looks of the tracks, it wasn't going to be easy.

"They've split seven ways from Sunday," Dan said. "No man rides alone. There's eighteen of us. We'll ride in twos. When you find a bunch, head 'em back this way and ride on. When they start to thin out, ride back, pickin' up each bunch as you come in. We'll get the nearest ones first, and then we'll all ride together for the rest of them."

It was slow work, and with the sun just an hour away from the western horizon, Dan ran a quick tally.

"We're still missin' three hundred, and I reckon we'll have to do a hell of a lot of ridin' to find the others. For sure we'll never find 'em before sundown, and we can't afford such a loss, so we'll have to hunt them tomorrow."

"Two days shot to hell," Wolf Bowdre groaned. "We purely can't afford any more stampedes."

They drove the recovered cattle back to the area where they had been bedded down the night before, near a small stream. After supper Dan called the men together.

"Until we have more men, I'm eliminating the third watch. There'll be only two, and we'll change at midnight. Those of you with the first ten numbers will take the first watch, and the rest, includin' me, will take the second. Does anybody object to that?"

"After last night," Rufe Keeler said, "I think it's a damn good idea."

Nobody disagreed with that. With Skull Kimbrough wounded, they had ten riders for each watch. Dan sat with his back against an oak, talking to Adeline. Lenore was within the shelter afforded by Sloan Kuykendall's extra wagon canvas, and Denny was elsewhere in the camp.

"It's been a terrible day in some ways," Adeline said,

"and a wonderful one in others. I'm just sick over the Chambers child being killed, and I'm completely mystified by Lenore's behavior. When I found she'd been shot, I don't remember what I did or what I said, but it was as though she didn't even know I was there. She seemed in shock, and she didn't come out of it until she saw you. Thank you for taking care of her wound. She had me so unnerved, I'm not sure I could have done it. She's taken to the Kuykendalls, and I'm going to leave her with them tonight. Why don't you go and say good night to her?"

When Dan stepped into the shelter, the Kuykendalls left him alone with the girl. While she had no greeting for him, she didn't turn away or blush.

"I just came to say good night and see how you're feeling," he said.

"I feel . . . kind of guilty. Alesia Chambers is dead, and I—"

"You're not to blame for that," Dan said. "Your suggestion was good, and we've sent for Chato and his men to ride with us throughout this gather, as well as for the drive to Dodge. Now you put all this out of your mind and rest." He turned to go.

"Dan?"

He turned, and found her leaning on one elbow. "I'm glad you came back to us," she said.

"So am I," he responded. He grinned at her and tipped his hat.

The following morning at first light, Dan called the riders together right after breakfast.

"These damn cows we're missing have to have water. Not countin' the Rio to the south of us, where's the nearest creek or river?"

"To the east, in Zavala County," said Wolf Bowdre, whose spread was in that direction. "There's the Nueces River, which is the closest sure water, and in the southwest part of Zavala, Cherokee lake. If the varmints have strayed that far, they'll favor the Nueces. It's brushy, with plenty of mesquite and prickly pear."

"That's where they are," Tobe Barnfield said. "Give cows a choice, and they'll head for the thorniest, meanest damn county in Texas."

"That's where we're going, then," Dan said. "We must find them today."

Wolf Bowdre led out. They rode north a ways to compensate for possible fanning out of the herd, and then rode eastward. The upper reaches of the Nueces was lined with live oak, pecan, and elm, and although there were tracks, they found no longhorns.

"This is my range," Bowdre said, "and these are likely the tracks of my cows. Way it's warmed up, they'll all be down yonder in the breaks. We're too far north."

They rode south along the Nueces until it became choked with head-high mesquite, where, with the exception of prickly pear, nothing else seemed to thrive.

"We'll split up in teams of two," Dan said, "and work both sides of the river."

It was slow, hard work, and many of the cows they drove out of thickets were unbranded. The animals with the circle star brand had drifted downriver to the southernmost stretch of the Nueces. By late afternoon they had gathered 320, thirty of which were unbranded.

"We'll cut them out and brand them after we're done with the Kuykendall gather," Dan said. "Let's get this bunch back to camp."

By the time they reached camp with the rest of the stampeded herd, it was suppertime, and Pablo Elfego had returned. He spoke to his father in Spanish, and Palo turned to Dan.

"Chato and his riders have accepted our terms," Palo said. "They will be here sometime before dawn. I am with the second watch. I will listen for the sound of their arrival."

That meant Chato would be arriving sometime after midnight. Dan began to consider his options, how he might best utilize these fighting men. Ledoux must eventually learn of their alliance with Chato, but Dan hoped by then his outfit might be finished with the gather and ready to begin the trail drive. Some of the other riders had questions as to the duties of the infamous Mexican band, and sought Dan after supper. Among the curious was Wolf Bowdre, and it was to him that Dan spoke.

"Get everybody together," he said. "If we're going to discuss Chato and what we aim for him to do, then let's do it before he gets here."

When Bowdre brought the men together, most of the women came with them. When they had all gathered, Dan spoke.

"Chato and his men will be here sometime tonight. I have some ideas as to what I'd like them to do, but I'm open to suggestions."

"You been right at every turn in the trail," Aubin Chambers said. "Tell us what you got in mind, and if any man don't like it, let him come up with somethin' better. Do any of you disagree with that?"

"All right," Dan said when they remained silent, "here's what I think we should do once Chato and his men get here. During daylight hours, while all our riders are roping cattle, Chato and his riders will conceal themselves unless they're needed. They'll virtually surround the area, protecting our camp and the cattle we've gathered and branded. At night we'll continue our two watches, but we'll ride closer to camp. Chato and his men will ride an outer perimeter, with orders to cut down anybody trying to infiltrate their line. In other words, that's all Chato and his riders will have to do, day or night. They'll take Ledoux's surprise attack and turn it around. Now if that rubs anybody's hide the wrong way, you're welcome to come up with somethin' better."

"I like it," Wolf Bowdre said, "but it's purely defensive. How much are we goin' to take before we hit Ledoux with a dose of his own medicine?"

"We're going to avoid any attacks on Ledoux," Dan said, "because that would give him a perfect excuse to send the soldiers after us. As long as he's attacking us, he's abusing his position and we're defending ourselves. He can't legally accuse us of rustling, because we're gathering only unbranded cows. Even a rustling charge won't justify bringing in Union soldiers. No, we'll defend ourselves, but we won't go looking for a fight. Now that can change, once we're out of Texas, where scalawags such as Ledoux don't own the law, but until then we can only defend ourselves. I hope all of you can see my reason for doing no more than that."

"I can see it," Silas said. "Even with Chato and his men, we can't fight the soldiers, but by God, we can make believers of Ledoux's night-ridin' killers."

"I'm satisfied," Aubin Chambers said, "as long as there are no more surprise attacks. This is what we should have done right from the start, and I'm sorry I opposed it."

"If there are no objections," Dan said, "this is what we'll ask of Chato and his riders."

The moon had set, and Dan judged it to be no more than an hour from first light when another rider from the second watch approached him. It was Palo.

"Chato and his men are here," he said softly. "I will ride and meet them."

Dan said nothing, and Palo was soon lost in the predawn darkness. Dan had heard nothing, and he wondered what Palo heard to alert him to the presence of the Mexican renegades.

"What would you have us do, senor?" inquired a voice from the shadows.

"Chato," Dan said, "let me tell you what's happened so far and what we are up against."

As briefly as he could, Dan told the Mexican of their race with time in the branding of cattle for the trail drive, of the sneak attack of the Ledoux riders, and of his plan to see that it didn't happen again.

"When these killer gringos come, we fight," Chato said.

"That's it," Dan said. "We don't go looking for them, but if they come after us, gun them down."

"*Si,*" Chato said. "You will not see or hear us, senor, unless we are needed."

With that, he was gone. Palo laughed, and then he spoke quietly.

"One can almost feel sorry for the Senor Ledoux's men," he said. "Chato and his *companeros* be Mejicano Indios. The *cuchillo* kills in silence."

Dan and his outfit soon learned that Chato's words had been no idle boast. The Texans saw nothing of the Indian renegades, not even during daylight hours.

"It's hard to believe they're here," Adeline said. "We've seen no smoke, no horses, nothing."

"Believe me, they're here," Dan said, "and from what Palo tells me, they don't always depend on guns. They carry Bowie knives and kill silently."

"Dear God," Adeline said, "that's terrible."

"No more terrible than Ledoux's bunch pouring lead into our camp in the dead of night and killing Alesia Chambers," Dan replied. "If they try it again, I want Chato and his boys to put the fear of God into them."

Uvalde, Texas. Friday, May 6, 1870.

Burton Ledoux was meeting with Campbell and Vance, two of his most trusted men.

"I want the two of you to pick eight riders," Ledoux said, "and sometime tonight, visit that cow gather again.

Take some more dynamite with you, and while you're stampeding the herd, have the others blast hell out of the camp."

"That's a lowdown, dirty way to fight," Campbell said.

"By God," Ledoux snarled, "I'm not paying you to like it, I'm paying you to do it. Anytime you don't favor my methods, you can be replaced."

"I ain't sayin' I don't favor 'em," Campbell said hastily.

"Then keep your mouth shut and do what I tell you," Ledoux said, easing his hand away from the butt of his Colt.

Less than an hour before sundown the ten men saddled up and rode south. Having plenty of time, they spared their horses, and Vance passed along the orders given by Ledoux.

"Me and Campbell will throw the dynamite," Vance said, "and when it lets go, the rest of you cut loose with your guns. Three volleys should be enough. By then they'll be shootin' at your muzzle flashes."

The wind was out of the northwest, and the ten riders smelled smoke from the supper fire long before they were anywhere close to the camp they sought. Vance and Campbell reined up, and Vance spoke to the rest of the men.

"We'll wait awhile. Give them that ain't on watch time to settle down in their blankets. We'll picket the horses and get some shut-eye ourselves."

An hour shy of midnight, Vance gave the order to mount up, and the ten rode out toward the east. Eventually Vance and Campbell angled off to the north, while their companions rode southeast with the intention of circling the sleeping camp. Somewhere ahead a cow bawled, and Vance reached for a match to light the dynamite fuse. Suddenly he froze. He had heard something, like a long sigh, and then there was silence.

"Campbell," he hissed, "where'n hell are you?"

Those were his last words. A burly arm caught him around the neck, and the muzzle of a Colt smashed against the side of his head. A keen Bowie slit his throat, silencing him forever. His horse trotted away, leaving him belly down, bleeding his life into the Texas sand. The rest of the riders waited, impatient for the dynamite blasts that would be their signal to open fire on the sleeping camp. But the blasts didn't come. Each of the eight riders was stalked by a silent shadow, and their awareness of the danger came much too late. Like Vance and Campbell, they died in silence, victims of the deadly Bowie. The camp slept on, except for the men on watch, and they were unaware that death had come into their midst and had departed in silence.

It was near dawn when Palo Elfego told Dan of the riders who had planned to attack the camp during the night.

"But we heard nothing," Dan said.

"Chato and his *companeros* use the *pistola* only when there is need for it," Palo said. "Those who came last night will not come again."

"All of them are dead?" Dan asked incredulously.

"*Si*, senor," Palo said. "It is as you wished."

"Ledoux will come looking for them and their horses."

"He will find neither," Palo said. "The *caballos* are in Mexico."

"And the dead men?"

"Do not ask, senor," Palo said.

Dan had some reservations about revealing the night's grisly deeds to the rest of the outfit, but knew that he must. Having hired Chato and his men, the Texans were responsible for the brutal retribution.

"They got what they deserved," Aubin Chambers said. "Chato and his boys done exactly what we hired 'em to do."

"Amen," Rux Carper said. "When Ledoux sends another bunch, give 'em the same damn treatment."

To a man they agreed, but Dan had his doubts. Ledoux could not—would not—ignore the disappearance of ten men and their horses. If nothing else, he would appeal to the Union army.

San Antonio, Texas. Monday, May 9, 1870.

Burton Ledoux waited impatiently in the outer office until the commanding officer, Captain Dillard, agreed to see him. Ledoux then presented his problem, telling the captain of his missing men and asking for help.

"Ledoux," the officer said impatiently, "this post is already undermanned. Yesterday, the Comanches attacked a patrol and two men were killed. I am in no position to send soldiers in search of cowboys who simply rode away and never returned. With continual trouble along the border, they should have kept away from it. What was their business there, anyhow?"

"There are ranchers in the area," Ledoux said, "and we're having trouble collecting taxes—"

"Good God," Captain Dillard shouted, "with the Comanches raising hell, and all of Texas short on soldiers and supplies, you expect the army to collect taxes? Get out of here, Ledoux. Get out."

Ledoux left Captain Dillard's office in a fury. He would hire more men, men who wouldn't ride away and leave him looking foolish. He went directly to the Broken Spoke Saloon, where he found Snell and Epps, an unsavory pair whose services he had bought before.

"I have a job for you," he told them. "I want you to hire eight more men. Fighting men. I'll pay fifty dollars to each of them, and a hundred dollars to each of you. Now here's what I want you to do . . ."

*   *   *

The outfit didn't finish Sloan Kuykendall's gather until the following Sunday, thanks to the stampede and the two days lost gathering the scattered longhorns. On Monday they branded a thousand and fifteen head, and at first light the next morning they moved on to Boyce Trevino's spread. Wolf Bowdre rode alongside Dan, and they talked.

"You know," Bowdre said, "since we can't come back to Texas, I've been thinking about claiming me some land in Kansas, or maybe the high plains, and startin' me a ranch. I could sell off half the herd at Dodge City, keepin' some cows and a bull or two."

"I think we should all consider that," Dan said. "If we don't, what are we going to do once we've sold our cows? A man needs roots, someplace to call home, and we've lost that in Texas."

"You reckon we've hurt Ledoux enough to keep him off our backs?"

"No," Dan said, "but I don't think he'll be able to drag the Union army into his fight. All he can claim is that ten of his men vanished without a trace. There are no bodies, and most important, no horses. He can't prove we've harmed them in any way, thanks to Chato. But he can hire more men. There are renegades aplenty, Confederate and Union. While Ledoux can't prove anything, he'll know we're responsible for the disappearance of his men, and he won't let any grass grow under his feet. I look for Chato and his boys to have more visitors one night this week."

Maverick County, Texas. Thursday, May 12, 1870.

Following the directions given them by Burton Ledoux, Snell, Epps, and their eight hired guns had no trouble locating Dan Ember and his outfit. It was near sundown, and the attackers had concealed themselves among the mesquite a safe distance from the gathered herd. Beyond it they could see the white of canvas shelters and the smoke from supper fires.

"Damnation," said one of the men, "they got enough people to start up a town."

"Just get some idea of how they're spread out and where the cows are," Epps said. "Once they're settled down for the night, we're to pour lead into the camp and scatter the cows from here to yonder. They'll have nighthawks, but we'll take 'em by surprise. We'll stay out of range of their pistols, and by the time they unlimber their rifles, we'll be gone."

But it didn't quite work out that way. The attackers waited until the stars said it was midnight, and then made their move. Approaching the camp, they split up, and it was their undoing. Chato and his *companeros* were swift, silent, deadly. Each furtive rider was swept from his saddle, knifed, and left to die. Chato and his men caught each horse before it became spooked and galloped away. With the dawn, only brown patches of dried blood would remain, swiftly vanishing evidence that death had come calling in the night.

The riders were saddling up for the next day's gather when Palo approached Dan with news of the past night's attackers and their grisly end. Palo held up both hands, the fingers spread. He then passed a finger across his throat.

"They come," he said, "and they die."

Dan didn't even bother inquiring about the bodies or the horses. After the day's gather was done, when supper was over, he told the rest of the outfit of the latest attempted raid. This time they seemed more shocked.

"My God," Monte Walsh said, "how long's he gonna keep sendin' men after us, and havin' none of 'em come back?"

"I doubt there'll be any more," Dan said. "Not at

night, anyway. I won't be surprised if we're visited by Mr. Ledoux himself, in daylight."

"What do you reckon that'll mean?" Tobe Barnfield asked.

"Two things," Dan said. "First, he hasn't been able to drag the army into his fight against us, and second, he'll be hopin' to discover how his killers keep disappearing without a trace. With that in mind, Palo, I have a message for Chato. Tell him if one, two, or three riders approach the camp in the daylight, to let them come. Chato and his *companeros* are to remain under cover. We're not ready for Ledoux to discover them, and they're far more useful to us against surprise attacks at night."

Maverick County, Texas. Monday, May 16, 1870.

"Rider comin'," Ward McNelly shouted.

It was suppertime, and the gather was finished for the day. Dan Ember turned to Wolf Bowdre. Bowdre would speak for the outfit, lest Dan be recognized. The single rider was Burton Ledoux, and Bowdre stepped out to meet him. He waited, offering no greeting, and didn't ask Ledoux to step down. Ledoux reined up and came right to the point.

"Some of my men rode down this way," Ledoux said, "and I haven't seen them since. Have any of you seen them?"

"No," Bowdre said truthfully, "we haven't. The last contact we had with your men, they shot up our camp in the middle of the night and stampeded our herd. Aubin Chambers's daughter was killed and some of our people were wounded."

"You have no proof my men did that," Ledoux said indignantly.

"Nobody else had any reason to," Bowdre replied. "Now get the hell out of here. You're not welcome."

Ledoux wheeled his horse and rode out.

"I got a feeling we ain't seen the last of him," Rufe Keeler said.

"But what can he do?" Kirby Wilkerson asked.

"I don't know," Dan said, "but he'll think of something."

7

Furious, Burton Ledoux rode back to San Antonio. He visited one saloon after another, talking to hard-eyed men who were drifters or on the dodge. Wherever he went, he was eyed with suspicion, and he soon learned the reason.

"I know Epps an' Snell," a bearded man told him, "an' last time I seen 'em, they was lookin' for gun throwers to ride for you. It was a one night job, an' they was comin' back here. It's been near a week, and I ain't seen 'em. The pay's short an' the job's damn permanent. Git away from me, Ledoux."

Ledoux stalked out of the saloon, at a loss as to where to turn. He had two men at the cabin near Uvalde, but of what use were they? Something had gone wrong, and he had no idea what the problem was or what he had to do to solve it. He bought a bottle at a saloon, took a room in a hotel, and got stinking drunk.

Following Ledoux's visit, the outfit settled down to roping cattle, and managed to finish Boyce Trevino's gather a day early.

"Accordin' to my figures," Silas said, "today's May twenty-second. We got three gathers done, and we're four days behind. That's figurin' five days for the gather and a day for the brandin'."

"We'll work like hell," Skull Kimbrough said, "and finish early on some of them gathers yet to be done. This damn wound kept me laid up, but I can ride and rope now."

"Skull not be with us," Palo Elfego said dryly. "That why we lose time."

On Monday, May 23, the outfit began Ward McNelly's gather, and by the end of the first day, Dan tallied 251 head.

"We'll gain another day here," Wolf Bowdre said. His gather would be next.

San Antonio, Texas. May 23, 1870.

Burton Ledoux awoke with a hangover for which there was but one sure cure. The Texas Saloon was the nearest to his hotel, and that's where he headed. He bought a bottle, was given a glass, and made his way to a table. It was nearly noon and the place was virtually deserted, for those who had more civilized places to be were absent. Ledoux downed one drink and was contemplating a second. He had ignored several men at the bar. Now one of them took his glass and sauntered toward Ledoux's table. He kicked back a chair, sat down, and poured himself a drink from Ledoux's bottle. Ledoux glared at him through bleary eyes.

"Who the hell are you," he snarled, "and what do you want?"

"Per'ap some talk," said the arrogant newcomer. He was Mexican, although he was dressed more like a Texan.

"Then talk," Ledoux snarled.

"You are the Senor Ledoux?" the Mexican inquired.

"I am," Ledoux said.

"I am Santos Miguel Montoya. I 'ave hear of you and your troubles, senor. Ah, but you are ambitious. Or per'ap I should say greedy."

"How the hell do you know so much about me?" Ledoux growled, becoming alarmed.

Montoya laughed softly, sipping his drink. "I know many things, senor. I know of the Tejanos who rope and brand the *vaca* for the drive north, and I know that you seek to stop them. Twice you 'ave sent men with guns, but these men and their *caballos* 'ave disappear. And now"—Montoya paused for that maddening laugh—"men fear you. To ride for the Senor Ledoux is to die."

"Damn you," Ledoux said, reaching for his Colt. He froze at the snick of a hammer being eared back.

"That is not wise, Senor Ledoux," Montoya said in a dangerously calm voice. "You are covered under the table. Per'ap we talk in a civilized manner, or must I keep the *pistola* in your belly?"

"Put the gun away," Ledoux said wearily. "What do you want of me?"

"You need men, Senor Ledoux, fighting men. I 'ave them, but there is a price."

It was Ledoux's turn to laugh. "Twenty men and their horses are gone, vanished. I'd be a fool to send you and your men to the same fate, and you'd be fools to go."

"Ah, senor," Montoya said, "you do not understand. We do not ride on your foolish raids. We 'ave, as you Tejanos would say, a proposition. Do you wish to hear it?"

"I'm listening," Ledoux said.

"We will not disturb the Tejanos who gather the *vaca* for a drive to the north," Montoya said. "When they are ready, you will ride with me and my *companeros,* and we will follow the herd. Before we 'ave reach the railroad to which they go, we kill them all, taking the *vaca* and *caballos.*"

"Then you bastards will gun me down and take it all for yourselves."

"Por Dios," Montoya said, eyeing Ledoux sadly, "you misjudge us, senor. We want only the *caballos* and fighting wages for the months on the trail."

"Misjudging you, hell," Ledoux said, almost sober now. "Gun pay's fifty dollars a month, and these damn ten cow outfits are short on horses. The few they have will be skin and bones by the end of the drive, if they make it at all. Now you tell me what you *really* want out of this, or get up and get the hell out of here."

"Ah," Montoya said, "that I cannot tell you, senor, without revealing information I will not give you for nothing. I 'ave nineteen riders, senor, and when you 'ave agreed to fighting pay while we are on the trail, then per'ap I tell you. For now, I tell you only that the *vaca* is yours and that there be many *caballos* across the Rio Grande, awaiting the start of the Tejano drive."

Ledoux pondered the situation. It seemed the bunch of shirttail ranchers were determined to complete the gather and take the drive north to the advancing railroad. From what he had seen of the gather, they seemed to be averaging at least a thousand head for each of the ranchers involved, and that could result in a drive of more than twenty thousand head. If they went for only thirty dollars a head—and they might bring even more—the eventual pot would be more than half a million dollars! Ledoux was by no means poor already, and the fighting wages this Mejicano was demanding would be a pittance when weighed against the vast herd of Texas cows.

"It's a deal," Ledoux said, "but you and your men will be paid at the end of the drive, when I've taken over the herd and sold it. Now, damn it, tell me what you're *really* getting out of this, and the information you refused to give me for nothing."

"Ah, senor," Montoya said, again adopting his sorrowful look, "but I 'ave second thoughts. For one to take his life in his hands, fifty dollars is a paltry sum. Per'ap we could raise the ante to, ah, twice that?"

"A hundred dollars?" Ledoux bawled. "Hell, no!"

Montoya kicked back his chair and stood up. "My regrets, senor."

"Sit down, you thieving bastard," Ledoux snarled.

"Senor Ledoux, if you ever call me that again, I will kill you."

Ledoux looked at the Mexican's clenched teeth, his hand hovering near the butt of his Colt, and swallowed hard. Montoya sat down, but on the edge of his chair, tense.

"I'll pay," Ledoux said, "but if you double-cross me, or even look like you're thinkin' of it, I'll do some killing of my own."

"Ah," Montoya said, with a grin that had no mirth in it, "we understand one another, senor. Now I shall begin by telling you what 'ave become of your men and their *caballos.* The men are dead, senor, and the *caballos* 'ave found new homes across the Rio Grande."

"I'd have been a fool, Montoya, not to have figured that out on my own."

"Per'ap," said Montoya, "but you would not know of that *bastardo,* Chato Guiterrez. Him and his riders 'ave kill your men, senor. With a *cuchillo* they kill quietly, swiftly. They are Mejicano Indios, *diablos de el noche.*"*

"I can believe that." Ledoux said. "But why? What did they have against my riders?"

"They are being paid fighting wages, senor, just as you are paying us."

"I see," Ledoux said, "and I suppose they'll be riding with the trail drive to the railroad."

"But of course," Montoya said. "We 'ave but one

* Mexican Indians, devils of the night

wish, and that is to get them out of the wilds of Mexico
and kill them to the last man."

"Am I allowed to ask the reason, without you raising
the ante again?"

"*Madre mia,*" Montoya said with a pained expression,
"we are fair men, senor. They are renegades who plun-
der and kill. Every man in my company 'ave lose *hijo* or
*hermano,** and they steal our women."

His words had the ring of truth, and Ledoux believed
him. The more he thought of the dastardly scheme, the
more it appealed to him. The ranchers had beaten him
with a bunch of knife-wielding Mexican Indians. By
God, he would fight fire with fire. He had gone about it
all wrong, fighting this damned gather. He would adopt
Montoya's plan, but take it a step further. Once the
ranchers abandoned their spreads, he could buy them
all up for the taxes due. However, he couldn't risk having the state take possession while he was away in Kansas. Slowly a plan began to evolve in his devious mind,
and he was brought back to reality when Montoya
spoke.

"We will know when the drive is to begin, senor.
Where are we to find you?"

"I have a place near Uvalde," Ledoux said. "I'll get
my horse from the livery and take you there."

Maverick County, Texas. Saturday, May 28, 1870.

"We gained another day," Sloan Kuykendall said as they
branded the last of Wolf Bowdre's gather.

"Yeah, if we can just keep doin' it," Garret Haddock
said. "You're next, Cash. Number six."

"That'll mean almost a third of the gather's done,"
Connolly said, "but we're just a month and two days
away from Ledoux's tax deadline."

* Son or brother

"I think we got the varmint buffaloed," said Walt Crump. "What do you think, Dan?"

"We've put a stop to his night raids," Dan said, "but don't underestimate him. Remember, he's got the law behind him, and if he's a mind to, he can force us to get permission to leave Texas. I think when his tax deadline has come and gone, we'll learn something. Not so much from what he does as what he fails to do. If we're allowed to finish the gather undisturbed, then we can look for trouble after we start the trail drive."

"We have taxes due in a month," Wolf Bowdre said. "Taxes we can't pay, and Ledoux damn well knows it. He knows we've abandoned our spreads, because we're takin' our families with us. If he wants our land, why can't he let us go in peace and foreclose after we're gone?"

"As I understand it," Dan said, "the law says you have to be off your place for a year before it can legally be sold for taxes. That means you could take the drive to Dodge, sell your herds, and return to Texas with gold in your pockets."

"Well, hell's bells," Chad Grimes said, "we're takin' our families with us. That don't sound like we're comin' back to Texas, does it?"

"Suppose you *did* aim to come back to Texas," Dan said. "Would you leave your family on a spread with the taxes past due, at the mercy of Ledoux's riders, while you take a trail drive to Dodge City?"

"Lookin' at it that way," Grimes said, "no. I'd take my family with me, and I'd have to agree with you. Even after we start the drive, we may still have that varmint houndin' us."

"That's what I expect," Dan said, "and that's why we'll have Chato and his riders with us. Before this drive is done, I think they will have more than earned their fighting wages."

* * *

San Antonio, Texas. Thursday, June 2, 1870.

Burton Ledoux was shown into the office of Judge Haynes Blackburn. The judge owed Ledoux some favors, and he greeted Ledoux without much enthusiasm.

"Judge," Ledoux said with feigned respect, "I need to talk to you."

"Quickly, then," Blackburn sighed. "I must attend a meeting." Actually, it wasn't until the afternoon, but Ledoux needn't know that.

"There are some ranchers who can't pay their taxes coming due July first," said Ledoux, "and I'm requesting extensions. Here are their names and their counties."

Blackburn took the list, regarding Ledoux with suspicion. The man was not known for his compassion. Blackburn quickly read the names and turned back to Ledoux.

"Hellfire and damnation, this is everybody from San Antonio to the Rio Grande. Why don't you just file for an extension for the whole damned state?"

"Four counties, damn it," Ledoux said, "and not a ranch that can raise enough cash to buy a sack of Durham. They're gathering cattle, but they need some time to get their herds to market."

"Six months," Blackburn sighed. "That's all anybody's getting. The word just came down from Fort Worth. Now get out of here. I have work to do."

Ledoux left the office satisfied. The ranches he expected to purchase for taxes were safe until the end of the year, and there was virtually no chance of his scheme being uncovered. The reconstruction authority was spread much too thin, and the military had its hands full with the Comanches. Ledoux had covered himself by telling Judge Blackburn the ranchers were taking a drive north. When they failed to return, their lands would be confiscated for delinquent taxes, and Burton Ledoux would be ready to purchase them.

Kinney County, Texas. Friday, July 1, 1870.

"This is the day," Spence Wilder said. "None of us has got a spread, and accordin' to law, I reckon we're ropin' cows that belong to the state."

"I dispute that," Dan Ember said. "According to range law, unbranded cows belong to the hombres that rope and brand them. It's always been that way, and no bunch of Yankee jaybirds is goin' to change it."

"By my tally," Wolf Bowdre said, "we got 10,540 head. Tomorrow we start our eleventh gather, at Hiram Beard's place. Give us two more months of decent weather and no trouble from Ledoux, and we'll be ready for the trail to Dodge."

But the weather didn't hold. The heat became unbearable, and by late Saturday a dirty gray bank of clouds hung heavy on the western horizon. The sun was swallowed early, and forked lightning did a silent, frenzied dance along the crest of the thunderheads.

"We could use the rain," Silas said, "but not the thunder and lightnin' that'll come with it."

"Every man in the saddle tonight," Dan said. "If this bunch of longhorns run, we'll be a week roundin' 'em up, and maybe not even then. If somethin' sets 'em off, look for 'em to run east, away from the storm. Head them if you can, but don't get caught in the stampede. We'll have supper early and try to bed them down before the storm comes any closer."

It soon became evident there would be a storm, and as the thunderheads came closer, so did the lightning. Soon there was a distant rumble of thunder, and a rising wind from the northwest brought the distinct smell of rain.

"There's rain comin', anyhow," Silas said.

The rain came first, gray sheets of it, driven by the wind. Lightning caressed the thunderheads with jagged fingers of gold, then flicking serpent tongues of fire toward the murky heavens. Thunder boomed in succession, each new rumble sounding like an echo of the last. Sensing the coming storm, the cattle had never settled down, nor did they intend to. A few began bawling uneasily, and like an eerie chorus, the others joined in. Their backs to the wind and driving rain, they began to drift. Dan got ahead of them, but his shouting was to no avail, the wind whipping the sound of his voice away. But the rest of the outfit could see what was coming, and following his lead, they galloped their horses ahead of the uneasy herd. Their one chance lay in turning the herd upon itself, to start the longhorns milling. But the herd was of a single mind, awaiting that terrifying something they knew must come, sending forty thousand hooves thundering across the prairie.

Thunder shook the earth and lightning leaped from low-hanging clouds. A hundred yards to the west, a giant oak exploded in a fury of fire and brimstone as the lightning struck. With a unanimous bellow the longhorns began running eastward, ignoring the riders trying to head them. Forced from the path of the charging herd, Dan and his cowboys rode alongside the lead steers, trying to head them. Repeatedly, riders drove the shoulders of their horses into the bodies of the stampeding longhorns, but the brutes refused to yield. Finally, the hard-riding cowboys fell back, knowing the cause was lost. They sat their saddles in the driving rain, watching the tag end of their herd disappear in the gathering darkness.

"Damn it," Rux Carper said, "come spring, we'll still be lookin' for them spooked varmints."

"Maybe not," Tobe Barnfield said. "After that one big blast, there wasn't that much lightnin'. They won't run that far."

"However long it takes, we'll have to round them up," Dan said, "but there's nothing we can do until morning. Settle down and get what sleep you can. Come first light, we'll go after them."

Even the families who hadn't brought wagons had brought extra canvas, and there was shelter for sleeping. But when the sodden riders returned to camp, everybody was awake, most of them discouraged by the stampede.

"Damn fool cows," Denny said in disgust. "We ain't never gonna get to the trail drive."

"Denny," Adeline said, "watch your language."

"Sorry, Ma," Denny said. "I shouldn't of said 'ain't.' I'll watch it."

Dan and Lenore laughed. From somewhere came the lonesome sound of a mouth harp, and thunder rumbled far off.

By daylight Dan and his riders were in the saddle, riding in the direction their stampeded herd had gone.

"This purely gets on a man's nerves," Kirby Wilkerson said. "Today we was to start Hiram Beard's gather. Now it looks like we'll spend a week on his range roundin' up the same varmints we've already roped and branded."

"Won't take that long," Hiram said. "Not if they kept runnin' straight. The Anacacho Mountains is to the southeast, and the Balcones Escarpment is to the north. If the varmints kept runnin' to the east, there ain't no place for 'em to hide but the breaks of the Nueces."

"In the mesquite, live oak, and cedar thickets," Spence Wilder said.

"God," Skull Kimbrough said, "I never knowed the Nueces was so long. No matter where the cows run, we always end up in the thorns and thickets along the Nueces, lookin' for the longhorned bastards. We lose this bunch one more time in the thickets along the same damn river, and I'm thinkin' we got a hex on us."*

"At least we have some idea where they are," Dan said. "This may not be so bad. When we take the trail with the full gather and they stampede, then we'll all have something to swear about."

Dan was right. Most of the herd hadn't run as far as the Nueces River, but they hadn't been part of the gather long enough to overcome their wild ways. They had been roped and branded, but had no desire to become part of the gather. More than a thousand had to be roped and hog-tied. Finally, when they had thrashed about and exhausted themselves, they were led meekly back to the herd. Working from daylight till dark, it took the riders five days to gather the stampeded herd. Dan had Wolf Bowdre, Monte Walsh, and Kirby Wilkerson running separate tallies.

"Still short at least thirty head," Bowdre said, "but we can afford to lose 'em. We're still five hundred head beyond what we set out to gather."

"Then we'll consider it finished and go on to Hiram Beard's gather," Dan said.

The weather continued hot and dry, but without disrupting thunder and lightning. By August first Rux Carper's gather—the fourteenth—had been completed. The outfit moved on to Kirby Wilkerson's range.

"We got to finish these gathers in four days," Boyce Trevino said. "We got so damn many cows already, we got to keep movin' 'em, so's they'll have graze."

It was true. Arranging graze and water for the existing gather became more difficult with each passing day. But Daniel Ember had looked ahead, making allowances.

"We're in Uvalde County now," he said, "and we're

* The Nueces River is 350 miles in length, flowing through or touching eleven counties before reaching Nueces Bay and the Gulf.

working our way south to Zavala. We'll wind things up with the DeVoe gather in Maverick, and take the drive west along the Rio Grande to Eagle Pass. From there we'll go north. Once we've crossed Maverick and Uvalde counties, it should be new grass all the way."

Without having to contend with Ledoux's unexpected night raids, nights around the supper fire became peaceful, a time to talk. Only occasionally was there a message from Chato, passed along through Palo Elfego, and as the enormous roundup drew to a close, excitement and optimism ran rampant. They moved south through Zavala County, finishing Spence Wilder's gather, the nineteenth. Finally there was only the DeVoe ranch, in Maverick county, along the Rio Grande. The gather was begun on August 25, and with the branding five days later, was over. There was jubilation around the supper fire, and Dan had to shout them down so he could speak.

"Tomorrow the drive begins. The wagons will take the lead, followed by the horse remuda, and then the herd. The men will take the flank and swing positions. Everybody else—ladies included—will ride drag. I realize it's the dirtiest of all, but it's also the safest. Palo, have you spoken to Chato about the horses he promised?"

"*Si*, senor," Palo said. "The *caballos* will be here at dawn."

"Wolf," Dan said, "do you have a final tally on the gather?"

"Twenty thousand, six hundred and ten," Bowdre said.

"By God," Silas Hamby shouted, "we done it. This has got to be the biggest damn gather anywhere, anytime."

"We can't afford to crow too loud," Dan said. "We still have to get to Dodge. Are there any questions before we call it a night?"

"Yeah," Walt Crump said. "Somethin' we ain't talked

about much. Since we don't know when the railroad's comin' to Dodge, what are we supposed to do with ourselves and this herd if we get there first?"

"We'll wait," Dan said, "even if we have to hold the herd fifty miles out of Dodge. Here's something all of you might want to consider. Some of us are planning to sell off maybe half our cows, and with the rest and a pair of bulls, file on some land and start ranching. Remember, you won't have any reason to return to Texas. There's still plenty of good range and grass to the north and west."

"From what I hear, there's still plenty of hell-raisin' Indians too," Aubin Chambers said.

"I reckon they can't be no worse than the Comanches," Ward McNelly said, "and God knows, Texas has more'n its share of them."

"Go where there's no Indians," Dan said, "and you'll find yourself neck deep in farmers and tax collectors like Burton Ledoux."

"By God, that's right," Cash Connolly said, "and I'll take the Indians. Even the Comanche."

Uvalde, Texas. Wednesday, August 31, 1870.

Santos Miguel Montoya dismounted before the cabin Burton Ledoux used for his headquarters. All that remained of Ledoux's gang—Black Bill and Loe Hagerman—waited on the porch, their hands near the butts of their Colts. They relaxed only when Ledoux spoke to Montoya. The Mexican eyed the gunmen suspiciously, and they stepped aside, allowing Montoya to follow Ledoux into the cabin. The excluded pair looked at the closed door, and Black Bill spoke.

"I hate Mejicanos."

"Hell," Hagerman said, "you hate everybody. Even me."

"Even you," Black Bill said, shifting the deadly whip

coiled about his massive left arm. He turned cold, hard eyes on Hagerman, and the gunman shuddered.

Inside the cabin Montoya ignored the chair Ledoux offered. The Mexican wasted no time, careful not to turn his back to the door where Ledoux's men waited.

"The *caballos*—the Tejano remuda—crossed the river just before dawn, senor. The drive begins today, I think. They follow the Rio Grande west."

"We're ready," Ledoux said, "and we'll ride back with you." He opened the door. "One of you saddle my horse," he said.

"You heard him," Black Bill said when Ledoux had closed the door, "go saddle his horse."

"Why not you?"

"I ain't no damn *pelado*," Black Bill said, fondling the heavy butt of the whip.

Hagerman stepped off the porch and trudged toward the barn. Black Bill laughed. It had been a while since he had killed a man with the whip. His hard eyes on Hagerman's back, he relished the thought.

8

Eagle Pass, Texas. Wednesday, August 31, 1870.

Just as Chato had promised, the horse remuda—a hundred strong—was brought across the river before dawn. At first light Dan and some of the outfit rode out to look at the herd.

"I'll give the varmints credit," Sloan Kuykendall said. "They damn well know their horses."

"From what I can see," Wolf Bowdre said, "there ain't a one of 'em got a brand. By God, that's what I call luck."

"Luck's got nothin' to do with it," Dan said. "Chato's no fool. We'll be at Fort Dodge, right under the noses of the military. Without brands, we can sell these animals for top prices, and nobody can question ownership. Now let's get back to camp, pick some horse wranglers, and take the long trail to Dodge."

Most of the outfit had been ready since the night before. Spence Wilder, Duncan Kilgore, and Palo Elfego all had sons as old or older than Denny DeVoe, and Dan had chosen the three of them and young Denny for horse wranglers. He still hadn't made the announcement, and when he finally got everybody quieted down, he spoke.

"Most of you know what you're going to be doing on this drive, but for four of you, I have a special assignment. Gus Wilder, Gid Kilgore, Pablo Elfego, and Denny DeVoe, come on over here beside me."

Unprepared, the four came forward, curious, self-conscious, and scared. Nobody knew what Dan was about to say except the three fathers and Adeline DeVoe.

"We now have a horse remuda," Dan said, "and we need horse wranglers. I'm asking the four of you to take on that responsibility from here to Dodge City, Kansas. You'll be expected to keep the remuda in line while we're on the trail, help unsaddle tired horses and saddle fresh ones, and you'll be spreading your blankets with the remuda every night, so they don't become spooked. But if you'd rather not do this, speak up. You can always ride drag."

The four stared at him big-eyed, eager, and in total silence. Some of the men laughed.

"All right," Dan said, "mount up, wranglers, and take your place with the remuda. Silas, ready your wagons, move out, and take the lead. All you wranglers trail the remuda behind the last wagon. Flank and swing riders take your positions, and those of you at drag get ready to swat some behinds."

Silas Hamby led out with the first wagon, the other six falling in behind. The newly appointed horse wranglers had no trouble swinging the remuda in behind the last wagon.

"Move 'em out," Dan shouted, waving his hat. Slowly, the massive herd fell into line, and those breaking away were headed and driven back to join their companions. It had been too long since the last rain, and dust quickly rose in clouds, hanging like smoke against the blue of the Texas sky. Despite the fact that most of the cows had been in the gather for a while, they seemed to revert to their wild ways once they were on the trail. The very size

of the herd made it all but impossible to keep them
bunched, and every cow that saw daylight took it as an
invitation to run for the thickets. Dan rode from one
end of the herd to the other and back again, looking for
potential trouble. There were gaps within the ranks, and
without their companions prodding them from behind,
the leaders slowed and tried to graze. Dan galloped
back to the drag, only to find the ranks closed. The
trouble was deep within the moving column, making it
difficult to reach the troublesome longhorns. The swing
riders were nearest the trouble spot, and Dan caught up
to Rux Carper and Tobe Barnfield.

"Some of these varmints are dragging their feet,"
Dan said, "and it's slowing the leaders. We're going to
have to fight our way through the outer ranks and get
these troublemakers bunched. Careful you don't get
yourself or your horse gored."

It was tricky business, with the horses having to force
their way into the moving column, matching their gait to
that of the herd. From there, the horses advanced a
little at a time, until they were behind the slow-moving
cattle. It being a mixed herd, the cows were the problem, their stride being shorter than that of a steer.
Slowly Dan and his companions worked their way into
the herd until they reached the lagging cows. The riders
doubled their lariats and began raining blows on dusty
behinds. With startled bellows the cows lurched ahead,
driving heads and horns into their equally startled companions. It created a gap, allowing Dan, Carper, and
Barnfield to begin working their way out of the herd.
The big steers behind quickly closed the gap, and with
continued pressure from the drag riders, the ranks were
closed tightly enough to keep the herd moving. Dan
rode to the point and found the previously slow-footed
leaders moving at an acceptable gait. He was more
thankful than ever for Chato and his riders, for they
were somewhere ahead, scouting for potential trouble.

Dan had warned them to avoid any confrontation with the military. He doubted so many Texans with so large a herd would ever be allowed to depart Texas without fully justifying the journey. He only hoped that when the time came, he and his companions would be equal to the task.

"God," Hiram Beard said when the troublesome herd had finally been bedded down for the night, "I never been so give out in my life."

"Is just first day," Palo Elfego said with a grin.

"Don't look for tomorrow or the next day to be any better," Wolf Bowdre said. "Them brutes ain't a damn bit more civilized than when we roped 'em out of the breaks."

"If the bastards stampede, I hope they run north," Skull Kimbrough said. "I ain't sure none of us will live long enough to round 'em up again."

"Hell, we'll be three more days just gettin' out of Maverick County," Kirby Wilkerson said. "I figure we come maybe seven miles."

"Yeah," Boyce Trevino said, "where there's no water except Las Moras and Indio creeks, and they only run in the rainy season. Ain't that some kind of a bad sign, when you spend your first night on the trail in dry camp?"

"We're not more'n seven mile from the Rio Grande," Monte Walsh said. "How'd you like to drive 'em back there?"

"How'd you like to be gut-shot?" Rux Carper inquired darkly. "Don't even suggest such a fool thing. One breath of wind from the south, and this whole God-awful day has been for nothin'."

"Not to mention the next two weeks," Cash Connolly said. "It'd take us that long to round 'em up again, and that's if we was almighty lucky."

"Well, by God," Wolf Bowdre said, "there don't none of us own a patch of ground big enough for a decent grave. We purely got to ride this damn herd down, if it takes a day, ten days, or a month."

"That's how it is," Dan said. "The first week will be the worst. Once the herd settles down, about the worst we'll have to contend with will be stampedes and Indians."

The second day was no better than the first, and in some respects it was more difficult. The day seemed longer, the sun seemed hotter, and tempers were definitely shorter. Again the drive progressed only about eight miles, and the runoff from the spring where they bedded down for the night was just adequate to slake the thirst of the massive herd. For some reason none of the riders understood, some of the longhorns were uneasy, bawling occasionally throughout the night.

The Nueces River. Wednesday, September 7, 1870.

"I'd say we've come forty-five miles," Wolf Bowdre said, "but the herd's settlin' down, becomin' trailwise."

"More important," Dan said, "we have water. This has to be the Nueces. How far north can we follow it?"

"A good fifty mile," Silas Hamby said, "takin' the east fork. Then it's maybe twenty mile till we reach the South Llano. We can foller it another twenty-five mile, I reckon. Beyond that, I can't say."

"Chato and his riders will be scouting ahead," Dan said. "If there's any doubt about water, they can guide us."

Their ninth day on the trail, Dan estimated they traveled twelve miles. Ready access to the river seemed to make a difference, and when the herd was bedded down for the night, the mood of the outfit had markedly improved. Just before sundown, near suppertime, the soldiers rode in. There was a lieutenant, a sergeant, and ten privates, and they came from the west. Dan met them and spoke.

"I'm Daniel Ember, trail boss. Step down and rest your saddles. We're about to have supper, and you're welcome to join us if you like beans and beef. There's plenty."

"We're obliged," the officer said. "Anything would be an improvement over field rations." He nodded to his companions, and when he dismounted, they followed suit.

"Unsaddle your horses," Dan said, "and our wranglers will loose them with our remuda."

"Thank you," the officer said. "I'm Lieutenant Winters, and this is Sergeant Foster." He didn't bother introducing the privates.

The soldiers seemed overwhelmed with the magnitude of the trail drive, and more than a little appreciative of Lenore and the younger women who served their supper. The Texans ate in silence, for there was tension in the air, the result of a confrontation that seemed imminent. Dan wondered how the lieutenant would lead up to the questions that must be foremost on the officer's mind. But Winters was tactful, at least at the beginning.

"You should know," he said, "that Quanah Parker and his Comanches are on a rampage. They're holed up somewhere on the Llano Estacado, and have hit most of the forts in West Texas."

"He didn't accept the Medicine Lodge Treaty,* then," Dan said.

* In 1867, the United States Congress created a peace commission, hoping to negotiate fresh treaties with the Cheyennes, Arapahos, Comanches and Kiowas. In return for the tribes remaining peacefully on reservations, the new treaty would provide rations, clothing, housing and vocational training. In October, 1867, the commission took a huge wagon train of supplies to a village in southern Kansas, called Medicine Lodge. But only Chief Black Kettle and his tribe of Cheyennes attended the meeting, and the congress that had created the peace commission refused it further support. Ironically, Black Kettle—who

"No," Lieutenant Winters said, "and if you're heading north, then you're taking your lives into your hands."

"We're bound for Dodge City," Dan said, "and this is the shortest way."

"I don't advise it," Winters said. "We're already spread too thin, and being short-handed, we can't offer you any protection."

"We're not expecting it," Dan said. "We know the risks."

"You should have reported to the commanding officer at San Antonio," Winter said. "He should have been told that you're leaving the state."

"We saw no need for that," Dan said. "The state's our reason for going. We have taxes to pay, and we have to get our cows to market. Is there a law against our doing that?"

"No," Winters said, "but under the Reconstruction Act, occupational forces—the military—must be made aware that you're leaving the state. One more thing. Those of you who fought with the Confederacy are not to bear arms, except on a conditional basis."

"I was with the Confederacy," Dan said, "so I reckon you'd better tell me what those conditions are. You wouldn't expect a man to go unarmed into Quanah Parker's territory, would you?"

"No," Winters said, "and if you'll comply with the law, you shouldn't have any trouble. Stop at Fort Griffin and tell the post commander you've talked to me and that you're following my advice. Tell him where you're taking your drive, and that you need your weapons.

had long sought peace with the white man—was brutally murdered in a pre-dawn attack on his village near the upper Washita River in what is now western Oklahoma. The attack was led by General George A. Custer and the U. S. Seventh Cavalry, taking place on November 27, 1868, a little more than a year after Black Kettle had signed the Medicine Lodge Treaty.

Those of you who are ex-Confederates will be allowed to sign papers stating that you won't take up arms against the Union again. That allows you to legally carry your weapons."

"Thanks," Dan said, relieved. "We'll stop at Fort Griffin. We sure as hell don't need any more problems. We have all we can say grace over, with this cantankerous bunch of longhorns."

The soldiers stayed the night, and after breakfast rode out toward the east.

"God, I'm glad that's behind us," Rufe Keeler said.

"It's not behind us," Dan said. "We still have to stop at Fort Griffin and talk to the post commander, but if Winters was tellin' it straight, we're gettin' off mighty easy."

"I believe the man gave us better advice than he realized," Wolf Bowdre said. "I still think Burton Ledoux may try to use the reconstruction law to get us in trouble with the military. Once we've cleared ourselves at Fort Griffin, we've pulled Ledoux's fangs."

"I won't consider Ledoux's fangs pulled until the sonofabitch is dead," Aubin Chambers said.

"That's somethin' you ain't likely to see," Rux Carper said. "Once we get out of Texas, we're done with him, and I'll settle for that."

The drive continued along the Nueces River, and the land became more mountainous. Huge cypress trees bordered the river. Five days took them as far as they could go along the east fork of the Nueces. Tomorrow they had to strike out for the South Llano River, the nearest sure water.

"No way in hell we can make it in one day," Wolf Bowdre said. "Silas, you sure of that distance?"

"Twenty mile," Silas said. "Maybe more."

"Palo," Dan said, "did you talk to Chato about water between here and the South Llano River?"

"*Si,*" Palo said. "Is only spring. *Vaca* too many, spring too small."

"Then we'll have to move on to the South Llano," Dan said. "We'll take the trail at first light, and we'll drive them hard."

"One whiff of that water," Walt Crump said, "and we won't have to drive 'em at all. They'll fog out like hell wouldn't have it, and we'll all be eatin' their dust."

South of the Llano. Tuesday, September 13, 1870.

Dan had the herd on the trail at first light. The horse remuda was already far ahead, traveling at the faster gait Dan had recommended. He joined the drag riders, swinging his doubled lariat against dusty flanks, forcing the unwilling cattle into a trot. Those ahead had no choice. It was move faster or have their rumps raked by the sharp horns of their companions. The herd was still lethargic from a night's rest, and not yet thirsty, so they rebelled at the unaccustomed fast gait, by breaking away at the slightest opportunity. Flank and swing riders repeatedly chased bunch quitters back to the herd, only to be faced with another wave of them. Cows from the tag end of the herd wheeled, hooking at horses and riders. To escape the deadly horns, Dan's horse reared. He leaned from the saddle, slamming his doubled lariat down on the angry cow's tender muzzle, and the brute ran bawling to catch up to the herd. Dan heard somebody swearing, and when he grinned at Adeline DeVoe, she only glared back at him. He rode to the aid of Amy Wilder, whose horse had reared and thrown her. He then rode after a pair of longhorns that had broken through the drag and were galloping down the back trail.

The sun rose higher, grew hotter, until every sweating horse and rider was yellow with dust. But the heat and the activity was taking its toll on the cattle. Fewer of them broke ranks, and they bawled their frustration as they surged ahead, but kept moving at the faster gait Dan Ember demanded. When the cattle at the tag end of the column were again responding to the efforts of the drag riders, Dan rode to the head of the herd, speaking to swing and flank riders as he went. He found the lead steers had closed the gap and were within a respectable distance of the horse remuda. Denny DeVoe waved his hat, and Dan waved back. He then rode down the other side of the moving column until he was again with the drag riders. Lenore smiled wearily at him through a mask of sweaty mud. He rode his horse alongside Adeline's, but she looked straight ahead, ignoring him.

"You look like a cowboy," he said cheerfully, "and you're startin' to sound like one too."

"If you don't like the way I sound, stay away from me," she snapped.

"I didn't say I didn't like it. What we've been through today would make a preacher cuss. Long as I'm working you like a cowboy, I won't complain if you talk and act like one. I would prefer that you don't strip down to the hide at the river crossings, though."

"I'm planning to do exactly that," she said defiantly. "It's the only way I'll ever get all this damn dirt off me."

"The worst of it's over," Dan said. "They're tiring."

"So are the rest of us. Do you really think we can reach South Llano before dark?"

"I don't know," Dan said. "If we don't, it'll mean dry camp. Tonight, if there's even the slightest breeze from the north or northwest, you'll see the damnedest stampede in Texas history."

"There's always a little breeze after sundown."

"That's why we're pushing the herd," Dan said. "If they stampede at the smell of water, some—probably the slower moving cows—will be gored or trampled.

They'll also be scattered for miles along the river, trying to get at the water."

"There's the horse remuda and the wagons ahead," Adeline said. "What's going to become of them?"

"I don't aim to leave them in the path of twenty thousand thirsty cows," Dan replied. "Two hours before sundown, I'll send the wagons and the horse remuda on ahead, to the river. The wagons can go on across, and when the horses have been watered, they can be taken across to graze. Then when the longhorns finally reach water, there won't be anything in their way."

"I like that," Adeline said, "except for one thing. What about Indians? I believe Lieutenant Winters was telling the truth."

"So do I. Chato and his riders are somewhere ahead of us, and we'll have to depend on them to defend our wagons and horse remuda, if need be. I believe they will, because the horse remuda belongs to them."

"I'd forgotten about that," Adeline said, "and I feel better. Whatever they think of us, they won't let the Comanches take their horses."

With the sun noon high, there still wasn't a breath of air stirring, and the heat seemed more oppressive than ever. That, combined with the dust, had the herd bawling for water. As their thirst and frustration grew, the brutes began hooking at one another, and some of them had bloody flanks.

"Damn it," Wolf Bowdre said to nobody in particular, "the blowflies will eat 'em alive."

When Dan judged the sun to be about two hours high, he rode ahead and talked to the horse wranglers.

"I'm going to have Silas set the pace," he told them. "Just follow the wagons. They'll go on across the river. Keep the horses moving, but don't let them run. When they've watered, take them across the river to graze."

Dan rode ahead, caught up to the lead wagon and explained to Silas what he was to do.

"What about them Comanche the blue belly was talkin' about?"

"Chato and his men are somewhere ahead of us," Dan said. "I think we can count on them. The horse remuda belongs to them, you know."

Silas nodded, grinned, and drove on.

The bawling, cantankerous herd plodded on, defying all efforts to prod them into a faster gait. It became a futile race with time, and Dan's eye was on the ever lowering sun. Since the wagons and the horses had gone on ahead, Dan rode to the point position. The longhorns had their heads down, their tongues lolling, but they still needed something or someone to follow. The oppressive heat seemed to rise out of the very earth, surrounding them, and not a breath of air stirred. The critical time would come after sundown, when a tantalizing wind from the northwest could bring a hint of water. In but a few seconds their cause could be lost, their efforts in vain, as the massive herd thundered across the plains, out of control.

Repeatedly, Dan turned in his saddle, watching the lead steers. The faster gait, which he had fought to establish at the start of the day, had dwindled, until the herd appeared to be moving even more slowly than before. But there was nothing more the riders could do. The brutes bawled in dismal cacophony as they stumbled along a trail that seemed endless. The westering sun seemed to rest on the distant horizon for a few minutes, and then began to slip away in a burst of crimson glory. Dan removed his hat, sleeving the sweat from his eyes. He judged they had maybe an hour before a treacherous wind might betray them. With that thought in mind, he distanced himself from the herd, riding far enough ahead that he might escape a thundering, thirst-crazed avalanche if he had to.

The sun was long gone and purple twilight approaching when Dan received the first hint of impending disaster. So weary was he that at first he didn't notice, but the thirsty longhorns did. Their frenzied bellows seemed to come simultaneously from twenty thousand parched throats. There was a gentle breeze from the northwest, cooling to Dan's sweaty, blistered face. There was a thunder of hooves as the thirsty longhorns responded, and Dan rode for his life. When the herd fanned out, they would come at him in a deadly swath a mile wide. He rode west until he was sure he was out of the path of the stampede. He waited until the danger was past, then rode back, catching up to the drag riders. Dejected, they sat their saddles amid the settling dust, watching the last of the herd vanish into the twilight.

"A hard day for nothing," Odessa Chambers sighed, "and God knows how many days rounding them up."

"One thing in our favor," Dan said, "they won't run beyond the water."

"No, but they might scatter the length of it," Adeline said wearily.

"That's something we'll have to contend with in the morning," Dan replied. "It'll be dark before we reach the river. Let's ride."

Dan estimated the distance at five miles. Eventually they smelled smoke, evidence that they were nearing the river and their camp. Silas had a fire going, and somewhere beyond it was the sound of cattle splashing around in the river.

"We got here with the wagons in time to fill all our pots and kegs with clear water," Silas said. "Them thirsty varmints is likely to muddy it up for the rest of the night."

"Let's hope they stand right there in it till daylight," Monte Walsh said. "Last time the bastards stampeded, it took us a week to round 'em up. Now we got twice as many."

Dan rode across the river to find the horse herd and see to the safety of the young wranglers. To his relief, he found them and their charges a quarter of a mile north of the river.

"They was all watered and out of the way when the longhorns hit the water," Denny said proudly.

"The four of you handled it just right," Dan said. "It's something to keep in mind. If there's a water problem somewhere along the trail, we may be faced with this again. The longhorns have settled down, so we can drive the horses a little closer to the river. By then supper should be ready."

Supper was mostly a silent affair. Nobody even wanted to think about tomorrow and the task of rounding up the scattered herd.

"Watches tonight as usual," Dan said, "but you can forget about the herd. Just stay close to camp, keep an eye on the wagons, and join the wranglers in seeing that nobody bothers the horses."

South Llano River. Wednesday, September 14, 1870.

Daylight found Dan and the outfit mounting up to gather the scattered herd. He sought out Wolf Bowdre.

"Wolf, you take nine men and ride east. I'll take nine and ride west. I reckon we'll find all these brutes strung out along the river, but there's so many of them, they may be scattered three or four miles in each direction. Ride as far east as you see any cows, and gather them as you return. The rest of us will ride west, gathering as we return. We'll meet, bringing as many together as we can. Once we have a tally and know how many are still out there, we'll go looking for stragglers."

The plan proved effective, and even with the large herd, more than half had been gathered by the end of the day.

"That was the easy part," Dan said. "The rest of them have wandered away from the river to graze, or they're hiding in the mesquite and the oak thickets. Tomorrow we'll go looking for them."

"Might not be all that bad," Garret Haddock said. "This is the closest water, and while cows ain't all that smart, they'll stay close enough to drink. When they're wild, they usually go to water in the early mornin', and this bunch ain't all that tame. If we're strung out up and down this river come daylight, we'll grab a bunch of 'em when they come to drink."

"That's right," Rufe Keeler said. "It'll be easier than draggin' the varmints out of the brush."

Supper was already under way when the big man on the black horse rode in. He wore polished black boots, Levi's, and a white shirt with a fancy black string tie. A gray Stetson completed his attire. He had jet-black hair, pale blue eyes, and a tied-down Colt on his right hip. Dan met him a few yards from the supper fire.

"I'm Clay Allison," the stranger said. "I have a place near Cimarron, New Mexico Territory."

"Step down," Dan said. "We're havin' supper, and you're welcome to join us if you like beans and beef."

"I didn't know there was anything else," Allison replied, dismounting.

9

Clay Allison proved a most interesting guest. He was a handsome man, not more than thirty, and seemed to enjoy the furtive looks he drew from the women. Conversation came easy to him, and when Dan spoke of the Indian situation, Allison expanded on it.

"I don't blame Quanah Parker and the Comanches for their hostility," Allison said. "He was right to back out of the Medicine Lodge Treaty. Not one provision of it was honored. The politicians in Washington promised food, clothing, and hunting grounds in return for peace with the Cheyennes, Arapahos, Comanches, and Kiowas. Not one of the promises were kept. When you're beyond Fort Griffin, you'll hear the boom of rifles to the west, and it won't be Indian rifles. White men have killed off the rest of the buffalo, and now they've invaded the hunting grounds ceded to the Indians."

"I don't doubt the truth of it," Wolf Bowdre said, "but you can't justify Quanah Parker and his Comanches attacking the forts and murdering whites who had nothing to do with violation of the treaties."

"I'm not tryin' to," Allison said. "What I'm saying is that the Indian makes no allowances for anything other than black or white. If you are not his friend, then you are his enemy. Let me give you an example of the white man's treachery that destroyed forever any hope of peace with the Indians. Black Kettle, a Cheyenne chief, brought his people together in support of the Medicine Lodge Treaty. In November 1868, a year after the failed Medicine Lodge conference, Black Kettle and some of his people were camped on the upper Washita River."*

Allison paused, staring into the fire as though remembering. Then he continued.

"At dawn there was an unprovoked attack on Black Kettle's camp. The U.S. Seventh Cavalry, led by the man the Indians call Long Hair. George Armstrong Custer hit the camp from four directions. Black Kettle and his wife were gunned down, along with many women and children. As a final insult, Custer allowed his Indian scouts to scalp Black Kettle. That's what the Indians have come to expect from the white man, and while I don't agree with what they're doing, I can understand their hatred."

"Put in those terms," Dan said, "so can I. The Confederacy is suffering under its own Washington treaty, called the Reconstruction Act."

"I'm familiar with it," Allison said. "I was there, along with some of my friends from Tennessee. When it was over, I came to Texas, only to learn I was about to end up under Washington's thumb. Before the blue bellies showed up, I pulled out. New Mexico Territory ain't all that bad."

"I reckon you're plenty familiar with Goodnight's drive through eastern New Mexico Territory into Colorado," Skull Kimbrough said. "Tough trail, I reckon."

"I wouldn't recommend it unless you're plannin' a ranch in the high country," Allison said. "I was trying to

* Now western Oklahoma

make a go of it in southeastern Colorado at the time, and I met some of Goodnight's pards in Santa Fe."†

"It's time for the first watch," Dan said, "and I reckon the rest of us had better call it a night. We have a hard day tomorrow."

"If you don't mind, I'll ride on to Fort Griffin with you," Allison said. "Kind of tedious, ridin' it by my lonesome, and there's always a chance I'll meet up with Quanah Parker and his amigos."

"You're welcome to ride with us," Dan said, "but you may be a while in gettin' there. Half our herd's scattered somewhere along this river, and we won't be goin' anywhere until we've rounded 'em up."

"I'm not in that great a hurry," Allison said. "I learned cow back in Tennessee. I'll lend a hand."

"He's a strange man," Adeline said when Dan had unrolled his blankets near hers. "I think there's more to him than meets the eye. If he lives in New Mexico, why is he going to Fort Griffin?"

"We won't know unless he chooses to tell us," Dan said. "This is the frontier, and you don't ask more of a man than he volunteers to tell you. But you're right about one thing. He does have another side. I heard of him while I was with the Confederacy. He was with a company of Tennesseans, and they fought like devils, Allison leading them."

"I like him," Adeline said. "Despite what Quanah Parker and his band are doing, Clay Allison spoke of them with compassion, and I liked that."

"If we have a fight with them, I hope he still feels that way," Dan said. "It's the kind of situation that depends mostly on whose ox is bein' gored."

Dan arose at midnight, taking his place on the second watch. Almost by the time he was in the saddle, there was the roar of a Colt. It came from the vicinity of the

† *The Goodnight Trail.* Book #1 in the Trail Drive Series.

horse remuda, and Dan and his riders arrived to find their four young horse wranglers standing over the body of a man.

"We didn't do it," Denny DeVoe said defensively as Dan and his companions dismounted.

"I did it," said Clay Allison from the shadows, "He was trying to get to the horses."

"You're a mite sudden with a gun," Dan said. "How did you know it wasn't one of our men?"

"He was afoot," Allison said. "Your camp was asleep, except for the men on watch, and they're all mounted. Turn him over and see if you recognize him." Allison lighted a match.

Dan rolled the man over and found himself looking into the swarthy face of a Mexican. The rest of Dan's riders from the second watch gathered around, along with most of those who had been awakened by the shot.

"Nobody I've ever seen before," Dan said. "What's a Mexican doing this far north, sneaking around our horse remuda in the middle of the night?"

"Bigger question is, how'd the varmint get past us and to the horses?" Silas Hamby asked.

"We didn't see or near nothin'," Gid Kilgore said, "till the shot was fired, and we wasn't asleep neither."

"Not the fault of you wranglers," Dan said. "Wolf, get a blanket. You and me will tote this hombre away from camp until we can bury him tomorrow. Those of you on the second watch mount up, and the rest of you get what sleep you can. Tomorrow will be another long day."

On the banks of the Nueces, some twenty miles south of the trail drive, Santos Miguel Montoya and his Mexican band had made their camp. A hundred yards to the south was a second camp, that of Burton Ledoux and his two men, Loe Hagerman and Black Bill. First light was just minutes away.

"That Mex that rode out last night ain't come back," Hagerman said. "What you reckon that means?"

"How the hell should I know?" Ledoux snapped irritably. Used to easier living, the discomforts of the trail were getting to him.

"I wish the whole damn lot would ride out and not come back," Black Bill said. "I hate Mejicanos."

"Along with everybody else," Hagerman observed.

"Watch your mouth," Black Bill said. "I ain't takin' nothin' off of you."

"Both of you just shut the hell up," Ledoux growled. "Here comes Montoya."

Black Bill eyed the Mexican with open contempt, while Montoya seemed to regard Black Bill with amusement. Montoya spoke.

"Diego has not returned, Senor Ledoux."

"I'm aware of that," Ledoux snapped. "What do you intend to do now?"

"Nothing, senor. If Diego lives, he will return to us. If he does not, then finding his dead body will accomplish nothing."

"We were stuck here on the damn riverbank all day yesterday," Ledoux fumed. "How much longer?"

"Two more day," Montoya said cheerfully. "Per'ap longer."

"Well, I'm damn tired of this inactivity," Ledoux said peevishly.

"Senor," Montoya said, "the Tejano herd is scattered, and gathering the *vaca* per'ap take days. We wait, senor, or you and your *companeros* may ride on alone." With that, he turned and walked away.

"Mouthy Mex bastard," Black Bill said, fondling the leather butt of his lethal whip. "I could cut that shirt off'n his back."

"I have a use for that bunch," Ledoux said. "Pick a fight with them, and if they don't gut-shoot you, I will."

Black Bill said nothing, but his pig eyes were on Bur-

ton Ledoux's back, and he continued fondling the butt
of the deadly whip.

South Llano River. Saturday, September 17, 1870.

Slowly, the scattered herd again came together. Clay
Allison became a source of amusement, his sense of
humor never failing him. He had forsaken his white
shirt and tie, donning an old flannel shirt from his saddlebag, and had replaced his fine gray Stetson with an
old black flop hat that had seen better days. He proved
adept at handling cattle.

"I'll hire you for the rest of the drive," Dan said, "if
you can make it without pay until we get to Dodge."

"No thanks," Allison replied, "and the pay's got nothing to do with it. I run out of patience with cows, and by
the time we reach Fort Griffin, then I reckon I'll have
had my fill."

While the scattered longhorns came to the river to
drink, some of them had found graze a considerable
distance away, and after a three-day gather, more than
two thousand were still missing.

"We'll have to find them," Dan said. "We've branded
them and driven them this far, and that's more than we
can afford to lose."

"I have a suggestion," Allison said. "Why not ride ten
miles west and form a skirmish line that crosses the
river, stretching a mile on either side? We should then
be able to comb the river from west to east and flush
them out, wherever they are."

"Good suggestion," Dan said, "except that we won't
have enough riders for a mile-long line on each side of
the river. We'll have to reduce it to half a mile. Let's
ride."

Allison's plan proved effective, and after a day's riding, the outfit had gathered more than half the missing
longhorns.

"By God," Sloan Kuykendall said, "one more day like this, and we'll have them all."

The following day, again using the skirmish line, they swept the river far to the east. Come sundown, Dan was convinced they weren't going to find any more cattle. He turned to Wolf Bowdre.

"Wolf, take three men and run a quick tally. I think this is going to be the end of the gather."

Bowdre chose Boyce Trevino, Palo Elfego, Chad Grimes, and Cash Connolly. The rest of the outfit gathered in camp, awaiting supper. It was almost dark when Bowdre and his companions returned.

"We differed some," Bowdre said, "but there wasn't time for a recount before dark. Comparing our tallies, we reckon that we're missing maybe fifty head, but no more than seventy-five."

"We can stand that," Dan said. "Tomorrow we'll move on. Allison, do you have any idea how far we are from Fort Griffin?"

"At least two hundred miles," Allison replied. "It's on the Clear Fork of the Brazos, a hundred and twenty miles west of Fort Worth."

"It's safe to say you've been there, I reckon," Dan said.

"Yes," Allison said, "I have business there occasionally. But I haven't been there in almost a year."

Dan wondered what that business was. Allison had ridden in from the west, which suggested he might have come through El Paso. By his own words, Allison had a place near Cimarron, but Dan had no idea where that was. It was a mystery why a man would ride so far, delaying his journey to ride with a trail drive. Allison had given Dan something to think about, insofar as the Indians were concerned. Since they were stopping at Fort Griffin anyway, why not seek the advice of the military as to the whereabouts of the hostiles?

* * *

On the trail north. Sunday, September 18, 1870.

At dawn, well-watered and -grazed, the herd again took the trail. Clay Allison chose to ride drag, to the delight of most of the women. Dan led the drive northeast, along the Llano River. Palo Elfego had conferred with Chato sometime during the night and was told they could follow the Llano twenty-five miles. There they must drive due north, and the next river was at least thirty-five miles. In between, the best they could expect were shallow creeks. As the herd fell in behind the horse remuda, Dan rode ahead, catching up to the lead wagon.

"Maybe two days on the Llano, Silas. See that all the water kegs are full, especially after tomorrow night's camp."

"I'll see to it," Silas said.

"One other thing," Dan said. "It's been a dry spring and summer, and we've had no troublesome river crossings. But before we reach Dodge, we'll be crossing rivers that are fed from the high plains. They'll be deeper and wider, and these wagons will have to be floated across. If they're not watertight, we'll have to spend some time on them or abandon them. I'm thinking Fort Griffin would be a good place to decide what must be done. What do you think?"

"I think there wasn't none of 'em built for fordin' deep rivers," Silas said, "but with enough pitch and patience, they can all be made to float. Us with no gold, you reckon we can talk them Yankees at the fort out of a bucket of pitch?"

"We can try," Dan said, "if there's any to be had. I'd purely hate to have to leave even one of the wagons. I also dislike having to spend too much time at the fort, but that can't be helped. We have to stop there and talk to the post commander anyway."

* * *

One hundred seventy-five miles south of Fort Griffin, Texas. Tuesday, September 20, 1870.

"When we take the trail tomorrow," Dan said, "We're thirty-five miles from the next river. Between here and there we'll have to depend on shallow creeks, both of which are about halfway. That means for the next two days we'll be looking at seventeen-mile drives if we're to reach water."

Nobody spoke, but the expressions on their faces said they were only too well aware of the impending trouble with a cantankerous, thirsty herd. But the dry spring and summer was behind them, and during the night there was lightning far to the west. At dawn the sky was overcast, and when the sun rose, it was but a pale yellow glow. The west wind had a chill to it, and the riders hunkered closer to the fire to eat their breakfast.

"We ain't got to worry about gettin' to the water," Silas said. "It's comin' to us."

"I don't remember it ever rainin' this early in the fall," Duncan Kilgore said. "Maybe it's got somethin' to do with the dry spring and summer."

"I reckon Texas can use the water," Garret Haddock said, "but we got some mighty big rivers to cross. That's all we need, for the fall rains to come early and raise the rivers another foot or two."

The rain began in the early afternoon. Strangely, there was no thunder and no lightning. Just torrents of water. The land was broken by hill ranges, with mesquite thickets in the draws. There was live oak, Spanish oak, and pecan, and after two hours of steady rain, wet weather streams abounded. Arroyos, normally dry, quickly filled with water, and low lands rapidly became quagmires in which the wagons sank to the axles. Mules had to be unhitched from one wagon and sent to the aid of another. Wagon after wagon bogged down, and the herd was forced to a standstill while the entire outfit, women included, went to the aid of the wagons. When they had finally been freed, everybody was exhausted.

"Damn it," Dan said, "I've had enough. Let's find some high ground and make camp."

They finally found some shelter among a stand of oaks on the lee side of a ridge. There was plentiful graze in the valley below, and a fast flowing creek whose bed had been dry the day before. Two wagons were lined up back to back and a canvas stretched between them to create a shelter for a cook fire. Silas had thoughtfully stretched a cowhide beneath each wagon box as a means of carrying dry firewood. The rain finally slacked sometime after midnight. Clay Allison was riding the second watch, trotting his horse beside Dan's, when Palo Elfego caught up to them.

"Indios campamento," he said. *"Muchos Indios. Comanch."**

"Where?" Dan asked.

"Norte, fi' milla."

"Fight?" Dan asked.

"No fight," Palo said. *"Muchos, muchos Indios."*

It was a message from Chato, warning them of a Comanche camp, of odds that were insurmountable.

"Thanks, Palo," Dan said. He rode on, saying nothing, his mind in a turmoil. They could expect no help from Chato and his men, for the Indian had sent him word the odds were impossibly high. It had nothing to do with courage or the lack of it. Only a fool fought when he stood to accomplish nothing but his own death.

"Sounds like Quanah Parker and his bunch," Clay Allison said. "I hear he can command seven hundred Comanche braves."

"A tenth that number would be the death of us," Dan said. "This trail drive could end right here."

"Maybe not," Allison said. "I met Quanah Parker

* Indian camp. Many Indians.

once, on the Llano Estacado. I can't promise anything, except that I don't think he'll shoot me on sight. We'll ride up there in the morning and powwow with him. Offer him a few cows as a gift. With the white man slaughtering all the buffalo, Indians are always hungry."

"Allison," Dan said, "you're a *muy bueno hombre*. You don't owe us a thing. You could circle that Comanche camp and be on your way to Fort Griffin, yet you'd ride into the midst of hostile Comanches and dicker for our scalps. I need help, and I appreciate your offer, but you could end up shot full of Comanche arrows, along with the rest of us."

"Luck of the draw," Allison said. "Maybe you can save my neck sometime."

While Dan didn't wish to alarm the rest of the outfit, he and Allison couldn't ride away without some explanation, so Dan told them the truth. He thought they regarded Allison with some doubt, but the big man was the only chance they had. Nobody said anything. He thought Adeline wanted to say something to him, but she bit her lip and remained silent. He and Allison saddled their horses and rode north, Allison taking the lead. Chato had given them correct information, for the ride took them less than half an hour. They saw and heard nothing, and suddenly they were surrounded by mounted Comanche warriors.

Allison spoke to them fluently in a tongue Dan didn't understand. The braves looked at one another, uncertain. Finally one of them nodded to Allison, and he rode on, Dan following. Dan started breathing again. They might yet be shot dead, but at least Allison had apparently gotten them an audience with Quanah Parker. As they progressed, Dan began to appreciate the wisdom of Chato's words, "no fight," for Comanches seemed to appear from behind every bush and tree. They reached a clearing where the cook fire still smoldered, an early morning breeze fanning the embers. A young Indian

stood before them, dressed in buckskin. He said nothing, and it was to him that Clay Allison spoke in what
apparently was the Comanche tongue. Dan couldn't believe the young chief was the notorious Quanah Parker.
He seemed no more than a boy.*

With his hands, Allison made the buffalo sign, and
then pointed to Dan. Allison then held up both hands,
spreading all his fingers, and pointed to the Comanche.
Quanah shook his head, raised both hands, spreading all
his fingers, then repeated the gesture. He then spoke to
Allison in that tongue Dan couldn't understand. Allison
replied, pointing again to Dan, and Quanah said nothing. Allison spoke to Dan.

"He says all white men deserve to die, just as Black
Kettle and his people died under the guns of Long Hair
and his soldiers. For a gift of twenty of the white man's
buffalo, he will allow you to go in peace, but you must
not come this way again. He vows all the men in the
soldier forts will die."

"Tell him he's welcome to twenty cows," Dan said.
"We'll cut them out and bring them to him, or he can
send some of his men back with us."

Again Allison spoke to the Comanche in his own
tongue, and Quanah gave an order. Four mounted
braves rode forward. Without another word Allison
rode out, Dan following, with the four Comanches behind him. It was an uneasy journey, Dan not daring to
look back. They avoided the camp, going directly to the
herd. The rest of the outfit could see the herd from their
camp, but they wisely stayed away. Quickly, Allison and
Dan cut out twenty steers, and the four Comanche
drove them away.

"By God," Dan said, sleeving the sweat from his
brow, "I reckon that's about the best swap a man ever
made for twenty cows."

* Quanah Parker was born in 1852.

Allison laughed. "I tried to get you off with ten, but he wouldn't have it. Believe it or not, he has a grudging respect for you Tejanos who raise cattle. He knows you're not responsible for slaughtering the buffalo."

Dan and Allison rode back to camp and found breakfast was ready. Nobody had wanted to eat until the crisis was resolved, if it could be.

"Mr. Allison swapped them twenty cows for our scalps," Dan said, "and for a promise we won't ever come this way again."

"That's a promise I won't have any trouble keepin'," Rufe Keeler said.

"Me neither," Monte Walsh said. "Let's get these brutes on the trail and move out before they have second thoughts."

"Silas," Chad Grimes said, "keep them wagons to the high ground. I purely ain't of a mind to spend the day haulin' them damn wagons out of the mud, with a bunch of Comanches lookin' over my shoulder."

"You'd better think some on that," Silas said irritably. "These wagons is carryin' our grub, ammunition, and dry bedrolls."

Silas led out with the wagons, followed by the horse remuda and then the longhorns. Silas kept to the ridges as much as he could, and there was no more trouble with the wagons miring down. Dan half considered taking the drive around the area where the Comanche camp had been, but changed his mind. Quanah Parker had known the drive would be coming, and when they reached the place where Allison had confronted the Indian, there was no sign of the camp. While the rain had ended during the night, the sky was still overcast, and the north wind was cold. Wet weather streams were still abundant, and would be until the sun appeared and sucked them dry. Dan rode ahead and caught up to the lead wagon.

"There's plenty of water, Silas, but I think we'll try to make it to the next river before dark."*

"Good idee," Silas said. "Sun comes out, these streams will be gone by mornin', if not sooner."

Since they had spent almost half the previous day dragging the wagons out of the mire, Dan doubted they had traveled more than ten miles. That meant the next river was twenty-five miles away, and the shallow creek Chato had reported would be another eight or nine miles. It posed a problem. If the drive stopped at the creek, they were assured of water, but it limited them to eight miles for the day. If they went on, and the sun dried up the excess water from the rain, they might be stuck in a dry camp a dozen miles south of the river. It seemed the other riders were having similar thoughts. Wolf Bowdre caught up to Dan, obviously something on his mind.

"The rain was a blessing," Bowdre said, "but we can't depend on these wet weather streams. Half a day of sun and they'll be gone faster than forty rod whiskey in a buffalo camp. It'll mean a short day, but I think we should accept our eight or nine miles for today, and save the drive on to the river for tomorrow."

"I think we'll save that decision until later in the day," Dan said. "If the sky stays cloudy, the temporary streams and water holes will remain another day. If they do, then we can forget this creek Chato spoke of, and bed down the herd wherever darkness catches us."

Bowdre started to speak, but thought better of it, dropping back to his position with the herd. Dan had wondered how long it was going to take before some of them began questioning his judgment, and he regretted it had to be Wolf Bowdre. He genuinely liked the man, and hoped it wouldn't come down to a question of who was going to be trail boss.

* The San Saba River

10

The drive reached the creek Chato had spoken of, and because of the rain, it was no longer shallow. The sky was still overcast, and thanks to the many wet weather streams, neither the horse remuda nor the herd was thirsty. Dan rode the length of the drive, speaking to the riders, saving Wolf Bowdre for last.

"We're going on, Wolf," Dan said. "There's a good four hours of daylight, plenty of water, and by dark we'll be within a day's drive of the next river."

Bowdre only nodded, and Dan rode on. The sky began to clear, but not until almost sundown. The wet weather streams would last until sometime into the next day, and the extra miles Dan had insisted upon would put them within reach of the next river. Dan was congratulated around the supper fire.

"Damn good thinkin'," Spence Wilder said. "If we'd stayed at that other stream, with just eight miles for the day, we'd of been facin' near twenty-five miles tomorrow, with the sun gobblin' up all this temporary water from the rain."

"Trail savvy," Kirby Wilkerson said, "is lookin' beyond water for today, and planning for tomorrow. We'd of been damn fools not to push the herd for as long as it was light enough to see, with plenty of water and the clouds keepin' the sun off us."

There were other favorable comments, but Dan shrugged them off. He half suspected they were for Wolf Bowdre's benefit, because Bowdre had made no secret of his wish to shorten the day's drive and stay with the sure water. Dan made it a point to speak to Bowdre, but the man seemed distant, as though he resented Dan's obviously successful decision. Since Silas Hamby was on the first watch, he waited until then to speak to Dan. Since the first day on the trail, Silas had taken it upon himself to seek out difficulties before they became insurmountable.

"Dan, we're needin' nails and shoes for all the hosses and mules. The bunch of cayuses Chato brought us was near barefooted when we got 'em, and every dang mule, includin' my own, is in bad shape."

"The whole bunch will have to be reshod by the time we get to Fort Griffin, then," Dan said.

"No later," Silas said. "Fact is, most of 'em need it now, but I know we ain't got the shoes or nails. I also know we got no money, even when we get to Fort Griffin."

"I've been thinking about that," Dan said. "We still have more than five hundred extra cows, and there'll be a sutler's store at the fort. What do you think of us selling maybe fifty cows and buying the things we need?"

"I think it's likely the best idee you've had so far," Silas said. "It's been nine year since I had coffee or sugar. 'Course we can live without that, but every damn hoss and mule in the outfit will end up crippled if we don't get shoes and nails, pronto."

"Silas, you've known these men longer than I have, and I think some of them are a little tired of everything coming from me. Talk to them, and let it be your idea that we swap some cows at the fort. If everybody agrees,

I'll talk to Clay Allison. He's been to Fort Griffin before, and can likely tell us something about the post and our chances of swapping some beef."

"I'll talk to 'em, then," Silas said, "but don't be takin' any back talk from some ungrateful varmint that thinks you ain't doin' things just right. I'll talk to them that's on the first watch, and mebbe hang around and palaver with them that comes on at midnight."

"Good," Dan said. "If everybody agrees, then you can talk to me like it's your idea."

One hundred fifty miles south of Fort Griffin, Texas. Thursday, September 22, 1870.

The cloud cover gone, the sun rose and quickly dried up all the wet weather streams, but thanks to Dan's foresight, the herd reached the river by sundown. Dan approached Silas as the old-timer was unhitching the mules from his wagon.

"I done it like you said for me to," Silas said, "and ever'body thinks it's the thing to do. I told 'em I'd mention it to you, and damn it, I purely don't feel right, takin' the credit for what you'd already thought of."

"Makes no difference who thought of it," Dan said. "The important thing is that we all agree on a means of getting the things we need at Fort Griffin. I'll talk to Allison and see what I can find out about the sutler's store."

Clay Allison seemed to shun inactivity, and often rode either the first or second watch. This night he rode the first watch, and Dan Ember rode with him.

"Silas suggested something to me," Dan said, "and since you've been to Fort Griffin before, I'd like your opinion."

"You got it, for whatever it's worth," Allison replied.

"We're needing many things," Dan said, "especially horse and mule shoes, and nails. We're thinking of sell-

ing maybe fifty head of cows to the sutler's store. Being
Rebs and out of favor with the Federals, do we have a
chance?"

"I don't see why not," Allison said. "These stores are
political plums handed out to civilians. Old varmint
name of Elwood Goldstein's got the one at Fort Griffin,
and all you got to be wary of is that he don't skin you.
I'd say don't offer to sell him any stock. You do, and
he'll beat your ears down, and then overcharge you at
the store. Ask thirty dollars a head, and take it all in
trade. But first I'd suggest you meet with the post commander and satisfy him as to your intentions."

"I aim to," Dan said. "We've already met some Union
soldiers and have been told we'll likely have to sign papers vowing not to take up our arms against the Union."

"It will be to your advantage to sign them," Allison
said, "so Goldstein can't refuse you guns and ammunition at the store. There's a new Winchester repeating
rifle that shoots seventeen times without reloading. Arm
yourselves with them, and you can stand off an army."

"Thanks," Dan said. "If they're available, we'll do
that."

"Shouldn't be a problem," Allison said. "Griffin's not
that far from Fort Worth, and everything's wagoned out
of there. It's the more distant forts that may be short,
because Quanah and his bunch have looted so many of
the supply trains from Fort Worth."

"I'm surprised the Comanches aren't armed with
Winchester repeaters," Dan said.

"Some of them are," Allison replied. "It's reached
the point where any arms or ammunition from Fort
Worth is so heavily guarded, it's a dead giveaway. The
Comanches know it's guns, ammunition, or both."

Dan said nothing to the rest of the outfit about what
Allison had told him. As it was, there would be speculation enough, with everybody expecting a beef sale at the
fort. Already, he feared most of them were reacting as

Silas originally had, thinking in terms of luxuries rather than necessities. The trail drive continued, often relying on water the elusive Chato and his men had located. Palo Elfego was the only man in the outfit who was contacted, and then only when it was necessary to relay some information about what lay ahead. There was some occasional grumbling about Chato, but Aubin Chambers quickly silenced it. He had not forgotten, and despite his early opposition, he now sided Daniel Ember.

Thirty-five miles south of Fort Griffin, Texas. Tuesday, October 4, 1870.

The country became more hilly, and there was live oak, post oak, mesquite, and cedar. The outfit spent the night near an unidentified lake, and from there sighted three substantial elevations.*

"Twenty miles south of Fort Griffin we'll come to another lake," Clay Allison said. "From there we'll follow the Clear Fork of the Brazos on to the fort."

"By my figurin'," Dan said, "we're maybe thirty-five miles south of the fort now. Tomorrow night we should reach this lake, and have sure water from there on to Fort Griffin."

"That's it," Allison said, "unless the fort or the Brazos has been moved since last year."

After supper Dan spent a rare hour with Adeline, Denny, and Lenore. It had been a while since they'd had any privacy, and Adeline had insisted on it.

"I ought to be with the horses, Ma," Denny complained.

"You had *not* ought to be with the horses," Adeline

* Lake Abilene is located a few miles south of what would become the city of Abilene, in 1881. The peaks, unknown to the riders, are Church Mountain, Bald Eagle, and East Peak.

said. "You sleep with them every night, and Dan's always with the first watch until midnight. I don't care what everybody else thinks."

"Denny's spent so much time with the horses, he eats, smells, and thinks like one," Lenore said.

Denny threw a boot at her, Dan laughed, and for just a little while they were a family.

Twenty miles south of Fort Griffin. Wednesday, October 5, 1870.

Dan found his estimate hadn't been all that accurate, and darkness was upon them before they reached the south shore of the lake Allison had said they would find, into which flowed the Brazos.*

"If you don't make the fort tomorrow," Allison said, "you'll be almost within hollerin' distance."

"I wish you weren't leaving us at the fort," Lenore said, finally overcoming her shyness. "I've gotten used to you, and I'm going to miss you."

"I take considerable gettin' used to, ma'am," Allison said, sweeping off his hat. "It'll sadden me when I go, havin' a pretty lady missing me, but I have some business here. Then I'll be back on my lonesome, ridin' back to New Mexico Territory, I reckon."

Since the day Allison had joined the drive, the Texans had wondered what was urgent enough to draw the big man all the way from New Mexico Territory. Not until they reached Fort Griffin would they discover the dark

---

* The Clear Fork of the Brazos flows into Lake Fort Phantom Hill, named for the fort established near the present town of Hawley, Texas, in 1851. Phantom Hill was one in a line of forts from Red River to the Rio Grande, offering protection to Forty-niners following the Randolph B. Marcy trail across Texas. But supplies had to be hauled all the way from Austin, and Fort Phantom Hill was abandoned in 1854.

side of Clay Allison, a shocking contrast to the gentleman he seemed to be.

Fort Griffin, Texas. Thursday, October 6, 1870.

"Rain come soon," predicted Palo Elfego, looking at the ominous gray mass of clouds far to the west.

"Our damn luck," growled Rux Carper. "A lake and the Brazos River waitin' for us tonight, and we get rained on all day."

"You'll be crossing the Brazos before you leave Texas," Allison said, "and then you'll have somethin' to be botherin' you. I hear it runs wide and deep, and except for the Red, it would likely be the worst."

"Something to look forward to, I reckon," Dan said. "Once we reach the fort, we have our work cut out for us. While some of us are shoein' horses and mules, the rest will be patching wagon boxes."

"Then I reckon Shakespeare was right," Allison said. "There's small choice in rotten apples."

"Is good we fix *carreta* at fort," Palo Elfego said. "How we know, when she cross deep water, she no sink?"

Palo was embarrassed and maybe a little angry when everybody laughed at what he had intended as a serious question. Silas came to his rescue.

"That's a fair question, Palo. We'll be right there on the Brazos, and when we reckon a wagon box is caulked good and tight, we'll float it across the river and back again. We'll weigh the wagon with rocks. The Brazos is a mean enough stretch of water that if there's any holes, the river will find 'em. We'd just better be lucky enough to find a blessed plenty of pitch at Fort Griffin."

"I expect you will," Allison said. "The military trains have to cross creeks and rivers, and I believe some of the buildings at the fort have flat roofs."

The rain wasn't long in coming. The drive hadn't been

on the trail two hours when the wind began to rise. While there was faraway thunder, there was no lightning, and all they had to contend with was the rain. It swept in from the west, the wind slapping it hard into man and beast. The longhorns wanted to turn their backs to wind and rain and drift with it. Dan pulled some of the flank and swing riders from the west flank of the herd, moving them to the opposite flank. As the wind and rain became more intense, there was a frantic effort among the longhorns to break away from their northern course, turning eastward with the storm.

"Hit 'em hard," Dan shouted, striving to be heard above the bawling of the cattle and the roar of the wind.

Water had begun to pool in low-lying areas, and Silas managed to keep his wagon to the ridges, the others following. Eventually the wind subsided and the rain became a steady, monotonous downpour. Without the wind slamming the rain into their flanks, the longhorns had no objection to trailing north. Their frustrated bawling ceased, and they slogged through hock-deep water without protest.

"This ain't bad," Skull Kimbrough bawled to anybody who cared to listen. "Is they any of you Tejano cow nurses that'd ruther have the hot sun?"

Riding drag, the women hunched over in their sodden clothes, following the herd. Lenore rode next to Adeline, and when the girl spoke, her teeth chattered.

"When we get to the fort, I hope we can get some warmer clothes. Cold as it is now, what will it be like when we're farther north?"

"Our behinds will be frozen to our saddles," said Amy Wilder, who had overheard.

"Nothing's been said about what we're going to try to get at the sutler's store," Adeline said, "except that I know we need shoes for the horses and mules, and nails. I'm not sure, but I believe Dan's waiting to see whether or not we can sell some cows. If we can, and can raise enough money, then I believe we'll all have a chance to get warm clothes and other things. That is, if the men all agree."

"Damn the men," said Hattie Kuykendall, who had ridden close enough to take part in the conversation. "There's not a man in this outfit that's any wetter or more miserable than I am. I know we need shoes for horses, mules, and nails, but after that's been bought, I'm havin' me some gloves, and some long-handled wool underwear."

"There is no such garment for a woman," Odessa Chambers said.

"That's what you think," Hattie replied. "I'm wearing Sloan's Levi's and shirt now, and I'd be wearin' his longhandles if he had any. If he's got the savvy God give a prairie dog, he'll get some at the fort, and I'll get a pair of them."

They all laughed at the salty woman, and it seemed to relieve some of the misery. The day wore on, and in the early afternoon the rain let up and the sky began to clear. Two hours before sunset, the sun was out, and not a rider complained. The warmth was welcome, and everybody's spirits rose. Ahead of them, seeming so close they could touch it, was a rainbow. Its red, blue, and gold seemed to touch the earth at the west end, while the other arced into the remaining clouds.

"That's off the lake," Allison said. "We'll reach the fort before dark."

"I think we'll wait until tomorrow before riding in," Dan said.

"That would likely be best," Allison said. "I doubt the post commander would see you before then, and I was serious when I said you should talk to him before going to the store."

"I'm taking your advice," Dan said, "and I'm obliged. Do you aim to ride in tonight?"

"No, I'll wait until morning," Allison said. "The hombre I'm looking for is a buffalo hunter, and tonight he'll likely be in the saloon in the back of the sutler's place, sloshed to the eyeballs. When him and me talk, I want him cold sober."

It was the closest Allison had come to revealing his business at Fort Griffin, and again Dan wondered what lay ahead. As Allison had predicted, the trail drive was within two or three miles of the fort before sundown.

"This is as far as we go tonight," Dan told them. "Since all of you are agreeable to selling some beef, I'll ride in tomorrow and see if we can. I don't aim to ride alone, but I don't think it's wise for twenty men to walk into the post commander's office. Likewise, we don't need or want the whole outfit haggling with this Elwood Goldstein over the price of beef. I aim to ask thirty dollars a head, not in cash, but in trade. Does anybody object to that?"

"I ain't objectin' to it," Rux Carper said, "but who decides what we're taking in trade from the store?"

"We'll all have a say in that," Dan replied, "after we've sold the cows and know we have some credit. How much we get, how much any of you receive, depends entirely upon how many cows we can sell. I'm suggesting fifty head."

"We got extra cows," Carper said. "Why not a hundred head?"

"Because that's three thousand dollars in credit," Dan said, "and we may not be able to get that much. We'll consider it, if it looks like Goldstein might be interested. Now, which four of you want to ride in with me in the morning?"

"You don't need us," Silas said. "You done said we'll have a choice in choosin' what we take in trade, and you'll be tellin' us how much credit we got, if we get any."

"Nevertheless," Dan said, "I'd prefer that some of you go with me. I'm not of a mind to have somebody disagree with whatever deal I can work out, and I think we can best avoid that if some of you are there to see and hear what takes place."

He had them in an embarrassing position. He knew some of them wanted to go, but to do so would reveal an obvious lack of confidence in their trail boss. Surprisingly, Wolf Bowdre came up with an acceptable solution.

"Silas," Bowdre said, "you been neck deep in this from the start. You cleaned out your store, usin' your goods and provisions to our benefit. Why don't you ride in tomorrow with Dan, and the rest of us will accept whatever the two of you can work out. Now, is there anybody that don't agree with that?"

Nobody objected, but Dan suspected there were several who would have liked to. It was a way out of a situation he had dreaded, and he nodded his thanks to Bowdre.

"I'll go, then," Silas said. "If we sell some cows, get some credit, we can all set down and do some talkin' and some figurin'. We'll figure out the things we got to have, such as hoss and mule shoes, and nails. That done, I reckon we'd best think about some warm coats, gloves, and such, since we're travelin' to the north country. And we can't overlook the need for guns and ammunition neither. Finally, with whatever's left, maybe we can add to our grub. When I say that, I don't mean we do it one family at a time. Up to now we been eatin' our beef and beans out of a common pot. I say we go on doin' that, but maybe add some flour, some meal, some sugar, and maybe even some coffee. Now that's how I feel. If there's anybody disagrees with that, then I'm backin' out, and you can send somebody else with Dan, not that he'll need you."

They all shouted their acceptance, even the women, and Silas said no more. Some of the men went a step further, making it a point to voice their approval to Dan and Silas. One of these was Wolf Bowdre. Generally the women kept silent, allowing the men to do their talking, but not this time. They gathered around like a covey of excited birds, and when Dan's eyes met Adeline's, he saw relief there. Dan felt as though a burden had been lifted from his shoulders, for not only had they all agreed on something for the good of the outfit, but he seemed to have regained some of the trust he feared he had lost. Now all they had to do was convince the post commander they had no intention of resuming the war against the Union, and to arrange for the sale of some beef to Elwood Goldstein at the sutler's store. Their difficulties were far from over, for much of the long trail still lay ahead, but Dan Ember believed they were finally coming into their own as an outfit. And that was all he asked.

After breakfast, Dan, Silas, and Clay Allison saddled their horses and rode upriver to the fort. Even from a distance Dan could see that it was much larger than he'd expected. Soldiers walked the parapets above the log walls, and the massive double gate that faced the south was actually two vertical sections of the log wall that swung inward. Even as the trio neared the fort, the gates swung open and half a dozen men exited. North of the fort, along the Brazos, mules and oxen grazed. Dan counted a dozen wagons, most of them with high boxes, loaded with weathered buffalo bones.

"You're in luck," Allison said. "They've killed off all the buffalo in these parts, else the wagons would be piled high with buffalo hides. When there was plenty of buffalo meat, Goldstein bought it for three or four cents a pound, and would have refused your beef. Now, I think he'll deal with you."

By the time they reached the fort, the gates had been closed and they had to wait for the sentry to challenge them. Allison spoke for them all.

"I'm Clay Allison, and I've been here before. These two gents are part of an outfit that's taking their cattle to market, and they need to talk to the post commander."

The gates remained closed while the sentry sent another soldier for the sergeant of the guard. Allison waited until the soldier returned, and when he did, his words were for Dan and Silas.

"Major Montgomery will see you," he said.

"I'll be seein' you gents later," Allison said, and he set off on his own.

Dan and Silas were led through an orderly room to a closed door beyond, where their guide knocked. Bid to enter, he did so, saluting. Dan and Silas followed. Major Montgomery had gray hair, a stern face, and hard blue eyes. He said nothing, waiting for Dan or Silas to speak. Dan did.

"I'm Daniel Ember, and this is Silas Hamby. We're part of an outfit of ranchers, and we're driving our cattle to market. A Lieutenant Winters and his command spent the night with us somewhere south of here, and he told us to meet with you, to tell you of our intentions."

For a long moment the officer said nothing. His eyes were on the Colts Dan and Silas wore. Finally his eyes met Dan's and he spoke.

"I presume the lieutenant told you that with Texas under Federal rule, you are not permitted to carry weapons."

"He did," Dan said, "with exceptions. He realized, as I'm sure you must, that we cannot undertake such a journey unarmed. We were told that we can sign papers allowing us to keep our weapons. We understand that it will be your decision, sir."

"That is correct," Montgomery said, a little less stuffily. "Where are you taking this drive?"

"Fort Dodge, Kansas," Dan said. "To the railroad."

"There is no railroad," Montgomery said. "It's

months away, and I must remind you that there is a government ban against commerce with anyone from a state that fought against the Union. Therefore, none of the forts to the north—in Indian Territory or Kansas—will be permitted to buy your cows."

"We understand that," Dan said, "and we have no intention of trying to sell to the government. We aim to wait for the railroad, if it takes a year."

"With that understanding, I'll permit you to keep your weapons, and it's my duty to tell you that there's an Indian problem we have been unable to reconcile. You may be fighting the Comanche, the Kiowa, the Arapaho, and possibly the Cheyenne. We're already spread too thin, and can't offer you any protection, and I expect the command at Fort Dodge is experiencing the same difficulty."

"We have twenty fighting men," Dan said, "and almost as many women, but we have almost no rifles. That's why we felt it necessary to reach some agreement with you on the weapons. We hope to do some trading with the sutler's store, arming ourselves with the new Winchester repeating rifles."

"I fear you'll be needing them," Montgomery said. "Good luck."

Dan and Silas had turned to go when Major Montgomery again spoke.

"The government can't buy your beef, Ember, but the sutler is under no such limitation. The store is civilian operated, and with the depletion of the buffalo, I suspect there is a need for beef at most of the forts on the frontier. If the government were allowed to buy, the going price would be twenty dollars a head, but that's too low. Don't take less than thirty."

Dan saluted Montgomery, and with a twinkle in his eyes, the officer returned it.

"By God," Silas said when they had left the building, "I never would of expected that from a blue belly."

"We fought them and they whipped us," said Dan. "I know Washington, with its politicians, regulations, carpetbaggers, and scalawags, is givin' us hell, but we can't fault the soldiers for that. Most of the soldiers are good men, with thankless, low-paying jobs, doing their best. We've been fortunate to meet one of them. I just hope Mr. Elwood Goldstein will be one-tenth as fair-minded, but I doubt it. Let's go take the varmint by the horns and find out."

11

⟨decorative divider⟩

$\mathcal{T}$he sutler's store was crowded, evidently with ex-buffalo hunters and bone gatherers. Dan and Silas made the rounds, finding all the items they would need, including the new Winchester repeating rifles. Men were grouped around the counter a dozen deep, and it seemed unlikely Dan and Silas would be speaking with Goldstein anytime soon.

"Come on," Dan said. "Let's wait awhile and come back. I'm not of a mind to have all these buffalo hunters gathered about when we finally talk to Goldstein. We'll have a look at the rest of the fort."

But they quickly discovered they didn't have the run of the place. As they left the store and passed the log building that housed the orderly room and the post commander's office, a corporal stepped out the orderly room door and halted them.

"It's a mite crowded in the store," Dan said, "and we thought we'd look around the post."

"Visitors only have access to the store," the soldier said. "Beyond that, you must have an escort. I'm Corporal Marler, and I'll be glad to show you around."

Dan and Silas followed the young soldier, and as they walked, he told them about the fort, how it began, and the government's plans for it.

"This post was established in 1867," Marler said, "as part of a chain of military posts along the Texas frontier, by Colonel Samuel Davis Sturgis and four companies of the Sixth Cavalry. It was first named Camp Wilson, but was later changed to Fort Griffin, in honor of Major General Charles Griffin, commanding the Department of Texas. For the time being, both officers and enlisted men are living in temporary wooden shelters. For instance, the commanding officer's quarters is a settler's cabin, hauled from a deserted ranch, and so is the building we're using for a post hospital. There are quarters for six companies and a band, eleven sets of officers' quarters, an adjutant's office, the hospital, a guardhouse, magazine, five storehouses, a forage barn, a bakery, four storage sheds, several workshops, and quarters for laundresses. Of course, there's the sutler's store and the blacksmith's, which are civilian operated. Some of the fort's early buildings were of stone, but the need for housing was immediate, and most of the existing buildings of wood are considered temporary. We have been promised a permanent installation, with proper stone structures."*

"It's an impressive layout, corporal," Dan said. "Now I reckon we'll go back to the sutler's and wait our turn."

The crowd in the store hadn't diminished all that much, but word of the trail drive had reached Goldstein's ears, and he obviously was expecting some of the riders to show up at the store. By now Goldstein had some help at the busy counter, likely a son, since the young man appeared to be a more recent version of Goldstein himself. When the storekeeper sighted Dan and Silas on the fringe of the crowd, he slipped away,

---

* Whatever Washington's intentions, the improvements were never made. With the end of Indian raids and the rapid advance of settlements, this and many other forts had outlived their usefulness. Fort Griffin was abandoned in 1881.

leaving the young man at the mercy of the buffalo hunters and bone gatherers.

"Here he comes," Silas said. "How'd he know us?"

"A good, solid guess," Dan said. "He knows by the look of us we're not buffalo hunters. A cowboy just looks like a cowboy, and there's no gettin' away from it."

"You are with the trail drive," Goldstein said when he reached them. "Are you the owners?"

"Two of them," Dan replied, and he said no more. It was Goldstein's move.

"I would be interested in buying some of them, perhaps, if the price is right."

"We might be interested in selling some of them," Dan said, "if the price is right."

"Twenty dollars a head," Goldstein said cautiously. "Cash."

"Thirty dollars a head," Dan countered, "but no cash. Trade only."

"Twenty-five dollars," Goldstein said, "and I'll take a hundred head."

"No," Dan said. "We can get thirty or more in Kansas, and you know it."

"Twenty-six," Goldstein said.

"Thirty," Dan said.

"Twenty-seven," Goldstein said.

Dan said nothing.

"Twenty-eight," Goldstein said, "and that's my final offer."

"Twenty-eight fifty," Dan said. "No less."

"Sold," Goldstein said, "but no cash. Trade only."

"Trade only," Dan agreed, "but no limitations. That includes having our horses and mules shod by your smithy. We've already spoken to the post commander, and we want two dozen Winchester repeating rifles, and ammunition."

"I'm not sure I have that many," said Goldstein.

"Major Montgomery believed you did," Dan said, "and so do I. Maybe you'd better look around some more. Give us two hours, and we'll have your steers here, all two-year-olds or better. I'll bring you a bill of sale, and we'll bring a wagon for the first of our provisions. Get word to your smithy about our credit. He can start with our horses and mules whenever he's ready, and the sooner the better."

With that, he turned and walked out, Silas following.

"That was slicker'n calf slobber," Silas said admiringly while they were mounting their horses. "Where you reckon Allison went?"

"His horse is still here," Dan said, "and since civilians aren't allowed to wander around the fort, I'd say he's in the saloon behind the store."

"We ain't gonna speak to him before we leave, then."

"No," Dan said. "We've made our deal, and I don't want Goldstein seeing us in there again until we have his hundred head of steers and a bill of sale."

There was jubilation within the outfit when Dan and Silas returned with the news, and immediate cries for food to supplement a weary diet of beans and beef.

"We have $2,850 credit," Dan said, "and we don't have to use it immediately. We'll be here a few days, with the time it takes the blacksmith to reshoe our horses and mules and for us to caulk all the wagon boxes. For starters, let me suggest this. We'll cut out a hundred steers and take them to the fort. Silas, take your wagon, and Wolf, you bring yours. Today we'll get the pitch we need to watertight the wagon boxes and the necessary tools. Then we'll load up on grub, with enough flour, meal, sugar, coffee, and bacon to last us to Dodge City. The rest of the time we're here, some of you can go in each day and choose the warm clothes you'll need as we ride farther north. Are there any of you unsatisfied with that?"

They kept their silence, and Dan continued.

"Tobe, Walt, and Monte, I'll need you to help me cut out the steers and drive them to the fort. Silas, you and Wolf follow us with the wagons."

The saloon behind the sutler's store was almost as large as the store itself. There was a bar on each side of the enormous room, each running the length of it, each with a pair of bartenders. Beer was drawn from huge kegs, and behind each bar stood row after row of whiskey bottles. There was a broad selection, everything from cheap forty-rod to expensive Tennessee and Kentucky bourbons. A full two dozen tables occupied the space between the bars, and there were men at every table, but not the man Clay Allison sought. He had chased Mort Suggs all the way from Tucumcari to El Paso, only to have Suggs get there a day ahead of him because Allison's horse had gone lame. Suggs could have fled west into Arizona Territory or south into Old Mexico, but when Allison had again picked up the trail, it led east. The trail had been rained out before Allison could catch up, forcing him to make a decision. For sure, Suggs hadn't ridden south into Old Mexico, for he had already forsaken that option. That left San Antonio, Austin, or some other destination to the north. Allison had pieced together that night back in Tucumcari, and thought he knew where he would find the elusive Mort Suggs.

Mort and his brothers, Julius and Felix, had been down-at-the-heels buffalo hunters, in Tucumcari for a hell-raising Saturday night. The Suggs brothers had bought into a poker game, and Clay Allison had withdrawn, accusing Mort Suggs of cheating. Allison was about to leave the saloon, accompanied by his longtime friend, Trinity Wells, when Allison dropped his hat. Just as he had stooped to retrieve it, Mort Suggs had lunged at him with a knife, and his brutal thrust had killed the girl. Knowing what would follow, Julius and Felix had leaped on Allison, starting a brawl that had allowed Mort Suggs to escape into the night.

A posse had ridden out at dawn, but had quit the trail after a fruitless all-day ride. But Clay Allison hadn't given up, and when he had joined the trail drive, he had fully expected to find the three Suggs brothers near Fort Griffin. Now he wondered if he had guessed wrong, if his ride had been in vain. There were no hides on the many wagons strung out along the Brazos, evidence enough that the buffalo on the plains of West Texas had all been slaughtered or driven away. With the buffalo gone, it was neck meat or nothing, and that accounted for the wagonloads of buffalo bones. It seemed some of the hunters had been forced to become bone gatherers. Might that not include the Suggs brothers?

Allison bought a bottle, slumped down at one of the tables and drank himself into a vile mood. It was possible the Suggs trio had withdrawn into Indian Territory, but with Indian hostility rampant, that wasn't likely. They would be hunkered down in the shadow of some fort, if not Fort Griffin, then maybe Fort Dodge. Suddenly Allison was struck with an idea, and leaning over, spoke to a man at the next table.

"Pardner, is there a camp on up the river? Been lookin' around in here for a gent I know, and can't seem to find him."

"Yeah," the stranger said, "there's a bunch sleepin' in their wagons and eatin' jackrabbit stew. They're too broke to come in here."

"When you get there with the cattle," Dan said, "hold them along the river until I find out where Goldstein wants them."

Dan then rode ahead to the fort, taking with him a prepared bill of sale. Reaching the store, he presented it to Goldstein in exchange for a written letter of credit for the amount of the sale.

"Take them three-quarters of a mile upriver," Gold-stein said. "There's a barn with an adjoining corral."

"Two of my men are outside with wagons," Dan said. "I'm going to have them come in and begin loading some provisions." He then spoke to Wolf and Silas.

Dan rode back, joining Tobe Barnfield, Walt Crump, and Monte Walsh, and the four of them drove the herd upriver to Goldstein's corral.

"This Goldstein's a more trustin' hombre than I'd be," Monte Walsh said. "There's a buffalo camp up yonder, and I bet them ex-hunters is hungry as a pack of lobo wolves."

"I reckon the varmints would like to have some of that buffalo meat they left to rot on the plains," Tobe Barnfield said.

Suddenly there was an uproar from the jumble of wagons as men shouted and cursed.

"Come on," Dan said, "let's ride up there and see what's going on."

They found Clay Allison with his back against an oak, the cocked Colt steady in his hand. Seven men faced him, and six of them had their hands near the butts of their Colts. The seventh man had no Colt, and although he was as big as Clay Allison, he looked scared.

"Allison," Dan said, "what's this all about?"

"Nothing to concern you," Allison said shortly, "but since you're here, you might as well know. I'm here to kill a man, but not without cause. This skunk—the one without a gun—killed a lady in Tucumcari, New Mexico. Miss Trinity Wells was my friend, and she took the blade this bastard intended for me. I should have gut-shot him when I caught him cheating at the poker table. He escaped after killing Trinity only because his pair of skunk-striped kin started a fight in the saloon."

"I didn't mean to kill her," Mort Suggs bawled. "She wasn't nothin' but a saloon whore nohow."

Allison's Colt roared, and Mort Suggs' left earlobe disappeared with a spray of blood.

"I ain't armed," Suggs screamed.

Four of the men were no longer hostile. One of them spoke to Allison.

"We ain't sidin' him, mister, if what you say is true."

"It's true," Allison said. "Now you three varmints," he continued, turning back to the Suggs brothers, "have a choice. This bastard that killed Trinity can face me man-to-man, or I'll gut-shoot the three of you."

"I ain't no gunman," Mort cried.

"Oh," Allison said mildly, "you're a knife man, so we'll do it your way. I've skinned a few skunks in my time. Ember, I'd take it as a favor if you hombres would keep an eye on this pair of Suggs while Mort and me mix it up with our *cuchillos.* Either or both of them would welcome the opportunity to shoot me in the back while I'm teaching little brother the error of his ways."

Allison eased down the hammer of his Colt and holstered the weapon. Removing his hat, he drew the rawhide thong over his head, removing a deadly Bowie that hung down the back of his shirt. Gripping the murderous knife in his right hand, he turned to face the trembling Mort Suggs.

"Get up, damn you," Allison said through clenched teeth.

When Suggs didn't move form the wagon tongue, Allison snatched the front of Suggs's shirt with a massive left hand, the deadly Bowie in his right. Mort Suggs screamed as Allison slit his shirt to shreds. Suggs broke loose and fell facedown on the ground. Allison hoisted him by his waistband and slit his trousers from waist to knee, then rolled him over and slashed the other side. With the terrible Bowie, he stripped Mort Suggs naked, Suggs whimpering like a whipped dog. Allison got astraddle of the naked man, the Bowie held high.

"You cowardly sonofabitch," Allison shouted, "I can't

make you stand up like a man, but by God, I'll make you wish you had. I aim to carve off some parts of your carcass that'll have you squattin' like a squaw for the rest of your miserable life."

Dan's companions had their hands on the butts of their Colts, but not to protect Clay Allison. Dan Ember was shocked, not so much by what Allison intended to do, as by the look in the man's eyes. He was mad, totally out of control, and Dan drew his Colt.

"That's enough, Allison. Back off. Let him go."

But Allison might not have heard. He was preparing to thrust the Bowie into Mort Suggs's belly, just below the navel. Dan's Colt roared, and the knife was torn from Allison's fist. Allison staggered to his feet and stood there looking dumbly at his empty hand. Dan turned to the terrified Julius and Felix, and his advice didn't have to be repeated.

"Get him away from here," Dan said.

The pair seized Mort, and as they dragged him away, he was screaming like a terrified child. Dan wondered if Allison hadn't extracted a vengeance more terrible than death itself, for Mort Suggs was behaving like a man whose mind had snapped. The other four buffalo hunters had long since departed, and Dan and his three companions rode quickly away. Dan looked back once, and Clay Allison seemed lost as he stood there staring after them. It would be the last time they would see him, a big, handsome man who rode a narrow trail. Ladies adored him, he had the ways of a gentleman, and was a friend to the Indians, but when he slipped over the edge, he became a brutal killer. . . .

When Dan and his companions returned to the sutler's, they found Wolf and Silas loading provisions into the wagons. They already had four barrels of flour, two barrels of cornmeal, and many sacks of sugar and coffee.

"Why don't we get a big load of dried apples?" Silas suggested. "Them dried apple pies is almighty good."

"Go ahead," Dan said, "but don't do that at the expense of the bacon."

"Let's get a coffee grinder too," Wolf said. "For an outfit like ours, it'd take half a day to smash enough beans just for breakfast coffee."

They bought sacks of salt and tinned goods, including peaches, tomatoes, and condensed milk. Dan filled one wagon almost entirely with hams and sides of bacon.

"Beef's all right," he said, "but nothing flavors a pot of *frijoles* like big hunks of ham."

Goldstein had kept a running total as they loaded the wagons, and when there was no more room, he presented the bill. It was six hundred dollars. Dan nodded and they all left the store. Dan, Tobe, Walt, and Monte rode back ahead of the loaded wagons, and never was there the like of the shouting and laughing that greeted them when they reached their camp. Denny and his wrangler friends rode out and escorted them in, and when Dan swung out of the saddle, Lenore and Adeline were waiting to greet him.

"By God," Duncan Kilgore shouted, "there *is* a Santa Claus."

"Is true," Palo Elfego said.

"Time to celebrate," Wolf Bowdre said. "Let's have a mess of fried ham, Dutch oven biscuits, and hot coffee with honest-to-God milk and sugar."

"But it's only three hours until suppertime," Fanny protested.

"What the hell," Bowdre laughed, "we'll have some more then."

"Sorry," Adeline said, "but no sourdough biscuits for a while. We have to set the dough to working."

"I know we have beans," Dan said. "Drop a ham in the pot, heat it up, and we'll have it with our coffee. I

reckon we'll have to wait on the Dutch oven biscuits,
but we have some celebrating to do."

The men slapped him on the back and all the women
made such a fuss over him, Dan was embarrassed, but
he soon overcame that. It became a festive occasion as
they savored the hot coffee and sugar most of them
hadn't tasted in almost ten years. The longhorns and the
horse remuda grazed along the Brazos, and despite the
realization that much of the hard trail still lay ahead of
them, the Texans rejoiced in their good fortune.
Through stampedes, storms, and dust they had brought
the herd this far, and now they were enjoying some of
the fruits of their labors. If they had done this well while
still in war-weary Texas, what might they accomplish in
Dodge City, with a railroad on the way?

Their celebration lasted on into the night, and they all
were still in high spirits the next morning, for they had
yet to go to the store for their new clothing. After
breakfast Dan announced the order in which they would
visit the sutler's store for their clothing.

"With all the buffalo hunters and bone gatherers at
the fort, we can't all go at once. Why not three families
at a time? I'm riding in to see when Goldstein's men can
begin shoeing our horses and mules, so the first three
can ride in with me. I believe half a day will be enough
time, and when you first three return, three more can
go. If you don't finish, we can always arrange for you to
go back another time. I think we'd better go by your
names, in alphabetical order. That means Bowdre,
Barnfield, and Beard will go this morning, and Carper,
Chambers, and Connolly will go this afternoon. The rest
of you can figure out the order, and in three and a half
days we should all have had a chance to go."

"Do you aim to go as Ember or DeVoe?" Boyce Trevino asked.

"I reckon I'll go as a DeVoe," said Dan. "That way,

I'll be able to go sooner." He laughed, and they laughed with him.

"We'll be going tomorrow morning," Lenore said, "and I just can't wait. I've never had new clothes before."

When Dan rode in, the Bowdres, the Barnfields, and the Beards accompanied him. Dan went directly to Goldstein's little office.

"There are four men at the blacksmith's," Goldstein said. "I'm assigning three of them to you for as long as it takes. They'll give you some idea as to how many animals they can shoe in a day, and it will be up to you to see that the shod horses are removed and those yet to be shod are brought in."

Dan nodded his satisfaction and went directly to the blacksmith shop. The man in charge was built like a grizzly and his name was McNaughton.

"I dunno how many we can do in a day," he said. "Depends mostly on the horse or mule. Some behaves themselves and some gives us hell. You can see they ain't no graze in the garrison, and water's got to be hauled from the river, so we can't keep 'em in here any longer'n it takes to shoe 'em. I'd say bring us a dozen head and we'll see how long it takes. Since you'll be on the trail, will you be wantin' extra shoes?"

"Yes," Dan said. "A full set on each animal, with one extra for the back, and one extra for the front."

"That'll take longer," McNaughton said.

"I realize that," Dan said, "but it can't be helped. I'll send some riders with the first dozen horses."

Dan rode back to the outfit and selected Boyce Trevino, Rufe Keeler, Duncan Kilgore, Skull Kimbrough, Garret Haddock, and Kirby Wilkerson.

"Each of you rope two horses needing to be shod and take them to the blacksmith," Dan said. "Begin with your own favorites and those of our other riders. Chato's remuda will be shod last."

"What about the mules?" Silas asked.

"They'll have a rest until we take the trail again," Dan said. "I think we'll have them reshod before we get to Chato's remuda."

"It kind of rubs me the wrong way, us spendin' that kind of money on a bunch of hosses that ain't even ours," Silas said.

"Don't let it bother you," Dan said. "We have the use of horses that we couldn't afford, just for the price of new shoes. Whoever they belonged to, and however Chato got them, we're obliged to him for allowing us to use them."

"If what this Major Montgomery says is true—that the government ain't allowed to buy from Rebs—you may be havin' some trouble sellin' all them hosses for Chato," Silas said.

"I've considered that," Dan said, "but with Dodge being a new town, I'm expecting a considerable market for livestock, without even bothering with the government. I think we'll have speculators bidding for our beef long before the railroad gets there."

"There's some things you forgot," Adeline said when she finally got Dan's attention. "It takes more than flour to make sourdough biscuits. We'll need at least a few potatoes and some baking soda for the starter."

"Write me out a list of what's needed," Dan said. "I'll be riding in to see how the shoeing of the horses is coming along, and I'll get the rest of your supplies."

It was near noon when the Bowdres, the Barnfields, and the Beards rode in from town. Dan had quietly spoken to the men, limiting each family to fifty dollars for clothing. Once he had gotten the new Winchesters from Goldstein, whatever credit was left could then be shared by the outfit, but there was no room for extravagance. Even with their fifty dollar limit, it seemed those who had been to the store had done well, and the second trio of families prepared to ride in. Dan waited until late afternoon before riding in to see about the horses.

"We'll finish this bunch today," McNaughton said, "and you'll have to get 'em out of here before dark. Bring a new bunch in the mornin', and unless I tell you different, a dozen at a time."

Dan returned to the sutler's, bought a pound of potatoes and several tins of baking soda, and returned to their camp on the Brazos. The Carpers, Chambers, and Connollys were just returning to camp, while Dan was preparing to ride in for the newly shod horses.

"There's an Indian scare at the fort," Cash Connolly said. "Three of them buffalo hunters was found dead maybe four miles north of the fort. All had their throats cut, but one of 'em had been stripped naked and mutilated somethin' awful. Soldiers are callin' it Comanche work, but nobody's seen any of the varmints."

Dan found Tobe Barnfield, Walt Crump, and Monte Walsh looking at him, but he said nothing. The four of them knew what the military probably would never learn. The Suggs brothers had come to a predictable bad end, but not at the hands of the Comanches.

The following morning Walt Crump and his wife, Palo Elfego and his family, and the DeVoes rode in to the store for their winter clothing. Dan went with the DeVoes. All he wanted was a sheepskin-lined coat. The DeVoes' needs were greater than his. Shirts and Levi's would satisfy Denny, and he knew Adeline wouldn't be hard to please, but he wasn't sure about Lenore. They lost her almost immediately after entering the store, and when they found her, she was among the women's fancy dresses and gowns.

"I like this," Lenore said, holding up a red frilly dress so Adeline could see. "What do you think, Ma?"

"I think," Adeline said, "if you mounted a horse

wearing that, every man in the outfit would give you his undivided attention."

Dan and Denny laughed, along with some other men who had overheard, and the embarrassed girl covered her face with the offending garment. Dan poked his head under it, made her laugh, and the four of them went looking for shirts, Levi's, and coats they would need in the north country.

12

Fort Griffin, Texas. Sunday, October 9, 1870.

"Silas," Dan said, "choose four men who are handy with tools to help us caulk the wagon boxes. Two of the men will work with you, and the other two will work with me. We'll want to allow the pitch a few days to harden before we put our work to a test in the river."

Silas chose Boyce Trevino, Spence Wilder, Skull Kimbrough, and Kirby Wilkerson. Skull and Kirby chose to work with Dan.

"Kirby," Dan said, "Silas and his boys are starting with his wagon, so we'll start with yours."

"I can't speak for the rest of the wagons," Kirby said, "but I reckon mine will need more than just a mess of pitch to keep the water out."

"The wood's not all that solid, then."

"No," Kirby said. "For crossin' deep water, I doubt we can make do with anything less than a new wagon box. I wasn't thinking ahead to these river crossings, or I'd of left the damn thing behind."

"I doubt the others thought that far ahead either," Dan said. "I reckon we'd better get with Silas and talk this over. We may need more than just one wagon box, and that means some good, seasoned lumber."

"My wagon ain't nowheres near perfect," Silas admitted, "but the box is solid oak. I reckon that won't be enough when it comes to water proofin', though. No matter how close them floorboards is fitted, you purely ain't gonna pitch them cracks tight enough to keep the water out."

"We need some long, flat oak strips, maybe four inches wide," Spence Wilder said. "Then we nail this new oak down solid, coverin' the cracks, using the pitch to seal the edges of this new wood to the original floor."

"That's an excellent idea," Dan said, "as far as it goes, and that brings us back to my original question. Silas, hadn't we better have a look at the rest of the wagons? Kirby believes he'll need a new wagon box, and there's a chance some of the other wagons will too. If we have to build one new box, then let's get the materials to build as many as we'll need, and be done with it. We're piling up an almighty lot of work for ourselves, but these wagons have been a blessing."

An inspection of the other wagons revealed that the Bowdre and McNelly wagons also needed new wagon boxes.

"There's a pile of sawed lumber inside the stockade," Silas said. "It's piled there at one end of the log house they're usin' for an orderly room, and it's pretty well weathered, so it's been there awhile."

"I expect it belongs to the military," Dan said. "From what the corporal told us, they've put up temporary wood buildings, expecting to replace them with stone. I'm going to talk to Major Montgomery and see if we can maybe use some of that wood for wagon boxes."

Dan called on the post commander and was again well-received. When he told Major Montgomery what he wanted, the officer didn't answer for a moment. When he did, it was favorable.

"Take what you can use," he said. "That's material left from the original construction, and officially it doesn't exist. Rumor has it that Fort Griffin is to become a permanent installation, with most of the present structures to be replaced with stone."

Most of the discarded lumber proved to be poplar or oak, seasoned and hard as stone. It proved difficult to saw, and nails bent quickly and often. The six men put in a week of hard labor building three new wagon boxes, and that didn't include the necessary caulking.

"We'll caulk every box," Dan said, "let them set a day or two, and then go over them again. In a week we'll float them across the river and back."

Dan began each day by taking horses to the blacksmith's, and concluded it by going after them. Everybody within the outfit had been to the sutler's for clothes and a coat and gloves. Finally, a week after the last caulking of the wagon boxes, Dan judged it was time to test them with a river crossing.

"We'll load them with rocks," he said, "and pull them across with ropes, just as we'll have to do on the trail. If they fail the test, there'll be more work for us."

"I aim to ride across in mine," Silas said. "If the varmint leaks, then I want to know where the holes is."

"I reckon one of us should ride across in all of them," Dan said, "and if there's more caulking to do, we'll be able to concentrate on the weak places. Silas, we might as well take yours first."

Heavy rocks were placed in all four corners of the wagon box, simulating a heavy load. Four lariats were tied together, one end tied to the wagon tongue, the other to Dan's saddle horn. He swam his horse across the river, and when the wagon was ready, he would pull it across. Wolf Bowdre and Tobe Barnfield would steady the wagon on the upstream side. Silas mounted the box, and Wolf Bowdre secured one end of his lariat to an iron ring anchored to the wagon box, just above the left front wheel. Tobe Barnfield tied his lariat to an identical iron ring bolted to the wagon box just above the left rear wheel. Sloan Kuykendall and Kirby Wilkerson had secured their lariats in similar positions on the downriver side of the wagon. From the wagon box, Silas waved his hat, and Dan urged his horse forward. The wagon began to roll toward the sloping riverbank, the four riders siding it keeping even with it. The wagon lurched forward as the front wheels left solid ground, righting itself as Dan's horse took up the slack in the line. The current seized the wagon and tried to carry it away, but Tobe Barnfield and Wolf Bowdre steadied it with their lariats on the upriver side. Slowly, surely, they guided the wagon across the Brazos until it lumbered out on the opposite bank.

"She ain't leaked yet," Silas crowed. "Let's take her back across."

The return trip was equally successful, and the heavy stones were shifted to Kirby Wilkerson's wagon. It crossed easily, with Rufe Keeler riding the wagon box and watching for leaks. This was a critical milestone in their journey to Dodge, and the entire outfit gathered to watch the testing of the wagons. There were shouts as each wagon crossed and returned, and when the seventh —Walt Crump's—returned safely, there was a delighted roar. Crump had ridden the wagon box across and back, and he was furiously waving his hat.

"Well, by God," Wolf Bowdre said, "whatever other problems we have on the way to Dodge, gettin' the wagons across the rivers won't be one of 'em."

"I'm feelin' a mite better about it," Silas said, "but I still aim to take a bunch of that pitch with me."

Except for the shoeing of the horses and mules, Dan had just one more piece of business with Elwood Goldstein. He still had to get the much-needed Winchester repeating rifles and a supply of ammunition. Goldstein was all business, unsociable, and about as friendly as a sore-tailed grizzly, and Dan looked forward to being free of the man. It wouldn't be any easier, he thought, if he waited until the last day, so he decided to be done with it. The morning after the wagons had been success- fully floated, he spoke to Silas Hamby and Wolf Bow- dre.

"I need the two of you to drive your wagons to the fort. I aim to get those Winchesters and some ammuni- tion, so we can cut ourselves loose from Goldstein. Whatever credit we have left—and I doubt there'll be much—we can take in extra grub, if nothing else."

Goldstein seemed to know it was time to negotiate for the Winchesters, and he greeted Dan with a total lack of enthusiasm.

"I'm not sure you're going to have that much credit, once all of your animals have been shod," Goldstein said.

"You know how many horses and mules we're having shod," Dan said, "and you've kept a running tally on everything else we've bought. Figure it out, and let's be done with this. I want twenty-four Winchesters, and a thousand rounds of ammunition for each of them."

"That's twelve hundred dollars," Goldstein said. "The Winchesters are forty dollars apiece, and the shells are ten dollars a thousand rounds."

"Then tally up what we've spent so far," Dan said.

Goldstein opened a ledger, and from the subtotals, Dan could see that the storekeeper already knew how much credit remained. However, he wrote a few figures and went through the motions of a tally.

"You have used $1,575 of your credit," Goldstein said, "leaving $1,275."

"Accordin' to my figures," Dan said, "there's a little more than enough for twelve hundred dollars' worth of Winchesters and ammunition. I have my wagons ready."

"Very well," Goldstein sighed. "What about the re- maining seventy-five dollars?"

"I'll take seventy-five dollars' worth of dried apples," Dan said.

Half the rifles and ammunition went on Bowdre's wagon and the other half on Silas's wagon.

"I reckon that took the rest of our credit," Silas said.

"Not quite," Dan said. "Here it comes now."

Goldstein brought out one gunny sack and went back for the second one. He left it on the dock, and without a word returned to the store.

"Dried apples," Dan said with a grin. "Seventy-five dollars' worth."

The trail north. Friday, October 28, 1870.

"Move 'em out," Dan shouted.

The last of the horses had been shod the day before. Silas had already led out with the wagons, the horse remuda following. It had taken a while to gather the longhorns, for the graze near the river had become scarce and the herd had scattered. Now they were reluctant to leave the good water and good grass, keeping the swing and flank riders on the run. Drag riders kept the herd bunched, and slowly but surely the long column strung out to the north, following the Brazos River. Dan rode ahead, catching up to Silas in the lead wagon.

"We got maybe a day's drive along the Brazos, Silas. From what Allison told me, we'll be crossing the Brazos twice. Once maybe fifteen miles north of Fort Griffin, with a second crossing about fifty miles north of the first."

"Nothin' to worry about," Silas said, "now that we got them wagons watertight. 'Course if there's rain enough, them rivers could overrun their banks, makin' it hard on us."

"I'm more afraid of snow than rain," Dan said. "It seldom gets that cold in South Texas, but it does on the Kansas plains."

Each of the men on the drive now carried a seventeen-shot Winchester in his saddle boot and a supply of cartridges in his saddlebag. Silas carried the rest of the ammunition and the three extra Winchesters in his wagon. At no time during their stay at Fort Griffin had Dan received any word from Chato, and when he spoke to Palo Elfego about it, the Mexican only shrugged. The outfit took their meals around a common fire, and Dan tried to end each day's drive so they could eat before dark. After sundown the wind—usually from the north or northwest—became cold, and families took refuge behind their canvas shelters. The exceptions, of course, were the young horse wranglers, who took pride in their constant guardianship of the horse remuda. Dan often came off his watch to find Adeline and Lenore awake, waiting for him. The cold and the canvas shelter afforded them some privacy, and Dan had come to enjoy the late night talks.

"I wish Clay Allison had gone on to Dodge City with us," Lenore said. "I wonder what became of him?"

"I'd say he finished his business at Fort Griffin and moved on," Dan replied. "He has a ranch somewhere in New Mexico Territory. He was a mite old for you, anyway."

Embarrassed, the girl kicked Dan in the ribs, and Adeline laughed.

The crossing of the Brazos to the north of Fort Griffin was without incident, but less than a dozen miles beyond, they reached what seemed to be a tributary.

"Looks like a west fork of the river we just crossed," Silas said. "Do we cross and go on, or make camp here?"

"We'll bed down the herd and stay here," Dan said. "I wonder why we got no word from Chato about this?"

Palo Elfego brought word from Chato that night, but it concerned water for the next night's camp.

For all the days Dan Ember and his outfit remained at Fort Griffin, Santos Miguel Montoya and his *Mejica-*

nos were camped a few miles to the south. South of their camp, Burton Ledoux, Black Bill and Loe Hagerman sat hunched over a small fire drinking bad coffee from a blackened pot. For the moment they were silent, Hagerman and Black Bill apparently tired of cursing one another, and Ledoux weary of shouting at them. But all hell broke loose before Ledoux caught on. The coffee pot sat precariously over the fire on a triangle of stones, and when Hagerman reached for it to hot up his coffee, Black Bill kicked the pot over. The coffee sloshed out, burning Hagerman's hand.

"You don' like that, eh?" Black Bill said with a malicious grin. He was on his feet when Hagerman rolled away from the fire and went for his gun. The whip in the Cajun's hand moved like a live thing, wrapping itself around Hagerman's throat like a noose. Hagerman's Colt roared, the slug thudding into the ground at Black Bill's feet. Black Bill suddenly found himself at the business end of Ledoux's cocked Colt.

"Get that damn whip loose," Ledoux snarled, "or I'll kill you."

"No," Black Bill said sullenly. Hagerman was reaching for the Colt he had dropped.

"Leave the gun where it is, Hagerman," said Ledoux. Hagerman paused, hating them both. Black Bill—deliberately slow—unwound the deadly whip. When he again had the whip coiled about his arm, he stood there with his right thumb hooked in his pistol belt, just above the butt of his Colt.

"Get up," Ledoux said. He barely nodded to Hagerman, keeping his eyes on Black Bill.

Hagerman retrieved his Colt and got to his feet, but did not holster the weapon. His eyes were on Black Bill.

"Holster the damn pistol," Ledoux roared. Even when Hagerman complied, Ledoux kept them covered, and when he spoke it was with such fury that Black Bill's customary evil grin vanished. "Now, by God," Ledoux

said, "I'll shoot the next man that pulls a gun. And you"
—he glared at Black Bill—"don't you *ever* unleash that
whip again without me sayin' so."

Ledoux's attention was drawn away from his troublesome companions by the approach of Santos Miguel
Montoya. If Montoya was surprised to find Ledoux covering Hagerman and Black Bill with a drawn Colt, he
didn't show it.

"The *Tejanos* and their cows have left the fort, *Senor*
Ledoux," Montoya said. "We will be riding west of the
fort in pursuit of them."

Montoya turned and walked away and Ledoux again
focused his attention on Hagerman and Black Bill.
"Saddle your horses. We're riding out."

Ledoux waited until Hagerman and Black Bill had
reached their horses before he began saddling his own.
Black Bill caught Hagerman's eye and winked.

"I think he don' kill nobody," the Cajun said. "When
the time come, it be jus' you an' me, eh?"

Black Bill laughed, an evil sound that chilled Hagerman's blood. The pair rode out, Ledoux following.

The Brazos River. Thursday, November 3, 1870.

The outfit bedded down the herd and the horse remuda
just before sunset, preparing for yet another crossing of
the Brazos the following morning. Supper was almost
ready when Denny DeVoe came riding in from where
the horse remuda had been grazing.

"Five riders comin' downriver," Denny shouted.
"They ain't Injuns."

Dan and the rest of the men got to their feet, having
been hunkered down enjoying first cups of hot coffee.
The five riders came on, and as they drew nearer, Dan
relaxed. They had ridden in from the east, and the setting sun winked off the emblems pinned to the lapels of
their coats. They all wore silver stars in a circle, the

badge of the Texas Rangers. They reined up, awaiting permission to advance or dismount.

"Step down, gents," Dan said. "The coffee's ready now, and supper's on the way."

"We're obliged," the lead rider said. "I'm McCullough, and the hombres behind me are Bell, Wallace, McKenzie, and McLean. The Comanches have been looting and killing along the Red, and by the time we picked up their trail, they had retreated into Indian Territory."

The five Rangers dismounted and approached the fire, for the sun was down and the wind was cold. Adeline DeVoe brought them tin cups, and they headed gratefully for one of the huge coffeepots the Texans had acquired at Fort Griffin.

"There's sugar and condensed milk there on the wagon tailgate," Adeline said.

"This is like manna from heaven," McCullough said. "We've had nothing but jerked beef and water for two weeks. Is that sourdough biscuits I smell?"

"It is," Dan said, "and there's ham, beans, and dried apple pie to go with them."

"I always hoped when I died I'd go to heaven," one of the Rangers said, "and it looks like I made it."

Fanny Bowdre, Amy Wilder, Adeline DeVoe, and the rest of the women in the outfit had devised an orderly means of turning out a meal in record time without it being overly hard on anybody. A dozen three-legged iron spiders straddled beds of coals over which hung two-gallon coffee pots. It was Lenore Devoe's turn to tend the coffee pots, putting on more water to boil as a pot was emptied. Fanny Bowdre had three women helping her tend the many Dutch ovens in which sourdough biscuits were baking. The ovens—huge iron pots with lids—sat on beds of coals, while more coals were piled on top. Every family in the outfit had brought one, distributing them among the wagons for transporting. Amy

Wilder was responsible for half a dozen enormous iron pots of beans, going from one pot to another, stirring them. Hattie Kuykendall had two women helping her turn the slabs of ham that sizzled in large iron skillets. Adeline DeVoe was preparing dried apple pies for the skillets when enough ham had been fried. Four large pots of dried apples had been boiled to perfection. A wagon tailgate had been let down, providing a table for Adeline's biscuit board. She prepared the pies rapidly. Rolling out a thin circle of dough as large as a plate, she filled half the circle with the cooked fruit, folded the rest of the dough over into a half-moon, and then crimped the rounded edges together with a fork. Each pie would then be fried in ham grease until the dough was crisp.

"Tarnation," one of the Rangers said, "I never seen so much cooking goin' on all at once or so spread out. Not even in the army."

"All the cook fires are laid out in a circle," Dan said, "and with so many things going at once, it takes a big circle. The wagon they're working from is left in the middle of the circle. Easier for everybody to get the supplies as they need 'em, and the wagon tailgate supports a biscuit board for cuttin' biscuits and rolling out dough for dried apple pies."

The meal that followed was an occasion to be remembered, especially by the half-starved Rangers. The five Rangers gratefully accepted an invitation to stay the night, and over many extra cups of coffee, the talk turned to the Indian problem.

"We ran into Quanah Parker and his Comanches south of Fort Griffin," Dan said. "They took twenty cows and let us go."

"My God," McCullough said, "you don't know how fortunate you are. It's unlike the Comanches. It's more their style to murder you, take your scalp and ride on.

They especially like to steal white women. Quanah's mother was white, you know. She was taken as a child and later became the wife of a Comanche chief, Peta Nocona. In December 1860, Rangers whipped a party of Comanches not too far from here. Cynthia Ann Parker was taken from them and returned to her family."*

"I've heard the story," Dan said. "What became of her?"

"After many years with the Comanches," McCullough said, "I fear she was more Indian than white. Soon after she was returned to her family, her child died, and she lived only a few months after that."

"You did her no favors, then," Dan said.

"I fear we did not," McCullough replied, "but we did what we thought was right. A man can do no more than that."

"When we cross the river in the morning," Dan said, "we will have crossed the Brazos three times since leaving Fort Griffin. What are our other crossings before we reach the Red?"

"Your next river will be the Wichita," McCullough said. "There's a north and south fork, and you'll be crossing them both. When you leave here, you'll be maybe twelve miles from the south fork, and once you've crossed it, about eighteen miles from the north fork. From there you'll be twenty miles or so from the Pease River. There's a confluence with the Red, but you won't be far enough to the east. You'll have to cross them both. Once you've crossed the Pease, depending on where you cross, you'll not be more than another twenty miles from the Red. After that, it'll be Indian Territory."

* The fight between Texas Rangers and Comanches took place on December 18, 1860, near the present-day town of Margaret, Texas, about nine miles northeast of Crowell.

"I know," Dan said. "We're looking forward to that. What can you tell us about it?"

"Nothing good," McCullough replied. "Except for an occasional foray along the Red, the Comanches generally confine their hell-raising to North, East, and West Texas. North of the Red, in Indian Territory, the Kiowas take up the slack. They're just about as compassionate as the Comanches. Another danger, once you've crossed the Red, is renegades. They were run out of Kansas and Missouri after the war, and most of them are holed up somewhere in Indian Territory. They masquerade as embittered southerners in rebellion, but mostly they're bands of thieves and killers who have taken advantage of the recent war. They have attacked some of the drives along the Chisholm Trail, murdering the cowboys and selling the cows to various forts."

"Well, by God, as a Texan, that burns my behind," Dan said. "Accordin' to these damn reconstruction laws, Union forts aren't allowed to buy cattle from Texans, but they can and will buy from thieving varmints who murder the owners and steal the herds."

"Obviously there are some inequities within this reconstruction law," McCullough said dryly, "but there are ways around them. If these renegades swoop down on you, empty their saddles and leave them for buzzard bait. This is still the frontier. If you have enough guns, and the guts to use them, the law is on your side."

"That's kind of the way we feel about it," Dan said, "but it's always good to hear it from men who have been through the fire."

After a bountiful breakfast and many thanks, the Rangers rode out the next morning. By now the outfit had their river crossing procedure down pat, and in less than an hour all seven wagons had been taken safely across the Brazos.

"My God," Silas said, "I never knowed there was so many rivers in Texas."

"It ain't there's so many," Kirby Wilkerson said, "it's how they twist and turn. You keep crossin' the same one. If the Brazos was strung out straight, it'd reach from one ocean to the other."*

"Hell, it ain't that long," Wolf Bowdre said. "It just seems that way, havin' to cross it so many times. From what I hear, the Red's the varmint that's likely to give us a ride we won't forget. If there's trouble ahead, that's where I figure we're most likely to get throwed and stomped."

There *was* trouble ahead, but within hours, not days or weeks. The dawn had broken under cloudy skies, the sun but a dim glow that soon was lost altogether. Riding into a cold north wind, the riders were thankful for their coats and gloves. The temperature began to fall, and an hour or two past midday tiny particles of ice stung their faces and rattled off the brims of their hats. Cattle hated trailing into a storm, and many of them broke away, seeking to take the back trail. Dan rode on ahead and caught up to the first wagon.

"Silas, we're in for it. I'm riding ahead looking for some shelter. It's already near impossible, driving the longhorns into the wind, and it's gettin' almighty cold."

"Snow's comin'," Silas said. "Won't be more'n another hour or two."

Dan rode ahead, seeking refuge from the north wind and the snow that was almost sure to come. And it did come, mixing with the sleet, much sooner than Silas had predicted. According to what McCullough had told them, their next river would be the south fork of the Wichita, at least twelve miles. Dan estimated they had traveled maybe half that distance, and with the temperature dropping by the minute, they couldn't possibly reach the river. Even if the snow held off—and that

* The Brazos is 840 miles long, the longest river in Texas. Sixty-five Texas counties are located in the watershed of the Brazos.

seemed unlikely—it would be virtually impossible to keep the herd moving headlong into a fiercer, colder wind. Dan rode on. The range was becoming hilly, with eroded brakes and head-high mesquite thickets. There was an occasional oak, its dead leaves long since stripped away by the prairie wind, its naked limbs stark against a leaden sky. But the land was becoming rougher, with draws and head-high escarpments. Finally Dan reached a fast-running creek, and following it west, found where it emerged from a canyon. Narrow at the mouth, the canyon grew wider as he rode deeper into it. Soon the north rim was high enough to provide relief from the wind, and ahead, along the creek, was the welcome green of willows. There was graze too. How much would depend upon the length of the canyon, and what there was would have to suffice for the duration of the storm. Dan watered his horse at the creek and rode back to meet the herd. When he rode out of the canyon and was again at the mercy of the pounding wind, it seemed colder than ever. The prairie was already white with snow, and his horse stumbled over stones that were difficult to see. It seemed like hours before he finally met the first wagon.

"Straight ahead," he shouted to Silas. "When you reach the creek, turn west. There's a deep canyon."

Dan rode on, knowing the herd would be fighting every effort to drive them into the growing storm. It was even worse than he'd expected, with the flank and swing riders galloping after bunch quitters, only to have more break away in the wake of the last bunch. Dan reached the drag and found the source of most of the trouble ahead. Cows were breaking away, galloping down the back trail, and as the female riders tried to head them, the rest of the herd had begun to lag. The resulting slack was allowing the longhorns to break away the entire length of the column in impossible numbers. Dan uncoiled his lariat as Adeline DeVoe threw up her hands in helpless frustration. Her companions weren't doing much better, torn between bunching the tag end of the herd and going after the brutes that trotted down the back trail.

"Forget the bunch quitters," Dan shouted. "I'll go after them. Move in close to the drag and keep the rest of the herd moving. There's a canyon just ahead of us."

He dared not tell them how far it was. He rode on, swinging wide to get ahead of the several dozen longhorns loping along the back trail. When he was ahead of them, the brutes began dodging left and right, determined they were not going to face the fury of the storm again. Dan needed at least another rider on a good horse, but had to make do. By the time he and his valiant horse had the stubborn longhorns headed north, the drag riders and the tag end of the herd were completely obscured by the swirling snow. Dan and his horse were exhausted, and he thought he was seeing things when a horse and rider emerged from the wall of white ahead of him.

"I thought you might need some help," Adeline shouted above the shriek of the wind.

"I never needed it more," Dan shouted in reply.

The two of them managed to keep the longhorns moving until at last they caught up with the drag. When the last of the herd finally turned west at the creek, Dan slumped in his saddle. Soon they were within the welcome confines of the canyon, with only flurries of snow coming in over the north rim. The longhorns and horses were strung out along the creek, and some of the riders had a fire going under the shelter of the canyon rim.

"Come on," Adeline shouted. "We'll have hot coffee in a few minutes."

13

The riders dragged down enough dead cedar from the upper end of the canyon to keep the fires burning, and the camp was comfortable. Although it wasn't even midday, the low-hanging clouds and swirling snow made it seem as night. The wind screamed through the upper reaches of the canyon, and some of the horse remuda drifted closer to the circle of light from the fires. For once, the young horse wranglers moved within the shelter of the camp, content to watch their charges from a distance.

"We'll keep watch tonight," Dan said, "but I see no point in riding from one end of this canyon to the other. We'll need to keep the fires going, and with the horse remuda at this end of the canyon, I think we can protect them from shelter. I can't imagine anybody trying to grab the herd during such a storm as this. Indians might come after the horses if they know we're here, but we've seen no sign, and there's been no warning from Chato."

"We got grub, a warm fire, and weapons," Duncan Kilgore said. "Why don't we keep the coffee hot, keep our guns handy, and rest our bones? That storm ain't gonna quit till she's ready, and by then there's likely to be plenty of snow. Horses, mules, cows, and wagons ain't goin' nowhere for a while."

"That makes sense to me," Sloan Kuykendall said. "This ain't home, but it's the best we're likely to have for a while."

Dan was reminded of something he had been intending to do, and now the young horse wranglers were in camp. Upon Dan's suggestion, Silas went to the wagon, returning with the three extra Winchesters and a supply of shells. Dan spread a blanket and divided the shells into three equal piles. Then he called for Pablo Elfego, Gus Wilder, and Gid Kilgore. When the trio stood before him, he handed each of them a Winchester.

"There's a supply of shells for each of you," he said. "Learn to use those weapons, keep them clean, and respect them."

"Yes, sir," the three shouted in a single voice.

Denny DeVoe refused to look at the grinning trio, turning reproachful eyes on Dan. But Dan seemed not to notice, and Adeline winked at him without Denny knowing. Looking up to Dan, Denny felt he had been betrayed, and before the entire outfit. His pride forbade him speaking to Dan, but he confronted Adeline after she and Lenore had taken their bedrolls and sought some privacy.

"I thought Dan liked me," Denny whined. "I liked him."

"And you don't anymore?" Adeline asked.

"Why should I? Everybody got a rifle except me."

"You have the Maynard carbine your father bought for you, and you have ammunition," Adeline said. "The other wranglers had no weapons at all."

"Now they got repeaters," Denny said bitterly, "and all I got is a damn old single-shot."

"You're used to it and you can hit what you're shooting at. I'd have been disappointed in Dan if he'd denied one of the others a rifle and given it to you. It's time you learned some tolerance and unselfishness, Denny

DeVoe. If you so much as mention this to Dan, I'll take your britches down and switch your naked behind before God and everybody. Do you understand?"

"Yes," Denny growled.

"Yes, what?"

"Yes, ma'am."

Denny retreated to the shadows, getting as far from Adeline as he could. She lay awake, watching him, watching Dan. After a decent interval, Dan sought her out.

"You must have been a mite hard on him," Dan said. "He looks like he just fell off the top of the world and had it roll over on him."

"You've just taught him a valuable lesson, but I fear he's still too young to appreciate it."

"I would have gotten him a rifle if he hadn't had one," Dan said.

"I know you would have," Adeline replied, "and he knows it too."

Santos Miguel Montoya and his Mejicanos had wisely remained at the Brazos, and had taken refuge along the river beneath overhanging banks. Three hundred yards downriver, Ledoux and his two companions shared a similar shelter. But none of them enjoyed as comfortable a camp as the Tejanos, half a dozen miles ahead. The wind-driven snow constantly found its way into their blankets, and they were half frozen from constantly stumbling through knee-deep drifts, seeking wood for their fires. There were especially vile words around Ledoux's fire, because he refused to join his disgruntled companions in the constant quest for firewood.

"I don' hire on wi' you to dig through the snow with my hands, seeking firewood," Black Bill said.

"Whatever needs doing," Ledoux said, "you'll do it. I got enough on you to have you hung six times, anywhere in Texas. Now get your mangy carcass out there and help Hagerman."

There was snow blowing into the canyon at dawn the next morning, but the worst of the storm seemed to have passed. The sky was still a dirty gray, and while it was well past sunrise, there was no evidence the sun would shine that day.

"It ain't over," Silas predicted. "She's slowed up to take another start, and she'll be blowin' again 'fore dark."

As unwelcome as the prediction was, there was no denying the look of the sky and the bone-chilling cold. Time hung heavy on everybody's hands, and nobody complained about the frequent forays upcanyon for more firewood. It was something to do. Within less than two hours, Silas's prediction became all too evident. Above the canyon rim, against the gray of the sky, the wind-driven snow looked like swirling smoke.

"We'd best take the horses and snake down every fallen log we can find," Dan said. "We're in for a blizzard, and we could be stuck here a week."

"You're almighty right," Silas agreed. "Thank God we sold them cows and loaded up on grub. In all this, if a body can eat decent and keep warm, that's enough."

The trail north. Tuesday, November 8, 1870.

After three days and nights the storm blew itself out, and a long absent sun emerged. The wind lost its bite, and the temperature rose as dramatically as it had fallen in the forefront of the storm.

"It'll be another two or three days 'fore enough of this snow's melted for us to get out of here," Silas said.

"That may be the case with the wagons," Dan said, "but these longhorn cows will have to be out of here in the morning, and that's pushing things to the limit. The graze is gone."

"The drifts at the mouth of the canyon won't be the only problem," Skull Kimbrough said. "When the thaw begins, it'll be the equal of a three-day rain, and anybody that thinks them wagons was mired down before ain't seen nothin' yet."

"I'm not playing down the need for the wagons," Dan said. "God knows, we've put enough into them, but they don't have to eat. The cows do, and if it takes a week to move the wagons, so be it. But we'll have to break a trail out of here and find some decent graze for the herd. We'll leave our camp where it is until we can take the wagons out."

A second day of sun made a difference, and the longhorns were driven out of the canyon the way they had come in. The open plain with only occasional mesquite was their salvation, for it was here that the sun was most effective in melting the snow. It would linger longest in the arroyos and low-lying areas where the sun's rays visited for only a few hours each day.

"Trouble with cows," Hiram Beard said, "is that they're so confounded dumb they can't kick through a little snow cover, gettin' at the grass below. If they ain't standin' belly deep in grass, they don't know it's there."

The herd and the horse remuda found graze a mile or two north of the canyon from which they had been driven. Every draw became a temporary stream and every depression a water hole, as the deep snowdrifts began to feel the heat of the sun and the effects of a rising temperature.

"Plenty of water now, with the melting snow," Kirby Wilkerson said, "but with the sun hot enough to melt the snow, it'll suck up all the water pronto."

"That won't hurt us," Dan said. "Remember, we weren't more than five or six miles from the south fork of the Wichita when the storm struck. If we have to, we'll drive the herd and the horse remuda on to the river, and come back for the wagons."

"I reckon we'd as well plan on doin' it like that," Silas said. "Then, if we have to, we can use every mule we got, bringin' one wagon at a time."

"We've got the herd and the horse remuda on good grass," Dan said. "Let's hold off moving the wagons for another day."

"I'll go along with that," Ward McNelly said, "and for more than just a possibility that wagons will bog down. The drifts have smoothed out the gullies and holes so's we can't see 'em. Drop a wheel in there sudden, and you got a broken wheel or a busted axle. I say we leave the wagons where they are for now, and move the herd on to the south fork of the Wichita."

Nobody argued with the logic of that. The longhorns and horse remuda were driven on to the river and loosed along its banks, and after another day of sun, the wagons were brought out of the canyon. By keeping to the ridges where the sun had cleared away the snow and the terrain was solid, all the wagons were taken to the south fork of the Wichita. While the temperature had risen, nights turned cold when the sun went down, and there was ice in the eddies along the riverbank. The fourth day after leaving the canyon where they had weathered the storm, Dan and the outfit were ready to cross the south fork of the Wichita.

"Water's a mite high," Wolf Bowdre said. "We got the snow to thank for that."

"I'm not concerned with it bein' high as I am with it bein' cold," Dan said. "I aim to ride across and back. If it's too cold, the horses and cows can't cross."

Dan rode across the river and returned. The horse shuddered, but the animal was game, and Dan judged the river safe for crossing.

"Wolf, Tobe, and Palo," Dan said, "I'll want you here with me when the leaders hit the water. The water's not that cold, but cold enough that they might try to turn back. It'll be up to us to see that they don't break to left or right. We get them off to a running start, and you drag riders hit them hard from behind. Once they're on the run, it'll be up to you flank and swing riders to see that none of them break away before they reach the water. We'll do the easy part first. Let's take the wagons across."

The wagons were crossed without difficulty, followed by the horse remuda. The longhorns were started at a great enough distance from the river that by the time the leaders reached the water, they were running. But the shock of the cold water slowed them, and the first few ranks were of a single mind. Despite the best efforts of Dan and Palo, the leaders broke downstream with the intention of returning to the riverbank they had just departed. Dan's horse knew what was expected of him, and the animal surged ahead of the rebellious longhorns. Dan drew his Colt and fired over their heads. Palo was right behind Dan, and with the two of them shooting and shouting, the lead steers gradually turned toward the north bank. The rest of the herd followed, and while they didn't emerge in a straight-across pattern, they did reach the opposite bank. Dan and Palo were ahead of them, forcing the leaders along the river until the tag end of the herd was out of the water.

"Head 'em up," Dan shouted, "and gather them near the horse remuda."

The fourth day after leaving the canyon where they had weathered the storm, Dan and the outfit crossed the north fork of the Wichita.

"McCullough said we'd be about eighteen miles south of the Pease River, and from there, twenty miles from the Red," Dan said. "That means a long drive tomorrow and another the day after, but the herd's had good grass and water. We'll move out tomorrow at first light and drive them hard. All of you know what that means.

There'll be bunch quitters galore. None of them will want to trail as fast as they'll have to, if we're to reach the Pease before dark tomorrow. It'll be a hard day, with another right on the heels of it."

North to the Pease River. Sunday, November 13, 1870.

It became a predictably bad day in more ways than they had anticipated. The warming weather brought another storm, and two hours into the day the temperature again dropped. There was no snow, but the cold rain came at them on the wings of a north wind. It took less than an hour to convince the herd they belonged on the back trail, the storm at their backs. The bunch quitting grew worse as the day progressed.

"By God," Wolf Bowdre said, "we haven't traveled a mile in the past two hours. Our horses are ready to drop, and we don't even have time to change mounts."

"Try to keep them bunched," Dan said. "I'll ride ahead and try to find a place where we can hold them until the storm lets up."

Dan rode on, dreading what might lie ahead. If the rain changed to snow, there might be another three-day blizzard. There had to be something—some kind of wind break—to hold the herd until the storm let up. Even then the brutes would try to get their backs to the wind and drift. The valley, when Dan came upon it, didn't look all that promising. He topped a ridge upon which there was nothing but mesquite, catclaw, and an occasional stunted oak, and the opposite ridge offered little more. The valley was deep, however, and the ridge to the north was a barrier to the cold wind. It was nothing like their canyon beyond the Wichita, but it would have to do. Dan estimated the distance back to the herd was at least five miles, and the rain seemed to be getting harder. Trailing the herd into the teeth of a storm for such a distance would be a cowboy's idea of hell, but they had no choice. When Dan reached the first wagon, he spoke to Silas.

"Valley ahead, Silas. Take the wagons up the farthest ridge a ways. No creek through there, but there could be later, if the rain continues. Get the wagons over, just in case."

Dan then rode back to join the drag riders. There were twenty-two women in the outfit. The wives of Bowdre, McNelly, Elfego, Grimes, Wilkerson, and Crump drove wagons. The rest—sixteen in all—rode drag, and while none of them had ever done anything of this magnitude, they had come together in a way that had amazed Dan Ember. They swung doubled lariats against bovine rumps, screeched like Comanches, and when things really went to hell, Dan heard some pretty salty language. He had a real affection for them all, and when the herd became the most unruly, he was always there to help them. And so it was today.

"Valley up ahead," he shouted. "We'll hold them there until the storm lets up."

It was a fight, keeping the herd moving into the storm until finally they topped a ridge and moved into the valley below. The rain was still cold, but without the wind, it was not a driving force, encouraging the herd to drift before it. Silas led the wagons across the floor of the valley and partway up the opposite side, just in case the rain continued and the water rose in a wet weather stream. Once the cattle and the horse remuda had strung out to graze, the riders converged on the wagons.

"Go ahead and put up your canvas shelters," Dan told them. "I look for the rain to continue today and maybe tonight, and with a cold wind from the north, it'll be near impossible drivin' the herd into it."

"Keeno," Cash Connolly said, "and we'll be damn lucky if it don't turn to snow."

"With that in mind," Dan said, "I think we'd all better

go in search of anything that'll burn. Nothing much in this valley. Split up into pairs and ride north. Nobody rides alone."

They were fortunate to find cedar and oak, some windblown and some that had been struck by lightning. These were snaked back across the ridge, and with an ax from each of the wagons, men began reducing the trees to firewood. Wagons had been positioned back to back or side by side, with canvas stretched between them, providing shelter for the cook fires. Cold wind still whipped into the valley, but the mesquited ridge broke the force of it. Water already had begun to flow down the normally dry valley floor, so there would be ample water for the horses and longhorns. While the animals had spread out down the valley, it was to take advantage of the graze. The rain continued, becoming harder at times, then slacking off to no more than a drizzle.

"If it goes on into the night," Silas predicted, "she'll change to snow, sure as hell."

Nobody doubted that. The temperature always seemed to drop at night, even if the sun had been out during the day. The day wore on, and there was hot coffee. The women began supper early, allowing the families to serve their plates and eat within their canvas shelters before dark. The rain continued into the night, but a little more than two hours after supper, it ceased.

"That could be the end of it," Silas said. "It's a good sign."

To everybody's surprise and relief, the clouds parted and a single timid star winked silver against the purple sky. Soon there were more stars, all seemingly scattered by a careless hand across a velvet plateau.

"We can't be more than eight or nine miles from the Pease River," Dan said, "and we'll be starting tomorrow with the herd well-grazed and watered. We'll drive them hard, and if we can reach the Pease early enough in the day, then I think we'll move on to the Red."

"You're saying tomorrow night might be a dry camp, then," Aubin Chambers said. "I don't like that."

"Me neither," Rux Carper added. "We got trouble enough with these varmints as it is."

"You're jumping to conclusions," Dan said. "From the information we have, once we reach the Pease River, we're a good twenty miles south of the Red. If we reach the Pease tomorrow at midday, we can be five or six miles closer to the Red tomorrow night. Once the herd's drunk their fill at the Pease, they won't be hurtin' for water again tomorrow night."

"Why, hell no, they won't," Silas said. "They'll be a mite thirsty before we get to the Red, but we'll be maybe thirteen or fourteen miles away, 'stead of twenty."

"I can't see coddlin' ourselves and the herd with a six or seven mile drive tomorrow, only to have hell all the next day, with a twenty mile run to the Red," Wolf Bowdre said. "If any of you hombres hanker to be trail boss, then we'll take a vote, but Dan Ember gets mine."

"And mine," shouted a dozen other men.

The men on the first watch mounted and rode out. The sky had cleared, and although the night wind had a chill to it, the riders were in good spirits. There had been enough rain for the temporary streams to have water, and even with the sun at its worst, the herd and horse remuda would by no means be dry when they reached the Pease River. Chambers and Carper were on the first watch with Dan, but they had nothing to say. When Dan left his watch at midnight, he found Adeline awake and waiting for him.

"Did Aubin Chambers and Rux Carper have anything to say to you?" she asked.

"No," Dan said. "Why?"

"Whether you realize it or not, the women on this trail drive have all the confidence in the world in you, and they're pretty well fed up with Chambers and Carper always trying to cut you down."

"I appreciate their confidence," Dan said, "but I think enough's been said."

"Odessa Chambers and Ellie Carper don't feel that way," Adeline said. "I think Mr. Chambers and Mr. Carper are catching hell just about now."

"That won't accomplish anything," Dan said, "except unite the two of them in some future devilment. I just want to be done with this drive."

"My God, yes," Adeline agreed. "Just to have some privacy."

"I could take a walk," Lenore said from the darkness.

"The time may come when we'll have you do just that," Dan said, "but not tonight."

The dawn broke clear and cold, with ice in standing pools of water. The wagons took the trail, followed by the horse remuda, and finally the longhorns.

"Keep them bunched and moving," Dan shouted as he made his way back to the drag. No such order was necessary for his drag riders. They knew what was expected of them, and they were right on the heels of the herd. Dan had some friendly words for every one, while Odessa Chambers and Ellie Carper made it a point to speak to him. Boyce Trevino, Palo Elfego, Chad Grimes, Garret Haddock, and Cash Connolly all had daughters near Lenore's age, and the girl had taken to riding with them. Dan trotted his horse alongside Adeline's. Hattie Kuykendall rode to Adeline's left, and Amy Wilder to Dan's right.

"This has to be the biggest bunch of drag riders for a single herd in the history of the world," Dan said.

"Why not?" Amy said. "Who's ever had a bigger herd?"

"We might not be the best," Hattie Kuykendall said, "but there's enough of us to make up the difference."

"I couldn't ask for a better drag," Dan said. "The flank and swing riders are important, but certainly no more important than any of you. Without you drag riders keeping the ranks closed, a hundred flank and swing riders would not be able to keep the column from breaking up."

The longhorns didn't like the faster gait, but they were forced to accept it, bawling their protests as they went. The sun soon began to make its presence felt, and the excess water that had collected on the prairie disappeared slowly but surely. The sun wasn't even noon high when the wagons and horse remuda reached the Pease River. The horse wranglers had wisely driven the remuda east far enough that they weren't in the way of the advancing herd. The longhorns were thirsty enough to trot, once they became aware of the water, and the river's bank was low enough not to be a danger. The lead steers broke for the water and the riders pulled back, letting them go. They had to cross the river anyway, and with the size of the herd, later arrivals would horn the earlier ones on across. Silas sat on the wagon box watching the steers and cows horn one another aside as they made their way to water.

"Water's not as deep as I'd reckoned," Dan said. "We might find a low enough bank and shallow enough water to just drive the wagons on across."

"I'm reckonin' the same thing," Silas said. "We know we'll have to float 'em across the Red, but maybe this once we won't have to."

Some of the cattle had given up reaching the water, and not being all that thirsty, had begun to graze. Some of the riders had ridden into the water, swinging their doubled lariats and shouting, seeking to drive some of the cattle on across and out on the opposite bank. Once their efforts began to succeed and the early arrivals were driven out, Dan and the rest of the riders began driving the grazing cattle on toward the water. The longer it took the herd to drink, the more time they would lose on their drive to the Red. The horse wranglers had found a suitable crossing and had driven the horse remuda to the opposite bank. Thinking it might be possible to cross the wagons there, Silas had headed his team upriver, the other wagons following. So large was the herd, many of the cattle had been forced into deeper water and were unable to linger in the river. Dan allowed the animals time to drink and then they were driven on across.

"Head 'em up!" he shouted. "We're moving out!"

There were seven of the Cheyenne—three braves, three squaws, and a boy still in his teens—and they had made their camp a hundred yards from the Red, near a popular crossing.* Finishing their supper well before dark, the supper fire was extinguished. The buffalo were gone, winter was nigh, and the seven were part of an exodus from the plains where the white buffalo hunter had encroached upon Indian hunting grounds. Circumstances beyond their control had torn their roots from the soil of their past and there seemed little or no future awaiting them. But the little party of Cheyenne were not alone, and the first hint of danger came at dawn, with the rattle of a wagon. East along the river it came, driven by a white man and followed by three others on horseback. They were former buffalo hunters, but their wagon was empty and their mules gaunt.

"Smoke," the lead rider said. The three drew their Sharps buffalo guns and rode on.

Ahead, the Cheyenne had put out their breakfast fire and the women were running toward a thicket where the horses had been concealed. The three Cheyenne

---

* Just north of present-day Vernon, Texas. The first house was erected in 1874. It became known as Doan's Crossing in 1879, when C. F. and Jonathan Doan built an adobe building and started a store.

braves stood their ground, buying a little time for their women. The boy refused to retreat with the women, remaining with the braves. As the white men drew near, the four Cheyenne gave the peace sign. But there was no peace. The buffalo guns roared and two of the braves fell, dead before they touched the ground. The third Cheyenne had seized his bow and an arrow, but they fell from his dead hands as heavy slugs from two of the Sharps ripped into his belly. The third Sharps cut down the Cheyenne boy.

"Come on," the man who had driven the wagon shouted. "Let's git them squaws."

The Cheyenne women hadn't moved fast enough and the buffalo hunters had seen them scatter into the thicket. The four men ran through underbrush. Leaving behind the heavy Sharps rifles, each man had drawn and cocked his Colt. They had taken Indian women before and bore scars as proof. Many a squaw had a knife and was adept in the use of it. But these Cheyenne squaws had only their hands and feet to defend themselves and the burly buffalo hunters used the muzzles of their Colts to knock the women unconscious. They each wore only a buckskin dress.

"Squaws ain't got but one damn thing goin' fer 'em," said one of the men. "They ain't all bound up in corsets an' such."

His three brutal companions shared his sentiments, and the women were quickly stripped of the little that they wore. There were crude jokes among the four as they had their way with the helpless Cheyenne women. Finished, they stood back to admire their handiwork just as the unfortunate trio were coming to their senses.

"Don't ever leave no witnesses, Injun or otherwise," one of the men said, drawing his Colt.

There was a roar of guns and the four men turned away from the bloody, violated bodies of the Cheyenne women. Quickly they found the horses that had belonged to the Cheyennes.

"Damn Injuns," said one of the men. "Nothin' worth the takin', 'cept fer the hosses, an' they ain't nothin' to git excited about."

Three of the men mounted their horses and the fourth climbed to the wagon box. Leading the stolen horses, they departed the scene of their crime, not even looking back at the bodies of the fallen Cheyenne braves who had only wanted peace. When the rattle of the wagon and the clopping of horses' hooves had faded, there was only silence, for when death came, even the birds fled the scene. When there finally was a sound, it came from the lips of the youngest Cheyenne. It was a groan of anguish that ended with a sigh, and the boy's left hand moved just a little. Life remained, but little more than a spark . . .

14

*T*he herd was trailing well, and Dan rode alongside the lead wagon, talking to Silas.

"We ought to make the Red easy," Silas said. "Give the herd and the hosses time to water, graze, and rest, and we can run 'em across first thing tomorrow."

It had the promise of a perfect day. While the longhorns hadn't been to water at the end of the previous day, they had watered at midday and hadn't been bedded down dry. Today they would be thirsty before reaching the Red, but thanks to Dan Ember's foresight, the drive wouldn't be nearly as long as it might have been. It was early afternoon when they first sighted the circling buzzards somewhere ahead.

"Something or somebody's down," Dan said. "Monte, pass the word along to take up the slack, keep the herd moving. I think Wolf and me will ride ahead, see what's happened."

Dan and Wolf Bowdre kicked their horses into a slow gallop, and in less than an hour had reached the Red. There was a gradual slope to the water, and another on the north bank where they would leave the river.

"I've heard a lot about the Red, and none of it's been good," Wolf said, "but this don't look too bad. Of course, it could be over the head of a man on a tall horse."

"Come on," Dan said. "We might as well find out."

Their horses readily took to the river and crossed without difficulty. As they neared the grisly scene, three buzzards flapped away, taking refuge in the upper branches of an oak.

"Shot down like dogs," Bowdre said angrily. "Look at that."

Even in death, the stiffened fingers of one Indian still made the peace sign.

"Four men," Dan said, "one of them driving a wagon. An empty wagon. I'd say it was buffalo hunters."

But that wasn't the worst of it. When they found the three Indian women, all had been shot in the back.

"To a lesser degree," Bowdre said, "it looks exactly like what Clay Allison told us was done to Black Kettle and his tribe."

"We'll have to bury these people," Dan said. "Ride back, meet the wagons, and bring some spades. I'll stay here and keep the buzzards away."

When Bowdre had ridden away, Dan walked toward the river where the men had fallen. Something about the scene bothered him. All four had been shot from the front, but the fourth lay facedown, and the exit wound was high up, near the left shoulder. Dan took the limp left wrist and found no pulse. He reached for the big artery in the neck, pressing hard. So weak was the pulse, he thought he was mistaken, but he tried again, and it was there. He rolled the Indian over on his back, and for a heartbeat the obsidian eyes met his own. The young Indian had been conscious enough, with the strength to turn over on his belly, protecting his eyes from the waiting buzzards. Dan's bedroll and blankets were in one of the wagons. He took his coat and covered the Indian, awaiting

Bowdre's return. When Bowdre rode in, Tobe Barnfield was with him.

"The herd was behavin' itself," Bowdre said, "so I brought some help."

"We'll need it," Dan said, "but not to dig graves. You and me can do that. One of these Indians—the boy—is still alive, but not by much. Tobe, I want you to ride back and bring the medicine chest Silas has in his wagon. Have Adeline and one or two of the other women come with you, and have them bring some blankets. *Rapido.*"

When Barnfield had ridden away, Dan and Wolf began digging.

"I think we'll just dig a common grave," Dan said, "deep enough to keep the buzzards and coyotes from getting at them. We'd be here a week, digging individual graves."

When Tobe Barnfield returned, he rode across the river alone, but he had a roll of blankets.

"I left the women across the river," Tobe said. "I didn't reckon they ought to see all the dead. We can hoist this Injun on some blankets betwixt two hosses, and take him over yonder where we'll be makin' our camp."

"Good thinkin', Tobe," Dan said. "You and Wolf take him on across, and I'll finish filling this grave."

When Dan finished his task and crossed the river, he found Adeline, Lenore, and Fanny Bowdre working over the critically wounded Indian. Fanny had brought her wagon on ahead, and there was little the men could do. Adeline already had stripped away the bloody old denim shirt and was cleansing the wound. From a bolt of muslin Silas had brought from his store, Lenore was folding a thick pad, while Fanny Bowdre prepared a second one. When the bandages were in place, the Indian was wrapped in blankets from his chin to his feet.

"I've made room for him in the wagon," Fanny said. "He shouldn't be out there on the damp ground."

"If there's room for me, I'll stay with him," Lenore said.

"He could be dangerous when he comes out of it," Dan said. "He was shot by whites, and that makes us the enemy."

"Not if he knows we're trying to help him," Lenore said. "I'm not afraid."

"Then go ahead," Dan said jokingly. "It's time you got yourself a man."

The girl blushed furiously, hiding her face in her hands. Dan, Wolf, Tobe, and Fanny laughed, but the time would come when Lenore's affection for the young Indian would be no laughing matter.

The herd reached the Red without difficulty, and the rest of the outfit was curious about the wounded Indian in the Bowdre wagon.

"We don't know anything about him," Dan told them, "except that it's not likely he's Comanche. These Indians tried to meet the whites in peace, and that's the last thing Comanches would have done."

"What are you aimin' to do with him?" Chad Grimes asked.

"I have no idea," Dan said, "beyond gettin' him well and back on his feet."

Lenore sat in the Bowdre wagon listening to the wounded man's ragged breathing. Had his mother and father been among the Indians who had died? She decided they probably had, and that meant he was an orphan. He looked no older than she, and now he was alone in the world. Lenore didn't want him to be alone, but suppose Dan was right? Suppose, when he came to his senses and was strong enough, he repaid her kindness by simply strangling her? She forced that possibility from her mind, filling it with alternatives that would have shocked Adeline DeVoe speechless.

* * *

Into Indian Territory. Monday, November 14, 1870.

While the wagons had to be floated across the Red, it was a natural crossing and there was no difficulty. The herd was kept bunched, and when the leaders hit the water, they swam readily to the opposite bank. Despite Adeline's pleading and Dan's warnings, Lenore remained in the Bowdre wagon with the wounded Indian. By the time the wagons had crossed the Red, Lenore needed help in getting some whiskey down her feverish companion. Out of his head, he spoke in a language none of them could understand.

Riding drag, the other women took turns trotting their horses alongside Adeline DeVoe, hoping to learn something about the mysterious Indian in the Bowdre wagon. What had really piqued their curiosity was Lenore's obvious interest. The girl had seemed so backward, so withdrawn, she had rarely spoken to the women, and now she was alone with an Indian. A wounded Indian, they conceded, but he was still a man. It bordered on the scandalous, and as well-liked as Adeline was, her companions couldn't resist the temptation.

"Dear God," Amy Wilder said, "if she was my daughter, I'd be scared to death."

"Of what?" Adeline asked. "The boy's been shot and he's flat on his back with a fever."

"Well, you know . . ." Amy's voice trailed off.

"Yes, I know," Adeline said wearily. "I also know the Indian's so sick and weak he's fouling his blankets, and likely will be for another week. I'm thinking of the possibility that the Indian might come to his senses and attack Fanny Bowdre while she's driving the wagon, which is another reason for Lenore being there. This is a trail drive, ladies. We can't spare a man."

She said no more, and the others drifted away, all too

aware that they had been raising questions that were none of their business.

"I'd say we've come about fifteen miles," Dan said as they bedded down the herd along a nameless creek. "From what Clay Allison told me, we're about a hundred and seventy miles south of Camp Supply. Fifty miles from here, we cross the North Fork of the Red. We're eighty miles from the Washita, and something over a hundred from the Canadian."

"That ain't all of 'em neither," Silas said. "From what I know, there's still the North Canadian and the Cimarron 'fore we leave Indian Territory."

The weather held, with cold nights and mild days, and there were numerous creeks. The drive was three days —about forty miles—into Indian Territory, when trouble struck, and then indirectly. Just before breakfast Palo Elfego brought a message to Dan, and it wasn't good news.

"Chato," Palo said. *"Lucha soldados ayer. Todo soldados muerto."**

"God Almighty," Dan said. "How many soldiers?"

Palo shrugged his shoulders. Chato hadn't said how many, or whether he had attacked or been attacked. Not that it mattered, Dan thought gloomily. The soldiers had likely been marching south, from Camp Supply, on the North Canadian River. Dan had no choice but to reveal to the rest of the outfit the macabre information Palo had delivered. He held nothing back, and there was a prolonged silence. Aubin Chambers broke it.

"Damn fool thing to do," Chambers said. "Are you sayin' we could be held responsible?"

"I'm saying nothing of the kind," Dan replied. "I've told you what was told to me, and that's all I know. This we *do* know. Chato and his band *are* Indians. Mexican Indians. The soldiers could have fired on them first, and

---

* Fight soldiers yesterday. All soldiers dead.

if the attack was unprovoked, they asked for what they got. I think we could be likely held responsible only if the military became aware of our arrangement with Chato."

"No way they could know," Cash Connolly said. "We'll just go on the way we're headed, and truthfully say we've seen no soldiers."

"It's about all we can do," Dan said.

"We didn't even have to know about this," Rux Carper said. "What's the point in this damn renegade tellin' us after the damage has been done?"

"If he and his men were under fire," Dan said coldly, "there was no time to get permission from us before shooting back. We're Texans, with no love for the blue bellies, and Chato knows this might put us in an uncomfortable position. Give the man credit. He's likely had to shoot himself out of a bad situation, and he's warning us as best he can."

"This is Indian Territory," Duncan Kilgore said. "From what I hear, it's full of renegades from both sides of the war. Why should the military try to lay these killings on us?"

"Because we're Rebs," Garret Haddock said, "and that may be reason enough, if they can't come up with anybody else."

"I doubt it," Dan said. "I've told you this not because there's anything we can do about it, but because I thought you had a right to know. We should have considered this possibility when we struck our deal with Chato, but we didn't. Now we have no choice but to play out our hand, and speculation is getting us nowhere. Let's move 'em out."

As the wagons led out, Dan realized he hadn't remembered to see about the wounded Indian, thanks to the disturbing news from Chato. Dan caught up to the Bowdre wagon.

"How is he, Fanny?" he asked.

"Fever's gone," Fanny said, "and he's asleep. Sweating something terrible, and I think he has a very, very bad hangover."

Dan dropped back to the herd, not looking forward to the days to come. The Indian would likely play possum until he recovered enough strength to make his move. True, he'd been stripped down to the hide and had no weapon, and Fanny Bowdre had a Colt revolver. Lenore was armed with nothing but her compassion and good intentions, and Dan doubted that would mean anything to an Indian whose last conscious recollection had been seeing his people gunned down by cruel white men.

The North Fork of Red River. Friday, November 18, 1870.

The Texas outfit crossed the North Fork of the Red, thirty miles south of the Washita. A cold rain had begun to fall just before dawn, but the herd took the trail as usual. If the rain worsened, joining forces with a storm-driven wind, the longhorns would balk, but until that became a problem, Dan kept the herd moving.

Within the jolting wagon, Lenore sat nodding, half asleep. The wagon's interior was dim enough, but today the canvas puckers had been drawn at front and back, because of the rain. Suddenly, Lenore was startled wide awake by a guttural sound, and she realized the Indian's eyes were open, staring into her own. He had freed his right arm from the blankets, and when the girl leaned close, his fist slammed into her left ear. She was thrown against an enormous barrel of flour, her head striking the heavy rim. The Indian tried to rise, found himself weak, and lay back. When Lenore regained her senses, the Indian lay there with his eyes closed, apparently asleep. The girl felt the cut on her head and wondered if the blow to her face would leave a visible swelling. Again she seemed to hear Dan's warning, and realized that her danger was very real. She had no business being alone with this young savage who might kill her for no reason other than that she was white. Suppose she told Dan of this incident? She knew he regarded her as his own daughter, and while he had readily saved the young Indian's life, Dan would tolerate no savagery from him. She couldn't tell Dan, at least not yet. But she didn't have to.

In the rainswept night that followed, the Indian would make his move.

Far to the south Santos Miguel Montoya and his band of Mejicanos crossed the Red, followed by Burton Ledoux and his companions. Montoya had paused at the common grave Dan Ember and Wolf Bowdre had dug, and was there when Ledoux and his men crossed the river.

"What do you make of that?" Ledoux asked.

"I think per'ap somebody die," the Mexican said. With that, he rode on to join his men, leaving Ledoux to reach his own conclusions.

"I don' like that mouthy Mejicano bastard," Black Bill said.

"You've said that ever' damn day for the last two and a half months," Loe Hagerman said.

"And I say it ever' damn day for the nex' two and a half months, if I want to," Black Bill snarled.

"Both of you just shut the hell up," Ledoux said. He mounted his horse and rode away, not caring whether they followed or not.

Dan estimated they were fifty-five miles into Indian Territory. When the herd and the horse remuda had been bedded down for the night, he spoke to Wolf Bowdre.

"Looks like the rain will be with us all night, Wolf. I'm a mite uneasy about this Indian Lenore's watchin' over. I think he's playing possum, and I look for him to slip away, maybe tonight. Frankly, I'd stake him to a good horse, if he'd ride and keep riding. I just want to be sure he doesn't hurt Lenore when he decides to leave. I'd like for you to swap with somebody and take the second watch, so you can stay close to the wagon when I'm gone."

"I'll do it," Bowdre said. "That's straight thinking. I've been about to say something about him ridin' in that wagon with two women. I figure us savin' his bacon won't be near as strong on his mind as the memory of those white men shootin' him and his people."

"That's how I see it," Dan said. "While he's not being held captive, I have trouble believin' he won't try to take revenge on some of us because we're white. Listen for anything that might mean trouble for Lenore."

Dan had taken the canvas shelter he shared with Adeline DeVoe and set it up near the Bowdre wagon. Adeline's worried eyes met his, as though she felt he knew or suspected something she did not. Dan said nothing, for he knew she was already concerned enough. When his watch ended, he spoke briefly to Wolf Bowdre.

"Not a sound," Wolf said, "but was I you, I'd take that *muchacha* out of there in the morning and keep her out."

Dan found Adeline awake, and he doubted she had slept at all. She wasted no time in sharing her fears for Lenore.

"This damn Indian may be a little weak yet," Dan said, "but I think it's time he was making tracks. Come daylight, I'm for putting him on a horse and letting him ride. We have problems enough without harboring another right under our noses."

"I was sorry for him," Adeline said, "but I'm afraid of him. I'm afraid of what he's already done to Lenore. After her father came home and slapped me around, after that indecent proposal by Burton Ledoux, she's been scared to death of men. Finally, when she turned to you, I thought she was coming out of it. Now, I don't know. She's become foolish, possessive, like this young savage . . . belongs to her."

"Not after tonight," Dan said. "She may end up not liking me, but—"

There was a scream, cut short, and then only the sound of the rain on the canvas. Having removed nothing but his hat, Dan was on his feet, his Colt in his hand. Adeline headed for the wagon while Dan went after the dim shadow that had emerged from it. There was a patter of hoofs as some of the men riding watch came on the run. While the rest of the riders converged on the wagon, Dan pursued the elusive shadow that ran toward the horse remuda. Horses nickered in fear and there were shouts as the horse wranglers became aware of the intruder. There was a confusion of arms and legs, and then the Indian launched himself at Dan like a cougar. Dan felt strong hands encircle his throat. He seized the Indian's long hair with his left hand, and with his right smashed his Colt against the attacker's head. In the darkness, one of the horse wranglers leaped on Dan.

"Damn it," he growled, "he's down. Get off me."

Dan fumbled around until he found the Indian's bare feet, and slung the unconscious man over his shoulder. "I'll take care of him," he told the wranglers. "Calm the horses."

When Dan returned to the Bowdre wagon, he found the tailgate down and a lantern lighted. He dropped the naked Indian on the ground, on his back.

"You've killed him," Lenore bawled, fighting to get out of the wagon.

"Not quite," Dan growled, "but it was a temptation. "What's he done to you?"

"N-Nothing," the girl sobbed, bowing her head.

Dan hunkered down so that he could see her face, and even in the dim light of the lantern, he saw the livid bruise that extended from her chin to her right ear.

"Take her with you, Adeline," Dan said. "Wolf, Silas, one of you bring me some rope. I reckon we'll have to hog-tie this young catamount until we decide what to do with him."

By the time Dan had the Indian's back to a wagon wheel, his wrists bound behind him, every man and woman in the outfit had gathered around.

"Somebody get a blanket for the naked varmint," Boyce Trevino said.

Fanny Bowdre brought one, and as Dan knelt to cover the Indian, he got a bare foot in his face.

"Blanco perro," the Indian spat.*

"The little varmint speaks Spanish," Wolf Bowdre said. "Palo, come here. You talk Espanol. Tell this loco Indio we mean him no harm."

Palo Elfego hunkered down before the Indian, speaking in rapid Spanish.

For a long moment the Indian said nothing, but the hard lines of his face softened. *"Nombre Aguila,"* he said.

Palo continued in Spanish, and the response came so rapidly, only Palo understood. When the Indian became silent, Palo spoke.

"He is Eagle," Palo said. "Cheyenne. His people wanted only peace with the white man, yet they have been betrayed and murdered."

"I can't deny that," Dan said. "Tell him we wish him no harm, that we found him near death. He is not a captive, and when he wishes to leave, he will be given a horse."

Again Palo spoke, and when he had finished, the young Cheyenne turned to Dan and spoke quietly.

"Ninguno lucha," the Indian said.

"He no fight," Palo said. "He want loose."

Dan loosed the rope. The Cheyenne rubbed one wrist

---

* White dog

and then the other, and then reached for the blanket, covering himself. That reminded Fanny Bowdre of something. She went to the wagon and returned with the Indian's buckskin trousers and his moccasins.

"The war's over," Dan said. "Back to your blankets, while this hombre makes himself decent."

The rest of the outfit drifted away, some to a second watch, others to get what sleep they could. Since they now had coffee, a pot was kept on the coals all night for the benefit of the riders on watch, and it was Adeline DeVoe who brought a hot cup of the brew, offering it to the Indian. He took it without a word, holding the tin cup with both hands, enjoying its warmth. There was movement from the shadows, and when Lenore realized Dan had seen her, she backed swiftly away. Dan pretended he hadn't noticed, speaking to Adeline.

"His name is Eagle, and he's Cheyenne. He knows we're friends."

"Thank God," Adeline said. "What are we going to do with him?"

"I don't know," Dan said. "He was hostile to us because his people have been betrayed by the whites. Wolf recognized part of his words as Spanish, and Palo convinced him we meant no harm. He'll be peaceful enough, I think, and I've promised him a horse if he wants to leave."

"Suppose he doesn't?"

"He won't harm any of us. But I reckon you're thinking of Lenore."

"I am," Adeline said, "and I don't mean physical harm. She didn't want him sent away, even when there was a possibility he might kill her."

"By frontier standards, Lenore's a woman," Dan said. "She'll have to make her own mistakes, and while this Indian may be one of them, can we fault him? I could put him on a horse and drive him away, but he's young, and I doubt he has anywhere to go. Do you want me to make it easy on all of us and just shoot him?"

"My God, no. I've felt sorry for him from the first, and I still do. I . . . it's just . . ."

"You don't want grandchildren that look like him," Dan said.

She said no more, burying her face in her hands. Fanny Bowdre had left a pair of blankets on the wagon's tailgate. Dan took the blankets, handed them to the Indian, and pointed to the underside of the Bowdre wagon. The Cheyenne nodded. Adeline had recovered her composure, and Eagle handed her the empty tin cup. *"Gracias,"* he said.

By the time Dan and Lenore returned to their shelter, the rain had let up. The sky had begun to clear, and in the starlight they could see Lenore sitting cross-legged, awake.

"It's two o'clock in the morning," Adeline said. "You should be asleep."

"I'm not sleepy."

"The Indian's name is Eagle," Adeline said. "He's Cheyenne, and we're in no danger from him. He's been given blankets, and he'll be sleeping beneath the Bowdre wagon. He no longer suffers from his wound, and you are not to go near him at night."

The girl said nothing, but she didn't need to. She had begun building a wall of hostility that would not be breached. Dan Ember had done battle with fists, guns, and knives, but never with emotions. He had quickly won Denny's trust and respect. Now, just when it seemed Lenore had begun to draw closer to him, he had lost her without striking a blow. He lay awake until first light, half expecting the girl to defy her mother and slip away to join the homeless Indian. Nor did Adeline sleep. Only Lenore did.

First light found the Cheyenne, Eagle, with his back to a wagon wheel, his blankets folded neatly on the tailgate of the Bowdre wagon. He seemed unconcerned, waiting for someone to tell him what was expected of him. There was standing water as a result of the rain, most of it iced over. Besides a new coat, Dan had left Fort Griffin with three flannel shirts. One of these he brought to the Indian, and Eagle accepted it without question. He readily accepted a tin plate of ham, beans, and biscuit, and a tin cup of steaming hot coffee. Lenore seemed to ignore him, and he never once looked at her, and that was enough to strike a new note of fear in Adeline DeVoe's heart. After breakfast, Dan roped and bridled a big roan horse, which he presented to the Cheyenne. He said nothing to the Indian about where he should ride, but when the herd moved out, Eagle took up a flank position behind Wolf Bowdre. Despite his early hostility, he not only sought to make a place for himself, but did a passable job of it.

"I think," Wolf Bowdre said, when Dan paused for a word with him, "this Cheyenne will make a fair to middlin' cowboy. After all the slick dealing his people have suffered at the hands of whites, he's got sand. If I was Indian and had seen my people shot down by whites, I'm not sure I could forget or forgive."

"I think that's all that separates a man from a lobo," Dan said, "and the color of his skin has nothing to do with it. My parents were murdered by the Comanches, and it would be easy for me to hate all Indians. But when I'm tempted, my mind force-marches me through centuries of brutality by the white man. Killers come in all colors, but so do men with compassion and guts."

While Dan and Wolf had no way of knowing Eagle's thoughts, the Cheyenne had reached some conclusions of his own, remarkably close to Dan's. While he had seen his people murdered by whites, and while he had been left for dead, he could not bring himself to condemn them all. These men and their squaws who drove the *vacas* had saved his life, fed him and had shown him kindness, even when he had returned that kindness with hostility. His people had been starved out of West Texas by the white buffalo hunters, and if they had killed all the buffalo on this range, had they not done so elsewhere? While Eagle did not understand where the cattle drive was going and why, it seemed to have some purpose, something his life lacked. Perhaps, now that he had no other, he could make a place for himself among these whites. They, like his people had been, were on the move, but they had some destination in mind. For the first time in his life there was food without days of fruitless hunting, and the eventual possibility that he might prove himself to the extent that he could own one of the white man's weapons. That in itself was reason enough to become part of the white man's world, but suddenly there came to him a new revelation that swept everything else aside.

Now that he had been accepted by the whites with whom he rode, would he not be permitted to move freely among the white man's villages? Despite the ordeal he had endured, the faces of four men had been burned into his brain as though with a hot iron. Somewhere the men who had murdered his people had to be walking free, and when he found them, he would not need the white man's deadly thunder stick. Eagle—the Cheyenne—would need only the cover of darkness and a well-honed *cuchillo . . .*

* Knife

15

The Washita River, Indian Territory. Sunday,
November 20, 1870.

*T*he herd and the horse remuda had been bedded
down on the south bank of the Washita; about
sixty-five miles south of Camp Supply, on the North Canadian, according to Dan's calculation. The soldiers—a
lieutenant, a sergeant, and nine privates—rode in from
the north just before sundown. Dan rode out to meet
them.

"Ride in and rest your saddles," he invited. "You're
welcome to join us for supper, and there's hot coffee
ready now. I'm Daniel Ember."

"We're obliged," the officer said. "I'm Lieutenant
Strait, and this is Sergeant Collins. I'll tell you a secret.
Soldiers don't eat all that well on post, and off it the
food becomes infinitely worse. We gladly accept the invitation to supper."

The men dismounted, unsaddled, and gratefully accepted tin cups of hot coffee. They canted their heads
like hunting wolves toward the Dutch ovens where sourdough biscuits were baking. They dug into supper as
though they were half starved, taking seconds of ham,
beans, hot biscuits, and dried apple pie. They emptied

two pots of coffee while two more were boiling. Finally, over fourth and fifth cups of coffee, the lieutenant got around to what Dan had been expecting.

"Two weeks ago," Strait said, "an eleven man patrol left Camp Supply, and haven't returned. To say we suspect foul play would sound foolish. They're dead and we know it, but what we don't know is how they have disappeared without a trace. There's been rain since, of course, and whatever trail there was is gone. Have you seen any sign that might be helpful to us, such as old tracks or ashes from old fires?"

"Nothing," Dan said truthfully. "The only camp we've seen is an Indian camp right after we crossed the Red. Seven Indians had been gunned down. We reckoned it was done by buffalo hunters, from shod horse tracks and the wagon tracks comin' out of the west."

"Likely you're right," Lieutenant Strait said.

"How far are we from Camp Supply?" Wolf Bowdre asked.

"A little more than sixty miles," Lieutenant Strait replied. "You should be there in four days, but don't expect a lot. We've been promised a fort, a permanent installation, but for the time being just about everything is in short supply. You'll find no weapons or ammunition for civilian use."

The soldiers stayed the night, and following a bountiful breakfast, rode south on their impossible mission. Dan and the outfit headed the herd and the horse remuda north, crossing the Washita.*

Lenore DeVoe took her old position riding drag, and appeared unchanged. She hadn't been overly friendly to

---

* This stretch along the Washita is now known as the "Black Kettle National Grassland," in memory of Chief Black Kettle and the Cheyennes who died there. George A. Custer and his U.S. Seventh Cavalry rode south from Camp Supply on November 23, 1868. On November 28, without warning, they attacked Black Kettle's sleeping camp, killing every man, woman, and child.

any of the other women, but she suddenly began riding close to Nakita Elfego. Nakita spoke English better than Palo or Tamara, and she was fluent in Spanish as well, and that was what interested Lenore. Nakita was near Lenore's age, and being the only Mejicano in the outfit, was as friendless as Lenore. Finally, when Lenore worked up enough courage to ask a favor, Nakita was responsive but curious.

"You are Tejano, and speak the most wonderful English," Nakita said, "while I work like the dog to master it. Why you wish me to teach you Espanol?"

"I can't tell you," Lenore said, "for two reasons. You would laugh at me, and you would tell, and I don't want anyone else to know."

"I would not laugh and I would not tell," Nakita said. "I think I know why, even if you do not tell me. You wish to talk to the Indio, and he knows no English."

"Damn you, Nakita," Lenore said, "if you breathe a word, I swear I'll kill you. Now you know my reason. Will you teach me?"

"Per'ap," Nakita said, "if you help me with the English. You see this Indio *desnudo*. He *bueno hombre*, no?"

"Like the *toro,*" Lenore said devilishly. "Now, when can we start with the Spanish?"

Palo Elfego had taken to riding with Eagle, and the Indian slowly began to learn some English. Even Adeline had become comfortable with him, and he seemed to have some vague recollection of her treating his wound. Often when he caught her eye, he grinned at her for no reason, as though they shared some secret. He had unusual habits, for an Indian. He didn't care how cold it got. Morning and evening he stripped off his shirt and washed himself. At some time in his life he seemed to have been around soldiers, for he walked and rode ramrod straight. He developed a habit of snapping Dan a military salute when they met, whether in camp or on the trail.

"Damned if I understand that Indian," Dan said. "He's had some civilizing somewhere along the trail. I'll be glad when he learns some English."

"Fanny says he already knows all the swear words," Adeline said, "and he can say 'Tejano.'"

The Canadian River. Monday, November 21, 1870.

The Canadian was just fifteen miles north of the Washita crossing, and the trail drive had made it easily by sundown. Now it was dawn, and all the wagons had been floated across the Canadian.

"How far to the next water?" Sloan Kuykendall asked.

"I have no idea," Dan said, "but we're not more than forty miles from the North Canadian, and with it that close, there should be plenty of runoffs to the south. If there's a water problem ahead, we usually get some warning from Chato, and I've heard nothing."

But Chato and his band were not ahead of the drive. In fact, they were concealed in the breaks along the Canadian, less than ten miles east of the position where the trail drive was crossing. Chato didn't know where the soldier fort was, and he had sent a man ahead to scout its location. While they waited, more soldiers had ridden south. The first group had stumbled on his camp, had attacked, and Chato and his men had been forced to kill them. Chato had considered ambushing the second group, but discarded the idea. If the soldier fort was near, he might bring down the wrath of the entire United States Army on himself and his men. Instead, he had sent a scout south, with orders to follow the soldiers. He had to be sure they didn't march just beyond the trail drive and double back along the flank, with mischief in mind. His experience with soldiers along the Rio Grande had all been bad, and he trusted none of them.

Sugato, the scout Chato had sent to follow the soldiers, had crossed the Washita and seen no evidence the eleven soldiers intended to turn back. Sugato had watered his horse and was about to ride north when he heard something downriver. Quickly he concealed himself and the horse, with his hand over the animal's muzzle. He watched in amazement as eighteen riders—all Mejicano—rode along the north bank of the river. He did not know them all, but he recognized the hated Santos Miguel Montoya as the leader. He waited until Montoya led his band north, the direction the trail drive had taken. Sugato waited, and before the Mejicano band was out of sight, three more riders appeared, following Montoya's band. Sugato recognized only the lead rider, for he was the *diablo americano* who had taken the Tejano land and sought to prevent the trail drive. Sugato led his horse downriver almost a mile before mounting. He then rode almost five miles to the east before reining his horse to the north. He then urged the animal into a fast gallop. Chato must know of this unholy alliance between Burton Ledoux and Montoya's killer Mejicanos. Even the uneducated Sugato realized that it was no longer just a case of Chato and his men protecting the Tejano outfit and their cows. Chato and his band of Mejicano Indios would be fighting for their lives.

Once the herd had crossed the Canadian and was headed north, it seemed nothing could go wrong. The sun had risen in a clear blue sky, and within two hours they crossed a clear running creek that angled in from the northwest. But far to the west, where the sun would bid the prairie good night, a dirty band of gray stretched from one horizon to the other. Somewhere—maybe over the Pacific—a storm was brewing, and for the time of the year, it could be rain, snow, or a combination of both. Dan was riding near the lead wagon, and Silas came up with one of his predictions.

"Ain't cold enough for snow, but that could change. If the temperature don't drop tonight, there'll be a frog strangler by mornin'."

"Given a choice," Dan said, "I'd almost prefer the snow. "This time of year, there's a real danger from ground lightning."

On the prairie any kind of lightning was feared by cattlemen, but the ground lightning was the worst. It came to earth as huge balls of fire, and brought with it a multitude of dangers. Even if the perilous blue and green spheres didn't strike a tree and explode, they had a way of terrifying horses and cattle. As the day wore on, the cloud bank grew, erasing the blue from the western horizon. The sun dipped lower and soon was gone, fanning out glorious shades of red and pink in memory of its passing. A chill wind rose out of the northwest, but there was no rain, no thunder, and no lightning. Near dawn there was a distant rumble of thunder, and breakfast was a hurried affair, with the expectation of rain. Even with the wind, the air seemed thick, oppressive. A cow bawled uneasily, and it seemed to have been a signal, as others joined in.

"Everybody in the saddle," Dan shouted. "Circle the herd and try to calm them." Dan could hear the horses nickering, and rode north west along the creek to the horse remuda. "It may be a bad one," he told the wranglers. "Hold them if you can."

Dan found Silas frantically harnessing his team to the wagon. Fanny Bowdre and the other women who drove wagons were attempting to harness their teams as well.

"We're movin' the wagons down the creek a ways," Silas shouted. "If they run, it'll likely be away from the storm and right through camp."

It was true. Dan leaped from the saddle and set about

helping Tamara Elfego with her team. There was a patter of rain and a roll of thunder as lightning flared from one horizon to the other.

"Here it comes," a rider shouted, and he wasn't referring to the rain, but the fearful lightning.

The glowing spheres dropped from the low-hanging gray clouds and went bounding across the plains like fiery tumbleweeds, some of them as big as wagon wheels. Silas was on the wagon box, flogging the mules, when a ball of fire broadsided the wagon. The wagon literally exploded, and there was a second blast the equal of the first as the keg of black powder from Silas's store detonated. The ground lightning would have been bad enough, but for the horses and longhorns the double blast was a scenario straight from hell. Being to the south of the herd, it drove the terrified longhorns to the north, taking the horse remuda with them. With the storm blowing from the northwest, the riders had expected the herd, if it stampeded, to run to the east, away from the storm. Thus some of the riders were to the north of the herd, and were caught between the stampeding longhorns and the horse remuda.

Dan had ridden eastward, hoping to get ahead of the expected stampede, and could only watch in horror as his companions rode for their lives. One of them was Lenore. Suddenly her horse stumbled, throwing her to the prairie. The horse limped away as she got to her feet, and Dan could see her terrified face as the thundering herd came closer. Adeline DeVoe reined up beside Dan, the sound of her anguished screams lost in the rumble of the stampede. Then from the west galloped a big roan horse, straight into the path of the twenty thousand rampaging longhorns. Eagle rode the horse like he was part of it, as though unaware of eighty thousand deadly hooves pounding toward him. On he rode, and when it seemed there was not a chance of his reaching the girl in time, he did. Without a break in the roan's stride, the Cheyenne caught Lenore up in his left arm and galloped on. But the danger wasn't past, for the herd had fanned out for more than a mile, and the valiant horse might yet be run down before it was out of the path of the stampede.

Dan and Adeline galloped their horses along with the running longhorns, aware that the stampede was losing momentum. The rain continued, but the wind, lightning, and thunder had abated. When Dan and Adeline met Eagle, the Cheyenne was leading his lathered horse. When Lenore saw Adeline, she all but fell off the animal. Adeline was out of the saddle in an instant, and when they met, Dan and the Indian were forgotten. The Cheyenne said not a word, but walked on toward camp, leading the weary horse. Dan rode after him, dreading what awaited them.

There was nothing left of the wagon but the wheels. There was a sickening odor of burned flesh, for the mules had died a fiery death along with Silas. What remained of him was covered with a blanket. The women who had driven the other wagons were in shock, and Tamara Elfego wept. The men were ill at ease, as though unsure as to what should be done. Death was a visitor with whom none of them were comfortable.

"Wolf," Dan said, "let's you and me dig a grave for Silas beneath that big oak down yonder by the river. The rest of you hitch up the wagons and move the camp upriver a mile or two. I reckon we'll be here awhile."

They needed something to occupy their minds and their hands, and they set about following Dan's orders as he and Wolf Bowdre took spades from the Bowdre wagon. The rain continued, but they hardly noticed. Finally, when they stopped, leaning on the handles of their spades, it was Bowdre who spoke.

"You know," he said, "I'll miss old Silas more than I'd miss any other man in this outfit. You got savvy, and you're one hell of a trail boss, but without Silas, I ain't sure you could have pulled all of us together."

"Neither am I," Dan said. "He gave it all he had, and damn it, I wish we could thank him with more than just a hole in the ground."

"He wouldn't expect more than that," Bowdre said. "I don't think he ever expected to see Kansas. What I regret most, and what I think is botherin' some of the others, is he was more a friend to us than we were to him. All of us laid out of the war, while Silas lost both his sons, but he never held it against us."

"What of his wife?"

"I reckon the war took her too," Bowdre said. "She died when she knew for sure her sons wouldn't be comin' home."

"I almost believe Silas wanted to do one more worthy thing, something he could be proud of," Dan said. "Thank God we're close enough to the finish that he could see the success of it. What better way for an old Texan to cash in, than on the trail with a herd of Texas longhorns?"

Beneath a gnarled oak on the Canadian River, they laid Silas Hamby to rest. Dan read passages from Hattie Kuykendall's Bible, and they all walked sorrowfully away, leaving Dan and Wolf to fill the grave.

Chato spoke not a word until Sugato had told the renegade leader all he had seen. "We kill?" Sugato asked.

"*Si,*" Chato said, "but when we are beyond the soldier fort. We have no fight with the army of the *americanos* if they do not attack us, and they do not attack us if they do not know we are here."

There was some grumbling, but Chato ignored it. They dared not run afoul of the law until they were ready to retreat into the wilds of Old Mexico, and that meant delaying their showdown with Montoya's bunch until they were much nearer Dodge City. Chato had every intention of collecting the money owed him for the trail drive and for the sale of the horse remuda.

The Canadian River. Wednesday, November 23, 1870.

"With rain all day yesterday and most of last night," Dan said, "there'll be plenty of standing water, so we'll have to go after the varmints. They won't have to come back to the river to drink."

"Anyhow, they're somewhere to the north of here," Spence Wilder said, "and that's where we're aimin' to take 'em."

"Yeah," Hiram Beard said, "but there's northwest, north, and northeast. They could be fanned out over thirty or forty miles."

"Cows scare easy," Dan said, "but they have short memories. I doubt they'd run more than four or five miles, unless the devil was on their heels snortin' fire and brimstone. But they'll drift some as they graze, so the sooner we start this gather, the less time it'll take."

"We're talkin' twenty thousand head," Aubin Chambers said. "Hell, we'll be here till spring."

"Maybe you will be," Dan said, "but I won't. Let's ride."

The first day's gather proved Dan correct, as they found a fourth of the herd grazing along the Canadian. Before the day was done, the sun came out and began drying up the standing water left by the rain.

"By this time tomorrow," Dan said, "the varmints will be huntin' water. Some of them will drift back to the Canadian, but we'll have to search the creeks and streams to the north of here for the rest."

The four young horse wranglers had gone in search of the horse remuda, and found nearly all the animals grazing along a creek that emptied into the Canadian. Eagle, the Cheyenne, had a fondness for horses, and went with them. The second day after the rain, the weather had warmed up, and the riders and their mounts were sweating. The women took advantage of the unseasonably warm weather and the sun, washing clothes and blankets. Dan stopped the gather an hour before sundown to allow time to drive the longhorns to the Canadian, where the rest of the herd grazed. Eagle rubbed down his roan and turned the animal loose with the rest of the horses. He then set off along the river, seeking the shallows upstream. The westering sun was still warm, and the water was pleasantly cool. Once there was a stand of willows between him and the camp, Eagle stripped and waded into the knee-deep water. Suddenly a twig snapped, and the Indian froze. Lenore DeVoe stood on the bank, not a dozen feet away.

"Eagle," said the girl. *"Aguila."*

"Aguila desnudo," the Cheyenne said. *"Licencia."**

"Ninguno," Lenore said. *"Vir Aguila desnudo en carreta."*

The Cheyenne glared at her. The stubborn Tejano squaw would not leave. While his mind was in the spirit land, she had seen him naked in the wagon, and had followed him when he came to the river to wash. Angrily, he splashed out of the water, pulled on his buckskins, his moccasins, and finally the shirt Dan had given him. Then, leaving Lenore standing there feeling foolish, he stalked back toward camp.

"Damn him," Lenore said, kicking a rock. "He thinks I followed him here to see his naked body again."

She walked slowly toward camp, so engrossed in her thoughts she didn't see Adeline DeVoe watching her. She also was unaware that Adeline had seen the Indian return just a few minutes ahead of Lenore. She said nothing to the girl. There would be time enough for that after Dan rode out for the first watch.

* * *

* Eagle naked. Leave.

After three days, more than half the herd was still missing. There was one other possibility Dan didn't like to face, but it must be considered.

"We're less than forty miles from the North Canadian," he said. "There's a chance we'll find the rest of the herd there."

"That don't make sense," Rux Carper said. "Why would they travel forty miles to water, when the Canadian River's at their backs?"

"Because they had standing water from the rain for a day and night," Dan said, "and since then, the wind's been out of the north. It might not make sense to you, Carper, but it does to a cow. If the wind brings the smell of water, you follow it, if it's fifty miles."

"That's gospel," Monte Walsh said. "I've seen the bastards stampede toward the smell of rain when it was somewheres in the Rocky Mountains."

That drew a laugh, for it was something every man had experienced at one time or another. Then, with a sigh, they mounted and rode out, faced with yet another day of brush popping. Dan thought it unlikely the longhorns would be found along the Canadian, as it wound its way toward the southeast, but it was something they couldn't afford to overlook.

"Today," he said, "I think we'll finish up on the Canadian. We'll cover both banks for ten miles to the east. That should account for any cows that have drifted back to water. The others have to be somewhere to the north, if not on the North Canadian, then along the creeks and streams to the south of it. Tomorrow we'll move the camp and the cows we've gathered. No use in our coming back here every night, when we'll be hunting cows somewhere to the north."

"Unless there's no water closer than the North Canadian," Aubin Chambers said.

"If I'm any judge," Dan said, "there'll be runoffs from the North Canadian. These missing cows have found water somewhere, and I don't think they've had to walk forty miles for it. If it's too far ahead, I think they would have drifted back here. Tomorrow we'll take what we've gathered and move a day's drive to the north."

Adeline DeVoe had wrestled with her problem for hours the night before, without gathering enough nerve to confront Lenore. She expected the girl to become angry, sulking the rest of the night, and she didn't want Dan dragged into the situation. At least not yet. Instead, she chose a time the next afternoon, while the riders were searching for the scattered herd.

"Come on, Lenore," Adeline said. "We'd better wash the rest of our blankets while we have the chance."

They found a place along the river where the water was shallow and the bottom was sandy. Once the heavy blankets were wet, it became a job for two people, just wringing the excess water from them. Finally the eight blankets were spread on the grass to dry, and the two women sank down to rest. With a sigh, Adeline said what was on her mind.

"Lenore, from now on, when Eagle leaves the camp, I don't want you going after him. For any reason."

"I'm almost seventeen," Lenore snapped, "and I'm a woman. What I do is my business."

"As long as you live with me," Adeline said, "what you do is my business, even if you're forty."

"You don't like Eagle," Lenore cried. "You never have."

"That has nothing to do with what we are discussing," Adeline said. "I know, just as everybody in the outfit knows, that the Indian finds a place to wash himself at the end of the day. That, I think, means that he takes off his clothes. Do you understand what I'm trying to tell you?"

"I wanted to talk to him, Ma, and there's always

somebody else around. Anyway, I saw him stripped after he'd been shot, so what does it matter?"

"You saw Dan stripped after he'd been shot," Adeline replied, "but I don't think it would be proper if you followed him for another look. Do you?"

"That wasn't why I followed him," Lenore said, refusing to look at her mother. "He saved me from the stampede, and I . . . I wanted to talk."

"How? He speaks almost no English."

"I know some Spanish," Lenore said.

"So what did he say?"

Lenore said nothing, still unable to face Adeline.

"Well?" Adeline asked.

"Oh, damn," Lenore sighed. "He was angry. He said he was naked, and told me to leave."

"Ah," Adeline said, striving mightily not to laugh, "and you didn't."

"No," Lenore replied, "and he . . .. he thought like you did, that I was just a foolish squaw, there to see him naked. He stomped out of the water, put on his clothes, and left me standing there, feeling like a fool."

"A homeless savage," Adeline said, "yet he's more a gentleman than you are a lady."

Lenore said nothing, her face averted, but Adeline wasn't finished.

"You're dead wrong about one thing, daughter. I do like the young Indian, Eagle. He's a man. An honorable man, and I'd like to know him better."

A fourth day scrounging the breaks along the Canadian produced less than two hundred longhorns.

"That does it," Dan said. "Tomorrow we'll take the drive north and continue our search there. We're still missing a dozen head of horses, and they're part of Chato's bunch."

"If he's somewhere to the north of us," Rux Carper

said, "he ought to know something about our missing horses and cows."

"They're not his responsibility," Dan said. "He made that clear before we took the trail. It's all up to us."

A few miles to the east, still camped on the Canadian, Chato had just had a report from a second scout. He now knew where the soldier fort was.

"Ah," Chato exulted, "soon we shall meet the Senor Montoya and his band of Mejicano *asnos* again. For the last time . . ."

16

Dan had their greatly reduced herd on the trail at first light, unsure as to where they would find water, but knowing there must be a source near enough to have attracted the elusive longhorns. Two hours from sundown they found it. A fast running creek angled in from the northwest, and there was a shout from the horse wranglers. The missing horses had been found.

"Good graze and good water," Dan said. "We'll make camp here and use the daylight that's left to hunt those missing cows."

"We ain't likely to find ten thousand on this creek," Rux Carper said.

"I don't expect to," Dan replied, "but we have to start somewhere. Do you have any better ideas?"

"Yeah," Carper said. "Let's just move on to the North Canadian, since we know that's where our cows are."

"We don't know that," Dan said coldly. "Suppose we skip these creeks and when we reach the North Canadian we don't find the rest of the herd? Do we then back-trail to the Canadian and search these creeks along the way?"

"By God, Carper," Wolf Bowdre said, "if you want to ride on to the North Canadian, go ahead. Dan's right. We might not find more than three or four hundred head along this creek, but it's more than we can afford to lose."

"I'll amen that," Sloan Kuykendall said. "What about the rest of you?"

There was a shouted chorus of agreement and some harsh looks directed at Rux Carper. Then the riders set out to search as much of the area as they could before dark. There were many mesquite and scrub oak thickets along the creek, and to everybody's amazement, the initial search produced more than four hundred head of longhorns. While it was still light enough to see, Dan, Wolf Bowdre, Chad Grimes, Cash Connolly, and Ward McNelly ran a tally.

"Give or take fifty head," Dan said when they had compared counts, "we have more than twelve thousand of them, and there may be more creeks before we reach the North Canadian."

The women of the outfit had long since divided themselves into two groups, taking turns cooking and cleaning up. When the meal was ready, the cooks then became servers, heaping the tin plates as the rest of the outfit passed along the serving line. Adeline DeVoe was serving each plate with a dried apple pie. On impulse, when Eagle reached her position, she placed two of the pies on the Cheyenne's plate.

"*Gracias,* Ma squaw," the Indian said solemnly.

The women on the serving line howled with laughter, and so did everybody else who heard. Those who didn't hear were later told by those who had, and from then on Adeline had to answer to "Ma squaw."

"He's heard Lenore call you Ma," Dan said. "You should be flattered. Except for Palo, he hardly ever talks to the rest of us."

The only one who didn't find the incident amusing was Lenore. She was still being taught Spanish by Nakita Elfego, and only Nakita realized and understood Lenore's frustration.

"He ignores me," Lenore fumed. "What must I do to get him to notice me?"

"In the night," Nakita said, "per'ap you creep naked into his blankets."

"You're no help, Nakita. I think that's what Ma expects me to do."

"She think you be *perra,* per'ap you become the *perra.* Why, no?"

"Because I'm not interested in him in that way," Lenore said. "Not yet. I just want him to notice me, to admit that I exist, but what does the damn Indian do? He adopts my mother."

"Per'ap you don' use right bait." Nakita giggled. "His belly become more excited than his other parts."

Indian Territory, North of the Canadian. Thursday, December 1, 1870.

Another day along the creek netted another two hundred head of longhorns, and the outfit again rode due north. Unfortunately, the rest of the streams they came upon were dry, running only after substantial rains.

"Suppose we ride more to the northeast," Wolf Bowdre suggested. "Even if the herd drifted due north, they still might have come downriver a ways once they reached the North Canadian."

"That's a possibility," Dan said. "If we bear to the northeast, we'll reach the North Canadian maybe ten miles nearer, and we can follow it all the way to Camp Supply. If we ride due north, after we reach the North Canadian, we'll still have to ride downriver, looking for cows."

"Well, hell," Rufe Keeler said, "let's just take the drive northeast to the North Canadian, follow it north, and look for cows as we go."

"I'm for it," Boyce Trevino said. "By reachin' the river this far south, we'll stand a better chance of finding the rest of the herd without back-trailin', and we'll have sure water all the way to Camp Supply."

"Unless somebody objects," Dan said, "we'll take the drive northeast to the North Canadian."

There were no objections. Only the crackle of the supper fires broke the stillness.

"In the morning, then," Dan said, "we'll head for the North Canadian, and hunt for cows as we go. This won't add more than ten miles to the distance we would have covered, and once we reach the river, we'll have water all the way to within a few miles of the Cimarron."

"We don't know for sure how far it is from here to the North Canadian," Rufe Keeler said. "I reckon that could mean dry camp tomorrow night."

"It could," Dan said, "but I doubt it. I can't imagine it being more than fifteen miles, and by starting early and driving hard, we can make it."

The evenings while Dan rode the first watch had become difficult for Adeline DeVoe, and likely, she suspected, even more difficult for Lenore. After supper was done, there was little to do except sleep, and Adeline was always awake until Dan returned at midnight. After Lenore's embarrassing rebuke by Eagle, and the Cheyenne's overtures toward Adeline, mother and daughter had little to talk about. This night was no different.

"I have to go to the bushes for a while," Lenore said.

"You shouldn't be going alone," Adeline told her. "I'll go with you."

"No need," Lenore said. "Nakita Elfego will go with me."

Adeline sighed. It was obvious she wasn't wanted, and she was damned if she would follow the girl, whatever the danger. Let the Comanches or the Kiowas have her. Lenore had become friendly with Nakita Elfego, but Adeline doubted the two would be together tonight. Lenore had used that as an excuse to escape her for a while. She had stopped short of warning Lenore not to go near the herd or the horse remuda in the dark. Lenore knew better.

Once free of Adeline, Lenore didn't go near the Elfegos. She didn't mind spending some time with Nakita, but not tonight. Eagle spent his nights with the horse wranglers or with the riders who circled the herd. Tonight he had ridden out with the first watch. The herd was bedded down on the other side of the creek, and three-quarters of a mile beyond was the horse remuda. Lenore began walking along the creek, unsure as to what she intended to do, knowing only that she was sick of the strained relationship between herself and her mother.

All I want, she told herself, is to be alone for a while, to walk along the creek. Maybe I'll see the riders as they circle the herd.

Liar, her conscience said. You're looking for the Indian.

All right, damn it, she said to the voice within, I'm looking for Eagle. What can it hurt if I stand on this side of the creek and watch for him?

You won't leave it at that, said the troublesome voice. You were told to stay away from the herd, from the horse remuda.

But as she neared the herd, she could see only a dark mass. She could be sure it was the drowsing herd only because a restless cow bawled. The night was so dark she was unable to see any of the circling riders. Suppose she crossed the creek and went closer, so she could see better? The trouble was, she had no idea how deep the creek might be. Her feet were bare, and she wore only a flannel shirt and Levi's. Feeling reckless, she skinned out of her Levi's and draped them around her neck. Wearing only the flannel shirt, she stepped into the creek. She caught her breath, for it was much colder than she had expected. But she continued, and finally she had to lift the tail of the shirt to keep it dry. She was about to climb out on the opposite bank when a strong hand caught her arm. She swung her fist as hard as she could and had the satisfaction of feeling it connect with a nose and mouth. But it cost her. She lost her Levi's in the swift running creek, and she felt the buttons pop off her shirt as her attacker seized the front of it. He dragged her out of the water and she drove a knee into his groin. That allowed her to break loose, but her antagonist caught the back of her shirt. Leaving him with it, she went head first into the creek, naked.

"Eagle," somebody shouted, "what'n hell's goin' on?"

"Cow in creek," the Indian said, thinking fast.

Lenore could barely move her arms and legs in the cold water. The Indian found one of her ankles and dragged her out on the bank.

"Th-Thank you, Eagle," Lenore said through chattering teeth.

"Damn *desnudo* squaw," the Indian said. He took to massaging her wet, half-frozen body with his big hands. He said nothing as he worked some feeling back into her. Finally he seized her, turned her belly down across the roan, and mounted behind her. He then crossed the creek, trotting the big horse toward the canvas shelter where the unfortunate Lenore would have some explaining to do. Lenore tried to slide off the horse before they were close enough for Adeline to hear the hoofbeats, but the Indian held her fast. The moon had risen, and combined with the starlight, the night wasn't nearly dark enough to suit Lenore. Eagle reined up before the shelter, and releasing his grip on Lenore, allowed her to slide off the horse. There was a chill wind now, and her legs were almost numb again. She landed ignominiously on her bare behind, only to find Adeline staring at her in total amazement. The Indian offered the only explanation he considered necessary.

"Fall in creek, Ma squaw. *Bonito pero torpe.*"*

With that he rode away. Adeline returned to their shelter and came out with a blanket. Gratefully, Lenore wrapped herself in it and stumbled into the shelter to escape the night wind. Adeline got more blankets, spread them over Lenore and began rubbing her feet. Finally she took a tin cup, went to the distant coffeepot, and returned with a steaming cup of coffee. Lenore took it, holding it in both hands, savoring the warmth. When the cup was empty, she put it down. Only then did she speak.

"I know what you're thinking. You might as well say it."

"If you know what I'm thinking," Adeline said, "then there's no point in me saying it."

"Oh, damn it, Ma, scream at me, take a switch to me, do *something.*"

"You want me to punish you so you'll feel better," Adeline said. "Well, it was you who told me you're a woman, so you'll not get out of it with a switching. I don't know what you did, how you did it, or why you did it, and I don't care. All that concerns me is that you may have caught your death from dunking yourself in the creek. I don't suppose I dare ask what became of your clothes?"

"He said I'm pretty, Ma."

"As well as clumsy," Adeline said, "and he had to see you stark naked to reach that conclusion."

Lenore was silent, and despite the girl's transgressions, Adeline smiled in the darkness.

The North Canadian. Saturday, December 3, 1870.

By Dan's estimate the drive to the North Canadian— driving northeast—was about twelve miles. It was too

* Pretty but clumsy

late in the day to begin a cow hunt, but to their surprise, almost a hundred head of their missing cattle had come to the river to drink.

"That's a good sign," Dan said. "Tomorrow we'll brush-pop both banks of the river, working our way northwest."

"There's a chance some of 'em may have drifted downriver," Walt Crump said. "It'd be easier, ridin' down there a ways now, than to have to double back."

"It would, for a fact," Dan said. "Suppose we take Walt's suggestion, and maybe four of us ride downriver another five miles or so? Do any of you object to that?"

"I don't," Wolf Bowdre said. "There's a chance we'll ride this river all the way to Camp Supply and still be missing more cows than we can afford to lose. I'd say let's cover another five—or even ten—miles downstream, so that we'll know we don't have to back-trail."

"That gets my vote," Skull Kimbrough said.

"And mine," other riders shouted.

"So be it," Dan said. "At first light I'll take Wolf, Skull, and Walt, and we'll ride as far as we have to, just to be sure we're not leaving any of our cows downriver. The rest of you will ride northwest. Any cows you gather, drive them back to camp, to the rest of the herd. We'll do the same. One more day and we should be ready to drive on to Camp Supply, rounding up our herd as we go."

Knowing that the soldier fort was only sixty-five miles to the north, Chato led his band northwest, bypassing the trail drive by many miles. One of Chato's lieutenants, Delgadito, listened as the renegade chief explained his tactics.

"We ride beyond the soldier fort," Chato said, "and there we wait for the Senor Montoya and his *perros.*"

"But what of the Tejanos and the *vacas?* We have agree to protect them."

"We do protect them," Chato said impatiently. "Why you think Montoya and his *bastardo perros* follow? They seek to kill the Tejanos, to steal the *vaca* and the *caballos*. To do these things, they must kill us, but they dare not until we are beyond the soldier fort. There, we will be waiting for them."

"Ah," Delgadito said, "the ambush, no?"

"*Si,*" Chato said. "We leave them for the *busardo* and the coyote to pick their bones."

To the south there was some disagreement between Santos Miguel Montoya and Burton Ledoux.

"Damn it, Montoya," Ledoux said, "the drive has turned to the northeast, while you and your men have gone to the northwest. Would you be kind enough to tell me just what the hell you have in mind?"

"The Tejano herd have stampede, senor," Montoya said, "and the Tejanos look for them along the river. How many times I tell you we do nothing until the drive is beyond the soldier fort? We follow Chato and the Mejicano Indios. You may follow the Tejanos and their cows to the soldier fort if you wish, but we do not."

With that, Montoya stalked angrily away. Loe Hagerman said nothing, but the antagonistic Black Bill turned on Ledoux.

"For three damn months I been layin' out in the brush eatin' beans and drinkin' bad coffee. Now I aim to stop by that soldier camp for a bait of decent grub and a shot of whiskey."

"Go ahead," Ledoux said. "You heard Montoya. Him and his bunch won't be going near the fort, nor will Chato and his men. So you go waltzing right in there, and you'll be mighty easy to remember. Montoya aims to ambush the Mejicanos and then the Tejanos. That kind of killing won't go unnoticed with the army sending out patrols. We'll follow Montoya, bypass the fort, and I don't want to hear another damn gripe out of you."

Loe Hagerman grinned, earning for himself a murderous look from Black Bill. The trio rode on, following Montoya and his bunch.

At dawn Dan took Wolf, Skull, and Walt, and the four of them rode along the North Canadian to the southeast, while the rest of the outfit followed the river upstream.

"I'll come off like a damn fool for suggestin' this," Walt said, "if we waste all day and ride in with no cows."

"It's a good idea, whether we find any cows or not," Dan said, "because we aren't sure where the cows are. If we moved on without searching this part of the river, there's always a chance we'd have to come back, and that would take even more time."

"Damn right," Wolf said. "It always takes longer when you don't do it right the first time."

"It's some aggravatin' not findin' any tracks," Skull said, "but there was plenty of rain after the stampede."

Despite the lack of sign, they began finding remnants of the scattered herd. First there were only a few cows, but the number grew as they followed the river southeast.

"We'll leave these bunches where they are," Dan said, "and ride on until they run out. Then we'll drive the final bunch upstream, adding the others as we go along. I think we're going to do surprisingly well."

And they did. Well before sundown, Dan and his companions drove eleven hundred head of the missing longhorns upriver. The rest of the outfit rode in with another nine hundred head.

"It's time for a tally," Dan said. "Tomorrow we'll take the herd upriver, adding to it as we go. We shouldn't be more than four or five days south of Camp Supply, and we'll have sure water all the way, so we can devote our time to gathering cows wherever we find them."

Wolf, Dan, Walt, Skull, and Palo ran individual tallies and then compared their totals. By the time they were finished, supper was almost ready. Dan announced the results.

"All of us agree on 17,300. That means there's twenty-seven hundred still loose, and that's if we settle for twenty thousand. Before the stampede, we had an extra five hundred and fifty."

"That's still too damn many to lose," Boyce Trevino said. "I say we find every blessed one of 'em before we quit."

"I'll buy that," Skull Kimbrough said, "as long as we find 'em along the North Canadian, between here and Camp Supply. If we don't find 'em there, we got nowhere else to search."

"That's how it stacks up," Dan said. "We'll have to take what we find along the river, on the way to Camp Supply, and let that be final."

Breakfast was usually a hurried affair, while supper was just the opposite. Riders lingered over coffee, while the women who had done the cooking for the day had their own suppers. On the days when Adeline and Lenore weren't part of the group doing the cooking, they took their supper with Dan. This was such a day, and to the surprise of them all, Eagle joined them. He said nothing, hunkering down with his tin plate in one hand and eating with the other. His first few meals he had eaten with his hands, but he had since developed a remarkable dexterity with knife and fork, simply by observing the others as they ate. He never seemed to get enough coffee. When he put down his tin cup, it was almost empty. Lenore took it to the nearest coffeepot, refilled it, and returned it to him.

"*Gracias,*" the Cheyenne said.

Dan winked at Lenore, who could scarcely contain herself. It was the first time the stubborn Indian had spoken directly to her without insulting her. When he had finished eating and had drunk the rest of his coffee, he took the tin plate, cup, and eating tools to the huge iron pot where they would be washed.

"I was startin' to wonder what you'd have to do to get that hombre to say something to you," Dan said. "Getting thrown in front of a stampede didn't work."

"She has a way about her," Adeline said innocently.

Dan laughed, and Lenore became embarrassed. Dan had said nothing, but Lenore almost knew Adeline had told him about Eagle bringing her in belly down across his horse, jaybird naked. Lenore was on the serving line at breakfast the next morning, and instead of the usual two biscuits, she gave Eagle four. He said nothing, but closed his left eye in a slow wink.

"*Hai,*" Nakita Elfego said, having witnessed the act, "Lenore bait Injun with biscuits."

Everybody within hearing laughed, Adeline the loudest of all, but Lenore didn't care. At least he knew she existed, and she thought he might be on the brink of seeing her as something more than a clumsy squaw.

Along the North Canadian. Monday, December 5, 1870.

The outfit took the trail at dawn. Now that Silas was gone, Fanny Bowdre drove the lead wagon. The wranglers had become adept at handling the remuda, and the horses took the trail readily. The lead steers were driven into line, and the rest of the herd followed. Accompanied by Eagle, Dan rode well ahead of Fanny Bowdre's wagon. Any of the missing cows Dan and Eagle flushed out, they would drive near enough for the flank and swing riders to simply run the strayed animals in with the moving herd. It worked extremely well. Some bunches of cows Dan and Eagle discovered were large enough to run in at the tag end of the herd. Dan tried to keep a tally in his head, but soon gave it up, as the cattle became more numerous. It began to look as though they

might recover all the missing longhorns, and wishing to
know their progress for the day, Dan halted the drive
early enough for a tally. For that purpose, he had left
the herd strung out along the river for a mile. He sent
Monte Walsh, Tobe Barnfield, Ward McNelly, Rux
Carper, Cash Connolly, and Chad Grimes to run the
talley. When it was finished, all the riders brought the
herd into a bunch, where they would be bedded down
for the night. Dan announced the results of the count at
suppertime.

"We added another fifteen hundred head, bringing
our total to 18,800."

"Another day like today," Kirby Wilkerson said, "and
we'll have 'em all."

"We may not have another day as good as this," Wolf
Bowdre said. "We're quite a ways from where that stampede started, and there's a limit to how far longhorns
will run from a storm. I'd say these brutes we're finding
now hit the river quite a ways south of here and just
grazed their way north, along the river."

"That may be the case," Dan said. "We did a good
search downriver, so I think tomorrow may be the end
of the gather."

"Riders comin'," Denny DeVoe shouted as he galloped his horse downriver, "and this bunch don't look
like Texas Rangers."

There was an even dozen of them. They rode in from
the east and looked like anything but lawmen. They
rode good horses, every man wore a Colt, and most of
them carried saddle guns as well. They reined up fifty
yards from the dying supper fire, apparently awaiting an
invitation to advance. But they didn't get one. Dan
didn't like the looks of them, and went to meet them on
foot. He didn't have to ask for backup. Wolf Bowdre
walked to his left, Monte Walsh to his right, and other
riders were behind him. The lead rider sat with one leg
hooked over his saddle horn, a gone-out cigarette dan-

gling from his lips. He wore range clothes, as did all the others. Dan and his companions halted a few yards away, waiting.

"I reckon," the man said, "you ain't invitin' us in."

"You're right," Dan said. "I'm not."

"That could be tooken as downright unneighborly."

"Take it any way you like," Dan said, "and unless you got some mighty convincing reason for being here, the bunch of you turn around and ride out."

"I'm Mitch Rowden," the stranger said, "and I ain't used to bein' talked down to. Fact is, me and my riders come by to do you a favor. I don't know where you're takin' them cows, and it don't make no difference. We got a kind of insurance business. For, say, ten cents a head, we can guarantee you that you'll git where you're goin'. Elsewise, come dark, some coyotes could just scatter them cows to hell an' gone, if you git what I mean."

The roar of the Colt seemed unnaturally loud, and Rowden's hat leaped from his head. Dan didn't return the weapon to its holster. Instead, he walked a step nearer, and when he spoke, his voice was cold, flint-hard.

"Any coyotes comin' near this herd will be shot dead or hung from a limb for buzzard bait, if you get what I mean. Now ride, the lot of you, and keep ridin'."

Wolf Bowdre's Colt roared, and to Dan's left a rider pitched out of his saddle, dropping his half-drawn weapon.

It was enough. The rest of them reined their horses around, careful to keep their hands clear of their weapons. One of the riders had caught the reins of the riderless horse. The fallen man was left where he lay, and the rest of them rode out.

"Damn it," Wolf Bowdre said, "where's Chato and his bunch when we need 'em?"

"They're likely scouting ahead," Dan replied. "We're

not much more than thirty miles south of Camp Supply, and I doubt Chato expected this kind of trouble, with the military so near. For that reason, I'm not sure we can count on them tonight, and maybe not until after we've passed the fort. They'll be shying clear of the soldiers. Tonight I think we'll all ride watch. We're gathering cows from the last stampede, and I don't even want to think about the possibility of another."

"Me neither," Skull Kimbrough said. "Let's take our Winchesters and cut them varmints down before they get within hollerin' distance of our cows."

His response was quickly echoed by the others. Dan stripped the dead man of his Colt, pistol belt, holster, and a Bowie knife. These he presented to Eagle.

"Gracias," the Cheyenne said, pleased.

"Kirby," Dan said, "you and Sloan drag that dead varmint off in some arroyo and cave some dirt in on him. Then we'll saddle up and wait for that bunch of coyotes. It'll be a long night, and when we break for coffee, we'll do it two at a time. Nobody rides away from the herd without the rest of us knowing. If we don't know you're gone, when you return, you could be shot by mistake. Ride careful, all of you."

17

*I*t was a long night, with no sleep for any of the riders. Most of the women were awake as well, and those who had guns kept them close at hand. But nothing disturbed the serenity of the night. Far to the west there was an almost constant blaze of lightning, and the wind grew noticeably colder. Even the stars seemed to withdraw, as the storm grew in intensity, and the first cold rain began three hours before dawn. The six wagons had been lined up in pairs of two. With canvas stretched from one to the other, there was a dozen feet of shelter between the two. There was then room for three cook fires and for the outfit to hunker out of the rain and eat. Despite the possibility of attack, Dan had those who were to do the day's cooking begin the breakfast almost two hours before first light.

"I want the herd moving as soon as it's light enough to see," Dan told the riders. "I look for this rain to change to snow sometime during the day, and we're in a poor position to weather a storm."

The wind and rain swept in out of the north, and with the herd trailing along the North Canadian to the northwest, it was purely hell with the lid off. The longhorns wanted to turn their backs to the storm, to drift with it, and their every move was dedicated to that end. Dan rode from one end of the herd to the other, encouraging the riders, and then rode upriver, ahead of the drive. There had to be a canyon somewhere to hole up and weather the storm. The wind and rain were bad enough, but when it changed to snow, forcing the longhorns into it would become impossible. While this was new country to them all, Dan had heard of these winter storms that swept down from the Rockies, dropping the temperature to zero and below across the plains of Kansas and Nebraska. Already his hands and feet were numb, and the fierce wind tugged at his tied-down hat, forcing frigid fingers beneath the scarf that protected his ears. The terrain became more rugged and the river widened, its banks becoming higher, but there was no overhang. Willows and underbrush crowded the river banks, offering sanctuary for the longhorns, but Dan rode on. Eventually he found what he was seeking. A broad canyon cut away to the south, a spill-off from the river when the water was high. Now, however, there was but a narrow stream, and while the canyon walls had no protective overhang, they were high enough to provide some shelter from the storm. Trouble was, there was almost no graze, not even enough for the horses for more than a day. But it would have to do. Already there were big, wet snowflakes mixing with the rain. Dan rode back the way he had come until he met the first wagon, reining his horse around until he rode alongside it.

"Fanny," he shouted, "there's a canyon ahead, a spill-off from the river. We'll take the wagons in there, but you'll have to circle to the south until the walls flatten out enough to get in. Drive straight on. I'll be back in time to guide you in."

Dan wheeled his horse and rode on. The rest of the wagons would follow the first. "Canyon ahead," he shouted to the horse wranglers. "Follow the wagons." Dan rode on, and the first rider he met was Wolf Bowdre.

"We can't hold 'em, Dan," Bowdre shouted against the wind. "The varmints are breakin' away and holin' up in the brush along the river."

"We'll have to drive the rest of them in there," Dan shouted, riding closer. "There's a canyon ahead for the wagons and the horse remuda, but not one-tenth big enough for the herd. Ride back to the drag and take word to the flank and swing riders as you go. Run the herd into the brakes along the river, and then be sure all the riders make it to the canyon ahead."

Dan rode ahead, catching up to the wagon Fanny Bowdre drove. Riding past it, he shouted to Fanny and then began a swing to the south. Reaching the canyon rim, he found it still too high for the wagons to descend. He had to wait until the Bowdre wagon caught up. He then rode south for more than a mile before the canyon played out. From there he rode north, enjoying the blessed relief as the canyon deepened enough to hold the storm at bay. When he looked back, he was able to see the wagons coming. He waited until the first one caught up.

"Fanny, go on until you're near where this spill-off breaks away from the river. There's a bend where it snakes off toward the southwest for a ways, and that's where we'll have the most protection."

Dan rode back along the canyon, passing the rest of the wagons. When he saw the first of the horses coming, he sighed with relief. Now he had only to guide the rest of his half-frozen outfit in out of the storm. He doubted the riders would have too much trouble driving the longhorns into the river brakes, since that was where they obviously wanted to go, but he rode north along the canyon rim until he reached the south bank of the river. Here the storm struck him with all its fury. The rain had ceased, and the snow blew so thick and fast he was unable to see more than a few feet downriver. From the stormy gloom a rider appeared. It was Eagle, and he

rode slowly, allowing others to follow him. Lacking a
coat, the Cheyenne had cut a hole in the center of a
blanket, allowing it to flow around him like a tent. Behind him rode the women from the drag, slumped in
their saddles, their heads down to keep the wind-driven
snow from their faces. Words were unnecessary. Dan
just pointed south, and Eagle turned his horse, leading
his companions along the canyon rim.

Dan rode downriver, concerned for the riders who
had been stuck with getting the troublesome longhorns
settled in along the river. While there was nowhere else
for the brutes to take shelter from the storm, they had a
cantankerous habit of doing exactly the opposite of
whatever was for their own good. Dan rode almost two
miles before he saw the first of the weary riders plodding toward him. They had their heads down, and he
couldn't recognize even one of the four.

"Canyon to the south," he shouted. "Follow it until it
levels out, then ride north to our camp." There was no
sign they had heard him, and he rode on. He hoped
Eagle had accounted for all the drag riders. That would
leave only the men, and four of them were on their way
to shelter. He must find fourteen more, and they appeared in twos and threes, plodding like specters from
an almost invisible wall of snow. Wolf Bowdre was the
last, and Dan was able to recognize him when he
shouted above the roar of the wind. Dan reined up,
turned his horse, and the two men rode side by side.
Reaching the canyon, Dan led the way south until their
horses could safely descend the rim.

"God," Bowdre said when they had escaped the
storm, "I thought we'd never get the varmints into the
brakes. Hated like hell to do it. We'll be a week chasin'
'em out of there."

"No help for it," Dan replied. "If we'd left them on
the plain, they'd have turned their backs to the storm
and drifted to God knows where. Besides, with them

dug in along the river, we won't have to worry about Rowden and his bunch delivering that stampede they threatened."

"You're dead right," Bowdre said. "We done the only damn thing we could do, and when the storm's done, we'll have to undo it. Until then, let's cozy up to a warm fire and get ourselves on the outside of some good grub and some hot coffee."

The hot coffee was ready, and although it wasn't quite midday, a hot meal was being prepared.

"Everybody's had a hard time of it," Fanny Bowdre said as Dan and Wolf dismounted. "We thought hot food and coffee would help ease the pain."

"You thought exactly right," Wolf replied. "It'll help get us through till supper. Soon as we've thawed out some, some of us can ride down canyon and snake in some more wood. I reckon we're gonna be needing it."

"We wouldn't have lasted another mile in this storm," Chad Grimes said, "so I ain't findin' fault, but by tomorrow this bunch of hosses will have et every blade of grass in this canyon."

"We'll have to hope this storm blows itself out," Dan said. "When it does, we can graze the horses somewhere else. Thank God horses and mules have sense enough to dig through snow to get at the grass."

The riders were forced out of the shelter of the canyon to find enough windblown and lightning-struck trees to feed their fires, but the temporary fury of the storm was bearable. Out of the wind and snow, with plenty of firewood, food, and hot coffee, they counted their blessings. The storm swept on, and they scarcely knew when day ended and night began. When they judged it was suppertime, they ate. Afterward, fortified with much hot coffee, Eagle took the whetstone Dan offered and spent the next several hours sharpening his newly acquired Bowie knife. While he seemed to appreciate the belt, the holster, and the Colt, the Bowie held a particular fascination for him. He swapped the big knife from one hand to the other in a border shift.

"By God," Rux Carper said, "I ain't sure it was such a good idea, him havin' that knife. He's startin' to give me the willies."

Eagle drove the Bowie into the ground and fixed hard eyes on Carper. He had mastered enough English to understand most of Carper's criticism, and he didn't like it. Carper flushed under the cold scrutiny, and Kirby Wilkerson laughed, enjoying Carper's discomfiture.

"The Indian don't like you, Carper," Monte Walsh said. "God only knows why." His sarcasm wasn't lost on the others, and Elanora, Carper's long-suffering wife, got up and slipped away in the darkness. While Dan was as fed up as the others with Carper's continual grousing, this was no time for such bickering among themselves.

"Being snowed in like this," Dan said, "I reckon we all get a mite cramped with one another's company. All of you are entitled to your personal gripes and aggravations. Just don't be so damn quick to air them at a time when you might rub somebody else the wrong way. I've given Eagle a Bowie and a Colt at no expense to any of us, and as part of this outfit, he deserves to be armed. None of you have been harmed as a result of that, and if you are, then you can blame me. Once we reach Dodge, those of you who don't like me or my decisions can go your separate ways. Until then, we're an outfit, and the will of the majority rules. *Comprender?*"

"Dan's right," Wolf Bowdre said. "Eagle's a *bueno hombre,* and he has as much right to his weapons as any of you."

Most of the others were quick to agree. Dan suspected that some—if not all—had seized upon this as much a means of showing their dislike for Carper as support for the Indian, but it didn't matter. The incident passed, and a better mood prevailed. Lenore refilled Eagle's tin cup with hot coffee, and produced grins and some crude jokes. Playing on the levity of the moment, the Indian winked at Lenore, and she became flustered. The laughter was at her expense, and everybody's good humor seemed restored. The storm roared on, the cold grew more intense, and there was nothing to do but wait.

In a similar camp a dozen miles downriver, Mitch Rowden and his ten men waited for the storm to let up. They played poker, using cartridges for chips, and cursed the storm. The clamor awoke Rowden, who had been trying to sleep.

"Damn it," Rowden shouted, "you're drowning out the storm."

"You ain't told us what you aim to do when the storm's done," growled one of his companions. "One of them cow nurses cashed in Gillis. You aim to let that pass?"

"Why not?" Rowden said angrily. "Gillis was a damn fool, pullin' his iron with all that bunch expectin' it. When this storm dies, we'll be stalking that outfit, but not to avenge Gillis. We're goin' after that horse remuda."

"I'm fer that!" one of the renegades shouted. "I didn't see a one of them cayuses that was branded. What you reckon's the reason fer that?"

"Who knows?" Rowden said. "We can trail them broncs to Fort Leavenworth and sell 'em to the army. Saddle-broke, they'll bring a hundred dollars a head. It'll be the easiest money we ever made. Near legal too, without brands."

It was something they all could appreciate, and they laughed, their good humor restored.

On the North Canadian. Friday, December 9, 1870.

By dawn of the third day after the storm began, it was over, but the wait wasn't. From the snowdrifts within the canyon, it wasn't difficult to imagine what they were like elsewhere. But the graze was gone, and the horse re-muda picked wistfully along the barren floor of the can-yon. There was water, and that had helped, but the animals were gaunt.

"We have to get them out of here where they can find some graze," Dan said, "and we have to do it today. The mules too."

"Let us do it," Denny DeVoe begged. "That's a job for the horse wranglers."

"That's a job for the wranglers and about five more good men," Dan replied. "We're talking about every horse and mule in the outfit."

"I don't think we ought to take 'em all at the same time," Tobe Barnfield said. "I don't like being left total afoot."

"Me neither," Ward McNelly agreed.

"I have no intention of taking them all at the same time," Dan said. "I aim to take everybody's favorite mount first. We'll bring them in at midday, replacing them with Chato's herd and the mules. For as long as we're snowed in, we'll swap them out every day, so that each animal gets some graze."

"That'll help," Wolf Bowdre said, "but they'll still look half starved until they're back on good grass full-time. Soon as the drifts are down, we got to get out of here."

"We will," Dan said, "but for now, we'll have to make do. Wranglers, you'll need some help. Palo, take Rufe, Monte, Kirby, and Walt. Ride with the wranglers and take the first of the horses to graze. I doubt they'll have their fill, but bring them in at midday so the others can have their turn. Don't take them any farther than you have to, and if there's trouble, fire three warning shots."

"All them damn cows got to be chased out of the brush," Aubin Chambers said. "When do we start?"

"When enough snow melts for them to see the grass,"

Dan replied. "It'll take that long to get the horses into any decent shape."

Three hours into the day an anemic sun crept out, but did nothing toward melting the snow. The bitter cold continued. A mile south of where the canyon played out, there was sufficient graze for the horses. At noon the first bunch was brought back to the canyon, then the first of the remuda. The rest of the horses and mules were then taken to graze. In the afternoon a new bunch of gray clouds marched across the western horizon, swallowing the sun two hours early. It was going to be a short graze for the horse remuda and the mules. As the gray of the sky deepened, Dan became anxious. He knew his riders were allowing the animals to graze as long as possible, but his unease got the best of him. Darkness was less than an hour away when he saddled his horse.

"I'm ridin' down there," he said. "They've been out too long."

"Eagle go," the Cheyenne said.

"Come on, then," Dan said.

But they were too late. The three warning shots shattered the stillness, and before the echo had died away, there was a rattle of distant gunfire.

"Come on," Dan shouted. His horse was off and running, Eagle's roan right behind him. Other riders were saddling their horses. The gunfire died away long before Dan and Eagle were near enough to join the fight. Dan feared the worst, and found his fears justified. The horse remuda and the mules were gone, leaving only the mounts belonging to the riders. Six of them knelt around the three who lay in the snow. Dan hit the ground running, and he saw the tragedy in their faces before anybody said a word.

"Dan," Tobe Barnfield said, "Gus Wilder's dead. Monte and Kirby are hurt bad. They hit us while we was split up, gettin' the string gathered."

Gus, Spence Wilder's only son, was just fifteen. He had been shot through the chest, and his dead hands still clutched the unfired Winchester. There was the thud of hooves as the rest of the outfit arrived, and they all sat their saddles in shocked silence as Spence Wilder fell on his knees beside his dead son. All of them—even Dan—had been shocked into silence. But not the Indian.

"Find," Eagle said. "Kill."

Without a word, Spence Wilder seized the Winchester that had belonged to Gus. He tossed it to Eagle, and the mounted Cheyenne caught it. Kicking his horse into a gallop, he followed the tracks of the stampeded horses. His act shocked the rest of the riders into action.

"Tobe," Dan said, "help Spence with Gus. Boyce, Rufe, Duncan, and Ward, rig some blanket slings and get Monte and Kirby back to camp. Gid, Pablo, and Denny, back to camp. The rest of you come with me. We have some debts to pay."

Already it was dark, but a rising wind had swept the clouds away. The starlight against the white of the snow left a trail anyone could have followed. They rode hard but never caught up to the Indian. Dan and his riders reined up. It was time to rest the horses. The moon was on the rise, and combined with the starlight, Dan could see clearly the grim faces of the eleven men who rode with him. There was Wolf Bowdre, Rux Carper, Skull Kimbrough, Chad Grimes, Hiram Beard, Garret Haddock, Sloan Kuykendall, Walt Crump, Palo Elfego, Aubin Chambers, and Cash Connolly.

"I don't like the looks of this," Bowdre said. "We're beggin' for an ambush."

"I don't think so," Dan said. "We have an ace in the hole. Eagle's out there, somewhere ahead of us. But you're right, Wolf. This bunch won't run too far. We've ridden about as far as we safely can without finding and disarming their ambush. We'll just stand pat for a few minutes."

He offered no explanation, and for a change nobody questioned his judgment. To a man, they knew the rustlers couldn't allow the pursuit to continue, and that meant an ambush. Suddenly, from somewhere ahead, there came a scream so agonized it might have emerged straight from the pits of hell. Just as suddenly it was choked off, its absence leaving the silence all the more intense.

"God Almighty," Skull Kimbrough said. "What was *that*?"

"Eagle's found the ambush," Dan said, "and I'd say he's just cut out the gizzard of one of the thieving varmints who was waitin' for us."

"Thoughtful of him to let the coyote sing for the others," Wolf said.

"That's the idea," Dan said. "Fear can be a more powerful weapon than a loaded gun. That should force the rest of them to run, and we'll ride the bastards down. But we'll wait a little longer. Eagle may not be finished."

There was a second screech as terrifying as the first, and again it was cut short.

"We can advance now," Dan said. "Hold your fire until somebody fires at us."

By moon and starlight, across the white of the snow, they could see the horseman coming long before they could identify him. He gripped the Winchester in both hands, holding it over his head. Dan and his companions reined up, waiting. Eagle didn't waste words.

"Two coyote die, two run," the Cheyenne said.

"Let's ride," Dan said. "We won't give 'em a chance to lay for us again."

Eagle led out, Dan and the rest of the outfit following without hesitation. They soon found tracks where two rustlers had fled the scene of the intended ambush.

They were riding hard to join their companions, and when the Texans topped a hill, they could see the stampeded horses being driven up a rise a few hundred yards ahead. There was a shout as the rustlers sighted their pursuers.

"After them," Dan shouted, kicking his horse into a fast gallop. "Ride them down and shoot to kill."

The rustlers realized the gravity of their situation, for they abandoned the horses they'd stolen and rode for their lives. Would the Texans give up the chase, settling for the recovery of their horses? They would not. The horses could be recovered later. Led by Eagle, the Texans rode hard. Aubin Chambers cut loose with his Winchester long before he was within range.

"Dámn it," Dan shouted, "hold your fire and ride."

To hit a moving target while firing from the back of a running horse was virtually impossible under the best of conditions, and all the more so at night. Dan could see the shadowy mouth of a canyon to the south, and it soon became obvious the outlaws hoped to reach this sanctuary. It was reason enough for Chambers becoming impatient with his Winchester, for once the rustlers reached the canyon, it would become a close-quarters fight. Dan and Eagle were well ahead of the rest of the outfit, and the Indian set the stage for the fight when he caught up to the last of the fleeing thieves. Eagle threw himself at the other rider, wrestling the man to the ground. The Cheyenne was on his feet, cat-quick, his Bowie flashing in the starlight. Dan drew his Colt and shot a rustler out of the saddle, only to have a third drop back and leap at him. Dan's left foot was caught in the stirrup, and he had to contend with his horse dragging him a few yards while he and his adversary fought for possession of Dan's Colt. The startled horse finally drew up, watching with interest as the two men wrestled and fought in the snow. The Colt roared, and Dan struggled to his feet, leaving his adversary dying. He managed to reach the trailing reins before the horse spooked and ran. Eagle hadn't been so fortunate. While he had slain his opponent in the hand-to-hand fight, the horse had run from the smell of blood, leaving the Indian afoot. Dan could see him running across the frozen snow toward two struggling men. One of the pair had a death-dealing advantage. Astride his opponent, Dan could see the flash of the Bowie's blade as it was drawn high for the fatal thrust. But the hand froze, losing its grip, as Eagle's thrown Bowie slammed into the man's chest. He toppled sideways and fell on his back. Eagle paused for only as long as it took to retrieve his Bowie, then went on, seeking one of the horses that ran loose. When Dan reached the fallen man, he found Rux Carper sitting there looking dazed.

"My God," Carper wheezed, "I was a dead man, but the Indian . . . he saved me. Why?"

"You'll have to ask him," Dan said. He rode on. There had been no more shooting. If there was more fighting, it had to be with the lethal Bowies. Dan could see a distant rider coming and reined up, unsure of the man's identity. The other rider reined up, identifying himself.

"Bowdre," he shouted. "Hold your fire."

Dan waited until Bowdre reached him. Wolf's shirt was ripped from the collar to the waist, a thin trail of blood marking the course of the knife.

"Two of the bastards outrode us," Wolf said. "Heavy mesquite thickets at the other end of this canyon, and they've had time to find cover. We nailed nine of them, but includin' the two he took out of the ambush, I reckon the Indian accounted for four. Three of our men are down."

"Bad?"

"Bad enough," Bowdre said. "Hiram and Sloan caught some lead, but nothin' in their vitals. Cash took a cut from shoulder to elbow. He was bleedin' like a stuck hog, but Palo and Skull was tendin' to him."

"Let's round up our mounts," Dan said, "and get the wounded men back to camp. With Kirby and Monte, that makes five."

"I wish to God that was the worst of it," Bowdre said. "There's Spence's boy, Gus. It's hell on Spence, but it'll damn near killed Amy."

"That's the worst part about two of the varmints escaping," Dan said. "We can't be sure that one of them didn't fire the shot that killed Gus."

Hiram Beard and Sloan Kuykendall had each taken a slug in the shoulder, Hiram in his left, and Sloan in his right.

"Good news," Sloan said, "is that we're alive. Bad news is, won't either of us be worth a damn on a cow hunt. Not for a good two weeks."

Cash Connolly leaned against his horse, his left arm hooked around the saddle horn. His right arm hung limp, swathed in bandannas.

"Cut deep," Palo said.

"Those wounds need attention," Dan said. "You men have lost some blood. Can you ride?"

"I can," Kuykendall said. "No bones broke."

"So can I," Hiram Beard said.

"I'll manage," Cash Connolly said. But he was weak, and it took three attempts before he was able to mount.

Palo and Skull had managed to catch the rest of their mounts, and they rode back the way they had come, picking up Rux Carper and Aubin Chambers. Neither man had accounted for himself very well in the fight, and Dan suspected that was the reason for their silence. Nobody mentioned the stampeded horses. Without the rustlers driving them, the animals would soon stop to graze, and becoming thirsty, drift north to the river. The horses could wait, but the wounded men could not.

"I ain't so sure them two escaped," Garret Haddock

said. "Last I seen of that Indian, he was hot on their heels."

"He's been more use to us than Chato's whole damn bunch," Skull said, "and he ain't cost us nothin' but a hoss, a knife, and a gun."

"He's a fighting man," Dan said, "but don't sell Chato short. There has to be some reason for his riding so far ahead. We took some nasty blows tonight, but it was nothing we couldn't handle. Except for Gus."

"God, yes," Cash Connolly groaned. "I feel guilty, ridin' in with just a cut arm, and the kid lying dead."

Dan said nothing, but he wondered how Rux Carper and Aubin Chambers felt. While Carper had made a poor showing, Dan suspected that Chambers had merely ridden into the canyon for show, and had not taken part in the fight at all.

18

While the wounds of Monte and Kirby hadn't been critical, the death of young Gus Wilder had shrouded the camp with an aura of gloom, and the arrival of three more wounded men did nothing to dispel it. Amy Wilder was in shock, her empty eyes staring into the fire. The rest of the women moved woodenly about, boiling more water, seeing to the hurts of the wounded men. There was little the men could do except watch helplessly. While the Texans had taken a terrible toll, there was no undoing the damage the renegades had done. The very spirit of the outfit seemed about to wither and die. The wounded men had been brought near the fire, and sleeping fitfully, they often cried out in pain. Spence Wilder was lost in a sorrowful world of his own, kneeling by the blanket-wrapped body of Gus. Dan hunkered down beside a silent Denny DeVoe. Adeline took his cup, filled it with hot coffee from one of the pots, and returned it to him. Wolf Bowdre joined Dan, and after a few moments of silence, spoke.

"My God, everybody's got a bait of the whim-whams. You'd think it was the end of the world."

"I reckon it is for Spence and Amy Wilder," Dan said, "and it's impossible for the rest of us not to share their grief. Any or all of the five wounded men might have died, and they still could. There'll be three days of fighting infection before they start to mend."

"Yeah," Bowdre said, "and it'll be another week before they can ride, if then."

"That won't matter, where the drive's concerned," Dan said. "We'll be lucky if we're able to gather the horses and longhorns by then. Tomorrow, I aim to go after the horses. After that, we'll start gathering the cattle. They'll be safe enough until the snow begins to melt. Then they'll begin to drift, looking for better graze."

"I know it's a painful time," Bowdre said, "but we need to get everybody together for some talk. There's a time for grief, but then you got to put it behind you and move on."

"I know," Dan said. "I reckon we'll have to bury Gus in the morning, and I don't feel right, getting anything else ahead of that. A burying is a thing that's got to be done, more for the sake of the living than for the dead. I aim to bring everybody together afterward. These folks are shocked, cut deep, but they're whang-leather tough. We'll pick up and move on."

It was a long night, the groans and incoherent mumblings of the wounded men making sleep almost impossible. The medicine chest that had belonged to Silas had gone up with the wagon, and all they had for disinfectant was the two gallons of whiskey Dan brought from Fort Griffin. There was just a little more than a gallon remaining when all the wounds had been treated.

"Wolf," Dan said, "take what's left of the whiskey and conceal it in your wagon. We'll need it for these wounded men when the fever takes them."

Dan hunkered down with Adeline and Lenore, wishing they had some privacy, some means of escaping the cries of the wounded. Lenore spoke to Dan twice before she got through to him.

"Where's Eagle?"

"I don't know," Dan said truthfully. "Two of the rustlers outrode us and escaped into a canyon. I suspect he went after them."

"He may be hurt," Lenore said. "I want to go look for him."

"You'll do no such thing," Adeline said.

"That's one Indian who can take care of himself," Dan said. "He killed four of that bunch himself, knifing two of them after they were forted up to ambush us."

"My God," Adeline said, "he's a savage."

"It's not savage, killing men who tried to kill him, to kill our riders," Lenore said. "That's noble and brave."

"He's that and more," Dan agreed, "and if he doesn't ride in tonight, I think we'll find him with the horses. We'll go looking for them in the morning."

Soon as it was light enough to see, the riders took turns digging a grave for Gus Wilder. When there was a burying, everything else waited. Even first coffee. The ceremony was sad and brief. Dan read passages from the Bible, and then stayed to help Tobe Barnfield and Walt Crump fill the grave. There had been a significant change in the weather during the night, and after the bone-chilling cold, the west wind seemed almost warm. There were gray clouds piling up to the west.

"There's rain comin'," Tobe predicted, "and it ain't far off."

"Let it come," Walt said. "It'll git rid of this snow."

"That means we'll have to gather the horses today," Dan said, "and be ready to go after the longhorns tomorrow. The graze along the river's been pretty skimpy, and as soon as they can see grass elsewhere, they'll drift."

Breakfast was a silent affair, the tragedy and the burying strong on their minds. When they were done, Dan spoke.

"There's rain on the way, and with the melting of the snow, we'll have to be ready to gather the herd. This morning we're going after the horses. Or some of us are. Some of you will have to remain in camp. Wolf, Skull, Palo, Garret, Chad, and Walt, you'll be riding with me. The rest of you—including the horse wranglers—will remain here, protecting the camp. Now those of you going with me, saddle up and let's ride."

Reaching the slope where the fight had begun, they found the coyote-ravaged bodies of the rustlers Dan and Eagle had accounted for, but riding into the canyon, they discovered the other bodies were gone.

*"Espectro,"** Palo said.

"They didn't leave on their own," Dan said. "They were dragged away for a reason."

Around a bend in the canyon a horse nickered, and Dan's horse answered. He drew his Colt, as did his companions, and they rode cautiously on. They relaxed when Eagle's roan rounded the bend. The Indian lifted his hand in greeting, and Dan responded.

"Find hoss," Eagle said when he had reined up.

"Bueno," Dan said. "All?"

"All," Eagle said, grinning. He then raised four fingers on his left hand and five on his right. *"Bandido hoss."*

"By God," Wolf said, slapping his thigh with his hat, "if that don't beat all. This *muy bueno hombre's* been out here all night, roundin' up the horse remuda, and he's added the nine cayuses that belonged to the rustlers."

"Eagle," Dan said, "you've done a night's work. Let's get these horses back to camp and roust you up some breakfast. I know of at least one *torpe bonito* squaw who'll cook it for you fresh."

That drew a sheepish grin from Eagle and a laugh from the rest of them as they rode on into the canyon

* Ghostly

for the horses and mules they had expected to cost them a full day's work.

"Eagle," Palo said seriously, "per'ap you ride out tonight, find cows for *manana*."

The Indian knew he was being hoorawed and laughed with the rest. Their early return to camp was unexpected, and it lifted everybody's spirits. Dan gave the Indian full credit for spending the night gathering the scattered horses, and Lenore had two other women helping her prepare Eagle's breakfast. The Cheyenne seemed amused with all the attention he was getting. The rain clouds swept in from the west and the rain began in the early afternoon. The canyon in which they were camped soon had a fast-running creek all its own.

"Tomorrow," Dan said, "we'll start the gather. With five wounded men, we'll have our work cut out for us. Some of you will have to stay and secure the camp. We'll swap it out, each of you taking a day in camp. God knows, we'll be a while gathering the herd, but we can't move on until our wounded are able to ride."

"I've been cowboy enough to eat drag dust all the way from South Texas," Adeline DeVoe said, "and I'm sick of being stuck here in camp. Since some of our men are wounded, I'll take the place of one of them in gathering the herd."

"So will I," Fanny Bowdre said.

There were a dozen others clamoring to ride, even the grief-stricken Amy Wilder. Dan laughed. It was exactly what they needed, some challenge to take their minds off yesterday's tragedy.

"You're on," Dan shouted. "You're a *bueno* bunch of Tejano cowboys, the lot of you."

The rain didn't let up until dawn the next morning. The women of the outfit had worked themselves out a schedule where half of them cooked and the rest worked the gather. Even with five wounded men, Dan still had more than twenty riders, half of them women.

After a bout with fever, hung over from whiskey, the wounded riders began their recovery. With all his fighting skills, Dan tried to leave Eagle in camp as much as possible, and to his amusement, the Indian seemed content to stay there only on the days when Lenore was one of the women doing the cooking. The rest of his time he spent with the horse remuda or in chasing cows out of the brush. Adeline mentioned it to Dan at the end of a day she and Lenore had spent helping with the cooking.

"Sooner or later," she said, "we're going to reach Dodge. What do you reckon this Indian is going to do?"

"Damned if I know," Dan replied, "but I have my suspicions. I think he'll be going wherever Lenore goes. I'm not sure he knows what's expected of him where she's concerned."

"That's what frightens me. Will my daughter end up hunched over an open fire cooking rabbit stew, with a child tied to her back?"

"Somehow I doubt it," Dan said. "While this hombre thinks and fights like an Indian, he learns fast, adapting to the white man's ways. Remember the first time you saw him eat, using his fingers? I doubt he'd ever seen a knife and fork in his life, and now he has better manners than some of the men in the outfit. He'll make one hell of a cowboy, if we can just get the little varmint to take to a double-rigged saddle."

After a week of rest, the wounded men had healed enough to ride, but it took twelve days to gather the scattered longhorns. The warming trend had continued, quickly melting the snow, luring the hungry cattle away from the river toward better graze. In one way, it was far easier than dragging the ornery animals out of the brakes, but in other ways it was more difficult. Without the snow hiding the grass, the longhorns scattered, forcing the riders to cover miles of prairie, rather than concentrating their efforts along the North Canadian.

"One thing in our favor," Hiram Beard said. "Once

we finally get all the varmints together, they won't be half starved."

It was true, and there was jubilation in the camp when they finally recaptured 20,350 of the brutes. It was enough, and Dan called the gather a success. They had come into this poor camp in a blizzard, still missing several thousand head as a result of the stampede. Now, with the exception of a few cows, the herd was as whole as it had been prior to the disastrous stampede.

"Tomorrow," Dan said, "we take the trail north to Camp Supply."

"I know we been told not to expect much from this soldier fort," Walt Crump said, "but I'd like to suggest somethin' that would put new life into our horses."

"If it's within our reach," Dan replied, "I'd favor it. Speak up."

"Workin' cows is hell on horses," Walt said, "and grass just ain't enough. Us, we eat plenty of beans, but we got to have some meat to go with 'em. If there's any grain—especially rye—at this fort, I'd favor tradin' some cows. A hatful of rye once a week will do wonders for a horse."

"Now that you mention it," Wolf said, "them soldiers we met to the south carried some grain behind their saddles."

"Rye," Walt said. "That's what brought it to mind."

"We'll see if they have any to spare," Dan said. "We've been on the trail goin' on four months, and there's no denying it would help our horses."

North to Camp Supply, Indian Territory. Saturday, December 24, 1870.

After breakfast, Spence and Amy Wilder spent a few minutes at the lonely grave where they would be leaving Gus. Amy then mounted the box of the second wagon, following the Bowdre wagon as Fanny took the lead.

Eagle, now one of the horse wranglers, was with the remuda as it moved into line behind the wagons.

"Move 'em out!" Dan shouted. There was a popping of lariats and the shouts of riders as the longhorns again took the trail north. Dan estimated they were a little more than forty miles south of Camp Supply. Driving along the North Canadian, there would be sure water for the journey. Dan figured they had traveled almost fifteen miles the first day. His watch was quiet, and when he returned just after midnight, he found Adeline and Lenore awake and waiting for him.

"Do you know what today is?" Adeline asked.

"Lacking four days, it's our fourth month on the trail," Dan replied.

"It's Christmas," Adeline said.

"Blast it," Dan said, "I forgot to ask you what you want."

"You could have asked me," Lenore said. "I know what she wants."

"Oh . . . How do you know?"

"Because it's the same thing she wants," Adeline said, "but she can't lure that damn Indian away from the horse remuda."

Dan laughed at the two of them, rolled into his blankets and was soon asleep.

They arose to a cloudless sky. The days were unseasonably warm with sun, but the nights were cold, and dawn found a thin sheet of ice along the eddies in the river.

"We can't be more than twelve miles from Camp Supply," Dan said.

It was sundown, the day after Christmas, and the herd had been bedded down for the night. Theirs was a good camp in the bend in the river. The wounded men had almost fully recovered, and there was excitement in the camp as they neared what seemed a milestone in their

journey. The night passed quietly, and only at breakfast
the next morning was Dan told there had been a visitor.

"Chato come," Palo Elfego said.

"It's about time," Dan replied. "What did he have to
say?"

"Stay one day, one night at *soldado* fort. No more."

"I hadn't aimed for us to linger," Dan said, "but why
just one day and one night?"

Palo shrugged his shoulders and said nothing.

Miles to the west of Camp Supply, Chato and his band
had just crossed the North Canadian and were scouting
the broken country beyond.

"Canon," Sugato said. *"Emboscada."**

Chato nodded. *"Si."*

This day, the Tejanos and their herd would reach the
soldado fort, and tomorrow they would move on. Senor
Santos Miguel Montoya and his Mejicanos were two
days behind. Once they reached this desolate canyon,
they would be many miles from the *soldado* fort. Here
Montoya and his Mejicano *perras* would die.

Far to the south, Montoya sought to raise the spirits of
his impatient men.

"Madre de Dios," he growled, "I have tell you why the
cursed *Indios* must be far from the *soldado* fort when we
kill them. *Bastante."*†

The grumbling ceased as they hunkered around a fire,
eating beans from a common pot. A few hundred yards
to the south of them, Burton Ledoux and his restless
companions shared an equally dismal camp.

"Four damn months," Black Bill groused. "Never
wanta see another bean long as I live."

* Ambush
† Enough

"I never wanta see *you* as long as I live," Hagerman said.

Burton Ledoux ignored them both. Camp Supply was behind them, and it was time for Montoya and his men to eliminate the Texans and the troublesome Mejicano Indios protecting them. Ledoux had seen a map of all the Federal forts while in San Antonio, and had some idea as to where Camp Supply was in relation to Fort Dodge. As he recalled, the two were about a hundred miles apart. Now Chato and his band were somewhere in between, waiting for the Texans to pass Camp Supply and catch up. Chato and his band would be as unwelcome north of the Rio Grande as were Montoya and his bunch, neither daring to go near the fort. The killing Ledoux had in mind—and that which Montoya and his men planned to do—would take on the proportions of a small war, and must not happen near enough to the fort for the shooting to be heard. Ledoux's cruel lips smiled in anticipation. Soon the killing would begin, and five days out of Dodge, the herd would be his. . . .

Camp Supply, Indian Territory. Tuesday, December 27, 1870.

The military installation was much nearer than expected, and two hours before noon, Dan and the riders could see the log palisades of the fort on the north bank of the river. The wagons had drawn up and the wranglers had the horses strung out to graze. Dan, Wolf, Palo, and Chad headed the lead steers, doubling the herd back to the south, and the animals took to grazing. With the horse remuda and the longhorns settled down, the riders gathered across the river from the fort's massive gates. Soldiers walked the parapets, watching curiously, but the gates remained closed.

"We'll stay here tonight," Dan said, "but we'll be moving out tomorrow at first light. We've been told this is one of the poorer posts and not to expect much here. I aim to talk to the post commander and the sutler. We can spare some more cows, if there's anything to trade them for. If nothing else, we need some grain for the horses. I favor swapping some beef for a little credit at the store, if they're well-stocked enough to be of any help to us. Does anybody object to that?"

"I don't object," Garret Haddock said, "but I'd like to suggest another possibility. Even if the sutler's got nothin' we can take in trade, these soldiers will be needin' beef. Why not just *sell* them a hundred head of our extra cows for gold? We'll be reachin' Dodge considerably ahead of the new railroad, and we may be needin' grub long before we sell any part of this herd."

Dan said nothing. They all had heard the proposal, and they shouted their approval in almost a single voice.

"Wolf, I'll want you with me," Dan said. "Does anybody think more than two of us ought to go?"

"Not if you do as well by us as you did at Fort Griffin," Aubin Chamber replied. "You aim to ask thirty dollars a head for the cows?"

Chambers drew some disgusted stares, and there was a shocked silence. Finally, when Dan trusted himself to speak, he did.

"Chambers, we've been told this is a poorly stocked post. You can see it's maybe half the size of Fort Griffin. Every man has two prices. The one he wants and the one he'll take. To answer your question, I want thirty dollars a head, but I'd take twenty-five, if it was up to me, if that's all the market will bear. Why don't we just head off any later misunderstandings and put it to a vote? Where do we draw the line?"

"Hell," Skull Kimbrough bawled, "take twenty-four, if that's all we can get. We're only talkin' maybe a hundred head, and that's extra stock."

There were shouts of assent, and some less than tolerant words directed at Chambers. Dan and Wolf mounted their horses and rode upriver until they found a place shallow enough to cross. The sergeant of the guard had been told of their presence and was waiting for them when they reached the fort's massive gates. They were opened just enough for Dan and Wolf to speak to the soldier. Dan spoke.

"I'm Daniel Ember, and this is Wolf Bowdre. We'd like to speak to the post commander."

The sergeant said nothing, the granting of permission evident by his stepping aside and allowing them and their horses to enter. Once they were inside the garrison, a private closed the gates behind them. As Dan and Wolf followed the sergeant, the overall seediness and decay of the outpost became evident. The buildings were all log huts, every one a loser in an unending battle with the elements. Entire sections of logs had rotted away and had not been replaced. Mud chinking had fallen from between logs and from mud and stone chimneys, leaving loose stones scattered about. When they reached the cabin that housed the orderly room and the post commander's office, there was a floorless stoop, but no steps. Protected by the overhang, growing out of the rotting logs nearest the ground, was an impressive stand of mushrooms and toadstools. The end of the cabin that served as an orderly room had only the crudest of furniture, and the floor was dirt. The sergeant knocked on a door, and when a voice granted entry, he opened the door on creaky hinges. He saluted, and the captain who sat behind a battered desk returned it. At least his office had a crude wooden floor.

"At ease, Sergeant," the officer said, getting to his feet.

"Sir," said the sergeant, "these men have a herd of cattle across the river, and they've asked to speak to you."

"Thank you, Sergeant. You're excused."

When the door had closed behind the sergeant, the

officer turned his attention to Dan and Wolf. "I'm Captain Chanute," he said.

"This is Wolf Bowdre," Dan said, "and I'm Dan Ember. We're taking a trail drive to Dodge City, to the railroad."

"You're only a hundred miles from Dodge," Chanute said, "and the rails are considerably farther."

"We know that," Dan said. "When it comes, we aim to be ready. We're in need of some grain for our horses, and we're hoping to find some here."

"I suppose the sutler will have some, but perhaps not enough to meet your needs. This is not a well-provisioned post. Everything has to be wagoned in from Leavenworth or Santa Fe. In West Texas and eastern New Mexico Territory, Quanah Parker and the Comanches have been killing our teamsters, our soldier escorts, and robbing us blind. Closer to home, here in Indian Territory, it's the Kiowa and bands of white renegades."

"We had trouble with some of your white renegades," Wolf said. "Varmint name of Rowden, and eleven others of the same stripe. They killed one of our riders, wounded five more, and rustled our horse remuda. We had to kill ten of them, and the other two got discouraged and rode out."

"By God," the captain said, "that's the best news I've had in a month of Sundays. I hope Rowden was one of the ten you cashed in. There's a price on his head in Missouri and Kansas."

"No," Dan said, "Rowden and one other of the coyotes hightailed it."

Suddenly, a large bug dropped from the ceiling, landing on its back on Captain Chanute's desk. The little creature struggled to its feet and began a slow trek across the desk. Fascinated, Dan and Wolf followed its progress with unbelieving eyes. Chanute laughed.

"Sometimes," he said, "when you're sleeping, they'll

drop on your face in the middle of the night. That takes some getting used to."

"I reckon it would," Dan said. "I'd take my blankets and move outside."

"Some of the men do, when the weather permits. We've been promised a permanent installation, with massive improvements. The hell of it is, all this is coming from Washington, and nobody's saying when."

"We can spare maybe a hundred cows," Dan said. "Is there a chance we might sell them here, either to the sutler or your quartermaster? We'd be glad to take some of it in trade, if supplies permit."

"I doubt that Stiverton, the sutler, can take more than a few head. Not in trade anyway, because our last supply train was ambushed. Again. Our quartermaster, Sergeant Harkness, buys beef when he can get it. But that —like all other appropriations—is limited. What's your asking price?"

"It was thirty at Fort Griffin," Dan said, "but we can make allowances here, I think. We really need some grain for our horses."

"I'll see that you get as much as we can spare," Chanute said, "if you'll work with us on the beef. God knows, we can use it."

"We'll drop our price to twenty-five dollars," Dan said.

"Go ahead and talk to Stiverton, then," the captain said. "I doubt he will take more than fifty head, if that many. When you're done with him, come back and see me. I'll talk to Sergeant Harkness."

"We're obliged," Dan said.

"We'll be obliged to you," Captain Chanute said. "Have you ever eaten the tinned stuff Washington calls beef, what they expect us to swallow?"

"No," Dan said.

"Then don't. And by the way, Stiverton's a civilian, so you're in no way bound by the price you've quoted me.

Thirty dollars a head is a fair price for a man who's not strangled by military regulations."

Dan and Wolf departed, leaving Captain Chanute to watch the slow progress of the bug as it continued its journey across the scarred expanse of his old desk.

19

Dan and Wolf found the sutler's store poorly provisioned, and Isaac Stiverton unwilling to trade for beef.

"Don't get me wrong," Stiverton said. "I could use the beef, but I can't afford to dicker away my goods when I don't know how far away we are from the next supply train. The quartermaster buys beef. Have you talked to Sergeant Harkness?"

"Not yet," Dan replied, "but we aim to. He's limited by regulations as to how much he can buy. Since you're in no position to trade, why not make it an outright sale? Then we can buy from you things we need. The sutler at Fort Griffin took a hundred head at twenty-eight fifty, and we'll make you the same offer."

"My God, no," Stiverton said. "I'd consider fifty head if the price was, ah . . . twenty-three dollars."

"Twenty-eight," Dan said.

"Twenty-three fifty," Stiverton countered.

"Twenty-seven fifty," Dan said.

"Twenty-four," Stiverton said.

"Twenty-seven," Dan said.

"I have my limit," Stiverton sighed, "and so have you. If we can deal, let's deal. If we can't, let's not continue

wasting your time and mine. I will go twenty-five fifty.
Do we have a deal?"

"We got a deal," Dan said. "We'll have the cows
across the river and a bill of sale in your hands before
noon. I know you're short on supplies, but we're in need
of some grain for our horses. Hopefully some rye. Do
you have any?"

"No," Stiverton said. "Not much demand for it. Army
buys for their own use. Some of the officers' wives have
horses, and the little grain I order goes mostly to them."

Dan and Wolf returned to Captain Chanute's dreary
office to find Sergeant Harkness there. After introductions, Harkness got down to business.

"I'd like fifty head," Harkness said, "but you're still a
few dollars over my limit. Can we negotiate?"

"We'll bend as much as we can," Dan said. "We'll sell
to you at twenty-four dollars a head. Now here's somethin' else that ought to make it a mite easier on you, and
it'll be a help to us. We're needin' some grain for our
horses, and Stiverton has none to sell. Throw in a sack
of rye, and we'll take another fifty dollars off the price
of your beef."

"That'll just about make the difference," Harkness
said. "I never know when we'll be shorted, so I always
ask for extra grain. The horses eat lots better than we
do."

"Have some men ready for the cows," Dan said, "and
we'll have them here before noon. Your bill of sale will
be for twelve hundred dollars. We won't mention the
grain."

"Thanks," Harkness said with a grin. "I suspect this is
a breach of military ethics. If we was caught, the captain
and me could be reassigned to some God-awful post.
Here, all we got to bother us is the Kiowas, the renegades from Kansas and Missouri, the bugs, and the bliz-
zards blowin' in from the Rockies."

Dan and Wolf returned to the outfit. Dan sent Kirby

Wilkerson, Boyce Trevino, and Rufe Keeler to cut out a hundred steers to be driven across the river. Dan found that Adeline had gotten the women to prepare a list of the supplies needed, if the store had them.

"We'll do the best we can," Dan said. "Whatever's lacking here, we'll have the money to buy when we reach Dodge. It's only a hundred more miles, and we should be there in another week."

Having delivered the cows and collected the money, Dan and his four companions walked the aisles of the poorly provisioned store. Most of the items on the list given Dan were to replenish their dwindling supply of food, and strangely enough, these were the things Stiverton seemed to have in quantity. There were no guns, no ammunition, no saddles, no boots, no hats.

"He's got them two gallon coffeepots," Boyce Trevino said. "We could use two more. The Indian needs one of his own."

"Get them," Dan said, "and speaking of Eagle, I'm going to buy him some kind of coat."

"Get him a couple of wool shirts too," Kirby said. "Them buckskin britches of his may last forever, but that one shirt won't. It's already out at both elbows."

"We're gettin' too anxious," Wolf said. "We got no way to tote all this stuff back to camp. I'd better ride back and bring a wagon."

"Do that," Dan said, "and while you're there, see how we're fixed for dried apples. Here's a barrel three-quarters full."

When Bowdre returned with the wagon, Dan, Kirby, Boyce, and Rufe had all their purchases on the loading dock behind the store. There was a barrel of flour, fifty pounds of brown sugar, forty pounds of coffee beans sacked in burlap, hams, sides of bacon, and a hundred pound sack of beans.

"Fanny says bring all the dried apples you can get. Sugar too," Bowdre said.

"Got all the sugar and coffee Stiverton would sell us," Dan said. "I'll see how much of this barrel of dried apples I can buy. Why don't you go to the quartermaster's and get our sack of grain?"

When Dan and the riders returned to camp, the outfit gathered around as supplies were unloaded from the Bowdre wagon and distributed among the other four. Fanny Bowdre climbed into the wagon to rearrange what was left, and shouted when she saw the almost full barrel of dried apples. There would be dried apple pie for supper. Dan took the wool shirts and the heavy mackinaw he had bought for Eagle and presented them to the Indian. Eagle wasted no time donning the coat, and everybody grinned at him except Rux Carper and Aubin Chambers.

"What the hell's the idea?" Carper demanded. "This ain't Christmas."

"Carper," Dan said, "you have an almighty short memory."

"That's partly my money you're blowin' on the Indian," Carper said, "and I don't like it."

"Carper," Wolf Bowdre said, "Eagle deserves that and more. If it bothers you that much, the little we spent on him can come out of my share."

There was an immediate clamor as the rest of the outfit sided with Bowdre. Elanora, Carper's wife, seemed mortally embarrassed over her husband's stringiness. Dan waited until the angry uproar died, and then he spoke.

"After what we bought at the store, we have twenty-two hundred dollars. I thought we had agreed this would be money for grub, money to last us until we sell the herd in Dodge. Well, I'm damned tired of having to account for every dime, like I'm stealing from some of you. Now I'm going to make an offer to Mr. Carper and anybody else of like mind. Equally divided, each of you is entitled to a hundred and ten dollars, and I'll give it to you right now, if that's what you want. But there's some strings attached. If you take your share and back out, you're on your own when we reach Dodge. That means you'll take your share of the herd and do as you like, and you won't be welcome at our cook fire. Either you want to be part of this outfit or you don't, and I don't aim to go through this again. Now, any man of you that's wantin' out, come on, and let's be done with it."

It was more than Elanora, Carper's long-suffering wife could take. She stalked over to stand before Carper, her hands on her hips, and spat out every angry word loud enough for everybody to hear.

"Rux Carper, the only reason I've come this far with you is because it seemed like we had a chance at somethin' better, because we was part of an outfit that cared if we lived or died. Folks has done the best they could, and all you've done is complain like a stove-up old granny. You pull out, and I promise you, you'll go without me."

Most of the men looked away, embarrassed. Carper stood there, teeth clenched, hands fisted at his sides, his face a mask of fury. Dan believed he would have struck the woman if he could have gotten away with it, but the rest of the women in the outfit had fixed their eyes on him in a manner that shocked him more than Elanora's outburst.

"I ain't backin' out," he said, his head down. "It's . . . I . . . I just don't always like the way things is done. . . ."

The moment passed and the men drifted away, uneasily aware that they had witnessed a thing that seemed contrary to nature. A man—if he *was* a man—didn't allow himself to be dressed down by a woman. While not a man in the outfit blamed Elanora, each felt as though he had lost something for having observed Rux Carper's degradation.

"Gracias, torpe," Eagle said as Lenore placed two dried apple pies on his plate.

She smiled at him, content that he was speaking to her, even if he did continue to refer to her as "clumsy." She sensed some feeling in him, some affection, yet he remained aloof. Nakita Elfego, damn her, had broken her word. Now everybody knew Lenore had been learning Spanish so that she could talk to Eagle, and the men grinned openly at him. The Cheyenne had his pride, and it bothered him when the whites laughed at him, whatever their reason. Lenore believed Eagle would be different once they had a ranch of their own, but suppose the Cheyenne chose not to remain with them? Indians being nomadic, it was one thing to be on the trail, forever on the move, and something else to settle down on a ranch. But they still had another week before reaching Dodge, and from what Dan had said, it would be many months before the railroad came.

Camp Supply, Indian Territory. Wednesday, December 28, 1870.

Without knowing the reason for it, Dan obeyed Chato's order. At first light the Bowdre wagon led out, followed by the horse remuda.

"Move 'em out," Dan shouted. The longhorns took the trail, following the North Canadian northwest. Half a dozen miles later they reached the shallow, sandy-bottomed crossing Dan had scouted earlier. Here they drove the wagons across, followed by the horse remuda and the longhorns. Catching up to the lead wagon, Dan spoke to Fanny Bowdre.

"Stay with the river, Fanny. Tomorrow we'll head due north, toward the Cimarron."

For the last time they bedded down the longhorns along the North Canadian River. Once they reached the Cimarron, they would have but to cross the river and their herd would be on Kansas grass. The night passed quietly, and none of the Texans were aware that one of Chato's men observed them. Delgadito had tied his horse a mile upriver, coming close enough on foot to be sure that the camp belonged to the Tejanos. Satisfied that it did, he returned to his horse, mounted, and returned to the hidden camp where Chato and the band waited.

"Tejano come," Delgadito said. "Leave *soldado* fort like you say."

"*Si,*" Chato said. *"Venir el alba, venir el perras, venir muerte."**

The canyon Chato had chosen for the ambush had served its purpose. The Mejicano, Montoya, had scouted it exactly as Chato had wished him to. Now Chato expected the Mejicanos to approach the canyon before dawn, an ambush of their own in mind. But they would never reach the canyon.

"Tiempo," Chato said as the rest of his men approached, leading their horses. Chato mounted and rode south, the others following. Half a dozen miles south of the fatal canyon where Montoya would expect to spring his ambush, Chato reined up. It was a flat stretch of prairie devoid of any cover except occasional mesquite. His men scattered into two groups, three hundred yards apart, leaving a broad expanse through which Montoya and his Mejicanos could ride. With their rifles, Chato and his Mejicano Indios settled down to wait for Senor Santos Miguel Montoya and his men to ride into a deadly cross fire. . . .

Two hours before first light, Montoya and his followers rode north, bound for the canyon in which Chato and his men had spent the last two nights.

"It is considerate of the Indios perras to choose so

---

* Come the dawn, come the dogs, come death.

beautiful a place for the ambush," Juan Panduro said.
"It be so simple a thing to kill them all from the rim."

"Per'ap you do not talk so much," Montoya hissed.
"You do not count the dead until the shooting is finish."

They rode single file, their rifles at the ready. Moon-
set wasn't far off, and the stars had already begun their
retreat into the majestic purple heavens that always
swallowed them just before the dawn.

Two miles behind Montoya's band rode Burton Ledoux,
Black Bill, and Loe Hagerman. A rear shoe of Black
Bill's horse nicked a stone, and in the quiet of the night
the sound seemed inordinately loud.

"Quiet, damn it," Burton Ledoux growled.

"It ain't my fault this cayuse can't see in the dark,"
Black Bill replied. "Why the hell we got to be right on
the heels of this Mex bunch, anyhow? In two hours it'll
be daylight."

"Come daylight," Ledoux said, "you'd better hope
we're far from here, on our way to Dodge. The wind's
from the north, and when the shooting begins, the
sound will carry for miles. Knowing that trail drive is
headed this way, the soldiers will come to investigate.
When they do, I want nobody in these parts but the
Texans and those dead Mejicano Indians. *Comprender?*"

"*Comprender,* hell." Hagerman laughed. "He
wouldn't know which way was north if he wasn't follerin'
you."

"Once we git to Dodge," Black Bill said ominously, "I
aim to let some of the wind out of you."

"You do anything in Dodge to draw attention to us,"
Ledoux said, "and you could become more valuable to
me dead than alive. You left Louisiana one jump ahead
of the law, and there's a price on your head. Keep that
in mind. That and the fact there's a United States Marshal at Dodge."

Loe Hagerman laughed, but it trailed off uneasily.

The Cajun said not a word, but his hate was so strong, an involuntary chill crept up Burton Ledoux's spine. . . .

Montoya and his band were downwind from the canyon where they expected to ambush Chato, yet there was no sound except the sigh of the wind in the mesquite and sage. For a certainty Chato would have lookouts posted, and it was inconceivable to Montoya that a man could remain so immobile there was not so much a hint that he existed. Yet these cursed Indios were capable of exactly that. They were nearing the canyon. Soon it would be time to leave the horses and creep to the canyon rim on foot. Montoya rode uneasily on, and when the surprise attack came, he was aware only of the first shot. He was flung from the saddle, dying as he fell. None of Montoya's men got off a shot. They were gunned down to the last man, nineteen of them dying in the deadly cross fire. Chato and his band had fired only twenty-one rounds, and so brief had been the encounter, an unsuspecting man might have believed his ears were playing tricks on him. But far to the south, on the banks of the North Canadian, Wolf Bowdre and his second watch companions heard the brief thunder of rifles and understood.

"Chato," Bowdre said.

Less than two miles south of the killing ground, Ledoux and his wary companions reined up, uncomfortable in the devastating silence. Suddenly, the plain ahead erupted in gunfire. The first shot snatched Ledoux's hat from his head while a second dropped his horse. A third shot burned Black Bill's horse, sending the animal galloping south. Ledoux sprang from the saddle of his dying mount and was given a hand up by Loe Hagerman. Hagerman kicked his horse into a gallop, and carrying double, the animal headed south. There was only one more shot, and the lead ripped

through Ledoux's upper left arm, shattering the bone.
Black Bill's horse couldn't maintain a fast gallop for
long, and even with Hagerman's mount carrying double,
they caught up to the Cajun. It was light enough for
Black Bill to eye Ledoux's bloody coat sleeve and use-
less left arm with some relish.

"I think," the Cajun said, "somet'ing go wrong."

"Don't do too much thinking," Hagerman said. "You
ain't equipped for it."

"Shut up," Ledoux shouted. "We have to find a place
to hole up, and quick. I'm hurt."

"I ain't," Black Bill said, "and with both of you
coyotes on just one hoss, you'll slow me down. Find your
own place to hole up."

"Damn you," Ledoux said, earing back the hammer
of his Colt, "you even look like you aim to run out on
me, and I'll kill you. Now lead out, and we'll be right
behind you."

Chato and his riders had reined up, looking south.

*"Seguir?"** Sugato asked.

Chato shook his head. *"Soldados* come." He wheeled
his horse, riding north, and wordlessly his companions
followed.

Distant shooting never went unnoticed on the frontier,
and every man in the Texas outfit had heard the gunfire.

"Bunch of shootin' up there to the north of us last
night," Chad Grimes said. "Somebody purely raised hell
and kicked a chunk under it."

"Must of been Chato and his bunch," Duncan Kilgore
said. "Do we scout ahead and see what happened, or is
it better if we don't know?"

"I think it's better if we don't know," Dan said. "I
didn't tell any of you this before, because I didn't know

* Follow

what it meant, if anything, but Chato sent word for us to spend just one night at Camp Supply before moving on. I think he pulled off one hell of an ambush last night, and I think where we were had something to do with it. That kind of shooting won't have gone unnoticed at Camp Supply, and I reckon we'll be seeing some soldiers pronto."

"Captain Chanute will think we've been hit by rene-gades or the Kiowa," Wolf said, "and when his detach-ment learns otherwise, it's unlikely the soldiers will ride any farther. I reckon it'll suit Chato's purpose if the military never learns what really happened."

"Nor us," Dan said. "He's removed some hombres who stood between us and Dodge, and that had some-thing to do with his being so far ahead of us when the rustlers struck."

The detachment of soldiers was small. There were only seven men, one of them Lieutenant Schorp, who was in charge. The enlisted men consisted of a sergeant and five privates. One of the drag riders brought word of their coming, and Dan rode back to meet them.

"Captain Chanute was concerned," Lieutenant Schorp said. "He feared you had been ambushed by renegades or Kiowa. Have you scouted ahead to deter-mine what might have happened?"

"No," Dan said. "Since we're headin' that way, we'll look around some. I've found it best not to mix into somebody else's fight when you can avoid it."

"That's a philosophy a man can live with," Schorp said. "Captain Chanute was concerned with your safety, and he said nothing about us riding any farther, so I'd like to ask a favor of you. If you find where last night's shooting took place, if there seems to be anything of interest to the military, will you report it to the post commander at Fort Dodge?"

"I will," Dan said.

"Then I see no point in us riding any farther afield,"

Schorp said, "since our post is already undermanned. I'll tell Captain Chanute. Good luck."

Dan watched them ride back the way they had come. He then rode ahead, talking to the swing and flank riders as he went.

Black Bill trotted his horse up a shallow draw, following a trickle of water that eventually led to a spring. Behind him, on a heaving horse, came Loe Hagerman and the wounded Burton Ledoux. Ledoux's cruel face was twisted with pain, but he still held the cocked Colt. Black Bill dismounted, drawing his Colt as he did so. Using the horse for a shield, he dropped behind the animal, firing under its belly. The slug slammed into the surprised Hagerman's chest, the force of it driving the dying gunman into Burton Ledoux. Ledoux went over the horse's rump, crying out in pain as he struck the ground on his wounded arm. Hagerman reeled out of the saddle and his horse trotted away. Ledoux tried to recover, but he was slow. Black Bill fired a second time, and the lead shattered Ledoux's right arm at the elbow. He bit his lips until they bled, and when he finally spoke, it was through painful, wracking sobs.

"You dirty . . . double-crossing . . . son of a bitch. I should have . . . gut-shot you . . . when . . . I . . . had . . . the . . . chance. . . ."

"But you didn't," Black Bill gloated, " 'cause you're a damn fool. You liked torturin' me, holdin' that rap in Louisiana over my head. Now, Mr. Big, I got a s'prise for you."

The big Cajun turned to his horse, removing the cruel blacksnake whip from his saddle. He uncoiled it lovingly, his cruel eyes feasting on the horrified expression on Ledoux's pain-wracked face.

"You . . . couldn't . . . be so . . . cruel," Ledoux panted. He tried to rise to his knees, an impossible feat with two shattered arms.

"Hell," Black Bill said, with an insane cackle, "I ain't human. You said so yourself. Now, by God, you're goin' to find out just how cruel I can be."

The whip took its first bite out of Ledoux's crotch, and his scream drew a fiendish laugh from Black Bill. He went after Ledoux's ears, cutting away at them until they were just bloody stumps. He then returned to Ledoux's crotch, shredding the trousers to the knees. From there he concentrated on Ledoux's shirt, ripping it from his body.

"Please," Ledoux shrieked, "in God's name . . . spare me. . . ."

But there was no mercy in Black Bill. When his right arm and shoulder grew tired, he swapped hands with the deadly whip. Finally Ledoux lapsed into unconsciousness, and it spared him the worst of a horrible ordeal. The terrible lash tore into his face, and his nose disappeared in a shower of blood. Black Bill laughed. That left only the eyes. . . .

Dan reined up, listening. There had been two more shots, maybe a minute apart, and then silence. Wolf Bowdre reined up beside him.

"Shots from a Colt," Wolf said. "Long after the fight at dawn, but I'm bettin' it's got somethin' to do with it."

"I reckon that would be a safe bet," Dan said. "Like I told the soldiers, we'll be goin' that way, and we'll look around some, but there'll be things we'll never know. And I reckon that's best."

Before leaving the grisly scene of death, Black Bill went through the pockets of Hagerman and Ledoux. He grinned in satisfaction when he found a little more than three hundred dollars in greenbacks on Ledoux. Hagerman had little of value, except his Colt, pistol belt, and holster. And of course, his horse. Black Bill mounted his own animal and, leading Hagerman's, rode out. While he had no idea who had gunned down Montoya and his men, Black Bill took no chances. He rode far to the west before again riding north. He would ride to the Arkansas River and approach Dodge City from the west. As he rode away, he studied the sky to the north. After the slaughter that had taken place, the sky should be black with buzzards, but there were none. It was more than he could comprehend, and shaking his head, he rode on.

The Cimarron. Thursday, December 29, 1870.

"By my figurin', we're a little more than sixty miles south of Dodge," Dan said.

"We still ain't come up on where all that shootin' took place," Ward McNelly said. "Kind of strange we ain't seen no buzzards."

"Maybe not," Wolf Bowdre said. "Chato and his boys is pretty handy at disposin' of the evidence. They've played it so's the army wouldn't have anything to get its teeth into, even if it was of a mind to try."

"It all happened somewhere north of the Cimarron," Dan said, "and I don't aim to go out of my way to look for any evidence. I can't see that there's anything to concern the military, unless Chato and his boys have gunned down a tribe of Kiowa."

"Somehow I don't think so," Bowdre said. "This is something that's been in the making since before we reached the North Canadian, and it took Chato a while to pull it off."

"There's the buzzards," Denny DeVoe shouted as he and the wranglers rode in for breakfast the next morning.

"Not that far ahead of us," Kirby Wilkerson said.

"We'll have to ride ahead and have a look," Dan said. "I promised the lieutenant. Besides, we'll have to take the herd on a wide swing around it. Take these brutes anywhere near the smell of death, and we'll have another stampede to contend with. We'll hold them here at the river until we see what's up ahead. Palo, you and Wolf will ride with me."

The coyotes and buzzards had been at the bodies, and several buzzards flapped sluggishly away as Dan and his companions approached. They reined up a few yards away.

"My God," Bowdre said, "I've never seen the like."

"I think," Dan said, "you're looking at the handiwork of the bastard who thought he had whipped me to death, and the last time I saw those fancy Mex boots, Burton Ledoux was wearin' them."

"He shot twice, other hombre shot once," Palo said. "We hear two shots."

"I reckon the brute that done the whipping fired those two shots," Dan said. "Ledoux likely took one of those slugs in the earlier fight."

"Then they holed up here," Wolf said, "and had a fallin' out of some kind. I'll lay you odds the bastard with the whip will be in Dodge when we get there."

20

❧❦❧

D an led the herd well to the east of the fateful draw where the buzzards still spiraled down to a macabre feast. Upon his return to the drive, he told the rest of the outfit only that they had discovered a pair of dead men. When they bedded down the herd on a creek fifteen miles north of the Cimarron, Dan and Wolf recounted what they had seen, what they knew, and finally, what they suspected.

"We found Burton Ledoux and one of his men dead," Dan said. "There had been a shooting, and the third man had ridden away."

"So that bastard Ledoux was somehow involved in all that shootin' that went on to the north of us," Chad Grimes said.

"It looks that way," Dan said.

"We have no proof," Wolf said, "but we think Ledoux had come up with some riders—maybe renegades from Indian Territory—and had planned to take the herd. After ambushing us, of course."

"So Chato and his bunch figured it out and set up an ambush of their own," Skull said.

Dan nodded. "That's about the way we've pieced it together. Looks like Ledoux and a pair of his men escaped, only to have a falling out among themselves. I believe the man who killed Ledoux and the other man is a brute with a whip who almost beat me to death after Ledoux took my spread. Ledoux had been cut to ribbons. We identified him by his fancy boots."

"All we know for sure," Wolf said, "is that if any trouble lies ahead of us, Burton Ledoux won't be the cause of it. I didn't see a thing that I'd think the post commander at Fort Dodge would find interesting."

"Neither did I," Dan said.

Fort Dodge, Kansas. Wednesday, January 4, 1871.

An hour before sundown Dan and the outfit bedded down the herd on the south bank of the Arkansas, within sight of Fort Dodge.

"That's it?" Fanny Bowdre asked, incredulous. "I thought there would be a town."

"There will be," Dan said. "From what we learned at Camp Supply, there's a town under way on the north bank of the Arkansas, eight miles west of here. I think we'll make our presence known to the post commander first."

Colonel McLean greeted them cordially.

"I don't look for the rails for at least another year," McLean said, "but that shouldn't stop you from selling your herd. Joseph McCoy's already here. You may have heard of him. He made a fortune when the first herds came up the Chisholm Trail to Abilene."*

"No," Dan said, "I haven't heard of him, but I'll track him down and talk to him. We aim to keep some of our herd for seed cattle and settle on some land, maybe to the north or to the west of here. I reckon the Indians are a problem."

"Unfortunately," McLean said, "but I look for that to change once the rails get here. There'll be more settlers,

* The Chisholm Trail. Book #3 in the Trail Drive Series.

and I've been promised more men, with better arms. If you're thinking about ranching along the Arkansas, then you'd best not waste any time getting to the land office. The speculators are already sniffing around."

"There's a land office?"

"You bet there is," McLean said. "There's even a hotel, a barbershop, a livery, and several decent cafes."

Dan and Wolf rode back across the Arkansas and took the time before supper to relay the information they had received from Colonel McLean.

"We can sell some cows here," Duncan Kilgore said, "but we don't have to ranch in the shadow of the fort. He's right about the railroad bringin' more settlers, and I purely don't like the sound of that. I reckon I'd as soon move on west, maybe to eastern Colorado Territory."

"That's kind of the way I feel," Kirby Wilkerson said.

"There's time enough to settle that," Dan said. "Once we've sold as much of the herd as we intend to sell, we can talk about where we aim to settle. I think tomorrow some of us ought to ride upriver to where the town's being built. If this Joseph McCoy made a pile in Abilene, then he should have the money to buy from us."

"That don't mean he'll pay a fair price," Boyce Trevino said. "If the railroad's more than a year away, he'll have a considerable wait for his money."

"That's why we have to meet with him," Dan said. "To see if he can pay us our asking price and make his money when he resells in the eastern markets."

"What *is* our asking price?" Aubin Chambers wanted to know.

"I'm considering starting at thirty-five dollars a head," Dan replied. "Do any of you disagree with that?"

"I do," Chambers said, surprising them all. "I think it's a mite high."

"Maybe," Dan said, "but you start high and come

down. If we could sell at thirty, without waiting for the railroad, I'd suggest we sell."

"*Si,*" Palo Elfego said.

The others shouted their agreement.

"*Bueno,*" Dan said. "Tomorrow, some of us will ride in and talk to McCoy."

But the Texans didn't have to ride to town. The next morning, following their arrival, men rode out on horseback, on mules, and in buckboards. Mostly they just looked in awe. Nobody had ever seen so many longhorns in one bunch. But one rider—a soldier from Fort Dodge—was more than an observer.

"I'm Sergeant Beckham," he said when Dan approached him. "I'm the post quartermaster, and I'm hoping you have some horses to sell."

"We do," Dan said. "Our remuda. Come along and have a look at them."

When they reined up near the grazing animals, Beckham whistled long and low. "How many, and how much?" he asked.

"A hundred," Dan said, "but I don't own them. I'll have to get with the owners and get back to you."

"Do that, please," Beckham replied.

It presented a problem, for Dan had no idea how much Chato wanted for the animals. When the quartermaster had ridden away, Dan went to Palo Elfego.

"Palo, I should have spoken to you about this much sooner. Do you know how much Chato expects to get for these horses he aims for us to sell?"

"Fi'ty *dollar,*" Palo said.

"I won't let them go for that," Dan said. "Broke to the saddle and no brands, they're worth twice that. Suppose Chato gets *more* than fifty dollars?"

Palo shrugged his shoulders. Dan rode to Fort Dodge and asked to see Sergeant Beckham.

"A hundred dollars a head," Dan said.

"I won't deny they're worth it," Beckham replied,

"but I can't pay that much. Suppose I buy them all. Will you take seventy-five?"

"Yes," Dan said, "but I'll need it in gold."

"That'll be a strain," Beckham said, "but I believe I can raise it. Let me talk to Colonel McLean, and I'll get back to you before the end of the day."

Nobody in the outfit—especially the horse wranglers —wanted to see Chato's horses go.

"Damn it," Denny DeVoe said, "why don't we buy them?"

"A little matter of us not having the money," Dan said, "and we don't know when we'll be able to sell the herd. If the army doesn't take them, and if we get no more offers, maybe we can hold on to them for a while. But in fairness to Chato, we can't refuse a decent offer."

Within two hours a private arrived bearing a message from Sergeant Beckham. Dan was to come to Fort Dodge, bringing a wagon.

"He has the gold," Dan said. "Wolf, Palo, Tobe, and Kirby, I'll want you riding along, and bring your Winchesters."

"We can handle it with a wagon," Tobe said, "but what about Chato? God Almighty, that's 37,500 double eagles."

"I reckon that'll have to be Chato's problem," Dan said, "and I doubt it will bother him near as much as tryin' to cash Yankee greenbacks. Eh, Palo?"

"*Si,*" Palo agreed. "*Oro muy bueno.*"

Dan and his five companions reached the fort's massive gates, and by order of Sergeant Beckham, the wagon was allowed to enter. Reaching Beckham's office, they found two corporals outside—one on each side of the door—their rifles at port arms. Beckham himself opened the door.

"Wait out here," Dan told his companions. He entered the office and Beckham closed the door behind him.

"Glad you brought some armed men with you," Beckham said. "Even with most of Dodge yet to be built, there's been killings and robberies. I hope you have a secure place to store all this coin."

"I aim to deliver it to the owners of the horses," Dan replied. "What they do with it is up to them. If you have pen, paper, and ink, I'll write you a bill of sale."

Using a corner of Beckham's desk, Dan wrote and signed the bill of sale. He then dated it and passed it to Sergeant Beckham.

"Now," Dan said, "after we've loaded the gold, come with me to the front gate. From there I'll signal my riders, and they'll drive the horses across the river."

The gold was in fifteen canvas sacks, 2500 double eagles per sack. Dan hefted one with both hands, barely getting it off the floor.

"You're welcome to count it if you wish," Beckham said with a grin.

"No, thanks," Dan replied. "You look like an honest man."

When the wagon reached the fort's gates, Dan waved his hat. Across the river the horse wranglers got the herd moving. Dan drove the wagon through the gates, clearing the way for the horse herd. Beckham stood on one side of the entrance and a corporal on the other, each of them taking a tally as the horses were driven through. Satisfied with the count, Beckham gave them a thumbs-up. Dan drove the wagon to a shallow crossing, followed by his four riders. When they reached the camp, he spoke to Wolf Bowdre.

"Wolf, since this is your wagon, I want you to take full charge of it and the gold until Chato claims it. Get Monte to join you, so you'll have a four-man guard. I have plans for Palo."

Palo followed Dan, and when they could speak in private, Dan reined up.

"Palo," Dan said, "you are our contact with Chato. Can you reach him sometime tonight?"

"*Si,*" Palo said.

"Tell him the wagon will be heavily guarded, and that he is to come to us alone. We will then remove our guards from the wagon, allowing him to take the gold in whatever manner he wishes. *Comprender?*"

"*Si,*" Palo said. He mounted his horse and rode south.

By the time Dan turned his attention to the herd, he found the curiosity seekers had all ridden away.

"None of them were serious," Boyce Trevino said. "With the railroad still months away, I doubt we'll find many takers. Not at our price."

"We came here prepared to wait for the railroad," Dan said, "and if that's what it takes, then we'll wait. That's how it is with speculators. They want to take advantage of our impatience, buying low and selling high."

Palo Elfego didn't return until almost dark. He spoke briefly to Dan and then went after his supper. Dan rode to the Bowdre wagon, which had been set well apart from the others, near a stand of cottonwoods.

"Chato and his boys will be here sometime after midnight," Dan told the guards. "Chato's been told not to approach the wagon alone or with any of his men until he's spoken to me. He'll come to the wagon with me, and then one at a time he'll replace all of you with his men."

Except for the four guards, Dan was careful to keep his riders well away from the Bowdre wagon. When the men saddled up for the second watch, Dan and Palo hunkered down by the embers of a fire where a coffeepot still simmered. Filling their tin cups, they waited, and at some signal only Palo heard, he got to his feet. Chato was coming. There was no moon, and the Indian seemed to suddenly appear from nowhere. Dan got to his feet. Palo spoke a few rapid words in Spanish and began a slow walk toward the distant wagon. Dan walked behind him, followed by the cat-footed Chato.

"Hold your fire," Dan said quietly as they drew near the wagon.

The four riders guarding the wagon came together with Dan and Palo, and Palo spoke to Chato in rapid Spanish.

"Gracias," Chato said.

Palo walked away, back the way they had come. Dan and the others were at his heels, none of them looking back. Not until they reached their camp did they again look toward the distant wagon. They saw nothing, not even a shadow. Palo said nothing until the next morning. Right after breakfast he spoke to Dan.

"Venir. You, me, Senor Wolf."

Having not the slightest idea what Palo had in mind, Dan saddled his horse and got Wolf's attention. They mounted and followed Palo south until they reached a secluded draw half a dozen miles away. From the draw a horse nickered, and Wolf's horse answered. Dan and Wolf slowed their mounts, but Palo rode on, unconcerned. Dan and Wolf reluctantly followed, unsure as to what lay ahead. The little draw was full of horses. Bays, roans, duns, and blacks, every one saddled. Dan counted nineteen of the animals.

"My God," Bowdre said, "Mex brands and Mex saddles. There's enough silver to start a mint."

"Palo," Dan said, "what are we expected to do with these animals?"

"Chato give," Palo said. "You take."

"But why?" Wolf wondered.

"You *honorado* Tejanos," Palo said. *"Mucho oro."**

"It's Chato's way of thanking us for the extra gold," Dan said. "He had asked fifty dollars a head, and he's getting seventy-five."

* Honest Texans. Much gold.

"He hasn't had time to count it," Wolf said. "How does he know?"

"I suspect Palo told him," Dan said with a grin. "Palo, these cayuses belonged to the hombres that aimed to ambush us, didn't they?"

"Si," Palo said. *"Mejicano bandidos."*

"Kind of far north for Mexican bandits," Wolf said, "unless they was followin' us."

"Si," Palo said. "That be so."

"That sneakin' bastard, Burton Ledoux," Wolf said. "He got himself a bunch of Mex bandits, aimin' to steal the herd from us once we got them near enough to Dodge."

"Si," Palo said. *"Mejicanos* hate Chato, *Mejicano Indios."*

"Let's get these horses back to camp," Dan said. "We can use them."

"No bill of sale, I reckon," Wolf said.

It was cowboy humor at its worst. They laughed and set about rounding up the horses.

"Ma," Denny DeVoe begged, "it ain't like I was askin' to ride to Wichita. I just want to ride into Dodge. Pablo's goin', Gid's goin', and Eagle will be ridin' with us. What could happen?"

"I don't know," Adeline replied. "All I know is that once you start carrying a gun, you're considered a man. When Dan returns, I'll talk to him."

"Oh, damn," Denny said, "the others will go without me."

"I don't think so," Adeline said. "Palo's with Dan, and I doubt Pablo will be going without his father's permission."

There was considerable excitement when Dan, Wolf, and Palo rode in with the nineteen horses. While Denny had an eye for the newly acquired horses, he wasted no time in beseeching Dan to plead his case with Adeline.

"I only want to ride into Dodge with Pablo, Gid, and Eagle," Denny said. "I never been to town in my whole life."

"I'll take your side," Dan said, "only if you leave your rifle in camp."

"Oh, damn," Denny said in disgust, "you sound just like Ma."

"She's been giving me lessons," Dan said. "That's the deal. Take it or leave it."

"I'll take it," Denny replied. "Can I go now?"

"After you've cleared it with your ma," Dan said. "What I've said don't mean doodly if she says no. Come on, I'll go with you."

Adeline and most of the other women were at the river, washing clothes in the shallows. Adeline got to her feet as Dan and Denny rode up.

"I don't think a ride to town will hurt him," Dan said, "if he leaves the gun behind."

"See that he does, then," Adeline said, "and he can go."

Dan took the rifle from Denny's saddle boot, and he went galloping away to join his companions.

"I'm a mite surprised at Eagle wanting to go to town," Dan said. "That's not usually the way of an Indian."

"Eagle's young," Adeline replied, "no more than a boy, and he's influenced by the others. I hope they don't get into any trouble."

"That's the painful part of growin' up," Dan said. "If they're going to become men, they'll have to learn to ride their own broncs. You just naturally get throwed and stomped once in a while. It kind of goes with the territory."

Gid Kilgore led out, followed by Pablo, Denny, and Eagle. The Cheyenne wore his Colt, and was the only one of the four who was armed. They followed the Arkansas west, crossing when they reached a shallow

place. They reined up when they came within sight of
the few buildings that comprised the new town. Most
were log huts, but the two-story hotel was built of lumber. They rode on, passing a pair of tents that served as
saloons. Next to the hotel was a hurriedly erected shack
that served as a cafe. A crudely painted sign simply said
Grub.

"I never been in a hotel before," Gid Kilgore said.
"Let's stop there."

There were three other horses at the hitch rail. Eagle's horse jostled one of the other horses, and the animal nickered. A heavy, dark-haired man with a whip
coiled on his left shoulder stepped out of the hotel. He
fixed cruel eyes on Eagle, and then he spoke.

"A damn Injun," he growled. "I don't like Injuns,
especially them that messes with my hoss. I aim to teach
you a lesson, boy." He began uncoiling the deadly whip.

"The Indian didn't hurt your horse," said a voice behind him. "Back off."

Slowly, Black Bill turned around, and found himself
facing two young men in town clothes, wearing narrow-
brimmed hats. It was the younger of the two who had
spoken, and he held a cocked Colt in his right hand.
Black Bill recoiled the whip, and when he spoke, his
voice wasn't much more than a vicious whisper.

"They's one thing I hate more'n Injuns, and that's
some damn tenderfoot with lace on his drawers pokin'
his nose where it don't belong. I ain't gonna be forget-
tin' you, mister."

"See that you don't," said the young man with the
Colt. "I'll be here a few days. I'm James B. Masterson,
and this is my brother, Ed. He'll keep an eye on my
back. Now whatever you have to do, you'll be doing it
elsewhere. Mount up and ride."*

Black Bill mounted and rode west, not looking back.

* William B. "Bat" Masterson became sheriff of Dodge City in 1877.

Masterson holstered his Colt. Eagle said nothing, and there was a painful silence. Denny finally found his voice.

"Thanks, Mr. Masterson. Eagle didn't do nothin' to him. We just rode in to see the town. Our outfit's down-river a ways, near Fort Dodge."

"You've seen about all of Dodge there is to see," Masterson said. "Maybe you'd better be going back. My brother and I have business at the fort, so we'll ride with you."

"Yes, sir," Denny said. They were young, but they had their pride, and it was Masterson's way of offering his help without seeming to. The big man with the whip might circle around and confront the four as they rode out. On the frontier, few would fault him for whipping the Indian, however trivial the reason. There was little talk until they were within sight of the huge grazing herd.

"Come meet our outfit," Denny said, "and stay for supper. You can tell us about Dodge."

They all rode in, Dan welcomed them, and, introductions in order, Denny told of the incident in which Masterson had taken their side.

"We're obliged," Dan said. "I know the man with the whip, and I have a score to settle with him. Unless you hombres have something more important to do, why don't you spend the afternoon with us and have supper?"

"I think I'd enjoy that," Ed said. "What about you, Bill?"

"So would I," the younger Masterson said.

The Mastersons had never been to Texas, and listened eagerly as Dan and his companions told them of buffalo hunting and of the daring attacks of the Comanches, led by Quanah Parker. Then the Mastersons spoke of the railroad. Having lived in Wichita, they were familiar with its progress, and to the surprise of the Texans, the

Mastersons were to take part in the completion of the line.

"We've taken a grading contract with the Atchison, Topeka and Santa Fe," Ed said, "and we're having a look at the terrain."

"We have a powerful interest in the railroad," Dan said. "We have twenty thousand head of Texas longhorns, and we may be stuck with them until the railroad comes. We've heard all kinds of rumors, most of them bad. Do you gents have any honest ideas as to how far away the rails are?"

"They've given us eighteen months to complete our section of the right-of-way," Ed replied, "and we'll be working west, toward Dodge. If the Indian trouble continues, I don't look for the rails to reach Dodge until sometime next fall, if then."

"The army's been sending troops from Fort Leavenworth," Bill said, "but they're too few and stretched too thin. Indians have ambushed so many supply trains, graders and track layers have been on starvation rations. They're refusing to work if they can't eat."

"You can't fault a man for that," Wolf Bowdre said. "I reckon we'll be here awhile. How's the range east of here?"

"Not suitable for ranching," Ed said. "Nothing wrong with the land, but the sodbusters will come like a grasshopper plague once the rails are down."

There was no denying the truth in that. The Mastersons stayed for supper, riding back to Dodge before dark.

"So far," Dan said, "I've been too busy to ride into town. Tomorrow, I aim to."

"You're lookin' for the big bastard with the whip," Denny said. "I wanta go with you."

"I aim to talk to some speculators about maybe buyin' the herd," Dan said, "and if there's trouble, I don't want to have to look out for anybody's hide but my own. You'll stay here."

Dan rode in right after breakfast and found both the tent saloons open for business. He found both full of bull whackers, and from listening to the talk, learned they had arrived late the day before. Part of their load had included an enormous tent which was to serve as a mercantile until the owners could erect a suitable building. The rest of the wagons contained an initial shipment of trade goods. Dan went to the hotel and inquired about some of the men who reportedly had an interest in the new town. He climbed the stairs to the hotel's second floor, to the room where he'd been told he would find Joseph McCoy.

"I reckon you're McCoy," he said when his knock was answered.

"I reckon I am," said the thin man with a receding chin and graying hair. "What do you want of me?"

"I have twenty thousand head of Texas longhorns," Dan said. "I hear that you bought cattle ahead of the rails in Abilene, and I thought you might be interested in doin' it here."

"I'm here to buy lots in the new town," McCoy replied, "but I'd consider an investment in cattle, if the price is right."

"Thirty-five," Dan said. "Twelve hundred pounds and up. Nothing under two years old."

"With the railroad a year and a half away," McCoy said, "I'd balk at twenty. So will everybody else."

"Thanks," Dan said, "and good luck with your investments in Dodge." He stepped out the door and closed it behind him.

He went down the stairs, disappointed. McCoy had been his best bet. He stepped out the door and collided with Black Bill. The big Cajun cursed and slammed a massive fist against Dan's head. Dazed, Dan steadied himself against the hotel's door and drove his right boot into Black Bill's crotch. The big man humped over, gasping, and flopped down on his back. Teamsters about to enter the cafe had paused, watching as Black Bill rolled over, getting to hands and knees. When he eventually got to his feet, he stood there rocking to and fro, like an oak in a mighty wind.

"You sonofabitch," he roared, "I've killed men for less'n that."

"I know you have," Dan said. "You've beaten them to death with a whip when they couldn't fight back. When I'd been shot out of the saddle and was unable to move, you beat me half to death. Now let's see how well you stand up to a man who can fight back. No whip, no fists. Draw, damn you."

Black Bill hesitated. He was accustomed to an advantage, and he had none. He had never lost a fight, and it was inconceivable that he might lose this one. Men were watching, and it was draw or take water. He hated this cocky bastard who had put him in so humiliating a position. His fury took control and he went for his Colt, but he never cleared leather. Daniel Ember's Colt roared four times, each slug slamming into Black Bill's belly just above his belt buckle. He crumpled and fell, dead before he hit the ground.

❧𝖜❧

*D*an turned to the teamsters who had witnessed the fight. "You saw what happened," he said. "If there are questions, will you testify for me?"

"Damn right," said one of the bull whackers. "That big varmint's been spoilin' for a fight. Ain't they no law here?"

"U. S. Marshal name of Deuce Yeager," said the clerk who had stepped out of the hotel. "You'll find him at Fort Dodge, and I'd take it kindly if one of you would fetch him. It'll be bad for business, a dead body layin' on the stoop. Especially this one."

Other men had been drawn by the shooting, and those who had seen it were happily answering the questions of those who had not. Some of the men had been insulted by Black Bill in the saloons the night before, and they were of a single mind: the burly Cajun had gotten what he deserved. Some of them had gotten up the nerve to take a closer look, and were amazed at what they discovered.

"By God," said one of the whackers who had seen Dan draw, "he waited for the big bastard to pull iron, then put four slugs in his belly. They went in so damn close, you can cover all four with a playin' card."

That prompted an examination by the rest of them,

and by the time the marshal arrived, Dan felt like a dancing bear in a circus. It seemed that each of the bystanders—even those who hadn't seen the event—wanted to be the first to describe it. Yeager proved to be a big man, wearing two guns, and he took his time with a cold appraisal of Dan. Finally he turned to the men who had gathered.

"How many of you," he asked, "actually saw what happened? Step forward."

Six men advanced.

"Now," Yeager said, "one at a time, tell me what you saw."

The six told their stories, clearly vindicating Dan's act. When they were finished, Yeager turned to Dan.

"This hombre seemed to have a mad on for somebody," Yeager said. "You and him met before?"

"In South Texas," Dan said, "but I don't think he remembered me. He left me for dead." He unbuttoned his shirt, peeled it off, and turned so that the marshal could see his whip-scarred back.

"I'd foller a man to hell for a beatin' like that," Yeager said. "You sure you didn't come here lookin' for him?"

"My bein' here had nothing to do with him," Dan said. "Have you seen the twenty thousand longhorn cows across the river from Fort Dodge? I'm trail boss, and I'll be with the herd if you have further need of me." Donning his shirt, he buttoned it, stuffing the tails in his Levi's.

"I can't see that I'll be needin' you," Yeager said. "Go on about your business."

Dan watched a crew of men fight a rising wind for possession of the big tent that would serve as a mercantile. A man in town clothes looked Dan over and finally spoke.

"I'll be needin' a guard at night. You lookin' for work?"

"No," Dan said. "I have all I can handle. Are you buying beef? I have twenty-thousand head."·

"Not today. See me a year from now."

Dan mounted and rode back to camp. He said nothing about the shooting, mentioning only his difficulty in finding a buyer for the herd.

"I think it's time for some serious talking," Wolf Bowdre said. "We come here with the intention of selling half the herd and taking up ranching with the rest. We ain't broke. We got money for supplies for at least another year. If all of us, includin' wives, sons, and daughters, filed homestead claims, we'd have nearly eight thousand acres. Why don't we have a look at that land office map and see what's available to the west of here?"

"Because a hundred and sixty acres ain't my idea of a ranch," Skull said. "If I had a wife and son or daughter —which I ain't—then I could get four hunnert and eighty acres. That ain't my idea of a spread neither. Besides, there's an hombre or two in this outfit I ain't hankerin' to have as neighbors."

"I hate to throw cold water on you, Wolf," Chad Grimes said, "but that's pretty much how I feel."

There was a chorus of approval, and some dark looks cast at Rux Carper and Aubin Chambers.

"Forget I mentioned it," Bowdre said. "I'd have to agree that the acres·a man can homestead don't make for much of a ranch, but the days of free range are numbered. Remember· what the Mastersons told you, because it's gospel. As the rails move west, so will the farmers, and what you're lookin' at today as free range will be a mess of farms. If you want a decent spread, somethin' beyond what you can homestead, then you got to buy and pay for it."

"I can't add a thing to that," Dan said. "There'll be free graze for a while, long enough for us to sell our cows. Then it'll be up to each of you as to where you

intend to settle. We'll drive the herd upriver a few miles
west of Dodge, setting up a permanent camp until we
either sell to speculators or until the railroad comes.
Does anybody object to that?"

"Nobody should," Boyce Trevino said. "That's what
we decided to do, even before we started the drive. Like
Wolf said, we got money for grub. Finally, when we sell
half the herd and we're ready to start ranchin', it'll be
every man for himself. Me, I aim to take some of the
money from the sale of the herd and buy me some land.
I reckon a homestead will do for a start, but Skull's
right. It'd be a poor excuse for a ranch."

"Tomorrow," Dan said, "we'll have to move the herd
to better graze. Why don't we just take them west along
the Arkansas a few miles and establish a permanent
camp?"

"If there's an Indian problem, we'll be giving up the
protection of the fort," Aubin Chambers said.

"There definitely is an Indian problem," Dan said,
"but with our twenty thousand head, we can't stay
within hollering distance of the fort. There's not that
much graze. As it is, we'll have to move them often, and
our camp along with them."

"That's right," Monte Walsh said. "Hell, we may be in
eastern Colorado by the time the rails get to Dodge."

"Any one of you wantin' to hunker here in the
shadow of the fort," Bowdre said, "cut your cows out
and stay. But Dan's talking sense, and I say we go ahead
and take the herd to some decent graze. Now, if there's
any man of you that don't like that, then you just tally
out your herd and do whatever you damn well please.
Speak up now."

There was only silence, and after a decent interval,
Dan spoke.

"Tomorrow, then, we'll drive west, following the Arkansas."

East of Fort Dodge the women had found a long

stretch of river with a sandy bottom, and were washing clothes and blankets. With far fewer horses in the remuda, Denny and Eagle had ridden along as lookouts. It was Eagle who first saw the riders and the wagon. He pointed, and far downriver Denny saw them coming. He wheeled his horse and rode for camp.

"Riders comin'!" Denny shouted. "Riders and a wagon."

"Come on, Wolf," Dan said. "Monte, Tobe, and Kirby too. Strangers ridin' in, and I'd as soon they don't get too close to our new remuda, with all those Mex brands."

Dan led out, with Wolf, Monte, Tobe, Kirby, and Denny following. They rode on beyond where the women were washing and reined up, awaiting the approaching party. Eagle followed, reining up next to Denny. The trio of horsemen were in the lead, the wagon following. Uncertain as to their welcome, they reined up fifty yards away from the waiting Texans.

"We're friendly," the lead rider said. "We heard they're buildin' a town here, and we come from Wichita lookin' for work."

Suddenly, there was a piercing whistle, and the spokesman's horse threw him. The animal nickered and galloped away, running straight toward Eagle. Deftly the Indian left the roan, straddling the dun. Palming his Bowie, he headed for the former rider, who was just getting to his feet.

"Eagle," Dan said, "no."

The Cheyenne reined up, and the four strangers froze, hands just above the butts of their Colts.

"I reckon you hombres have some talking to do," Dan said. "Eagle and some of his people were gunned down near the Red a few weeks ago. Gunned down and left for dead by four men, one of them in a wagon. You, afoot, where did you get the horse?"

"Found him wanderin' on the plains," the stranger said. "You can't prove nothin' agin us."

"Get in the wagon," Dan said, "and the lot of you get out of here. And circle wide. I don't want you goin' even close to our camp."

With wary eyes on Eagle, the man afoot climbed into the wagon and the four of them veered away to the south. Eagle trotted his dun after them.

"Eagle," Dan said, "no."

The Indian turned his horse and rode back to face Dan. "They kill," the Cheyenne said. "Eagle kill."

"Eagle," Dan said, "you have no proof. It would be your word against theirs. The law would hang you."

Eagle turned away, watching the departing wagon and the riders for as long as he could see them. The women had left their washing at the river and had reached the scene in time to see Eagle recover his horse and go after the recognized killers.

"Eagle!" Lenore cried. "Eagle!"

Slowly, the Indian turned back to face his companions, his obsidian eyes telling them nothing. The others soon forgot the incident, but Eagle did not. After supper, when the first watch had ridden out to circle the herd, the Indian crept away into the gathering darkness, afoot, leading his horse. Once he was well away from the camp, he mounted and rode west, the way the four strangers and the wagon had gone. Lenore was the first to miss Eagle when he wasn't there for breakfast.

"He's gone after those men!" Lenore cried. "What are we going to do?"

"There's nothing we can do," Dan said. "He recognized them as the men who gunned him down and left him for dead. One of them had his horse. That was proof enough for me, but it won't be for the law. Those men are likely dead by now, and if Eagle has any chance at all, he'll have to keep riding."

*   *   *

Eagle had no trouble finding his quarry. They made their meager camp not more than a mile west of Dodge, beside the Arkansas. Not having money to belly up to the bar, one of them rode in and bought two bottles of rotgut at one of the tent saloons. In the darkness, a few yards away, Eagle patiently waited for them to drink themselves senseless, and having had experience, it was a feat that took them only about two hours. One by one Eagle slit their throats, and their lives drained into the sandy bank of the Arkansas. The Cheyenne's only emotion was regret. Regret that the four hadn't been conscious of his act or of the vengeance that had prompted it. He mounted his horse and rode back along the Arkansas, toward Dodge. Finally he reined up, thinking of Daniel Ember's words. Whatever the provocation, when white men died at Indian hands, there was trouble. He thought of the trail drive, of the good food, and of the white squaw. While these men had deserved the justice he had meted out to them, their deaths had cost him. He turned his horse and rode west along the Arkansas, unsure of his destination, knowing only that he could not return to the Tejano camp.

The outfit was just finishing breakfast when Marshal Deuce Yeager rode in. He dismounted, accepting a cup of hot coffee from Fanny Bowdre. Wasting no time, he turned to Dan.

"I fanned through some wanted posters," he said, "and found one on that varmint with the whip. A Cajun, Black Bill Shatika. Killed a gent in New Orleans, and there's a thousand dollars on his head. I'll get in touch with the law there and collect it for you. Are you aimin' to be around here for a while?"

"Until the railroad comes, I reckon," Dan said, "but we'll be movin' west a ways. Takes lots of graze for twenty thousand longhorns."

"Reckon I ought to warn you," Yeager said. "Four

men were killed almost within sight of Dodge, sometime
last night. One of them rode in, bought a couple bottles
of whiskey, and they all got drunk. Somebody slit their
throats. I'm inclined to think it was Indian work, but it
don't add up. Their horses wasn't taken, they still had
their sidearms, and two of them had rifles on their saddles. That's where most of our Indian trouble originates,
to the south and west of here."

Nobody said anything until Yeager had ridden away.
Lenore stood there, white-faced, big silent tears rolling
down her cheeks.

"Well," Hattie Kuykendall said, "we're rid of the Indian, and it's just as well. We've no business harboring a
murderer."

"It was all right when he killed for us," Lenore said
bitterly, "but when he kills to avenge his people, he's a
murderer."

"Lenore, hush," Adeline said.

"No," Lenore bawled, "I won't hush. I'd have gone
with him, if I could."

She stomped off down to the river and stood there
looking westward. It was Wolf Bowdre who finally
spoke.

"One thing in our favor. Yeager never saw Eagle, so
at least we don't have to account for where he is. He
served us well, and I don't fault him for what he's done.
The law wouldn't have helped him, because it would
have been his word against that of four whites, so he
done it the only way he could. One thing for sure, them
hombres bein' drunk had nothing to do with it. He
could have taken then stone cold sober. I'd welcome
him back, when and if he's of a mind to come."

"So would I," Rux Carper said. "He never hurt any of
us."

So rarely had Carper agreed on anything, that drew
more attention than Eagle's questionable deed.

"Mount up," Dan said. "We're moving out."

The herd moved west, along the south bank of the Arkansas, and when they passed Dodge City, all activity ceased. Men lined the north bank, watching the longhorns trail past. Some of the observers shouted and waved, and the riders waved their hats. Darkness caught up to them eight miles west of Dodge. Come sundown, the wind always turned chill, but this time it had a familiar, ominous feel. Far to the west, a mass of dirty gray clouds swallowed the sun an hour early.

"We're in for another bad one," Skull Kimbrough said. "That wind tells me that anything comin' at us is gonna be trouble."

"That means we'll have to find a valley, a canyon, someplace where we can bunch this herd," Dan said. "Otherwise, they'll drift all the way to Wichita."

The temperature dropped drastically during the night, and the outfit hurried through breakfast. Great gray clouds rolled in from the west.

"We'll leave the herd where it is," Dan said, "and scout ahead for some shelter. Wolf, you ride the south bank and I'll ride the north. We'll stay as near the river as we can, for the sake of water, but shelter comes first. We'll limit our search to five miles, because that's about as far as we can take the herd before the storm breaks. We'll compare our findings and take the best of the lot."

Dan and Wolf rode west, Wolf along the south bank, Dan along the north. Dan rode a mile north and then west, paralleling the Arkansas. He could see the land becoming rougher, laced with ravines, but nothing that suited their needs. They needed a valley running north to south, offering them a lee slope that blunted the fury of the storm. What bothered Dan was the possibility that neither he or Wolf would find a suitable sanctuary before the storm was upon them. He rode on, his hat tied down with piggin string, his head bowed against the rising wind. First drops of rain fell, and they were cold. He rode on, finding nothing but shallow gorges and arroyos. Suddenly, somewhere to the south, there was a shot. Dan reined up, listening for a second and a third. But there was no more, and he rode south at a fast gallop. One shot was intended to get his attention. Three would have meant trouble. Probably Wolf had found something promising enough to end the search, and he knew their time was short. Dan reined up at the Arkansas as Wolf came riding along the south bank from the west.

"Valley to the south," Wolf shouted. "Spill-off from the Arkansas, and there's graze."

"Bueno," Dan responded. "Nothin' over here. Let's ride."

The cold rain had begun in earnest by the time they reached the herd, and the longhorns wanted to mill, with their backs to it. The riders shouted, fired their Colts and swung doubled lariats until finally the cantankerous brutes lurched into a trot.

"Keep the varmints bunched," Dan shouted. "At least we don't have to cross the river."

The rain became mixed with hail, and stones as big as double eagles made it hell for animals and riders. The longhorns bawled their misery and tried all the harder to turn their backs on this added discomfort. But somehow the riders kept them moving, knowing that when things changed, it would be for the worse. Hail usually was a sign that the rain was done, and on the heels of the hail there would be snow. While rain and hail was troublesome, the snow was the killer. It hid the grass, robbing the longhorns of their graze, and it set them adrift. Unchecked, they would simply wander, seeking to escape the storm, until they literally froze to death. This storm was the worst of all, for it roared out of the west and the herd was being forced into the very teeth of it. The one advantage the riders had was that the Arkansas was a barrier, allowing the outfit to concentrate all its efforts along the other flank of the herd. At one point the south bank of the Arkansas leveled off enough for some of the steers to seek the river as a means of escape. But the water was ice cold and the brutes were forced back into the herd.

Dan had fallen back to the drag, allowing Wolf Bowdre to take the point. Before reaching the canyon, the herd had to be turned south for entry, and it would depend on Wolf and the swing riders. Once the longhorns were turned away from the river, the riders would again be fighting both flanks against bunch quitters. In this particular instance, Dan had reversed the order of things. The longhorns must be sheltered from the storm in all possible haste, so the herd had taken the trail first. Behind it came the diminished horse remuda, followed by the five wagons. It proved a blessing to the drag riders, as steers of a mind to hit the back trail found it full of horses.

Dan left the drag, getting between the moving herd and the river, as ever so slightly the longhorns veered to the southwest. They were approaching the valley Bowdre had found. It was far more than Dan had expected, long enough that the runoff from the Arkansas became a trickle before reaching the end. Dan sighed with relief when the last of the herd was driven in. The horse remuda and wagons followed. The valley broadened as they traveled north toward the Arkansas, and the runoff from the river became a decent stream. The grass was good, but there was little other vegetation except sage and mesquite.

"We're going to have to scramble for some firewood," Dan said when all the riders had come together. "Let's all take our ropes and snake in all we can find."

They needed windblown and lightning-struck timber, and they had been in Kansas long enough to know that was expecting a lot. Mostly it was just flat plain, with little or nothing to *become* windblown or lightning struck. They foraged four or five miles before finding anything substantial enough for firewood. By the time they returned to camp, they were half frozen, and when the fire finally took hold, they hunkered around it, warming their hands.

"By God," Monte Walsh said, "I never seen territory that just didn't have no trees at all. It must drive dogs plumb crazy."

"We ain't seen no dogs neither," Denny DeVoe said.

The storm grew in intensity, and during the night, the outfit heard a sound more bone-chilling than any of them had ever experienced. It was the distant mournful cry of prairie wolves. Dan heard them during the first watch, and again after midnight, when he was awakened by them.

"Dear God," Adeline said, "they're coming closer."

"They're hungry," Dan said. "Before this storm's done, we'll likely be shootin' the varmints to keep them away from the cattle."

"Eagle's out there somewhere," Lenore said wistfully.

"He'll survive," Dan said. "He's one hard Indian to kill."

"I wish there'd been a preacher in Dodge," Adeline said. "We could just bundle up together and stay warm."

"Just as well there wasn't," Lenore said. "I think I'd refuse to take a walk tonight."

"Give the place another month or two," Dan said, "and I think it'll be some kind of town, railroad or not."

West of Dodge, on the Arkansas. Saturday, February 4, 1871.

The storm continued, becoming a veritable blizzard. The second day, it became necessary for the riders to seek more firewood, for the cold became more intense, and each night it seemed the wolves came closer. Even the runoff from the Arkansas froze over, and ice had to be broken for the cattle and horses to drink.

"God Almighty," Hiram Beard said, "why would a man start up a ranch in the flatlands, where the wind cuts you in half and there ain't enough wood to pick your teeth? Me, I want me a place in Colorado, where there's trees and mountains."

As the wolves drew nearer, Dan called the outfit together. With the overcast sky and swirling snow, a night watch was no longer sufficient.

"We'll have to ride the valley day and night," Dan told them. "There's too many cows, too strung out. We'll leave our first and second watch as is. You'll be on watch six hours and off six until the storm blows itself out and we're rid of these wolves."

After midnight the third night, the wolves invaded the valley, killing a steer. The predators were unable to enjoy their kill, but only one was shot. Three others escaped, and from somewhere to the west their quavering howls mingled with the scream of the wind. When more wood was needed, only a few riders could be spared to seek it. Most of the outfit had to ride the valley, lest the wolves again come after the cattle.

"The wolves won't make no difference if this storm don't let up soon," Duncan Kilgore said. "This graze won't last much longer, and if these brutes has been kilt by wolves or starved to death won't make no difference."

Sometime before dawn the storm abated, with only fine flurries of snow. But the wolves became more persistent, more bold, and the continual howling began to wear on everybody's nerves.

"Damn it," Monte Walsh said, "them of us that ain't on watch, why don't we saddle up, take our rifles and shoot us some wolves?"

"I'm game," Skull said. "This howlin' is givin' me the heebie-jeebies."

"Might rid us of some of the varmints," Sloan Kuykendall said. "Dan, what do you think?"

"I think we'll be wasting our time," Dan replied, "but I'll admit it might be better than another day of their infernal howling. After breakfast we'll ride out and try our luck."

Dan took Monte, Palo, Skull, Chad, Hiram, and Walt, promising the others they could ride out at other times if the tactic worked. The seven riders were forced to ride all the way to the south end of the valley because of the drifted snow. It was hard going until they reached the plains along the bank of the Arkansas. While the snow had drifted deep in protected areas, the incessant prairie wind had blown it far and wide. The going was difficult, but not impossible.

"By God," Hiram said, "it's like the varmints know we're lookin' for 'em. They ain't howled once since we saddled up."

"In a way, they're smarter than people," Skull said. "They know when to keep their mouths shut."

"I doubt we'll even see one of them," Dan said. "The drifts will be bad, and this kind of riding won't be easy on our horses. Let's give it maybe two hours, and then we'll ride in. Fire three shots if you get in trouble."

Dan had his doubts about the wolf hunt, but the animals had begun to get on everybody's nerves. After being snowbound for three days, captives to the continual howling, it felt good to be doing something, however futile the result. Dan found a shallow place, forded the river, and rode along the west bank. Suddenly he reined up. Wolf tracks! Two wolves had swung in from the northeast, and heading west, paralleled the river. Dan followed. He hadn't expected to sight any of the animals, and now it looked as though he might actually get a shot at a pair of them. To his dismay, the snow started again, big, wet flakes blowing into his face. But the excitement of the hunt overcame his alarm, and he rode on. He would at least follow the tracks until they were snowed out. Then he would be forced to turn back.

Somewhere ahead of him a wolf howled. Dan un-shucked his rifle, kicking his horse into as fast a lope as it could achieve in the snow. Suddenly, Dan's horse screamed and the earth seemed to fall away before them. He was flung over the animal's head into a snow-filled arroyo. He went facedown in the snow, the ponderous weight of the horse on top of him, and knew no more. . . .

〜✖〜

22

Dan wasn't out more than a few minutes, belly down in the snow. The depth of it had saved him as he was trapped under the body of his horse. The animal was dead, having broken its neck in the fall. Dan found only his left hand, arm, and head free. He wriggled, trying mightily to free his right arm, to reach his Colt. On the back of his hand, the back of his neck, he could feel new snow. Already the snow would be covering the tracks of his horse. How long before it covered him and the horse as well? With or without a warning shot, the outfit would come looking for him, but his mind was a ticking clock. There was no feeling in his hands or his feet, and his face felt wooden. Involuntarily, his eyes closed, and he awoke terrified, unsure as to how long he had slept. He wanted only to drift back into the comfortable sleep, knowing if he did, it might be his last. He began shouting, trying to keep himself awake, to attract the attention of those who would come looking for him. The wind whipped his voice away, and the only sound he heard was the cry of the elusive wolves.

Skull and Palo were the first riders to reach the camp in the valley, and dismayed to learn that none of the others had returned, they rode out again. They reached the bank of the Arkansas and, straining their eyes into the blowing snow, could see four shadowy riders coming. The four reined up, their heads bowed. Skull and Palo rode close enough to be heard against the shriek of the wind.

"Dan," Skull shouted. "Dan ain't rode in."

"We'll have to find him," Hiram said. "His horse may be down, and he's afoot, or he could be hurt. Won't be no tracks. We'll have to fan out in a circle."

"Make that a half circle toward the west," Monte shouted. "That's the way he rode out. We ain't got that much time."

They rode west, Skull, Palo, and Hiram crossing to the north bank when the river became shallow enough. They rode in a race with death, knowing the deepening snow could conceal a fallen horse and rider in a matter of minutes. The expanse ahead of them seemed unbroken. Palo reined up, listening.

"What is it?" Skull shouted. "You hear something?"

"Think it be voice cry for help," Palo replied. "Per'ap it be only the wind."

Dan's throat had grown dry and his voice had become weaker. He managed to get a mouthful of snow. Again he tried to free his right hand and arm, to reach his Colt, but he could not. Again a wolf howled, and it seemed a lot closer. That suggested a new possibility far more terrifying than freezing to death. There was a ray of hope that the howling of the big predators might bring his friends to him, but a disturbing possibility that the wolves might arrive first. He doubted that the wolves would ignore him and tear into the carcass of the dead horse. The human scent would be too strong. They would kill him first. While he was mostly covered by the body of the horse, they could get at his throat, and that would be enough.

A few miles to the west a horse plodded eastward along the Arkansas, its rider slumped low. Four days

322   *Ralph Compton*

Eagle had been without food, for after the storm had
struck, he hadn't been able to raise even a jackrabbit.
He had no idea where the herd was, only that he must
find it. He felt some shame, realizing that he needed the
white man's grub. But there was something else that
drew him. Black Kettle and the old ones were long
dead, and he had no people, nobody to whom he could
turn. Nobody but the Tejanos who had found him while
a spark of life remained, and had tried to make him one
of them. But did he wish to become one of them? These
lonely nights and hungry days he had pondered the
question. When he had claimed his horse from the
white man, he kept the saddle. He intended to discard it
after leaving the camp of the Tejanos, but for some reason he had not. There was a lariat, a boot for his rifle,
and once he had gotten used to it, the contraption
seemed surprisingly comfortable. The Tejanos had given
him a knife, a revolver, and a rifle, with ammunition.
True, there were several of the Tejanos who didn't like
him, but they weren't that well-liked themselves. Finally
he thought of the young squaw. She had seen to his
hurts after he was shot, had fed him more than his
share, and had learned another language so she might
talk to him. These Tejanos knew and respected fine
horses, and they made their living driving the *vaca* to
market. The buffalo would soon be gone, if they were
not already, and what was the Indian to do? Eagle had
seen his people turn from the white man's ways, and
now they, like the buffalo, were gone. Was it wrong for a
Cheyenne to become part of a Tejano outfit, driving and
roping the white man's buffalo? He had nowhere to go,
no people except the Tejanos who had welcomed him.
He would return to them, claim the young squaw, and
take his place among the Tejano riders.

Suddenly he reined up, listening. The wolves had set
up a clamor that Eagle recognized as a hunting or feed-

ing cry. He kicked his tired horse into a lope, drawing the Winchester from its boot.

Dan heard the snarling of the wolves and realized the moment he'd been dreading had arrived. Being face-down, he had no idea what the animals were doing. The little of him that wasn't covered by the carcass of the horse was likely covered by snow, and there was a small possibility that the wolves were not yet aware of him. He lay still, hardly daring to breathe. There was more growling, and he wondered if the animals were about to fight for possession of the horse. He wondered how many there were. Judging from the growling, he thought there must be at least three or four.

Eagle topped a rise and sighted four huge gray wolves snarling at one another. Something was dead, and it seemed there was some disagreement as to the owner-ship of it. Perhaps it was a *vaca* from the Tejano herd. These were predators who, if they weren't already caus-ing trouble, would do so at some future time. Eagle raised the Winchester and fired once, twice, three times. He killed two of the wolves, but the other two vanished like smoke. Sheathing the Winchester, the Indian trot-ted his horse ahead to see what had attracted the wolves. The horse snorted, refusing to go near the bod-ies of the dead wolves.

The triple bark of the Winchester was the most glori-ous sound Dan had ever heard. Almost immediately a horse snorted, but when Dan tried to cry out, his throat was dry and there was only a croak. Frantically he took another mouthful of snow and was able to make a noise that at least sounded human.

Dan's weary companions were exhausted and half fro-zen when they heard the three rapid shots from the Winchester. It drove new life into them, and they turned their horses into the wind.

Eagle tied one end of the lariat to the saddle horn, looping the other end over the hind legs of the dead

horse. He had no idea who was trapped beneath the
horse, and it was hard to tell who was more surprised
when Dan finally faced the Indian. Dan got to his knees,
then unsteadily to his feet, and accepted a hand out of
the ravine.

"*Gracias,*" Dan said.

Eagle said nothing, his hand on his Colt, for six riders
were approaching. Finally the Indian relaxed, for he
recognized the riders and they recognized him. Nobody
spoke. They were exhausted, numb with cold. Eagle
mounted, gave Dan a hand up behind him. Dan was
missing his saddle and Winchester, but they would have
to wait. Eagle followed the other riders to the secluded
valley, to the warmth of the fires, to hot coffee.

"Eagle," Lenore shouted joyously as they rode in. She
didn't even seem to notice that Dan didn't have a horse.
She flew to the Indian the moment he had dismounted,
and he didn't seem all that embarrassed as she fussed
over him.

Dan shucked his coat and stood before the fire, rubbing his arms. Skull and the rest of the riders who had
gone on the futile wolf hunt were describing Dan's
ordeal and telling of Eagle's rescue. While Lenore de-
voted her attention to Eagle, the other women prepared
him some hot food. He devoured it all and was given
more.

"I think," Dan said, when he felt like talking, "we'll
leave the wolf hunting alone. By the time they've finished with my horse, the storm will have blown itself out
and the snow shouldn't be a problem."

The storm did ease up before the day was over. The
wind swept the clouds away, and for several hours the
long-absent sun made an appearance, blinding them
with its brilliance against the white of the snow. By sundown even the wind seemed warm. The temperature
had risen to the point that most of the riders shucked
their coats.

"Another day like this," Cash Connolly said, "and we'll be able to take the herd out of here."

"We got no choice," Garret Haddock said. "Another day here and they'll be too weak to get out. They're so gaunt you can count their ribs."

"No worse than the horses," Monte Walsh said. "That's what bothers me about ranching on this plains country. Suppose it was to snow like this for a week or more, and a hard freeze kept the snow from meltin'? Hell's fire, a man could be wiped out."*

"It'll take some planning ahead," Dan said. "You'll have to build hay sheds, and during the summer and fall fill them with hay. Cattle and horses can stand the cold. It's the lack of graze that'll get them."

"We be farmers," Palo said.

"Farmers as well as ranchers," Wolf Bowdre said. "I'll cut and store hay before I'll watch my stock starve to death in deep snow."

The next morning at first light the riders began driving the cattle and the horses out of the valley. No graze remained, and while the snow had only begun to melt, patches of grass were visible. The horses and mules wasted no time pawing away the snow to reach the graze beneath it.

"I reckon we'll just leave our camp where it is," Dan said, "at least until spring. It'll be far easier to ride watch on the herd than to move them to and from graze morning and night."

Following the thaw, Dan and Wolf took a wagon to Dodge to replenish their supplies. To their surprise, despite the snow, the town had grown remarkably.

* It happened during the winter of 1886–87. The temperature dropped to sixty degrees below zero, and in the plains states more than twenty million cattle froze to death or starved during the blizzard, which lasted many days.

Wagonloads of lumber had been dropped at various locations, and at most of them men labored to erect buildings. Already the walls of the mercantile had begun to rise around those of the enormous tent. When the roof went up, the tent would come down. Even as Dan and Wolf watched, yet another caravan of wagons approached from the east, following the Arkansas.

"With all this activity," Wolf said, "there just ain't no tellin' what we'll find in that store."

Before reaching the store, they encountered Yeager, the U.S. Marshal, and he had some news for Dan.

"Drive on out to the fort before you leave," Yeager said. "I told you there was a reward for that varmint you shot. It's waitin' for you. All I'll need is for you to sign a receipt, and you can have it."

"Thanks," Dan said. "I'll see you before we leave."

"That's what I call gettin' even," Bowdre said. "You gunned down the hombre that tried to kill you, and then collected a bounty on the bastard's hide. For all my years in Texas, I never saw a thousand dollars all in one pile."

"I don't take any pleasure in money for killing a man," Dan said. "Not even a varmint like Black Bill. But I reckon I'll take it. If I can find what I want at this new mercantile, I'll have need of it."

Dan reined up the team off to one side of the mercantile tent. Having made their purchases, they could then back up the wagon to load it. A pair of teamsters came out as Dan and Wolf started in.

"Better stay out of there," one of the bull whackers said. "A preacher's in there, and he's beggin' money to build a church."

"You ought to contribute," Wolf said, grinning at Dan. "You're goin' to be needin' a church and a preacher, from what I hear."

"You know a hell of a lot about my business," Dan said. "Who's talking?"

"Who do you reckon? The women are practically layin' bets as to how long it'll be until Adeline proves up her claim and snares you."

"Damn it," Dan said, "I don't know as I like havin' everybody in the outfit decidin' what I'm about to do before I've made up my own mind. We've been together for months. Adeline's kept to her blankets and me to mine, and by God, if anybody's said anything to the contrary—"

"Whoa up," Wolf said soothingly, "and don't get your tail all twisted. Nobody's sayin' anything's improper. Adeline's a handsome woman, and I reckon everybody in the outfit would like to see the two of you in double harness."

"I appreciate their feelings," Dan said testily, "but I don't like somebody behind me with a prod pole, forcing me to jump before I'm ready."

Sure enough, before they'd had a chance to more than get through the door, they encountered the new preacher.

"Gentlemen," he said, "I am the Reverend Augustus Littlefield, and I—"

"Do you perform weddings?" Dan interrupted.

"Well, I . . ." the man stammered, looking from Dan to Wolf.

"Oh, not me and him," Dan said, disgusted. Wolf roared with laughter.

"Yes," Littlefield said, recovering his composure. "I perform weddings."

"Then when I'm ready, consider mine paid for," Dan said. He handed the surprised preacher a double eagle.

"We'd make quite a team," Wolf chuckled as they progressed through the tent mercantile, "although I reckon it'd shock hell out of Fanny and Adeline."

"Oh, shut up," Dan said.

The new store even had week-old copies of the *Wich-*

ita Tribune. Dan took a dozen copies, and Wolf began reading the front page of one.

"The rails are thirty miles west of Newton," he said, "and a little more than a hundred miles from Dodge."

It was good news, but Dan still had in the back of his mind what they'd been told by the Masterson brothers. The store was well-stocked, exceeding Dan's expectations. There was a locked glass showcase of assorted jewelery and pocket watches. Surprisingly, the mercantile didn't have boomtown prices. Dan and Wolf went beyond the necessary supplies, buying a few luxuries such as tinned peaches and tomatoes. They bought two hundred pounds of potatoes and fifty pounds of onions.

"Everything we need for beef stew," Wolf said. "It's likely against the law for a Texan admittin' this, but I'm damn tired of beef cooked over an open fire."

"Won't be long," said one of the storekeepers, "till you can get fresh bacon, ham, and sausage. Gent just north of here, up on Duck Creek, is raisin' hogs. He aims to bring in chickens, soon as he can figger a way to keep the damn coyotes and wolves from gettin' em."

When they were finished at the store and had the wagon loaded, Dan drove on to Fort Dodge.

"We'll just leave the wagon outside the gate and you can stay with it," he told Wolf. "I shouldn't be more than a few minutes."

He found Marshal Yeager in his office.

"You'll have to take a bank draft," Yeager said. "You can cash this at the store. I've already told them you have the money coming, so you won't have any trouble."

"You're a gent who thinks ahead," Dan said. "Thanks."

On their way back to camp, they had to drive through Dodge, past the mercantile, and Dan reined up there.

"I want to cash this bank draft," he said. He had no trouble doing so, and it was the perfect opportunity to purchase something he wished nobody else to know about. He had to gamble on the size, and he still needed to talk to Eagle, but he would be ready when the time came.

By the last week in March the grass began to green. It would be an early spring. Eagle had proven himself more than adequate as a cowboy, and could "drop a loop" with the best of them. As the weather warmed, the Indian and Lenore often rode off together.

"That girl's just asking for trouble," Dan said. "I reckon I'll have to talk to Eagle."

Adeline said nothing, turning away, and he had the distinct impression that she knew something he did not. . . .

"April fourteenth comes on Saturday," Dan said. "I think that would be a good time for you and me to ride into Dodge."

"For what reason?" Adeline asked, surprised.

"There's a preacher there that owes me twenty dollars," Dan said, his eyes twinkling, "and I thought we'd just take it out in trade."

It was suppertime, and just about everybody heard his proposal. There was shouting and laughing, and it took a moment for Adeline to comprehend what he was suggesting. Finally she threw her arms around him, laughing and crying in turn. Only one of the outfit seemed not to share her joy. Lenore looked alone and forlorn. Dan almost spoke to her, but Eagle's eyes were on the girl, and Dan said nothing. Something had to happen, and the next day, just after supper, it did. . . .

A warm wind whispered through the young cottonwoods and willows along the river, and most of the women were washing clothes in the shallows. The grass was already high enough for the cattle and horses to go after the young shoots hungrily. By midday the women who were doing the cooking already had four huge iron pots spidered over the cook fires. There was an aroma of onions, potatoes, and beef simmering. Supper would be early, allowing the first watch to reach the grazing herd before dark. Dan watched Lenore, and the girl ate nothing. Such had been the case for almost a week. Eagle ate rapidly, but for once not for the purpose of taking seconds. There was tension in the air, an uneasiness they all felt. Eagle got to his feet, went to Lenore and took her hand. She rose, and they walked to where Adeline sat, Dan beside her.

"Eagle take squaw," the Indian said. *"Esposa."**

Nobody spoke. There was only the sigh of the wind. In Lenore's eyes there was mute appeal, in Eagle's nothing. Dan thought Adeline would get up and go to the girl, but she didn't. When she finally spoke, it was to Eagle.

"Eagle take squaw," she said. *"Esposa."*

Again there was utter silence. Nobody seemed to know whether to laugh or to cry. Dan got up, and taking the gold band he had bought at the mercantile, took Lenore's left hand and placed it on her ring finger. The girl reacted in a way none of them expected. She threw her arms around Dan and sobbed until there were no tears left. Eagle waited, expressionless, saying nothing. When Lenore turned away from Dan, it was to the Indian, and he led her away. Those elected to ride the first watch seemed eager to leave, and began saddling their horses. The rest quickly recalled tasks that needed doing, and moved rapidly away. Even Denny hurried away to his horse, leaving Dan and Adeline alone.

"That took a lot of courage," Dan said.

"Not really. We do what must be done. There's a lot of savage in him, but he's all the man any woman could ask. He's a good man, and someday he'll be a better

---

* Wife

one. But he'll never be the equal of you. You're so much more than a cowboy, Daniel Ember. That ring meant more to her than anything that I could have said or done. How . . . how did you know?"

"She'll never get him before a preacher," Dan said. "That's all she'll have. That and Eagle's word."

"That should be enough," Adeline said. "It had to be his choice, and I forbade Lenore to try and force him."

"He's an Indian," Dan said. "Force him how?"

"He's a man, and he has pride," Adeline said. "Before snow flies, Lenore will have his child."

The days and nights were warm. Lenore and Eagle took to spreading their blankets far enough away to afford them some privacy. Denny continued spending his nights with the horse remuda, leaving Dan and Adeline pretty much to themselves. They spent their nights talking. Or Adeline did. Dan mostly listened.

"When we stand before the preacher," she asked, "will we be alone, or do you aim for the rest of the outfit to be there?"

"Just us," Dan said. "Won't take more than a few minutes, and since the reverend don't have a church, we'll have to use the chapel at the fort. When that's done, we'll take us a room at that highfalutin hotel, and the fewer folks we have around, the better."

"It would be nice," she said, "not to spend our first night on a blanket beside the river. Already I'm missing the old cabin beside the Rio Grande. It all seemed so simple. Drive our cattle to the railroad, sell them, and then take up ranching. Now we find the railroad is months away, and we'll be facing another of these terrible winters that I don't think any of us expected."

"No, we won't be spending another winter in the open," Dan said, "because we can't wait for the railroad. Chato appreciates what we did for him with the horse remuda, but Palo tells me Chato and his men wish to return to Mexico. They won't wait another year or more for the railroad."

"But we don't have the money we promised them."

"We're going to," Dan said, "because after that last trip to town, I know something I didn't know before. The rails have already passed through Newton, and it's less than a hundred and forty miles east of here. I aim to ride out of here with one of these wagon trains and find us a cattle buyer in Newton. The part of the herd that we aim to sell, we can drive to Newton. We can make it in two weeks, easy. We'll just follow the Arkansas, and there'll be water all the way."

"Oh," she cried, "it's a wonderful idea. When will you go?"

"Not until after the fourteenth," he said, laughing. "I aim to lay this before the rest of the outfit, maybe to-morrow, and be sure they approve."

"I don't know why in the world they wouldn't. It'll mean we can settle on some land and have some kind of roof over our heads before another winter."

"And we won't have Chato and his boys becoming more impatient by the day," Dan said.

Dodge City, Kansas. Saturday, April 14, 1871.

Amid the shouts and laughter of the outfit, Dan and Adeline set out for Dodge. After months on the trail, nobody questioned their wish for privacy.

"First we'll stop at the mercantile," Dan said. "A woman ought to have some finery on her marryin' day, and we'll need a ring."

"Why, I . . . I never expected such," Adeline said. "Is . . . is this our money?"

"Every peso," Dan said.

Adeline swapped her boots for slippers, and her shirt, Levi's, and hat for a stylish dress and bonnet.

"You'll have to change at the fort," Dan said. "I won't have you ridin' astraddle in that."

From the display, Adeline chose a ring that fit, and they rode along the river to Fort Dodge. The Reverend Littlefield was waiting for them in the marshal's office. Deuce Yeager had ridden to Wichita.

"We'll need a place for Adeline to change out of her ridin' clothes and into her finery," Dan said.

"She can use the chapel," Littlefield replied. "We'll wait here."

It took Adeline only a few minutes to change, and just a little longer for Littlefield to perform the brief ceremony. Dan gave the preacher another double eagle.

"I don't charge a fee," Littlefield said. "Besides, you've already given to the church."

"Then I'm giving to it again," Dan said. "I'd like to keep you all dressed up," he told Adeline, "but you'd better change back. We have to ride to the hotel."

Already Dodge had a livery. Dan and Adeline left their horses there and began the short walk to the hotel. They had ridden past the two tent saloons, and as they neared the first one, a man stepped out.

"Mister," he shouted, "them two hosses belonged to me and to my outfit."

"You're accusing me of horse stealing, then," Dan said.

"That and murder," the stranger said. "You owe me, and it's pay-up time."

"I owe you nothing, Rowden," Dan said, "except the same dose of lead the rest of your thieving bunch got. Give the lady time to get to the hotel."

"Dan, no!" Adeline cried.

"To the hotel," Dan said. "Quickly."

Numbly, she obeyed, and Mitch Rowden stepped out into the street. His Colt was tied down on his left hip, butt forward for a cross-hand draw. He seemed a bit too cocky, like he had an edge, and Dan recalled that two of the rustlers had escaped. Where was the other man? Somehow he had to draw the second man into the fight, buying a few seconds before Rowden could draw and fire. Firing to his extreme right, he would have to snatch the Colt from his left hip and make a hundred eighty degree turn. Dan judged the other man would be inside the second saloon tent or on the farthest side, where he had only to step around the corner. Rowden seemed in no hurry to draw, and when there were twenty-five yards between them, Dan made his move. He threw himself as far to Rowden's right as he could, drawing his Colt as he went. Belly down, ignoring Rowden for the moment, he saw the second man step out from beside the tent, leveling his Colt. Dan shot him once and the man stumbled back against the tent. The move had caught Rowden off guard, and his first slug flung dirt in Dan's face. Dan's lead slammed into Rowden's shoulder, staggering him. Rowden tried to raise the Colt but could not, and the lead tore into the ground at his feet. Dan shot him again and he dropped the Colt. He stumbled backward until his knees gave out, and he slumped in the dirt street before the tent saloon. Men boiled out of the tent saloons.

"God Almighty," one shouted, "I never seen such shootin'. They was goin' to ambush him, and he kilt 'em both. Hey, mister!"

Daniel Ember didn't hear them. He holstered his Colt and started for the hotel, but Adeline wasn't waiting. She ran to him and he caught her up in a bear hug. They walked on to the hotel, neither of them looking back.

Dodge City, Kansas. Sunday, April 15, 1871.

Amid much hoorawing, Dan and Adeline returned to the herd. Dan wasted no time in calling the entire outfit together.

"End-of-track is a hundred and forty miles east of here," Dan said. "I'm proposing the we decide how much of the herd we want to sell, and drive them to the railroad, instead of waiting for it to come to us. Driving the cattle directly to the railroad, we can find a buyer in Newton. The rails have already passed through there. Mind you, this is not something you have to do. You can sit here and wait for the railroad and the cattle buyers to reach Dodge, provided you have your share of the money we need to pay Chato and his riders. Me, I need to sell some cows."

"It's decision time, then," Wolf Bowdre said. "I aim to sell half my herd, keepin' the rest to start me a ranch, but I don't want it even close to here. With the railroad comin', there'll be farmers in droves."

"Let's make it easy on everybody," Dan said. "I propose we drive half the herd to Newton, sell them, pay off Chato, and divide what's left equally among us. Likewise, we'll equally divide the rest of the herd, and each of you can take it from there."

"Where do you aim to take your herd?" Sloan Kuykendall asked. "I don't aim to be meddlesome. But we all been together for so long . . ."

Dan laughed. "We're an outfit. Wolf Bowdre and me are taking our cows north, to Dakota Territory. We kind of like that Circle Star brand. With enough cows, all of us usin' that common brand, we could have us some kind of ranch. What do you reckon, Wolf?"

"I'd welcome any man from this outfit that wants to take the trail north," Bowdre said. We're all Texans, ain't we?"

There were shouts of approval. The Circle Star would ride together . . .

EPILOGUE

Clay Allison was born in Waynesboro, Tennessee, in 1840. Allison joined the Confederacy shortly after the outbreak of the war, serving in various Confederate outfits. After the war, Clay and his brothers moved to Texas. Allison cowboyed for a number of outfits, including Charles Goodnight's, and established a reputation as a hard drinker, mean with his fists and fast with a gun. Allison could be a gentleman, but he had a cruel, sadistic streak, often abusing the corpse of a man he had killed. Strangely enough, he didn't die by the gun. He fell from the box of a freight wagon and the huge front wheel broke his back. He was just thirty-seven.

Four years before his death on the Washita, Cheyenne chief Black Kettle had survived the infamous massacree at Sand Creek, Colorado Territory. Colonel J. M. Chivington, a former Methodist minister and commander of the Military District of Colorado, led the attack on November 30, 1864. Chivington reported five hundred Indians killed. Actually, only 123 died, ninety-eight of those women and children.

In September 1874 the army broke the back of the Indian rebellion. Colonel Ronald MacKenzie was sent specifically to subdue Quanah Parker and his band. MacKenzie and his soldiers attacked a camp of Comanches, Cheyennes, and Kiowas in Palo Duro Canyon, on the headwaters of the Red. Fourteen hundred horses and mules were captured, and MacKenzie ordered them all shot. It was too much. One by one the hostiles surrendered. Quanah Parker and his band held on until the last, giving up in 1875.

Thirty-four-year-old Cynthia Ann Parker was welcomed back by the whites, but her tragedy didn't end. Repeatedly she ran away, seeking her sons. Four years after her return to civilization, her little girl died with a fever. Cynthia Ann never recovered, and starved herself to death.

The Masterson family moved to Wichita about 1867. Bat and his older brother Ed came to Dodge City and took a grading contract with the Atchison, Topeka & Santa Fe Railroad. Bat later went to Texas to hunt buffalo, and on July 27, 1874, fought Quanah Parker and his Comanches at the battle of Adobe Walls, in the Texas Panhandle. Masterson was born in 1853, in Quebec, Canada, and died in New York in 1921. In his time, he worked as a farmer, laborer, army scout, buffalo hunter, gambler, saloon owner, law officer, gunman, sportsman, prizefight promoter, and finally, as a sports writer. Despite the legends and tall tales surrounding his life, there is a record of Bat Masterson having taken part in only three gunfights. He killed just one man, and wounded three others.

FOLLOW *THE OREGON TRAIL* WITH RALPH COMPTON—THE NEXT GREAT NOVEL OF THE WESTERN FRONTIER, FROM ST. MARTIN'S PAPERBACKS. AN EXCERPT FOLLOWS:

The herd again took the trail, and within an hour the lead steers were nearing the slow-moving wagons. The terrain allowed them to travel four abreast. The herd split, some of it trailing to the farthermost side of the fourth wagon. But some of the longhorns, aggressive brutes that they were, loped between the moving wagons. Some of the wagons were drawn by teams of mules rather than oxen, and some of the mules began to bray in fear as the longhorned interlopers ran loose among them.

One old bull, annoyed by the braying mules, reacted in typical longhorn fashion. He hooked one of the offending mules, raking its flank with the tip of a murderous horn. The animal screamed and the rest of the team lit out like retribution with the fuse afire. Women screamed, men shouted, and there was a grinding crash as a rear wheel of the runaway wagon ripped off the rear wheel of another. Teamsters with oxen managed to hold them, but two other mule-drawn wagons followed first, wreaking havoc as they went.

The first wagon came to a shuddering stop when a left front wheel smashed into an upthrust of stone and the lathered mules could drag it no farther. Before the other mule teams could be halted, their wagons had smashed into other wagons. When the run finally ended and the dust settled, six wagons had been disabled. Four of them had been toppled and dragged, doubletrees ripped loose, wheels torn from the hubs. By some miracle, nobody seemed to have been hurt. Men and women got shakily to their feet, dusted themselves off and stared unbelievingly at their damaged wagons. The wagons ahead had halted, as men tried to calm their teams.

"Come on," Lou Spencer shouted. "Let's get those cows out of there."

Incredibly, only a dozen longhorns had wrought all the destruction. The crazed braying of the mules and the clatter of runaway wagons had spooked the rest of the herd, and the brutes had veered north, bypassing the strung-out wagons.

"Lou!" Waco shouted, "Look out!"

The shot came from somewhere behind Lou, the slug ripping through the crown of his hat. Lou wheeled his horse, his Colt drawn and cocked, but Waco already had the angry teamster covered.

"Damn you," the man snarled. "Damn you!"

"Put the gun away," said Lou to the man who had fired the shot. He holstered his own Colt and then he spoke to the many whose angry eyes bored into him. "If you're looking for somebody to blame, then blame your wagon boss. He deliberately slowed you people down, believing he could force us to become part of your train. When you made the decision for the cattle to follow you, it became your responsibility to stay ahead of the herd."

The last of the herd, followed by the drag riders, had passed the wrecked wagons when Landon Everett came galloping back to the scene of the disaster. Dillard Sumner, Waco, and Dub Stern had joined Lou in separating the longhorns from among the emigrant wagons. The four cowboys now lounged in their saddles, thumbs hooked in their pistol belts. After glaring furiously at them, Landon Everett turned his eyes to the rising cloud of dust that marked the arrival of Jesse Applegate's wagons. Ignoring the Texans, Everett rode to meet the approaching wagons. Lou nodded to his three companions and they followed. If there was an account to be settled, Applegate wouldn't have to settle it alone. Applegate saw them coming, and when he nodded to Higdon and Quimby, the three lead wagons stopped, halting the train. Forty yards away, Landon Everett reined up, and when he spoke, his voice shook with anger.

"Jesse Applegate, how could you allow this to happen?"

"You *know* why it happened, Landon," Applegate said mildly, "and it wasn't our doing. We've maintained the same gait while you slowed yours. You wanted a cattle column, with the cattle trailing your wagons, and that's what you have. You were two days ahead of us, and if there's anybody to blame, it's you."

"We'll be a week repairing these wagons," Everett growled.

"Take your time," said Applegate coolly. "That will give us time to get well ahead of you, and I promise you we'll stay ahead."

He said no more, veering his teams past the tag end of the Everett wagons. The Higdon and Quimby teams followed, the rest of the Applegate train trailing behind. The cowboys riding drag had already reclaimed the errant steers that had run rampant among the wagons. Lou Spencer and his three companions rode on ahead to catch up to the herd.

"Jesse," Sarah Applegate said reprovingly as she walked beside her husband, "that was a terrible thing to do. Some of those people could have been killed."

"Their choice," said Applegate. "I refuse to be intimidated."

Reaching the point position, Lou guided the herd well away from the strung-out wagons. The Applegate wagons followed, and behind them came the horse remuda. Soon they had left Landon Everett and his crippled wagons behind, and Lou led the herd back to within sight of the Little Blue. Come sundown, the Texans bedded down the herd and the horse remuda half a mile north of the Little Blue, while Applegate circled his wagons near the river. The emigrants were subdued, their minds still on the near-disaster that had taken place earlier in the day. During supper there was an uneasy silence, while some eyed Applegate accusingly. But Lou Spencer had something to say, and he set down his tin coffee cup.

"I reckon it's time I reminded you folks that Mr. Applegate, with all of you in agreement, asked us to lead the way with the herd. Now you're all hunkered around the fire feelin' guilty, thinkin' that if we'd tried, we could have kept them cows away from the tag end of Everett's wagon train. You're right, damn it, we could have. But is there a man or woman among you that don't know why Everett's wagons suddenly got in the way of our herd?"

"They slowed down a-purpose," said young Jud Applegate, "so we'd have to throw in with 'em."

"Exactly," Applegate said, getting to his feet. "There was no way our teams could get past theirs as long as they were on the move, because our teams are not faster than theirs. It's been a hard lesson, but I'm learning. This is the frontier, and we do what we must, even if it means somebody gets hurt."

While some of them plainly didn't like Applegate's hard-bitten attitude, they seemed to understand the wisdom of his words. Dillard Sumner and his outfit rode out to begin the first watch. Lou hadn't been in his blankets long enough to fall asleep when he found Sandy beside him.

"Some of the things about the frontier I don't like," she said softly.

"There'll likely be a lot more before you get to Oregon," Lou said.

"They wanted us to trail our wagons with theirs because they're afraid," said Sandy. "We all fear the unknown, and they don't know what lies ahead. They want you and your cowboys taking the lead for them as you're doing for us."

"Damn it," Lou said, irritated, "we hired on to trail these cattle to Oregon, not to wet-nurse two hundred and fifty families. We've never been to Oregon, and there's not a man of us that knows any more about the trail ahead than any of you."

"But you're not strangers to the frontier. Can this be any more dangerous than driving hundreds of wild cows from Texas to Missouri? Would it be all that bad if you and your riders took the cattle on ahead, like you're already doing, and allowed all the wagons to follow?"

"It would for us," said Lou. "I've talked to my outfit, to Dillard Sumner and his riders, and we're all of the same mind. We already got all the responsibility we can handle, and we don't aim to take on any more. Landon Everett's bunch booted you out. Now they got a killer within their ranks, they've discovered the trail's a hell of a lot tougher than they expected, and they're wantin' somebody to hold their hands from here to Oregon."

"It seems I have misunderstood you," she said hotly. "You are a selfish, insensitive brute."

"I reckon," he said coolly, "but it's kept me alive."

She slipped away in the darkness, and from somewhere nearby Vangie Applegate laughed softly.

THE OREGON TRAIL—AVAILABLE FROM ST. MARTIN'S PAPERBACKS!